# Code Blue

# BY PAT NICOLETTE

Code Blue For Murder © 2007 Pat Nicolette

ISBN-13  978-1-60145-114-9
ISBN-10  1-60145-114-8

Printed in the United States of America.
Published by BookLocker.com, Inc.

The characters and events in this book are fictitious. Any similarity to real persons, living or dead, is coincidental and not intended by the author.

Also by Pat Nicolette

Nick Mercante Mysteries:

The Caruso File
The Trinity Church Murders
Twin Killing: The Gemini Plot

Plays:

The House on the Hill
The Brother
In the Best of Families

# DEDICATION

To the Memory of Dr. William H. Elliott, Jr.
Brilliant and Innovative Surgeon

# ACKNOWLEDGEMENTS

Many thanks to my dear friend and editor-in-chief,
Barbara Webster Black, for her hard work and insights,
And, of course, to my wife,
Susan Elliott, for her support, encouragement,
and introducing me to Bill

Pat Nicolette, January 2007

# PROLOGUE

## SATURDAY, FEBRUARY 28

A solitary figure walked slowly toward the exit of the darkened hospital, a slight frown creasing otherwise pleasant features. To be sure, events were coalescing favorably. Yet, despite the months of planning, success was not at all assured. The competition was formidable, some might say invincible. But defeat was not acceptable. The opportunity was now. Time was no longer a friend.

Outside, the frown hardened in the cold night air. The moon playing on the doorway lights turned the figure into a grotesque shifting shadow as it hurried toward the parking lot. A few moments later, the silence was broken by a car engine starting. As the heater worked its magic, the face behind the wheel relaxed. *I just have to be patient. The party is only two weeks away and I should know more. Then Philadelphia--the launching point for murder.*

The car began to move, its headlights sweeping the hospital complex as it glided toward the gate. Those buildings would bear witness to many killings in the days ahead. The names of the victims would shock everyone.

# ONE

## SUNDAY, MARCH 14

For the nearly five years he had been chief executive officer of Washington's Clara Barton Memorial Hospital, Robert Kramer had hosted a St. Patrick's Day party in his spacious home on Riverview Heights in Potomac, Maryland. An invitation was considered a plum by those on the staff lucky enough to receive one. Tonight, although it was well after eleven, more than 70 people were still partaking of Kramer's generous buffet and open bar as they wandered in and out of the downstairs rooms and danced to the unobtrusive music of a six-piece ensemble.

A handsome man stood idly watching the dancers, sipping a glass of champagne. Several women on the dance floor smiled in his direction, hoping to catch his eye. Dr. Peter Thorpe was an established star in Clara Barton's phalanx of fine surgeons and, perhaps more importantly, his black hair and cobalt blue eyes placed him at the top of the hospital's most eligible bachelor list.

Hearing a familiar voice, Thorpe turned to see Father Brian Cahill hot on the heels of their host. Robert Kramer walked faster, trying to extricate himself from the clutches of the hospital's portly Assistant Director of Pastoral Care.

"But, Mr. Kramer," Thorpe heard Cahill say, "our patients don't know what opting out of the census means. Their families can't get in touch with them."

Kramer stopped a few steps from Thorpe, nodding politely as he listened to Cahill. Finally, he ran a hand through his sandy brown hair. "Father, this law wasn't my idea. We protected patient privacy just fine before HIPPA. Why don't you complain to your old friend, Bill Clinton? They passed the thing on his watch."

"I'm not blaming you, Mr. Kramer, but we need special intake staff to explain this to our patients so they can make a considered judgment."

"We don't have money for that right now. Didn't Ms. Ellis explain that to you?"

"For about ten seconds. And that's part of the problem around here, if you don't mind my saying."

Kramer's hazel eyes flashed behind his wire-rimmed glasses, but he kept his voice even. "Look, Father," he said, backing away a step, "this really isn't a good time to discuss this. Why don't you give Ms. Ellis a call early in the week?"

"I would if I thought she'd listen," Cahill huffed, again following Kramer who was now moving off. "Can't you tell her...?"

Had Thorpe not been watching Cahill, he might have seen Cynthia Ellis reach the foot of the stairs fresh from the second floor powder room. A tall, striking brunette wearing a purple cocktail dress, her gray eyes surveyed the crowd and spotted Cahill trailing after Kramer. Serves Bob right, she smiled to herself, then continued scanning. Now where is Peter?

"Care to dance, Ms. Ellis?"

Despite her height, Cynthia had to look up to meet the dark brown eyes. "Dr. Monroe! I'd be delighted, but aren't you afraid people will talk?" she asked in her throaty voice, accepting his hand and walking toward the rectangular wooden dance floor set up in front of the band.

"Because I'm black?"

"Perhaps," she chuckled. "More likely because you shouldn't be seen dancing with the enemy."

"I thought we all have the best interests of the hospital at heart," he said, as they began to move with the music.

"If only all our surgeons felt that way. Are you enjoying the party?"

"Very much," Monroe said. "This is my first. Bob Kramer must be very well off."

"Doesn't need to work another day in his life."

"So why does he put up with all the crap? Running the hospital can't be much fun."

"It has its moments."

"And you enjoy being his chief of staff?"

"For now," she said.

"Ah hah," he smiled, dipping her body easily as he shifted their direction. "Then the rumors are true."

"What rumors?" Cynthia asked deadpan.

"You're going to apply for CEO because Kramer's vulnerable."

"Isn't this where I say no comment?"

"If you like. My views really don't matter."

"Unless I were seeking your support."

"I don't have a vote," Monroe said.

"You have a voice. The trustees aren't deaf."

"And are you soliciting me to make a speech?"

"I might, but don't you have to be loyal to your own?" she asked, glancing to where Dr. Stanley Jacobi was bending over Vivian Pershing's wheelchair talking in her ear.

Monroe followed her eyes. "Dr. Jacobi's a good administrator."

"I agree. And he should remain chief of surgery."

Monroe laughed. "Now, I know you're courting me."

"Maybe I am at that," Cynthia said, moving her body closer to his while straining to hear what Jacobi was saying.

"Vivian, I truly haven't decided," Jacobi said, not wanting to tip his hand but still eager to gain her backing. Vivian Pershing was Clara Barton--the longest serving member of its board of trustees and its chair for over a decade. Her tenure had earned her the sobriquet of the Czarina--except no one dared call her that to her face.

"You'd better make up your mind, Stanley," she said. "Cynthia Ellis is bound to apply and she's damn good. I can't very well influence the board if you're only lukewarm. That is, if I were to endorse you."

"You'd abandon Kramer?"

"I'd throw you overboard if it helped Clara Barton."

"Well, I'd like to see the third quarter figures before I commit."

"So would I, Stanley. But remember, there may never be a better time for you. The board may be ready for a doctor to take command."

"I appreciate your insight, Vivian."

"And I'd appreciate another drink. Come along, I've got a funny story to tell you."

Jacobi followed Pershing as she maneuvered her electric wheelchair through the crowd toward one of the two long tables that served as bars for the evening.

Thorpe had watched the pair from across the room, fairly certain what they'd been discussing. Then his eyes shifted to Cynthia and the other attractive women on the dance floor, some of whom he'd never seen before or only in lab coats or nurse garb.

None, however, was lovelier than the woman who walked toward him now in a breathtaking, electric-green dress that hugged her curves and complemented her blonde hair and blue eyes. Laura Prentice was Robert Kramer's executive assistant.

"Good evening, Dr. Thorpe. Buy a lady a drink?"

"Be glad to, Ms. Prentice. Champagne? I was just about to freshen mine."

"Then I'll help."

He took her arm and they strolled over to one of the tables, behind which stood a pair of very attentive college-aged young men. "Two champagnes," Thorpe said to one of them.

"Yes, sir." The young man's hands flew into action.

"You look beautiful," Thorpe said softly. "Am I the first to say that tonight?"

"Just the most important. Miss me?"

"Not so loud," he murmured.

"Doesn't matter," Laura smiled. "I happen to know there's a lip reader in the band."

"Then I'll choose my words more carefully." He nodded his thanks to the young man and handed her one of the glasses.

"Of course, to your question," he said, guiding her toward a draped window recess.

"Really? I saw you ogling all the sweet young things parading around. Like Nancy Kwan," she said and nodded toward the middle of the dance floor.

Thorpe looked over to the new head of the medical records office, who had just taken it upon herself to do an Irish jig--solo. Kwan's red rhinestone sheath barely contained her.

"She is something," he said. "How does that bodice stay up, anyway?"

"As if you didn't know. Word has it she's a fitness freak and has a thing for doctors. And if I'm not mistaken, she was chatting up one of our best surgeons in the cafeteria the other day."

He smiled. "She was telling me about her exploits at volley ball."

"And you definitely looked interested."

"You know I love sports."

"Stick to golf," she said. "Peter, I have news."

"Happy to change the subject."

"Cynthia's on the prowl and you're the target. So pay

attention if she comes stalking."

"She'd better hurry. I'm out of here in a few minutes. I've just been waiting to bid you and my host good night. Surgery tomorrow."

"You and your Mondays."

"Not this time," he said. "It's Ann Lyman's case. A tough one. She asked me to assist."

"Then you're not coming over tonight."

"I'll make it up to you Friday."

"I have to wait that long?"

"My week's jammed up, babe. So what's with Cynthia?"

"I spoke with her upstairs. She's definitely going after Kramer's job."

"No surprise. You know what they say. Hell hath no fury and all that."

Laura shook her head. "She knows better. The trustees only care about the balance sheet."

"And?"

"Cynthia overheard Al Jennings tell Kramer that the third quarter results might be worse than they thought."

"That's why he's chief financial officer. So?"

"So the word's bound to get out to some of the trustees. Cynthia thinks unless Bob can work a miracle, they're sure to pare back his budget proposal for next year."

"He won't like that," Thorpe said.

"Exactly. She said if that happens, he might not ask for a new contract in July. He could resign."

"What does all that have to do with me?"

"Everything. Cynthia's sure Jacobi will try for CEO too."

"I was afraid of that. He was just talking to Pershing. I'll never get to be chief of surgery if he's CEO. He'd kill my chances with the trustees. The guy hates me."

"He's jealous. Cynthia wants to cut Jacobi off at the knees. And guess who's going to be her sword?"

"Me?"

"None other."

"What am I supposed to do?"

"She didn't say. Listen, I have more to tell you, but I think I should circulate."

"You're leaving me here wondering?" he asked, feigning

distress.

"I'll make it up to you Friday," she winked.

"Cute. I might ask Nancy Kwan to dance with me."

"I'm sure she can't wait to show you her serve."

"She may want me to drive her home."

"Do it. Give the rumor mill something to churn on. Just stay out of her bed." She touched glasses and moved off, Thorpe admiring the sway of her hips.

They had started seeing each other in November when he'd saw her waiting for a bus outside the parking lot and he pulled over. She told him the afternoon's freak thunderstorm had somehow damaged her Taurus because it kept dying out when she started it.

He offered her a ride home and, after a moment's hesitation, she accepted. The drive to her small colonial on Brandywine Street led to cocktails and dinner at Caballeros, her favorite Mexican restaurant, a couple of blocks away on Wisconsin Avenue.

More dinners followed. Tacitly at first, then by agreement, they kept their relationship secret, though she convinced him she should be free to tell her parents and he his mother since all three lived out of town.

Now, when passing in the hospital corridors, they nodded politely, nothing more. They arranged to meet by phone, didn't even use e-mail. And, apart from their first dinner, they were careful not to be seen together, eating out rarely and then in remote locations, making liberal use of Caballeros's delivery service when they were at her house.

But no visit tonight, he thought, as Laura disappeared in the crowd. He glanced once more at Nancy Kwan's bouncing figure, then went looking for Kramer.

## TUESDAY, MARCH 16

"This doesn't look good," Vivian Pershing said to the figures on her computer screen. She clicked the mouse on Print and hit OK. She backed her Rover wheelchair away from the desk and moved to the other end of her study to wait for the financial statements to come off the printer.

Nearing 70, Vivian was still a handsome woman with clear skin, curly salt and pepper hair and green eyes. She had been only

32 when she replaced her father on Clara Barton's board of trustees, two months after he was killed in the same auto accident that fractured three of her lumbar vertebrae and damaged her spinal cord. The injury caused her to lose the use of her legs, which in turn prompted her lover Andrew to stop seeing her and not leave his wife as he had promised.

None of these events or the fact that she had spent half her life confined to a wheelchair had diminished her energy or her interest in life. And tonight she was irritated.

Taking the sheets from the printer, she maneuvered the Rover to the dining room where she spread them on the table. She poured herself a small bourbon and water and studied each page. The projected results for the third quarter were dreadful. The hospital's cash flow was hemorrhaging like some patients in the ER.

She took her cell phone from its compartment in the Rover and punched in Elmer Woodworth's number.

"Hello?"

"Woody, Vivian here. Got a minute?"

"Sure thing. Missed you at the meeting today."

"Had a check-up with Dr. Patterson. I assume you got Al Jennings's preliminaries for the third quarter?"

"Yes. I left a set for you in the volunteer office." Vivian volunteered Thursday mornings at the hospital information desk.

"I already have them. Cynthia Ellis was delighted to call me this evening and e-mail them."

"They don't look too hot."

"They're awful. Woody, if things don't turn around, I may personally lead the charge to change CEO's."

"Gee, Vivian. You're the one who wanted Kramer here with his experience and all."

"And I may have made a mistake. Maybe we never should have hired someone from a medical center."

"He's made a lot of improvements, Vivian."

"That's the problem. We're a community hospital. We don't have the money for some of his projects. The new research department's a black hole."

"Is it that bad?"

"Look at the numbers. Woody, can I count on you if I support someone else this time around?"

"Well, I almost always go along with you, Vivian, but we're

coming to the end of the fiscal year and Kramer's contract's up right after that."

"So?

"I don't think there's enough time for a search. Someone would have to step in as interim CEO."

"What about Stan Jacobi?"

"A doctor?"

"I hear he's interested."

"He is pretty smart."

"And he's been here forever. Think about it, Woody."

"Well, sure I will, Vivian, but, you know, maybe you ought to talk to Kramer. Give him some warning."

"Oh, I intend to. And, as vice chair, you should too."

"All right. I'll give him a call."

"Good, keep the pressure on. Nice talking to you, Woody."

"My pleasure, Vivian. Good night."

Vivian clicked off. Elmer Woodworth was a lot smarter than he made out, but no match for Bob Kramer. She took a sip of her bourbon and turned back to the financials.

## FRIDAY, MARCH 19

Thorpe had been a frequent guest in Laura Prentice's bed since New Year's Eve. Tonight, lying in her arms, he listened attentively as she recounted her conversations with Cynthia Ellis at Kramer's party and during the week.

"So," she said, "Cynthia figures you're stuck with Jacobi running the department unless he retires or gets Kramer's job."

"She's right," Thorpe said.

"And if he becomes CEO, she thinks he'll torpedo you as chief surgeon."

"Just as I told you."

"But she believes then you'll look for another hospital."

"No, I quit one when my brother was killed. I don't want to leave Clara Barton."

"But Cynthia doesn't know that. So if you help her win, she promises to get rid of Jacobi as chief. I know the CEO sits on the medical committees, but could she really do that?"

"If she's learned anything from Kramer," Thorpe said.

"He is popular with the surgeons."

"It's no accident. He's budgeted money among the departments as best he could and gone for state-of-the-art equipment. He also squeezes a few more dollars to help us in recruiting. So we listen to him when he has a personnel recommendation. And that's important to the trustees."

"He's more shrewd than I thought."

"Cynthia will have to be too. She'll also need a good plan to beat him and Jacobi."

"Guess that's why she wants to talk to you."

Thorpe moved a strand of blond hair away from Laura's eye. "Why did she tell you all this?"

"Because I've agreed to be her mole in Kramer's office."

"Ho-ho! And I thought Cynthia was ambitious."

"All's fair," Laura smiled.

"When did you climb on her bandwagon?"

"Last week. If Cynthia wins, I'll replace her."

"She promised you chief of staff?"

"Has a nice ring, doesn't it?"

He moved another strand of her hair. "When did you two become so chummy?"

"Since we made love."

"What?"

"You heard me. Don't look so surprised."

"You and Cynthia? You're bisexual?"

"Peter, it's not a dirty word. It happens."

"I've studied psychology, Laura. How did it happen with you?"

"When I was at boarding school at St. Vincent's. No boys around, so girls did what girls do. Some of us, anyway."

"Circumstantial bisexualism."

"Is that what they call it?"

"Yes. And you've experimented ever since?"

"Not often," she said. "More since my divorce."

"When with Cynthia?"

"Last fall at Coolfont."

"The admin staff retreat?"

"Mmm-hmm. We found ourselves skinny dipping in a spa."

He smiled. "I'd love to have seen that. And I suppose it wasn't her first time?"

"God, no. She was the curious type growing up. Now it's

more when the spirit moves her. Sort of like me, I guess."

"Have you...been with her since?"

"A couple times, but not after you and I got together. She did ask me again, but I begged off. Where are you going?" Laura said as he climbed from the bed.

"To the john."

"You went ten minutes ago. Are you okay?"

"I'm fine. You want anything?"

"No, thanks."

She watched him amble toward the bathroom, thinking back to their first dinner dates. Aware of his reputation as a ladies man, she decided she wouldn't sleep with him, unwilling to become another entry in his black book. To her surprise, he was content to talk or listen to music when they were together. Maybe he welcomed the novelty of a woman who wasn't eager to be a doctor's wife.

When they finally did make love on New Year's Eve, it was as explosive as the thunderstorm that had blitzed her car. But, given her own caution, she had willingly abetted the secrecy of their relationship. It was as though each of them was afraid to break the spell, waiting for the other to tempt the fates. Neither did. Only in the past few weeks had they broached the prospect of revealing their affair to the world.

Now, as he returned to the bedroom carrying a small brandy, she had a fleeting thought about a future with him, but pushed it away. And, as he sat on the edge of the bed, she sensed a change in his mood.

"You're not angry, are you?" she asked.

"More like flummoxed. This is a new one for me."

"You only think so," she said, stroking his thigh lightly. "Lots of women experiment, but don't advertise."

"Not to me anyway. Look, about you and Cynthia. What happens to this CEO stuff if she learns about us?"

"What do you mean if? We've agreed to go public."

"Correction--when she finds out. Won't it upset her plans, and yours?"

"Why should it? We're all on the same side."

"It could get complicated if she wants to go on making love with you."

"I don't want to now," Laura said.

"Suppose she gets jealous?"

"I'm not engaged to her, Peter. We had some fun together. We both like guys, you know."

"Still, she could change her mind about making me chief. That would put you in the middle."

"Don't be silly. But if she should start in after you, I'll tell her all bets are off."

"I'm not so sure."

She kissed him. "You come first. Let's not fight over nothing, okay?"

"No, that's not what I meant. I'm not sure you can trust her. Or I can."

"Peter, I'm not naive. Cynthia's ambitious. So are we. This is a chance for all our careers. It's what I want. It's what you want."

"I suppose."

"Suppose? You forgetting all that talk about wanting to honor your father's and brother's memory?"

"I'm just trying to think this through, okay? We might lose leverage if we tell people now."

"Leverage?"

"Yes, this idea of you being Cynthia's mole. Suppose she asks you to come on to Kramer to get information?"

Laura sat up. "That's not the deal."

"But he's not the bashful type. Cynthia can vouch for that. Hasn't he ever made a pass at you?

"Sure, he's looked, but never touched. Everyone's not like you, Peter."

"Hey, that's not fair."

"I'm sorry. That was out of line."

"Okay, but don't forget, he's a man and you're a beautiful woman. You might be more effective if he thought you were available."

"Talk about Cynthia, it sounds like you want me to sleep with him."

He took her hands in his. "I just think we should do what it takes to get what we want."

"You'd let me make love to Bob?"

"I didn't say that. But you don't have to take yourself out of the running too soon. If I shouldn't mind about you and Cynthia, why get upset over a little flirting with Kramer?"

"I'm not sure I like this."

"Let's sleep on it. I may think differently in the morning or when I hear what Cynthia wants me to do."

"Knowing her, it could be anything."

"Yeah, and that's what worries me."

## FRIDAY, APRIL 2

Dr. Stanley Jacobi was in a hurry as he exited the elevator. It was nearly five and he didn't want to be late for his last meeting of the day. A thickset six-four with a large baldhead, he projected boundless energy despite his 57 years. These days he needed it. The administrative side of being chief of surgery increasingly claimed more of his time. But truth be known, he enjoyed the budget and personnel battles more than surgery. If his great-great grandfather had a grave out in the hills of Maryland, he was probably rolling over in it.

Melvin Jacobi had been the first in the line of family physicians. A Civil War battlefield surgeon with the famous Iron Brigade, he was one of 300 men in the 6th Wisconsin regiment who fought at Antietam in September 1862. Nearly half were casualties, including Melvin who died from his wounds. He left behind a nineteen-year-old wife pregnant with Stanley's grandfather, Ira, who moved to Pennsylvania with his mother three years later when she remarried.

If the Civil War had prematurely ended medical careers, a less violent but equally destructive force was at work today. The cost of malpractice policies and the difficulties in fee collection from health insurance companies and Medicare had driven many doctors to early retirement. While Ira Jacobi had been able to practice medicine and run a hospital in Hagerstown, Maryland into the 1930's, it was said you couldn't do both jobs anymore. But his grandson Stanley was ready to try.

God knows he could do better than Bob Kramer. All he had to do was convince the trustees. The thought of Kramer's ineptitude quickened Jacobi's stride. If I had his job the first thing I'd do--.

"Dr. Jacobi! Do you have a minute?"

Jacobi turned to see the rotund figure of Father Brian Cahill scurrying toward him. Just what I need, he thought, the Vatican Doughboy. "Father," he smiled warmly. "What's on your mind?"

Assuming you still have one.

"I'd like your help, doctor. Have you seen my request for new locks for the chapel doors?"

"I'm not sure. Isn't that for building and grounds to pass on first? The budget committee has no jurisdiction over such details."

"Oh, I know. It's just that...well, you know. You being so important these days."

Jacobi decided to have a moment's fun. "These days, Father?"

"Well, I hear things."

Jacobi smiled. "What exactly?"

Cahill actually blushed. "I shouldn't say. I mean--."

"Never mind, Father. Look, I have a meeting I must get to." He started to step away. "Please send me a copy of your request. I'll take a look at it."

"Wonderful. And I was wondering?"

"Yes?"

"Can I talk to you later this week? I have some concerns about hospital security, but Mr. Kramer doesn't want to listen."

Jacobi raised an eyebrow. "Security, you say? Listen, Father, why don't we meet for breakfast soon. I'm usually in by six."

"Can we do it a little later? I try to get to the fitness room when its not crowded. Got to take care of the old ticker."

"Certainly, just leave me a voice-mail with some possible days you'd like to meet. I'll set it up."

"Splendid. And perhaps we might discuss some other matters which are troubling me."

"Of course. I'm always willing to listen to your point of view."

"You won't be sorry. There are things happening here that border on malpractice and worse."

What's he driving at, Jacobi wondered. "I didn't know of your interest in medicine, Father."

"Oh, I've studied some over the years since I took this assignment."

"Indeed."

"Yes, and I've learned a great deal observing and talking with the staff. Some of you work miracles, but others...?"

"Miracles are more in your line, Father. We simply try to practice good medicine. Let's continue this over breakfast, shall we?"

"Of course. Jesus bless you, doctor. Oh, I'm sorry, I didn't mean--"

"Not to worry, Father. I won't tell my God if you won't tell yours."

Cahill smiled and rubbed his hands together in a washing motion as he watched Jacobi stride down the hallway.

Tugging at his white collar, Cahill walked toward the chapel that was on one side of the lobby. He pushed through the glass doors into the dim interior, always a cool place even in winter when the hospital temperature could be so high as to be stifling. He went down the short center aisle and knelt at the altar, eyes fixed at the simple cross in the center of the sacristy.

He prayed to his Lord, asking forgiveness for his sins and failures, giving thanks for His patience, and seeking guidance on how he might yet succeed in the mission God had asked of him here: to stop those who prescribe birth control, use embryos to extract stem cells, murder innocent fetuses, and turn away the homeless and uninsured because money and new machines were more important than saving lives. Either the policies had to change or the policy makers. He knew he couldn't do it alone, but with God's help it would happen at Clara Barton.

## PHILADELPHIA, SUNDAY, APRIL 4

Carefully obeying the speed limit, the killer's drive from Washington had taken nearly three hours. While Amtrak would have been quicker and more comfortable, train tickets meant names in a computer and showing ID. After parking near Penn Station, the killer grabbed a carryall from the back seat, took the subway to East Market, and now walked through Galleria Mall, recalling how this day and city had come into play.

In early December the killer had faced the dark reality that had nagged for weeks: there was only one sure way to succeed. It would require an act most would consider heinous, contrary to what the hospital stood for--healing others, confronting illness, cheating death if only temporarily. Victory might require murder.

But would that be so terrible? Everyone dies eventually and too often it is an untimely, senseless tragedy. Even at Clara Barton, some patients would have survived given greater care, a larger staff, better training. On the other hand, some deaths would be welcomed, even cheered.

The outlines of a plan began to form. Where, how, when. By the mid-January the details were essentially in place. But important, unresolved issues remained. Others who had tried had failed, indeed, been caught. Should help be sought? Would chances improve? Could someone be found...trusted...?

Difficult questions, but the answers were available, thanks to the public library, the Washington Post archives and the Internet. Months of research reduced to weeks. The effort had proven invaluable, prompting changes to the plan, bolstering confidence and uncovering an array of notorious murderers, their motives, methods and cunning, as well as their missteps and stupidity.

Reaching the glass doors of the Mall, the killer exited into bright noonday sunshine, donned a pair of sunglasses from the carryall, and began walking down Market Street, occasionally dodging a Palm Sunday shopper intent on finding Easter bargains. At Third Street, the killer turned right.

The weeks of research had also strengthened the sense that, in order to completely eliminate risk, one must act alone yet still avoid the hidden pitfalls that had trapped so many. Which led the killer to Philadelphia and Timothy Parnell: the one man who knew criminal techniques better than anyone and who had put many murderers in jail until he himself had made one mistake.

It took only a single call from a pay phone to arrange today's meeting. Once again, the Internet proved a great resource, providing detailed driving directions from Washington to Parnell's house. Now it was time to see if the plan was complete or if there was more to learn. After a few more minutes, the killer stood in front of the low stoop of a row house on Van Dyke Street and was about to ring the bell when the door opened.

"Come on in. I was beginning to think you weren't coming." Parnell was a ruddy-faced man wearing worn slacks and a short-sleeve polo shirt. The former D.C. detective had aged a good deal more than the dozen or so years since the photo of him leaving the courthouse had appeared in the *Post*.

"Aren't you going to ask who I am?" the killer asked, stepping into a small but well-furnished living room, with a staircase off to the right.

"Why should I?" Parnell said. "I don't have any guests

scheduled today."

"Guests?"

"This is a B&B. Sign in if you'd like," he smiled, pointing to a register on the coffee table.

This could be mean trouble. "Is anyone here now?"

"Wish there were," Parnell said, shaking his head. "Too early in the season. Haven't had any traffic since the flower show in March."

The killer relaxed and looked around. "Quite a switch. Solving homicides to serving breakfast to gardeners."

"It was my mother's business. I took it over when she died two years after I...left Washington. Have a seat." Parnell gestured to a long sofa along the front wall. "I was about to have a beer. Can I get you anything?"

"I'll join you."

"Really?"

"Surprised?"

"Yeah, even in those jeans you look more like the white wine type. Beer's for slobs like me."

"Well, when in Rome."

Parnell looked puzzled, then shrugged and turned. "Whatever. Be right back."

He limped through a wide archway into an adjoining kitchen, twice the size of the living room with a dining table across from the refrigerator. For the guests no doubt, the killer thought, angry for not having asked Parnell whether he usually had visitors. A B&B no less.

Parnell returned carrying two long-necked Budweisers and a glass. "Here you are," he said, placing one bottle and the glass on the coffee table.

The killer ignored the glass and took a long swig from the bottle.

"You're full of surprises," Parnell said.

"I'm just starting. Are you ready to talk?"

"After we settle up."

"Of course," the killer nodded, then reached into the carryall and handed over an envelope.

Parnell counted the bills. "To the penny," he said, raising his bottle in a half toast. "Still can't figure why your magazine would pay $2,500 to rehash an old story."

"They probably wouldn't. I don't work for them and I know every detail of your story."

Parnell's eyes narrowed. "Who are you?"

"Who is not important. Why I'm here is."

"You a cop?"

"No. I may have to commit a murder."

Parnell didn't blink. "You're not sure?"

"I'm in the middle of this sort of contest. Things look promising, but you never know."

"And you want to eliminate one of the contestants," Parnell said, taking a swallow.

"There could be an obstacle that needs moving."

Parnell sat back in his chair. "Why tell me?"

"I'd like your help."

"Me?"

"You're the expert."

"I'm not for hire."

"I'm not asking for that. I want to learn how to fool your old friends back in D.C."

"That's worth a hell of a lot more than $2,500."

"I agree. I'll double it if you tell me what I need to know."

"No sale. I could get in trouble."

"No more than when you stole cocaine from the evidence room."

"That was a set up. I was an honest cop."

"Is that what you told the two girls from St. Benedict's who died using the crack you put back on the street?"

"No one proved I did a thing."

"But you didn't take the stand to tell your side, now did you?"

"I listened to my lawyer. And I got off." Parnell lifted the bottle again.

"On a technicality. And then you were invited to retire early."

"That was my idea."

"I'm sure. Look, I don't care about all that. You have nothing to worry about from me. How much more do you want?"

Parnell took a sip of beer. "Say another $7,500. Ten thou all told."

The killer gave Parnell a small smile, fished through the

carryall, then took out three more envelopes and slid one across the table. "Here's another $2,500. If I like what I hear, I'll hand over the rest. If not, you'll still have twice what you bargained for."

Parnell glanced into the envelope without counting. "Where do I start? You want to ask me questions?"

"No, tell me what the police look for, what stymies them, why some cases don't get solved. I'll stop you if I have questions." The killer leaned back. "So talk."

"Well, the toughest case is the random killing. No witnesses or premeditation. Street robbery, for example."

"I know that. Next?"

"All right. Well, we always ask who profits, who has a motive."

"Listen, this isn't a rerun of Law and Order. I've done my homework, I know my victim, I have a motive and the police will figure it out. Now, how do I get away with it?"

Parnell took a swig of beer and leaned forward. "You working alone?"

"Yes."

"Then your best bet is to rig an accident or a poisoning and not be around when it goes down. Be out of town. Now, that can get tricky, but it's doable."

"I don't like that. I have to stay close."

"That's your call," Parnell shrugged. "Then get help. You seem to have the money. Contract with a pro to take out your target and set up an air tight alibi."

"That's a recipe for blackmail, isn't it?"

"Not if you go through the right channels. There are honest brokers out there. I could give you a name or two."

"If you know who they are, why aren't they in jail?"

"Because they're good. They know people who don't leave clues and neither do they. They've been arrested, sure, but they always walk. Nothing sticks to them."

"Now you're up to two people who would know."

Parnell shook his head. "Depends on the broker. If you go to the right man, you only deal with him. The pro doesn't know or care who you are. He just wants to get paid."

"I don't know," the killer said, having read about this tactic and eventually rejecting it.

"I'm telling you it's safe. Here." Parnell pulled the guest

register toward him and ripped out a page. "Call this number," he said, writing. "This guy can take you where you need to go. Tell him Mrs. Peabody referred you."

The killer studied the sheet, noting "Parnell's Bed and Breakfast" and the Van Dyke address at the top, then slipped it into the carryall. "Maybe, but I don't think so. What else?"

"Well, if you insist on flying solo, there's always misdirection. Get the cops looking at other things, other people."

"You mean frame someone," the killer said, becoming impatient.

Parnell nodded. "That's the usual way, but there's a neat twist not many know about."

"I'm listening," the killer said, hearing something new for the first time.

Parnell hunched forward. "You kill a stranger."

"Someone I don't know?"

"That's best, but it doesn't matter. Just so it's a person you have no motive to kill, but your real target does. Like say your man has a big insurance policy on his wife. You take care of her, you plant a little evidence, and the cops take care of him. You walk away clean."

The idea held a hint of promise. "Let me think about it, but one problem is finding the right substitute. My victim's not in that kind of a relationship. You have anything better?"

Parnell swallowed more beer, then put down the bottle. "How much of a stomach do you have for killing?"

"You mean can I cause pain or see blood?"

"Not that. Can you do more than one?"

"What are you talking about? I want to lower my risks."

"That's what I'm saying."

"I don't get it."

"Neither do the police. You make them think you're a serial killer. You give them a bunch of victims but in fact only one's your real target."

"Go on," the killer said, dubious but intrigued.

Parnell proceeded to talk for several minutes, starting a second beer in the process, then sat back with satisfied smile. "See? It's really easy."

"So you don't stop with the real target?"

"Never. You make sure there's at least one more killing after

your man goes down.  And don't do your guy early on.  Third out
of four is best."

"But serial killers always seem to get caught."

"Sure, the ones who can't keep their mouth shut. They boast,
send letters, seek attention. You never read about the others
because they finish their business and keep quiet."

"How come you know about this angle?"

"I worked a case like it back in D.C. Everyone thought a
serial was nailing women joggers in the park.  But I was sure this
banker killed them and his wife so he could play house with his
secretary. Never could prove it, but he married the babe two years
later."

"What made you think he did it?" the killer asked.

"All the victims had some of their clothes ripped off except
the wife. Just her shoes were missing."

"Sounds like a great theory, except for the sex idea. That
won't work for me."

"You don't need sex," Parnell said. "All you have to do is
find what your man's into.  Say he's a golfer or a lawyer. Then you
take out two like him and bingo."

"So everyone has some kind of link," the killer said,
exploring the point.

"Not always," Parnell wagged his finger. "The pattern's the
key. Locale, weapon, day of the week. Just give the cops something
to chew on.  They love trying to connect the dots."

The killer sat there a moment, thinking. "I might not be able
to come up with just the right connection."

Parnell took another sip of beer. "Well, you could do a
random thing. The cops will never find your guy mixed in there."

"I don't follow you."

"Remember those Beltway snipers who had everyone down
in D.C. and Maryland scared shitless?"

"Sure, including me."

"Well, the victims seemed to be picked at random. Maybe
they were. But there was another part of the story."

"Which was?"

"That one of the snipers was really after his ex-wife.  She'd
be killed and everyone would think she was just another victim. It's
a great ploy if you can pull it off.  No one would suspect you even if
you had a motive and no alibi."

The killer nodded thoughtfully, then squinted at Parnell. "Look, I might not know if I have to commit the murder until pretty late in the game."

"Then it's tough to set up multiple killings."

"That's my point. So let me ask you a question."

Parnell swigged his beer. "Shoot."

"Suppose it isn't only homicides. Would the police still figure one person was doing it?"

"You mean a series of other crimes?"

"Right. A robbery, for example."

Parnell tilted his head. "That's an interesting spin. Let's see, the random idea wouldn't work. You'd need some kind of link to help the cops see the big picture."

"But if I had it?"

Parnell's considered then shook his head. "Won't fly. You can't do it with only one killing because then your guy would stick out. Why would you suddenly get into murder?"

"Maybe I planned it that way? Make them think I had to resort to extreme measures to get attention? I'm some kind of psychopath, right? Let them figure what's in my head. So long as they can't find me."

"I think it's too risky. I still say go with a pro, kill a stranger or do a few victims if you have the time."

"All right. Listen, may I use your bathroom? This beer seems to have gotten to me."

Parnell grinned. "Maybe you should have had the wine. First door on the right in the kitchen."

"Thanks," the killer said, picking up the carryall and standing.

"You taking that to the john? What's the matter, don't trust me?"

"Just being careful."

Inside the bathroom, the killer took a hypodermic syringe from the carryall, removed a protective cap from the needle, held it to the light and pressed the plunger to remove any residual air. The killer replaced the cap and put the syringe in a back pocket, smiled into the mirror and flushed the toilet, grasping the handle with a paper towel, using it also to wipe the door knob and then placing it in the carryall.

Parnell raised his bottle when the killer returned. "So did

you like what I had to say?"

"You've been very useful," the killer said, placing the carryall on the sofa but not sitting. "It seems to take a lot of planning."

"That's why it can work.  You out think them up front. They react like puppets. You stay in control all the way. Your schedule. I'd like the other five thousand now."

The killer smiled. "Do you think you've earned it?"

"Don't you?"

"Yes, I do."  The killer reached into the carryall and removed the other two envelopes and a cell phone. Tossing the envelopes on the table, the killer began working the phone's keypad.

"Have to make a call," the killer said, stepping past Parnell back toward the kitchen.

"Take your time," Parnell said, reaching forward for the envelopes.

The killer whirled and clamped an arm around Parnell's neck in the "sleeper hold" once favored by police. Applying pressure to the complex formed by the carotid arteries, jugular veins and the vagus nerves, the killer watched Parnell sink back in his chair stunned, but still conscious.

Laying the phone on the coffee table, the killer took out the syringe, removed the cap, expertly squeezed Parnell's left arm to expose the vein and rapidly injected 500 mg. of a 10% solution of lidocaine hydrochloride.

"Hey," Parnell croaked, twisting to one side, "what is this?"

"End of the road," the killer said, recapping the syringe.

"What...who?" Parnell struggled to his feet.

"Easy now," the killer said, taking a step away, the syringe in one hand and the phone now in the other. "It'll be over soon."

Parnell took two steps and seemed to lose control of his limbs.

"You'll feel a little giddy, then dizzy," the killer said, but it won't be painful."

Parnell stumbled around like the stricken animal he was, the killer easily staying out of his way.  After a few moments, Parnell began to convulse, then crumpled to the floor, his breathing erratic, becoming shallower and then undetectable. The killer watched and waited, then returned the syringe and phone to the carryall, put on latex gloves, and removed a stethoscope, tweezers and several clear plastic envelopes, each labeled with a name.

Selecting one of the envelopes and replacing the others, the killer knelt and checked Parnell's pupils, placed the stethoscope on his chest, listened. Nothing. Fatal cardiac arrest. Using the tweezers, the killer removed a strand of hair from the plastic envelope and placed it on the rug near Parnell.

Still wearing the gloves, the killer tore another sheet from the guest book, retrieved the four envelopes and the beer bottle and put them in the carryall with everything else. After looking around the room, the killer opened the door, checked outside, then wiped off the doorknob and put the sunglasses back on.

"The toughest case--a random hit with no motive," the killer said, nodding to Parnell's body before closing the door.

# TWO

## THURSDAY, APRIL 22

Vivian Pershing usually arrived at the hospital well before 8:30 on Thursdays. But today there had been an accident on Little Falls Parkway and it was after nine when she worked the special hand controls built into the steering wheel of her Toyota Sienna and eased into a handicap space in the parking lot.

She turned off the engine and set the parking brake by touching a button on the dashboard. She put the Rover, which doubled as her car seat, into reverse, executed a right turn and punched a button on the dash. Instantly the side right-hand door of the van slid open and a ramp extended out and lowered to the pavement.

Driving the Rover slowly down the ramp, she then pressed a button on her key ring and was well away from the van before the ramp whined back in place and the door snapped closed. She drove to a sloping section of the curb, paused momentarily to check for cars, and sped across the driveway to the staff entrance and through the glass doors held open for her by a one of the nurses.

She cruised down the middle of the hallway and turned left into the volunteer office where she took her red cotton blazer from the rack. Male volunteers had been wearing the jackets forever. But now, thanks in no small part to her efforts, women could choose whether to abandon their traditional candy stripe smock for the blazer.

Slipping the blazer over her white nylon blouse, Vivian signed in using the touch screen on the computer. Before leaving she checked for any messages on the bulletin board. Occasionally a volunteer would call in sick or with a conflict, and another volunteer would be asked to pinch hit. Vivian often substituted at the surgical waiting desk, but there were no messages for her today.

Driving through the lobby, Vivian saw Connie Vacarro and the other volunteers behind the semicircular information desk busily answering phone calls from those seeking to talk to hospitalized friends and relatives. Connie was a vivacious redhead and, although new, she and Vivian had become fast friends. They shared a common interest in arts and crafts, and Vivian was envious that Connie had a degree from New York City's Pace College, painted in oils, and made glazed ceramic tiles.

Connie worked downtown as a bartender and Vivian was also pleased that they shared an affection for good bourbon. It was over drinks at Vivian's house one Saturday afternoon that she learned Connie had recently suffered through a devastating love affair. Vivian admired Connie's spirit in getting on with her life just as she herself had done years before when Andrew walked out of hers.

She maneuvered the Rover behind the desk and eased into her station at the first computer, squeezing Connie's shoulder.

"Afternoon, sleepy head," Connie said.

"Up yours," Vivian winked. "You finish your rounds already?"

"Yes, ma'am. Fastest paper girl in D.C." One of the volunteers' daily tasks was to distribute about 200 copies of the *Washington Post* to patients and certain staff throughout the hospital. Connie arrived an hour ahead of the others so she could deliver the newspapers that awaited her on a cart.

Vivian smiled. "Bet I'd beat your butt by ten minutes if this chair had a sidecar for the papers."

"I'd lose the way you drive."

"You sucking up to me?"

"Of course. I know my place."

"Hi ladies," a voice said.

They looked up to see Ramon Vargas, who ran the gift shop, holding a bouquet of flowers. "These go to 3 East. Room number's on the card."

"I'll take them," Connie said.

"Pretty aren't they?" Vargas said, leering at her.

"How goes it, Ramon?" Vivian asked.

"Getting by," he answered, his eyes fixed on Connie. "You?"

"Fine, since they amputated my arm."

"That's nice."

"Thought you'd think so."

"Good, good," Vargas said. "Well, see you beauties later," he smiled, waving and showing a perfect set of teeth.

"God, what a creep," Connie said. "Does he really think he's sexy?"

"Lot's of women here do. Bare their soul to the guy. Some other parts too."

"They must be desperate. Hope I'll never be like that."

"Not with your looks," Vivian said.

"Not so sure with my luck."

"Luck has nothing to do with it."

"Thank you, mother. Listen, I'd better deliver these."

When Connie returned a few minutes later, Vivian was in the middle of a phone call. She waited until there was a lull, then tapped Vivian's arm. "Guess who I saw in the cafeteria this morning?"

"I'll bite."

"Your favorite pair, Prentice and Ellis head to head in a veddy earnest conversation. And I could swear they were holding hands a second under the table."

"Aha! I knew those two were up to something."

"Sexual hanky panky?"

"That's only part of it. I'm sure they're plotting against Bob Kramer. Ellis's really pushing for his job. You should have heard her on the phone when she called me last night about the financials. Talk about sucking up."

"Can she really be CEO?"

"Sure. She's smart and has the credentials. A Master's from Arizona State in hospital administration and a couple years nursing training to boot."

"Wouldn't Albert Jennings be in line before her?"

"No way. He's good, but happy crunching numbers. Her real competition's Stan Jacobi."

"Jacobi? Doesn't he have enough to do being chief of surgery?"

"Oh, he'd have to give that up and scale back his practice. Kramer may not know it, but he's fighting a two-front war."

"You're in his corner, right?"

"I'm wavering. The third quarter results came out Monday and I don't know if he's still the right man for the job."

"From what I've heard he seems like a pretty sharp guy."

"He is. But maybe not for Clara Barton. Anyhow, I'm going to pay him a visit today to shake him up."

"Well, just tell me who you're backing before I put my money down."

"You'll go far here, Vacarro."

---

"Not at all, Woody," Kramer said soothingly into his phone that afternoon. He pushed his glasses to his forehead and rubbed his eyes with his thumb and forefinger as he listened to the voice on the other end of the line.

"I totally agree," he said, "and the research department should pay its own way soon. Several promising leads for genetic therapies. Yes. A whole menu of experiments, some with live animals. I'm hopeful we won't have to dip into the endowment next year. Absolutely. Look, let's get together for lunch before the next meeting. Good. I'll look forward to it. Regards to Helen."

Kramer swiveled his chair toward the window and replaced his glasses, looking out at the horseshoe-shaped driveway where patients came and went every day as they had for the past five years. During that time he had taken this sleepy, country club of a hospital kicking and screaming into the 21st century.

Clara Barton was hardly immune to the problems plaguing all hospitals, but Kramer had the knack for dealing with the complex issues of modern health care: government policy, labor problems, insurance reimbursement negotiations, departmental bickering, and the allure and expense of technological advances. And what had been his reward? Skepticism, controversy, and, for the past six months, definite signs of a hostile takeover. Just when he was so close to making it all work.

Sure, the numbers were bad. He'd never promised otherwise. But give him two more years--three at the outside--and Clara Barton would no longer take a back seat to Inova Fairfax, Georgetown or any other Washington area hospital. He'd match them in facilities, grant money, equipment and personnel. But first he needed to get a new budget passed and his contract renewed. And to do that he had to ward off the circling buzzards: his former playmate, Cynthia Ellis, and the CEO-in-waiting, Stan Jacobi.

Kramer turned back to his desk. They must think him either blind or a fool. He might not know Washington all that well, but the cutthroats at his other hospitals were no different. Indeed, his ex-wife Roberta and the others on the staff at Erie County General in New York could teach them a few dirty tricks. He still bore the scars to prove it. Never again. This time he had plans in place. He was a step ahead of Cynthia and Jacobi and would beat them.

There was a knock at the door of the adjoining office. "Come in, Laura." he called.

She entered smiling. "Woodworth's head must be spinning," she said. "You almost had me convinced."

"That's the idea. Did you get it all down?"

"Better yet. I had the tape running."

"Good. You can erase my promise about the research department," he smiled. He went over to the wet bar he'd had installed when he took the job.

She leaned against his desk, quite stunning in a tight navy skirt and cream-colored silk blouse open at the collar. "You starting happy hour early?"

"I deserve a drink after talking to Woodworth. Care for a sherry?" Laura had been very friendly lately. Was it compassion or collusion?

"I'll pass," she said, "and so should you. You have one more meeting and she's camped in my office. The Czarina."

"Pershing? When did I set that up?"

"You didn't. I've been fending off her calls all afternoon, but she drove in like a small tank while you were on the phone and demanded an audience. Her words."

"She say what she wanted?"

"Three guesses."

"Never mind," he sighed. He turned back toward his desk. The timing was fortuitous. He decided to throw Laura a piece of bait. "Look, could you do me a favor before you leave for the day?"

"Sure."

"Run off a copy of the P&L projections for next year that assume the same level of receipts as through the third quarter. Bring it in while I'm with Pershing."

"You going to show it to her?"

"I might. Then she can see what we may be up against if my new projections don't hold."

"That's not how you pitched it to Woodworth."

"Pershing's a lot smarter," Kramer said.

"Sure you don't want me to hang around?"

"No, that's okay. Can I phone you tonight? I may need you to come in early."

"I'll be home. Rain check on the sherry?"

"Say when. All right," he said and put down his glass. "Show in the old bear, and watch out for her wheels."

# FRIDAY, APRIL 23

Cynthia sat at her bathroom vanity brushing her long black hair. She had always loved looking in the mirror, aware of her beauty since she was a toddler. Her older brother Rick had often called her a flirt when she would follow him around trying to impress his pals in the schoolyard. In fact, she was as athletic and fast as some of them and could play ball better than most. She even grew a tad taller than Rick, though she admitted he was smarter, a brilliant lawyer who was deputy inspector general at a federal agency. If only their father were still alive. He'd be proud of them both, especially when she became CEO.

Of course, Dad would have handled things differently, but then he was a man and played by the old rules--you worked harder than the next guy and, if you had smarts and were lucky, success would inevitably come. And it had for him, appointed president of a Fortune 500 company at age 44. But he had paid a huge price: long days stretching into nights, weekends traveling, a disintegrating marriage, an alcoholic wife who left him with a teen-age son and daughter, and a massive heart attack in his fifties.

Rick had worked just as hard, but he was still waiting for promotion to the top job. She wasn't going that route. She'd use her brains and energy, sure, but every other angle too. She'd plot every step, cut every corner, seek every edge, use her beauty and be affable when it helped, and ruthless when it didn't. Her way might not be as pretty, but she'd get there and be alive to enjoy it.

She lay down the brush and checked her image one more time. Into the arena, she winked, adjusted her skirt and halter-top and walked through her house to the combination porch and deck where she'd left Peter sipping an after-dinner cognac.

"Why are you sitting in the shadows?" she said, switching on a lamp. She took the opposite chair and crossed her legs, making sure some thigh was showing.

He turned to her. "And God saw the light and called it good."

"That's blasphemy."

"Not at all. Ask Father Cahill."

"No thanks," she said, taking a sip of her cognac. "I've seen enough of him lately. Didn't know you were a fan."

Thorpe shrugged. "We've chatted in the fitness room is all."

"Yeah, he's a treadmill freak. Wish he'd spend more time there and less in my office."

"Maybe he's trying to convert you," Thorpe smiled.

"Me? I'm his personal Satan. He's forever complaining we're too indifferent to charity cases."

"He told me that once too. I reminded him we're not a free clinic."

"Cahill doesn't care. Says we should do more. Instead we spend money on wicked programs."

"Tell him to talk to Kramer."

"Bob won't meet with him anymore. Wants me to deal with him."

"You should. I hear some trustees think he's great. Why not butter him up? Tell him you're going after Kramer's job."

"Won't help. He thinks I'm part of the problem. My guess is he'll be a cheerleader for Jacobi. Dr. Wonderful can move mountains, haven't you heard?"

"Jacobi won't listen to Cahill's babbling."

"Wrong. He'd use any ammunition he can when he makes his move. Which won't be long, now that he's seen the financials."

"That bad?"

"Worse. The deficit's way larger than the projections. Kramer must be going nuts, but he'll fight like hell."

Thorpe put down his snifter and leaned forward. "So, it's like you figured, you'll be up against him and Jacobi."

"And I've given that a lot of thought. Peter, I have to attack Jacobi where he's strongest." She moved her chair closer. "Put on a trustee's hat for a minute. Why would you be fed up with Kramer?"

"Because he's losing money."

"Why is that?"

"God, there's a host of reasons. It's not easy to run a hospital."

"Some do it successfully. Why not Kramer? He knows his stuff."

"He's spending too much in the wrong places."

"Bulls eye," she said. "His programs are too ambitious. But you bear some responsibility. You're a trustee and passed his budgets. What do you do?"

"I vote to change course."

"Yes, but you won't turn to me because...fill in the blank."

"Because Kramer hired you."

"And I'm trained the same way he is. Master's in hospital

administration. I'd try to run Clara Barton like a business and make it a more modern hospital same as him."

"You have to in today's world."

"And deep down the trustees know that," she said, her knees now touching his. "But some of the graybeards still long for the good old days when doctors ran everything."

"Enter Jacobi."

"Correct. And that's where we beat him. We go after his reputation as chief of surgery."

"Hold it. Wouldn't I--I mean the trustees--simply look for some other physician?"

"Not enough time. Besides, there aren't many out there who can or want to run a hospital. Jacobi's the only one they'd go for without a nationwide search."

"Assume you're right," Thorpe said, standing. "How do we hit him?"

"That's where you come in. I've heard some negatives about him. Have you?"

"The usual complaints," he said and moved toward the railing. "Scheduling screw ups, mismatching surgeons and nurses, techs bitching over hours and procedures. But you can't keep everyone happy. Anyway, that's all administrative stuff, not medicine."

"The nurses say he's abusive in the OR."

Thorpe laughed. "Cynthia, we all blow up in there. I've done it plenty."

"But you apologize. And that's not all, Peter. I've checked. The number of incident reports filed about him is way up from last year. Maybe he's spread too thin."

"He's a workaholic. But look, even if he's stressed out and the nurses and surgeons are griping more, I can't very well be the one to ask the committee or Kramer to take some kind of action."

"Of course not. Anyway, Bob wouldn't dare--the trustees would crucify him. We need something stronger. What about the debriefings?" she asked.

"The post-op conferences?"

"Yes. Dr. Monroe mentioned to me that Jacobi's been criticized lately."

Thorpe nodded. "There've been a few technical lapses. We all go through it."

Cynthia walked over to him. "More than usual?"

Thorpe looked thoughtful a moment. "Now that you mention it. But nothing really bad. He's still a fine surgeon."

"Does he admit he screws up?"

"He's responsive to the critiques, but, of course, he defends himself."

"How?" she asked, edging closer.

"Same as we all do. You recite the book and how you followed it, then acknowledge there could have been an unanticipated problem and try to avoid it next time. Jacobi's no different."

"Christ, Peter, you're making this hard."

He gazed into those lovely gray eyes. "Complications happen, Cynthia. That's why we have patient consent. And sometimes surgeons make a mistake. But we don't call each other out unless there's something really egregious."

"Like what?"

He paused. "Gross negligence or an ethical issue. Those would be serious. Jacobi's clean on that score."

"You sure?"

"I know what I've seen and heard. There's not a blemish on his record."

"Maybe you can find one."

Thorpe smiled. "You mean create one."

She put her hands on his shoulders. "That's not a bad idea." She moved away, picked up her glass and took a sip. "What's some of the worst things a surgeon can do to a patient?"

"That's easy. Operating on the wrong patient or wrong body part."

"Jacobi's not that bad. What else?"

"Unnecessary surgery if you can prove it," he said, "but that's almost always a judgment call."

"Nope. Keep going."

"Well, showing up drunk or on drugs."

"Jacobi like his cocktails, doesn't he?"

"Sure. You've seen him at the open house."

"Cool. That's a possibility."

"Oh, sure. I'll slip him a gin and tonic while he's scrubbing at six in the morning, then tell him to stand down."

"Nothing so obvious. Just do me a favor. Examine the recent cases where he lost a patient and the family wasn't too happy."

"There aren't that many, Cynthia."

"Then it won't take you long, now will it?"

"What's the point?"

"I know a lawyer who might be willing to file a lawsuit claiming that Jacobi wasn't fit to operate that day."

"Who is he?"

"She. Marcia Davis and she owes me a favor."

"Lawyers don't give favors."

"This one does. My brother Rick dated her for awhile after her hubby left."

"Did it work out?"

"Got her back feeling good about herself, but then pfft. He's another lawyer."

"See what I mean?"

"Peter, a well-publicized lawsuit could put Jacobi's golden reputation in doubt and help me. Marcia can always dismiss the case later."

Thorpe shook his head. "I don't think a trumped-up case would impress the trustees. In could even backfire and generate sympathy for him."

"Fine, Peter. You play fair like King Arthur, but Jacobi won't. That's how he got to be chief. I read the file. He practically called Emerson an incompetent."

"I'm aware of that, but a malpractice suit's not the answer."

"Then come up with a better idea. Otherwise, he's going to be your next CEO and you'll still be tying sutures while he looks over your shoulder."

Thorpe put down his glass. "Thanks for dinner. I'll get back to you. Maybe there's another way."

"I'm willing to listen, but we don't have much time. He's gaining momentum." She stepped over to him. "Don't go away angry. Stay a little longer."

"Clock's ticking, Cynthia. We've got things to do."

# THREE

## SUNDAY, APRIL 25

The sun was setting when Dr. Edward Monroe walked out of Clara Barton that evening. Dinner with that hot new lab tech would be delayed, but Monroe was glad he'd visited Mrs. Warren. He liked to assure himself that his patients were comfortable the night before surgery.

On Peter Thorpe's advice, Monroe often scheduled surgery on Mondays since there were usually plenty of empty slots in the OR. He smiled as he recalled Peter's explanation: "Many patients don't want a Monday because they're afraid nurses and doctors are hung over from the weekend. And I've seen a few who were."

Monroe was in a good mood and with reason. Fourth in his class at GW medical school, he was one of the few black doctors who had made it big in this part of the city and the first named an oncology staff surgeon at Clara Barton. At 34, he was hitting his professional stride and was seriously thinking that marriage might finally be a realistic choice for him.

But not yet, he thought, anticipating what might follow tonight's dinner with the tech. He stepped up his pace when he reached the doctors' parking lot, heading toward the back corner. He chose the remote location even on weekends to avoid some cowboy late for a tee time nicking one of the fenders of his vintage Jaguar XKE convertible.

Monroe had reached the car and was unlocking the driver's door when a menacing, electronic voice called out off to his right.

"Turn around, blackie."

The killer emerged from the hedges, wearing a gray sweat suit and a Darth Vader mask equipped with voice changer and carrying a large tote bag in one hand and a 9mm. Beretta in the other.

Monroe stared at the gun. "Look, I don't have--."

"Shut up!" The killer snapped through the voice changer. "Empty your pockets, and I want your watch, bracelet, pager and cell phone. Put it all on the ground and toss those keys away."

"Anything you say."

"Do it." The Beretta waved.

"Hey, I'm cooperating," Monroe said, briefly raising his hands. He went through his pockets and removed the other items as instructed. He placed everything on the ground.

"The keys," the killer said, taking a step forward. "Then get in your car and stay put till I'm gone."

"Relax, okay?" Monroe said, turning slowly and opening the door. Suddenly, he spun back with a scream, kicking out and forward in a karate move and hurling the keys directly at the killer.

Startled, the killer jumped back, but Monroe's foot slammed into a knee and his hand chopped at the killer's forearm, causing the index finger to jerk the trigger.

The bullet smashed into the right side of Monroe's chest. He fell back and collapsed against the car, his head slamming into the side of the front seat. He struggled to breathe through the pain, but drew blood into his badly wounded lung. He gasped and coughed up pink foam, only vaguely aware of the killer's legs moving toward him as he lost consciousness.

The killer studied the wound. It looked very serious. You fool, why didn't you just get in the car? Pushing Monroe's cell phone aside, the killer quickly scooped the wallet and other items into the tote bag along with the gun. Opening the phone, the killer moved toward the hedges, turning slightly to catch more sunlight, then spotted a woman in nurse's scrubs running toward the parking lot. Even better than 911, the killer thought, removing the mask and disappearing through the hedges.

---

Several minutes after Dr. Monroe was shot, police detective Tawana Briggs and Lieutenant Sam Witkin reached the bottom of the front steps of the small but elegant Tudor on the 5200 block of Palisades Avenue, a short drive from the hospital. They turned back to look at the brick facade of the house.

"What do you think?" Tawana asked.

"The family was nice to let us stop by so late," Sam said.

"Sammy, I want that house," Tawana said, a beautiful woman of 30 with chiseled features, light mahogany skin and reddish brown hair swept into a pony tail.

"And I want a raise." Sam was only slightly taller than Tawana, in his 40s with swarthy skin and dark brown hair and eyes. "It's a great house, but we can't afford it." He took her hand and started up the street toward his old Volvo.

She took a last look at the house before following. They both worked homicide and had met two years before when he was a sergeant and she a rookie. His boss and longtime friend, Frank Stephens, had solved the problem of Sam dating a subordinate by becoming her direct supervisor. The fact that Sam was white and Tawana was black was not an issue.

"Sammy, I know it's more than we talked about, but it's the perfect size, it's near the church and close enough to the hospital so Gail can pop over anytime." Gail Stephens was Frank's wife and a senior triage nurse at Clara Barton.

"Uh-huh."

"And Nick and Kathy live within walking distance."

"Oh great," Sam said, rolling his eyes. "Just what I always wanted, Nick Mercante for a neighbor. Anyway, you've seen that house of theirs. They're loaded."

"They're not. Kathy and her first husband bought it at the right time and she held on. Paid a lot less than we'll have to."

"We don't have to do anything. It's too much money."

"After tax and interest deductions, it'll only be a bit more a month than we're paying Mrs. Copland in rent."

"What about when you go on leave when the baby comes?" he asked.

"We'll manage for a few months."

"You're forgetting day care. And where will we come up with a down payment for that place? You happen to have an extra fifty grand in your pocket?"

"We can scrape it together. My Mom said she'd help."

"Since when?"

"Since I called last night and told her about the house."

"She hasn't seen it."

"Yes she has," Tawana said. "She accessed the listing picture on the internet."

He shook his head, smiling as he opened the Volvo's passenger door for her. "Your generation's too much."

"My generation? She's nearly 70." Tawana eased herself carefully into the front seat even though she was only four months pregnant.

Sam climbed in and started the engine.

"Anyway," Tawana continued, "she'd like us to be in a house

before much longer and so would I."

"But, T, you don't know how the game is played. We suddenly come up with that kind of cash in our account and the bank will know somebody's fronting the down payment."

"Stop being dense. People do it all the time. I know it's a stretch, but real estate's a good investment. It only goes up in value. Like your antiques."

"I'd never sell my furniture," he said, making a right off Arizona Avenue.

"That's how I'll feel about that house."

"You sound like the wife in that movie War of the Roses."

"This house doesn't have a chandelier."

"There are other ways of offing your husband."

"Listen to you. Sammy, let's drive by the church on the way home."

They had been married three weeks before at Trinity United Methodist Church in a ceremony performed jointly by the minister and a rabbi whose name Sam had found in the Yellow pages. Not a religious man, he was nonetheless aware of his roots. And while his mother and father loved Tawana and the thought of becoming grandparents, his father would have chewed him a new one if the wedding tradition had been ignored.

"Samuel," his father had said, "I don't mind that she's black and a shiksa, but you're a Jew. Don't forget that."

"Pop, I haven't been to a synagogue since I was 15."

"It's never too late, Samuel. God teaches that. You must have a rabbi perform the service. So tell me, how are you going to raise the baby?"

Sam had left the answer for another day. Now they swung by the church and once again admired its graceful lines. Cathedrals this size were a thing of the past, and Tawana had fallen in love with the place the first time she saw it when she was investigating the Trinity murder case.

"Sammy, if we buy the house, I think I'll become a member here. Would you mind?"

"Of course not. You can join even if we buy that condo I like."

"I want a garden, not Astroturf next to a pool."

"Hold on!" he exclaimed, pulling over sharply when a police cruiser turned into their street and raced toward them, its siren wailing and its canopy lights flashing red and blue. A second cruiser followed closely behind.

"Something nasty going down," Tawana said, as the cruisers screamed past.

"And you wanna live in this neighborhood."

---

Minutes later, the police cruisers careened to a stop outside the emergency room entrance at Clara Barton. After conferring briefly with a security guard, two of the officers hustled over to Monroe's car to secure the crime scene. The second pair went through the doors over to the intake clerk. Unlike some weekend nights, the waiting room was fairly quiet, a woman was pacing and wringing her hands while a young boy trailed behind her, whimpering.

"Hiya, Liz, is he conscious?" the taller policeman asked, taking out a small notebook from his shirt pocket.

The clerk shook her head. "I wouldn't count on a statement any time soon. They've taken him to a trauma room."

At that moment, Dr. Emily Harris entered the third of the ER's six trauma rooms and slipped on a fresh mask and pair of latex examination gloves. As a junior resident, she was used to working Sundays, but was glad her shift was almost over.

She hurried over to the operating table where Monroe had been placed. Shock trauma teams didn't stand on ceremony. For the past several minutes, a team had been working feverishly, attaching electrical and IV leads, checking his vital signs, and trying to keep him warm.

"My God! It's Dr. Monroe," she said, reaching his side.

"Yes, doctor," Gail Stephens said calmly.

Harris looked at the steady brown eyes above Gail's mask and nodded. "Okay, what do we have?" she said evenly, pulling the blanket down. Monroe's shirt had been cut away. Blood was seeping into a pressure bandage that had been applied.

"Likely gunshot," Gail said. "He's already lost a lot of blood, and I think the lung's collapsed."

After Harris shifted the bandage, four pairs of eyes stared at the gaping wound in Monroe's chest from which blood oozed.

"BP when he came in?" Harris asked.

"Seventy-six," Gail replied, giving only the systolic blood pressure reading. "We've started a Ringers, Dextran and a unit of blood."

Harris glanced at the IV pole. The electrolyte-glucose solution and drug being infused into Monroe's leg were standard measures to stabilize blood pressure. Then she noted the unit of blood.

"Why O-positive?" she asked.

"All we have," a technician at her shoulder said, "but we've sent for negative."

"Good decision. We can risk a case of hives right now. And give him 80 mg of gentamicin."

"Yes, doctor."

"When did it happen?" Harris asked Gail, taking out her stethoscope.

"Ten, fifteen minutes ago. We got lucky. Priscilla was taking a smoke break in the gazebo and thought she heard a shot."

Harris glanced at the monitor. Heart rate 122. She listened to the rapid and erratic beat a moment. "He's not getting enough air. We have to intubate."

Monroe coughed up some blood as Gail handed Harris an endotracheal tube, which she maneuvered carefully down his throat and into the trachea. Another nurse attached the tube to a respirator to help Monroe's labored breathing.

"BP?" Harris asked.

"Sixty-eight."

"He must be hemorrhaging. Start another unit of blood stat."

Harris bent over and heard the faint hiss of air moving in and out of the hole in Monroe's lung, the signature of a sucking chest wound. "Damn, it's a sucker," she said.

She moved her stethoscope around the wound. "It's a pneumothorax, all right. Get a tube ready. We've got to close that hole."

The team worked expertly and quietly, the only sounds in the room the steady rhythm of the respirator and the beeping of the EKG monitor. Harris reached down and fingered Monroe's chest until she reached the fifth rib. She lifted her finger and Gail immediately wiped the area with an antiseptic and another nurse handed Harris a scalpel.

Harris made a neat one-inch incision through the chest muscle on a line directly below Monroe's armpit. Using her fingers, she spread the tissues wide enough to accommodate the chest tube, which was about the size of her index finger. "Ready," she murmured.

Gail instantly placed the tube in Harris's hand. She carefully inserted it into the chest between the rib and muscle wall and the collapsed lung, then connected the other end to a suction bottle in order to clear out the chest cavity.

The next step was to locate the bullet, repair and stabilize the lung, and stop the blood loss. "Okay, get an x-ray," Harris said.

A nurse began moving the portable machine toward the table when the EKG monitor alarm sounded.

"Fibrillating, doctor," Gail said, immediately starting resuscitation by pressing Monroe's chest rhythmically as the other nurse pushed the x-ray equipment aside and pulled a crash-cart from the wall.

"Call a Code," Harris ordered, studying the chaotic waves on the EKG monitor.

"There's a team right outside," a technician said, "but we're down a surgeon."

"Get them in here. Where's Mallory?" Harris asked, taking the defibrillator paddles from the top shelf of the crash cart.

"Working a stabbing next door."

"Get me anybody in house."

The technician hit a button and spoke into a wall speaker.

Almost instantly the hospital's public address system blared into life:

*Code Blue, Any surgeon, Trauma Room 3.*
*Code Blue, Any surgeon, Trauma Room 3.*

Harris pressed the paddles against Monroe's chest. "Clear!"

Everyone moved back as 1800 volts of electricity shot into Monroe's body. The EKG monitor didn't change. The respirator continued to ventilate his lung.

The Code team rushed into the room and hovered near the table--a pharmacist, anesthesiologist, and two nurses.

"Clear!" Harris worked the paddles again, then once more. Still no change.

"Epinephrine," Harris ordered and the pharmacist injected 10 mg into a 100 cc bottle and hung it to run through tube carrying the Dextran.

The seconds ticked by as Harris kept working the paddles, Gail continuing to pump Monroe's chest between attempts. Harris was about to try once more when suddenly the EKG waves went flat and the monitor emitted a steady tone.

"We'll have to go in," she said. "Where's that damn surgeon?

"Right here, doctor," a man's voice answered.

She turned. "Dr. Jacobi! I didn't--"

"It's all right. I happened to be in the building."

"Yes, sir." She stepped away from the table.

Without a word, Jacobi moved forward. It was now his decision whether they should break into the chest wall and try to squeeze Monroe's heart to life.

Jacobi bent over and shined a penlight into Monroe's eyes, which were lifeless with fully dilated pupils. He shook his head. "There's nothing more we can do." He stood erect, towering over Harris. "Good work, doctor," he said, then smiled. "Thank you for asking me in." He turned and left the room.

Harris took off her mask and turned to the team. "Thanks, everyone. Gail, can you tend the body and call the police?"

"They're already here, doctor," Gail said, lowering her mask and revealing her smooth ebony skin.

Harris walked wearily to the door, removing her gloves. "Okay. I'll speak with them."

## MONDAY, APRIL 26

At six-thirty that morning Thorpe was putting on scrubs in the surgeons' locker room, thinking through the radical mastectomy he was about to perform. The procedure was now routine for him though devastating for many patients.

The door opened and Dr. Ann Lyman walked in, a petite brunette in glasses who looked more like a college student than the veteran surgeon she was. She came over and put her hand on Thorpe's shoulder.

"Peter, I'm so sorry."

"About what?"

"Ed Monroe."

Thorpe studied her face. "What about him?"

"You haven't heard?"

"I'm running late. What's going on?"

"He's dead."

"Dead? Jesus, what happened?"

"He was shot in the parking lot last night. Pneumothorax. They got him right to the ER, but he'd lost too much blood."

"Shot here? Who examined him?"

"Harris. Looks like he was robbed."

"Geez. Was he in any pain?"

"I don't know if he was conscious. Perkins just told me about when I looked at the case board. Asked her why Ed's surgery had been canceled."

"She still outside?" Dorothy Perkins was a nurse manager on the surgical floor.

"At her desk."

"Listen, Ann, thanks for telling me. I have to scrub."

After completing the surgery, Thorpe spoke to Perkins, visited a patient, then went to the cafeteria to take a break with a cup of coffee and the *Post*. The cashier smiled as Thorpe took his change. Women usually did.

He was settling down at a table next to the windows when his pager went off. He glanced at the display. What took you so long, he thought. He reached for his cell phone and keyed in Kramer's direct line.

"Peter?"

"Good morning, Bob."

"You've heard about Ed Monroe?"

"This morning. Why didn't you call me last night?"

"They didn't catch up with me until after ten, and when I checked the roster, I saw you had surgery this morning. Peter, I'm sorry. I know how much you liked Ed and valued his work."

"You could have sent me an email."

"I would have, but I've been in a meeting since I got in. Peter, there's a blurb in the Metro section. I've asked Laura to draft a statement."

"I see."

"The police think it was a robbery."

"Yeah, Perkins said Ed never regained consciousness after the ER nurse found him. Did anyone else see or hear anything?"

"Not that we know of. Look, we need to think about a

replacement. Jacobi's already asked for the last cut of applicants from when we hired Mallory."

Jacobi. "That was fast."

"He was at the meeting this morning. All department heads were. And he answered the Code they called for Monroe."

"What was he doing here on a Sunday?"

"Ask him."

"The man never sleeps."

"Tell me about it. Peter, can you look over the applications before he convenes the committee? I don't want him ramming somebody through."

"Neither do I."

"Good, then I'll have Laura send you a set. God, we don't need this right now."

"No. No, we don't."

"Listen, I have to run. I'll be in touch."

Thorpe broke the connection. He pulled the Metro Section from the paper. The single paragraph was at the bottom of page 3.

*Doctor Killed at Clara Barton*

*Edward Drew Monroe, an oncological surgeon affiliated with Clara Barton Memorial Hospital, was shot to death in the hospital's parking lot yesterday evening, an apparent robbery victim. The body of Monroe, 34, who lived at the Waterside Apartments in the 500 block of O Street, Southwest, was discovered next to his car by an emergency room nurse. Monroe was a graduate of Howard College and George Washington University Medical School. He is survived by his parents, Mr. & Mrs. Charles Drew of Richmond, and an older sister, Eunice Talbot of Fredericksburg. The incident is under investigation, a police spokesperson said.*

Thorpe reread the piece, shaking his head. Poor bastard. Ed's whole future had been ahead of him. If only he'd gone back to Virginia, he'd be alive today. But he'd wanted the big time Washington practice. Thorpe looked at his watch, picked up his cell phone and keyed in the familiar number.

"Administration. Prentice."

"Morning, Laura."

"Peter. Did Bob reach you about Dr. Monroe?"

"Yes."

"Isn't it a shame? Everybody liked him."

"I know, so did I. Listen, Laura, somebody should call his parents to make arrangements for the body."

"I just got off the phone with his sister."

"Good," he nodded. "And would you remind Bob about the applications we just talked about? Jacobi's making noises about a replacement already."

"Sure. Peter?"

"Yes?"

"Can you come over tonight? It seems like ages."

"I have a bear of day ahead, babe. Then the post-op conference and a couple patients at the office. I'll be bushed."

"I miss you, darling."

"Me too. Look, let's try for tomorrow night. I'd be better company anyway."

"Don't have another date with Cynthia?"

"You'd know if I did. Play fair, okay?"

"Just teasing. Tomorrow then."

"Okay. Bye for now."

Laura hung up and went to the window, gazed out to the horseshoe-shaped driveway, again wrestling with her conflicted feelings about Peter. They were more about her than him, the result of a disastrous marriage, a sordid affair with a woman, and exhausting therapy. After all that, Laura had promised herself she would be more cautious and avoid surprises.

A Bethesda native, she was the only child of a veterinarian and a gynecological nurse who had waited until their late 30s to start a family and then suffered through a pair of miscarriages before Laura was born. Around medicine and hospitals all her life, she also had a head for finance. This led to a business degree from Rutgers University in New Jersey, followed by a job in a Newark hospital for four years.

Her career path was interrupted when she met and married Doug, a domineering Seton Hall law professor, who six months later insisted she stay home and get pregnant and then left abruptly when she refused to do either. Returning to Maryland, Laura went to work in her father's clinic and sought solace in the arms of Allison Bradley, a friend from high school.

The relationship with was comforting at first, but Allison became more intense and possessive, and Laura began to feel dominated again. When she tried to break it off, Allison refused and began to stalk her. Laura was able to escape only with the help of the police after obtaining a court order. Subsequent therapy had done little to heal the wounds of either relationship.

Feeling it was time to resume her career, Laura received a master's degree in public health administration from Ohio State University, then took an entry-level job at a Columbus hospital that led to her current position at Clara Barton a year and a half ago. Although hospitals were fertile grounds for romance, she had avoided any until her encounter with Cynthia and her dinner with Peter.

The intercom brought her out of her reverie. She went to her desk. "Yes, Bob."

"Laura, I see where the Washington Times phoned. Can you deal with them? I want to call some of the trustees."

"I'll handle it. And I should have a draft of the Monroe e-mail ready soon."

"Thanks. If my phone button's lit, just pop in with the hard copy."

"Fine." She checked the number for the Times and picked up the receiver. It was one of those days grad school didn't prepare you for.

---

Cynthia finished editing a memo for Kramer and reached for the phone to tell Laura to come pick it up when her private line rang. She saw it was her brother.

"Rick, how are you?"

"Fine, Cindy, but I read about the shooting. How are you holding up over there?"

"Had more peaceful mornings, but I'm okay. Staff's a little worked up, though."

"Did you know this Dr. Monroe?"

"Yeah. Sharp guy. Good looking, real comer."

"Damn city's going to hell.  Makes me want to go south or somewhere."

"Away from the action?" she smiled. "Who'd you investigate? Arkansas Moonshiners?"

"I'll leave them to the ATF. Gimme good old white-collar crime. Got a hot one going right now. I'd love to talk to you about it, but you know I can't."

"Big shot. Then tell me about your love life. How are you and Joyce?"

"Off and on. Mostly off."

"Rick, you really ought to settle down."

"Look who's talking--Miss Executive."

"Well, we both work too hard."

"It's in the genes, Cindy."

"Yeah, I was thinking about Dad this weekend. I almost called you."

"But you were too busy, yada, yada."

"Listen, let's do lunch soon. Can you get up here?"

"No way," he said. "I did that last time. You get your butt downtown."

"I promise. Soon as I can."

"Sure you will. Call me, okay?"

"Yes. Love you, bro."

"Me too. Watch out for muggers, Cindy. You're all I've got."

Rick was right, Cynthia thought pressing down on the receiver button. She had to keep him closer, more in her life. But not today, she sighed, lifting her finger to dial Laura. Then she changed her mind. Picking up the memo, she straightened her light green skirt, went down the hall to Laura's office and entered without knocking.

"See if he has a problem with this," she said, handing Laura the memo.

"Why don't you come in?" Laura said.

Cynthia ignored the jibe. "Helluva morning. Shows how screwed up Bob's priorities are.  He should never have cut security funding last year."

"I doubt another weekend guard would have saved Dr. Monroe."

"You never know."

"Come on, Cynthia, they never go near the parking lots unless somebody asks them to check on a car with its lights on."

"The trustees won't see it that way."

Laura leaned back. "You almost sound pleased Dr. Monroe was shot."

"Hey, I liked the guy. But you have to admit, this won't do your boss any good."

"Which helps you."

"Which helps both of us."

Laura looked away a moment, then, "I suppose, but I don't feel I'm contributing much."

"You are. Just keep being Bob's adoring assistant and tell me what you pick up about his contacts with the trustees. Only three more months, honey."

"And you really think they'll kick him out?"

"Wait till they see the year-end results. They'll never renew his contract. You talk to Peter today?"

"Yes."

"He mention looking into Jacobi's cases?" Cynthia asked.

"No, only that Jacobi's eager to replace Monroe."

"Perfect. Let him obsess on new surgeons while Peter digs up some dirt."

"You have it all figured out, don't you?"

"That's why I'm chief of staff," Cynthia said, sitting on the edge of the desk.

"And here I thought Bob was just after your body."

Cynthia smiled. "And he got his wish. But now I just scare him."

"Sometimes you scare me."

"I thought I turned you on."

"That too," Laura admitted.

"I was beginning to wonder." Cynthia leaned over and began fondling Laura's breast through her nylon blouse.

"Careful," Laura protested. "Bob might stick his head in."

After a slight squeeze, Cynthia hopped off the desk. "Some day I can do that and not worry. Another perk of being CEO. Direct access to your office."

"Wrong. I'm getting yours, remember?"

"We'll have to renovate."

---

At the buzz of his private line, Captain Frank Stephens tossed aside the report he'd been struggling to read. It must be Gail, he thought, pushing his bulky frame from his rocking chair and moving across the office. He was nearly as light on his feet as when he was a wide receiver at Marshall University 30 years before. He reached the phone before the third ring.

"Hello?"

"Hi, sweetie."

"You feeling any better?" he asked, concern showing on his handsome black features.

"Much. Sorry I was so wound up last night."

"Why wouldn't you be?" Not only had Gail been massaging Monroe's chest just before he died, she was a close friend of Priscilla Turner who found him next to his car. "At least you got some sleep. You were out cold when I left this morning."

"Thanks to the little blue pill. Do you have any more word on what happened?"

"Boys in robbery haven't talked to everyone yet, but so far none of the employees saw anything. And the radar units and cameras didn't pick up any strange traffic or speeders in the area. Looks like your basic street thief lurking around. They did find out Monroe knew karate. They think he might have tried to resist rather than just hand over his wallet. Big mistake."

"The poor guy. Frank, did I tell you he pinch hit in the ER one night?"

"Good man."

"I got to work with him. He was real savvy and so pleasant. You know why his middle name was Drew?"

"No. Should I?"

"Charles Drew was his hero."

"All right, I give up. Who was he?"

"A black surgeon born right here in D.C. a century ago. He discovered blood plasma. Saved thousands of lives in World War II."

"Back then? With the discrimination and all?"

"Not only that. He convinced young blacks to go into medicine. This is such a waste, Frank. We can't afford to lose people like Ed Monroe."

"You might still have him if he'd parked closer to the building. Fancy cars in empty parking lots is just asking for trouble."

"But, we're a hospital."

"And doctors have expensive cars and jewelry and often carry lots of cash."

"God, I hate this city sometimes."

"No more than me. What are you doing today?"

"I've got three days off. I intend to pamper myself and do some shopping. I'm going to call Priscilla to see if she wants to join me."

"Good idea."

"Life goes on, huh?"

"At least today," he said.

"I'm glad you don't work the streets anymore."

"I'm getting fat."

"I'll make us a nice dinner and keep you that way. Lamb chops?"

"Never turn them down. Will the boys be eating with us?"

"I'm not sure," she said. "You know how it is when you're 14."

"I can't remember. I'm losing my memory too."

"Hope you haven't forgotten what I look like."

"You are feeling better."

"I'll prove it tonight."

"Never turn that down either."

"I love you, Frank."

"Same here. Have a good day."

Frank hung up smiling. He might be able to concentrate on that report now.

# FOUR

## THURSDAY, MAY 6

Nick Mercante didn't like the looks of the darkening sky moving in from the west. He was worried Kathy would be so immersed in her garden, she'd be unaware of the approaching storm. It happened once before. She'd been terrified when lighting struck very close by, but thankfully the bolt missed her and took down a tulip poplar.

He pressed the gas pedal and increased the speed of his Camry to slightly above the limit as he cruised down Dalecarlia Parkway. The first drops were spattering the windshield by the time he pulled in behind Kathy's red Mazda B2300. She had long coveted a pickup truck and this spring they had decided it was time.

Now she couldn't believe she'd ever lived without one. It was perfect for her home and church projects that required trips to plant nurseries and a local quarry for cement, sand and bluestone--the fodder of a serious gardener and landscaper. There were enough trades people coming and going that her truck blended perfectly with day-to-day life of the neighborhood. Still, it seemed slightly out of place in the driveway of the beautiful house she and her former husband had bought in 1981.

A decade later and divorced, Kathy had met Nick at NASA where they were employed in a secret project, she as a computer programmer, he as an historian. They had married and he moved into the house and helped raise her adolescent daughters. These days, he worked mostly at home and she had also started telecommuting, which gave her more time in her garden where she might be at the moment.

The rain was coming down harder as Nick climbed out of the car. He was a short man in his late fifties, with graying black hair and brown eyes that now searched the front and side gardens as he carried the groceries up the flagstone walk toward the kitchen door. Kathy was nowhere in sight. A clap of thunder galvanized him to put down the bag and hurry to the back of the house.

There she was on a ladder in yellow-striped overalls and coral tee shirt sawing the top limbs of the crepe myrtle that grew at the edge of the roof outside their bedroom window.

"Hey get down from there," he called, "it's going to storm."

"Hold on, I've got to cut back this top branch," She was a pretty blonde with light blue-gray eyes and a classic ski jump nose. At moments like this, she was a fair replica of Julie Andrews as he often told her.

"I thought you wanted the bush tall."

"But I should have pruned this side more in February. Don't worry, it'll grow back by summer."

"You won't live to see it if you don't come down."

"Be right there," she said and resumed her attack on the branch as the thunder moved closer and grew louder.

"Come on, Kathy, the gods are on the prowl."

"What? I don't need a towel."

"No, what you need is a hearing aid."

"Patches gets one first," she said, referring to their increasingly deaf English springer spaniel.

"At least she's smart enough to stay out of the rain."

"Then who's that next to the day lily bed?"

He turned his head. Sure enough the dog was watching from the grass.

"Nicky, watch out!"

He jumped back as the branch tumbled past him just as another thunderclap boomed just overhead.

"Kathy, get down. Now." He steadied the ladder as the clouds opened and a drenching rain began. "Hurry up."

"Okay, here I come, and no cracks about my butt."

"Cracks? Butt? Hmm."

"Stop it. Watch your foot." She joined him on the ground and nuzzled his neck. "You're standing here getting soaked. Why?"

A half hour later they were sitting on their enclosed porch, looking out at the garden. The rain had passed and the day lily plants glistened in the late afternoon sun. Patches was now studying a drip from a holly bush.

"Gail called just after you left," she said.

"Oh yeah?"

"Good news. Sam and Tawana got the house."

"Terrific. When's the settlement?"

"Middle of June."

Nick took a sip of his Heineken. "We should get them a

housewarming gift."

"Tawana wants to have a party in late summer, but she's worried she may not be up to it because of the baby. Gail asked if we'd pitch in. You game?"

"If Sam doesn't kick me out."

"Thought you two had buried the hatchet."

Nick smiled. "I keep mine handy just in case."

"Juvenile. You should call and congratulate him. "

"I might. I owe Frank a call too." He and Frank had become friends during the Caruso case that Nick had helped solve. Sam had balked at Nick's assistance and, while his resistance had lessened during later cases, it had not entirely disappeared.

"Nicky, I think it's time we all got together again. We don't have to wait till the fall."

"Fine with me."

"Good, because I suggested we do a summer barbecue. Maybe a garden party. We could invite some neighbors and other friends. I've been wanting to show my day lilies."

"Maybe you can start a tradition."

"Gail's going to check with Frank. Said she could use a party. She's pulling extra shifts in the ER. Budget crunch."

"At Clara Barton? I thought the place was a cash cow."

"Not to hear her tell it. The nurses are even making noises about a union."

"Gail would never do that."

"No, but she sounded grumpy."

"Maybe she's still in a funk over Dr. Monroe. She mention it again?"

"Not a word."

"Well, that's plus. So when would we do this barbecue?"

"Around the Fourth? The blooms should be at their peak if the deer don't eat them."

"Put up a net like you did last year."

"What we need is to build that fence."

"Will it keep out Sam?"

## FRIDAY, MAY 7

Jacobi took his change from the cashier and carried his breakfast tray to the cafeteria dining room, oblivious to the familiar clusters of medical staff. Many had their faces buried in newspapers or chatted with colleagues, while ingesting food and hot coffee to prepare for the busy morning ahead or to replenish from hours already worked.

The usual members of the public were also there: weary, expectant fathers who'd been up all night waiting for their wives to finish their nine-month journey; predawn arrivals who had driven friends and relatives for outpatient procedures and would make the return trip this afternoon; and the anxious who sat quietly, waiting for the news on the fate of a loved one or trying to cope with the verdict they'd already received.

Jacobi spotted Cahill at the back of the room near the window. He made his way through the tables and managed a smile in response to the clergyman's wave. The man really ought to lose some weight, his professional gaze told him. Slipping into a chair, he noticed the plate on Cahill's tray bore traces of maple syrup.

"Good morning, Father," he said.

"Dr. Jacobi. So good of you to give me a few minutes out of your day. Forgive me for starting without you, but I can't abide cold pancakes."

"We all have our crosses to bear, Father," Jacobi winked, spooning into his poached egg. "So what can I do for you? You seemed somewhat distressed the other day."

"I'm worse now because of Dr. Monroe."

"Yes, of course. A terrible tragedy. A real loss for the hospital."

"It didn't have to happen, doctor. I've told Mr. Kramer to increase surveillance in the parking lots."

"You have?"

"Several times, but he and Miss Ellis don't seem to care. I hate to bother you, but I don't know where else to turn."

"That's quite all right, Father. Perhaps I can help. What else is troubling you?"

"Almost everything, but it all boils down to how we're spending our money. We're more worried about buildings and equipment than in helping God's children."

Spare me, Jacobi thought. "Ah, can you be more specific?"

"Oh yes," Cahill said, leaning forward. "Let's start with inside security. You know we're no longer allowed to put calls through to a patient unless the caller knows the first and last name."

Jacobi nodded. "The new HIPPA law."

"Yes, but any stranger can still come in off the street carrying all sorts of packages and no one stops them at the front door."

"Father, these are visitors bringing candy or gifts. We can't very well search everyone."

"But since 9/11 shouldn't we be more careful? We could post security at the doors and at least ask whom they're visiting. And what's worse even some florists don't always stop at the front desk like they're supposed to. They could be disguised terrorists carrying bombs. I've heard some of the volunteers talking."

"I see," Jacobi said, beginning to fidget.

"I'm telling you we worry about innocent phone calls and ignore real risks. If Mr. Kramer spent more money on background checks, we wouldn't have hired that lab tech who committed identity theft."

"Yes, that was a blunder." The man had stolen identification from a dying patient who had in fact lived. He was caught when the patient began receiving thank you letters at home for opening new credit card accounts.

"And take this new research wing," Cahill said. "A total waste of money on unproven theories. University hospitals should do that kind of thing. We're supposed to be helping the afflicted."

"You're absolutely right, Father," Jacobi said, trying not to sound bored.

"Not to mention they're interfering with God's law. Using embryos to extract stem cells--murder, pure and simple."

Jacobi finished his egg and poured skim milk on his cornflakes. "Yes, well, that's open to debate. But I see your overall point."

"I thought you would. We're even turning patients away if they don't have insurance."

"Father, we're not a public hospital," Jacobi said and stole a glance at his newspaper.

"But we're required to provide a reasonable amount of service without charge or at a reduced rate for the indigent."

At least Cahill knew the rules, Jacobi thought. "To be sure, but that doesn't mean everyone gets in for free or at a discount."

"But Mr. Kramer's policies are egregious. Are you aware the ER's been turning people away because they don't have an insurance card in their pocket?"

Jacobi looked up. This might be interesting. "The ER, you say?"

"Can I give you a few examples?"
"Please."
"We used to fill all prescriptions for outpatients."
"Until this fiscal year," Jacobi said.
"But now we won't provide medicine unless the patient can pay directly or through insurance."

"Father, lots of hospitals require that. It's sound business practice."

"It kills. Last December a pregnant homeless woman showed up at the ER spitting up blood. Turns out she had pulmonary TB."

"I assume we treated her with antibiotics."

"Gave her enough for three days. But when we released her we told her to go to a drug store to get her prescription filled. We wouldn't do it."

"We don't under the new policy."

"But she had no money even to get to a clinic. So when she stopped taking drugs, her symptoms worsened. By the time she got help, her condition was more complicated. She survived but lost the baby."

Jacobi shifted in his seat. "Go on."

"Then there was the woman whose doctor stopped seeing her when her husband got laid off and lost his health insurance. She later detected a small growth in her breast, but delayed getting an examination hoping her husband would find work. When she finally came here, the ER wouldn't give her a second look."

"No doctor referral, no insurance and her condition wasn't life-threatening."

"Exactly. But how much would a mammogram and diagnosis have set us back? Anyway, after several months she finally saw someone at a county hospital where her sister lived. By then the cancer had metastasized. Her prognosis isn't great."

Jacobi nodded. While neither case violated any laws or ethics codes, they did represent distasteful outcomes. "Tell me, Father, how do you know so much about these patients?"

"I have friends in the ER who've followed up on them and talked to me in confidence. I've assembled data on over two dozen such episodes in the last ten months."

"Two dozen? Did you discuss them with Mr. Kramer?"

"I've tried. That nice Laura Prentice is sympathetic and has made appointments for me, but Miss Ellis is deaf and Mr. Kramer says it's out of his hands. Claims the budget and policy are set by the trustees."

Which is only technically correct, Jacobi thought. Kramer proposes the budget; the board just tweaks it. "Father, you've made a powerful argument. I'd like to help you do more for God's children."

Cahill beamed. "You think you really can?"

"I'll do my best. Now, can you put all this in writing? Say in the form of a report with your recommendations for change?"

"Oh yes. It's all on my computer."

Jacobi patted the other man's arm. "Then all you need do is polish it. Feel free to include your security and other concerns, but be sure to highlight every one of those unfortunate ER cases. Could you have a draft to me by the end of next week?"

"With God's grace."

"Good. That'll give me time to look it over so we can make any needed...refinements. Then I could present it to the trustees on the budget committee when it meets in a few weeks."

"You'd do that?"

"I give you my word. Of course, as you know, the final decision's up to the full board. But if you make a good case and the committee likes what I say, I'm sure all the trustees will go along."

"Bless you, doctor, that's wonderful," Cahill said, his right hand making an almost imperceptible sign of the cross on his chest.

"Now, let's not get too far ahead of ourselves, but there is one thing you could do for me."

"Of course."

"I don't want you to breach any confidences, mind you, but you mentioned hearing positive things about me. I'd like you to reflect on that and suggest what more I might do to engender support if I decide to make myself available for chief executive officer."

"I can jot down some notes today."

"Oh no. Your first order of business is that report. Then you and I can talk politics."

"You're right." Cahill pushed away from the table. "I'll start on it this morning."

"Go to it, Father."

"I will." Cahill took a step away and then paused. "Oh, I almost forgot. Is the surgical staff planning anything special to memorialize Dr. Monroe?"

Jacobi frowned. "Far as I know, there's nothing in the works."

"So you won't mind if I have a service in the chapel next week? Non-denominational, of course."

"By all means. Whatever you think appropriate, Father."

"Thank you, doctor. God bless you."

"Well, let's pray He guides your important work."

"Yes, yes. Have a good day."

"You too," Jacobi smiled as Cahill bustled off. It's already been a fine day, he thought, flipping open his Wall Street Journal.

As he turned toward the elevators, Cahill looked back to Jacobi now immersed in his newspaper. He's so transparent, the priest thought. He's only after power. Still, getting him as an ally was a piece of the puzzle that had been missing. Now to my computer. I'll compose a quick e-mail to thank him again for meeting with him.  It was the polite thing to do. It would also make the record clear in case anyone asked later.

Cahill saw that the up button had been pressed by an attractive nurse who was tapping her foot impatiently. She reminded him of his sister Janet whose husband had been tragically killed four years before.  The couple had been walking home from church when a car trying to dodge a speeding fire truck jumped the curb, impaling him against the front of a building.

Despite Cahill's prayers, a bitter Janet had stopped going to church until last year when she was caught in a department store fire. Ironically, she was now back attending Mass and dating the fireman who had saved her when he carried out of the smoke-filled building.

Cahill smiled and let the nurse precede him when the elevator arrived.  As always, if one is patient, the Lord will work His will.

---

Laura backed her new green Ford Escape out of the hospital parking space and turned on the air conditioner. Summer was threatening to come early to Washington. The parking lot attendant waved her through and she sped out of the driveway, but soon slowed, aware how easily the peppy SUV bumped up to the speed limit.

She switched on the radio and began to hum, reveling in the feel and smell of the new car. The down payment had been a surprise Valentine's present from Peter who insisted she needed a more reliable vehicle. "Now you can bury the Taurus to commemorate our first date," he joked at the time.

Laura eased to a halt for a stop sign held by a member of work crew trimming trees. She had been thrilled yet unsettled by Peter's gesture. Her parents reinforced her mixed feelings when she called them that night in Naples, Florida where they had retired.

"Laura," her mother said, "you haven't sounded this happy since you met Doug."

"It feels good, Mom."

Her father chimed in on the extension, "But how can you accept such a gift after only a few months?"

"He insisted, Daddy, and he can afford it ten times over."

"Be careful, honey, Doug started out nice too."

"Stop lecturing, Stuart," her mother said, "Laura's perfectly capable of living her own life."

"Mom's right, Daddy, and Peter's not at all like Doug."

"Well, I don't like that he keeps your relationship a secret. It's as though he's ashamed of you or something."

"It's complicated, Daddy, and part of it's my own doing. But I am watching my step, really."

"So when do we meet him?" her mother asked. "I'm sure it's freezing up there. Can't you fly down for a weekend? It's beautiful this time of year."

"I don't want to rush him, Mom. Or me. If things keep going like they are, well, I'm sure we'll visit this summer."

The workman switched the sign to Slow and Laura moved forward. Soon she turned left down Arizona Avenue, went through the intersection on MacArthur Boulevard and into the First Security Bank parking lot. She saw Cynthia's black VW Passat at the far end and eased into the adjoining parking place.

A moment later she climbed into the Passat's passenger seat. "Your day as crazy as mine?" she asked.

"Yeah, Bob was in rare form. He's running around like a bitch in heat."

Laura smiled. "He might be at that. I caught him looking at my boobs a couple of times. I think I'm getting to him."

"Good," Cynthia said. "What size are they, by the way?"

"34C and every inch is mine."

"Thought so." She squeezed Laura's thigh through her white linen skirt. "But don't give yourself too much credit, sweetie. Right now the numbers he's most concerned about are in the P&L."

"He should be, but he's not talking much about it. You think he suspects me?" Laura asked.

"You're not pressuring him are you?"

"Not at all. It's just that before this week he would talk

specifics. Now he's vague and seems to be placing fewer calls when I'm around. So I don't always know when he's phoning the trustees."

"You still listen in, don't you?"

"If I can. I pick up as soon as I see his extension light, but not if I'm unsure how long he's been on. He could hear a click."

"Smart girl," Cynthia said. "Look, don't worry. He's got a lot on his plate right now."

"Yeah, he does. Like tomorrow. Are you set for the meeting with the nursing reps?"

"You know about that? We just scheduled it."

"Bob asked me to come in," Laura said.

"On a weekend? Doesn't sound to me like he's suspicious. Will you be sitting in?"

"No. He just wants me around in case he needs some info from the files."

"Did he tell you we're meeting over in Cabot?" Cynthia asked, referring to the building adjoining the main hospital.

"Sure. You'll need the space."

"This is perfect. That'll give you a chance to check his office to see if there's anything new we should know about."

"I peek through his desk every day," Laura said.

"But tomorrow he'll be tied up for at least a couple of hours. The reps have lots on their mind and we'll listen to everything they have to say. We don't want them forming a union."

"So I can take my time searching."

"And you can hit the file cabinets too," Cynthia said. "If he leaves to go to back to his office, I'll call to warn you."

"Great. I finally get to be useful."

"Too bad Peter isn't."

"No news about Jacobi?" she asked, already knowing the answer.

"No, that's what I wanted to talk to you about. He's taking too long finding someone to sue Jacobi."

"Maybe there isn't anybody."

"He's not looking hard enough. I even tried getting him into the sack to motivate him."

"You came on to him?"

"He's a hunk or haven't you noticed?"

"I'm not blind," Laura said, annoyed Peter hadn't mentioned this.

"Anyway, I think I have an idea to get him moving, but I need your help."

"What can I do that you couldn't with those legs of yours?"

"I'll get back to you on that," Cynthia smiled, "but for now, I want you to tell Peter you saw a note on Bob's desk that Jacobi may replace Monroe with a senior surgeon who can step in to be his successor as chief."

"He will?"

"Not that I'm aware, but Peter doesn't have to know that. You can say you found it in your search tomorrow."

"Suppose he confronts Jacobi?"

"Let him. Jacobi would deny it even if he had thought of it."

Laura shook her head. "God, I'd hate to be your enemy."

"Yes, it's much better to stay on my good side." She leaned over and kissed Laura, darting her tongue into her mouth. "And a lot more fun. Now you'd better go before we embarrass the night depositors."

## SATURDAY, MAY 8

A few minutes after four, Cynthia called Laura to alert her the meeting was over and Kramer was on his way back.

"No problem," Laura said. "I finished a while ago, and I think I found something interesting."

"Good, but I can't talk now. I've got a ton of work to do thanks to his nibs. Call me tonight."

Moments later Kramer walked into Laura's office.

"How did it go?" she greeted him, standing.

"Better than I thought. They were loaded for bear, but we dug in our heels. Thanks for coming in. I should have sent you home long ago when I realized I didn't need your help."

"And here I thought I was indispensable," she said, leaning against her desk, her figure nicely outlined in white slacks and yellow cotton sweater.

"Labor negotiations your specialty?" he asked, admiring her.

"I could learn," she smiled.

"I may need you down the road now that you mention it. Listen, I've already ruined your Saturday. Suppose I make amends and claim your rain check from the other day. I'd like to bounce some ideas off you if you have time for a drink."

She'd have to call Peter. "Sure, I'm free."

"How about Lardiere's? It's right down the road."

"I've been there. Let me make a quick call."

"Fine. I'll need a moment to organize these notes."

"Okay."

"See you in a couple minutes," he said, moving toward the inner door that led to his office.

Once inside he went to his desk and waited until he saw a phone button light, signaling that Laura had started her call. Then he reached down and eased open the top left drawer.

The manila folder labeled "Trustees" was right on top where he had left it. Taking a ruler from the center drawer, he measured the distance from the bottom of the folder to the front of the drawer. Two and three-eighth inches. Close but no cigar. He had left it precisely three inches from the front.

He gently opened the folder and looked at the sheet of memo paper on which he'd written enough to be provocative but not to disclose much. The memo no longer rested exactly on the third line of the blank page of a legal pad he had placed underneath. So while the mouse had been away, the cat had indeed played. Smiling, he closed the folder and drawer. Drinks with Laura might prove interesting.

---

Thorpe came out of the bathroom drying his hair and noticed the blinking light on his answering machine. Stepping over to the bed, he saw that Laura had called from the office a few minutes before. He tied the towel around his middle and pressed the play button.

"Peter, Bob's asked me out for a drink and I think I should go. Call me if you get this message in the next ten minutes."

He hit Call Back.

"Peter, where were you?"

"In the shower. What's up?"

She told him.

"All right," he said. "Play interested. Stay and have dinner if he wants. Maybe you'll learn something useful."

"I already have. I found a note in his office today and made a copy. We'll have to study it."

"I assume it's not the one where Jacobi's going to handpick his successor."

She chuckled. "Cynthia's little ruse? Tell her I said I found it if you think it'll make her feel better."

"I'll pretend I'm worried. Maybe it'll get her off my back."

"As long as you stay off hers."

"What's that mean?"

"When were you going to tell me she asked you to sleep with her?"

He paused. "What difference does it make? I wasn't buying. Anyway, I seem to recall you haven't been bashful with her."

"That's different."

"Why?"

"It just is, and besides, I told you about it."

"Look, Cynthia's hormones aren't really the issue. Let's stick to the plan."

"Peter--"

A beep in his ear interrupted her.     "Laura, hold on, I've got another call coming in."

"Hello," he answered after pressing Flash.

"Dr. Thorpe? It's Marguerite. Sorry to bother you, but now might be a good time for a chat."

"Can I call back in a couple minutes?"

"That's fine. I'm in her room."

He pressed the button again. "Laura, my mother's calling. Let's finish this later, okay?"

"I'd better go anyway. I didn't mean to be catty."

"It's all right. Call me when you get home."

Thorpe tossed the towel into the bathroom hamper, slipped into a pair of jeans and an old blue dress shirt, and went downstairs. Settling into his favorite easy chair with a small Scotch, he looked across the room at the desert photographs taken in Saudi Arabia in 1991 after the first Gulf War. A set also hung in his mother's tiny apartment though it was unclear she ever understood what they were. Nor, when she was told, did she apparently comprehend that her son William died tragically in Dubai soon after those photos were taken.

Thorpe's mother had Alzheimer's and had lived in a nursing home in St. Louis since 1990, only months after a stroke killed her husband. Dr. Joseph Thorpe had been a successful internist in the small town of Bunceton, Missouri, where he and his wife Eleanor had raised two sons. Like their father, William and Peter had gone to the state medical school in Columbia, Missouri. But he urged them to broaden their horizons. They did.

William was several years older and settled in Springfield, Massachusetts. Besides a thriving surgical practice, he became an expert on mental health issues and caught the eye of a local member of Congress. The congressman often consulted him on medical matters, including post-traumatic stress affecting the military. William accompanied the congressman on a fact-finding trip to the Gulf shortly after the end of the war.

On the day he was to return to the States, William was killed instantly when a truckload of supposedly-disarmed land mines exploded outside the hotel where he was standing waiting for a ride to the airport. That was what Thorpe told the world. It was a lie; he would never tell the truth.

In fact, after William returned home in June, reports began to surface that the congressman and unnamed accomplices, perhaps organized crime figures, were at the center of a huge Medicare fraud scheme and about to be indicted. One Friday night in August, the propane tanks at the congressman's beach cottage on Cape Cod exploded, trapping two men and a woman inside where they were burned to death beyond recognition. However, William's car and that of the congressman's wife were found at the cottage and the next day police uncovered evidence in William's home of his participation in the scheme. The police suspected the explosion might have been rigged, but no arrests were ever made.

In the meantime, Peter had started his own promising career, becoming an established surgeon at the Larimer County Medical Center in Fort Collins, Colorado. He was so well thought of among his peers and staff that in record time he rose to assistant chief of surgery. In the chief surgeon's evaluation, Peter was "destined for the top post at the hospital of his choice."

But only days after the details of William's death and his relationship with the congressman became public, the chief surgeon received a telegram from Peter asking for a leave of absence "in order to comfort my mother and to work through my own grief." The request was of course granted, but the telegram was followed several weeks later by a letter of resignation. Peter "could not find the inner resources to return to the practice of medicine for the foreseeable future."

It was more than two years before Thorpe applied for a surgical position at Clara Barton. Now, with the help of Cynthia and Laura, he fully intended to become chief of surgery. Jacobi be damned.

Taking a swallow of Scotch, Thorpe reached for the phone and dialed his mother's number.

"Dr. Thorpe?"

"Yes, Marguerite."

"Hold on."

Thorpe waited. "Peter. Where are you? The pot roast's almost ready."

"I'll be there soon, Mom. I have to get gas for the car."

"Don't be late. You know how hungry your father gets this time of day."

"Yes, Mom."

"You sound tired."

"I am," he said, realizing it was the truth.

"You're working too hard, just like Bill. He had to rush off and couldn't stay for dinner."

"That's too bad."

"When are you coming to visit?"

"Soon. This summer."

"So long? That's almost Thanksgiving."

"I'll stay for a week, how's that?"

"A whole week?  Can we go to St. Louis and visit Aunt Henrietta?  She can't drive anymore, you know."

"Sure we can."

"Could I tell her?"

"Absolutely."

"She'll be so happy. I think I'll call her right now."

"Good. Give her my best."

A long silence. "I have to check the roast now. You know how hungry your father gets this time of day."

"Yes. You take care, Mom. I'll call you Sunday like always, okay?"

A longer silence. "Dr. Thorpe, she's nodded off."

"How's she doing, Marguerite?"

"Holding her own."

"Thank you. She wants me to visit."

"She mentions it often. I know you can't count on her knowing you, but it has been awhile."

"I'll have some time late this summer. Maybe I'll get her on a good day."

"Just let me know when you're coming."

"Sure. Thanks, Marguerite."

"Be well. God bless you."

Thorpe stood and took his father's old medical bag from its place on the bookcase. It was his good luck piece and he once took it everywhere, but now only to the hospital on days he had surgery. He sank back into the chair and removed the blood pressure cuff from the bag, waited a few moments then took a reading: 126 over 81. Slightly elevated, but nothing remarkable. Could be the Scotch.

He took another sip, the amber liquid easing down his throat. Wonderful stuff. He drummed his fingers, wondering what to do about dinner with Laura out of the picture. He could call Cynthia, but that wouldn't be smart.  His relationship with the two women was challenging. They were both strong and determined. Dealing with one would be difficult for anyone; keeping up with both was daunting.

Cynthia had her own agenda, and he suspected Laura did as well. He wouldn't delude himself into thinking either was being completely honest with him. Perhaps they felt the same way about him. Life in fast lane. He put down his glass and went to the kitchen to find a steak. What he needed was protein, not problems.

## SUNDAY, MAY 9

"Why didn't you call last night about this?" Cynthia's voice was angry in Laura's ear.

"I did," Laura said. "Your line was busy and you haven't been around all day." She shifted the cordless phone to her other hand and leaned back in her tub, luxuriating in the hot water. "Anyway, I've told you now. What difference do a few hours make?"

"Depends what Kramer's note means. You sure you have it right?"

"I read you my photocopy."

"Read it again real slow so I'm sure I have it all."

"Fine, but listen this time, will you?" Laura said, taking the sheet of paper from the edge of the tub.

*"Mtg. w/ Pershing 4/22, pitched next yr turnaround. get her support if... need $ from lot 4"*

"Got it, now?" she asked.

"Yes. Did you bring up Pershing during dinner with him?"

"Of course. I was there when she came to Bob's office that day, remember?

"And?"

"And he thought she's being more sympathetic, but he didn't give me any details. Like I told you he's been with me lately."

"You think the Czarina would really support him or is this note just wishful thinking?"

"It's not clear."

"Dammit, Laura, I know that, but what's your sense? You

were the one drinking wine with him."

Laura took a breath. "Look, I'm not a mind reader. I said he was vague. Just like this damn note. I can't figure out who or what the dollar sign has to do with this lot four, whatever that is."

"It's the last vacant parcel the hospital owns. It adjoins the edge of lot three where the research wing was built."

"Okay...maybe he wants to sell the lot to get her support."

"The trustees wouldn't permit it."

"Well, then he might sell it to her for cash. Have the hospital give her a mortgage."

"Laura, that parcel's worth millions. Pershing's rich, but she doesn't have that kind of money."

"Maybe Bob promised her to use the lot for something she wants."

"That's a possibility," Cynthia said after a moment. "Pershing was lukewarm over the research department."

"There you go," Laura said. "Does she have any pet projects?"

"Yeah, world peace and the betterment of man. Laura, you need to keep after Bob on this. I have to know what he's up to."

"I'll nose around, but I don't think I can ask him anymore about Pershing without making him suspicious."

"All right, but keep your ears open. Meantime I'll make nice with her. I should do that anyway. Look, you did a good job. Sorry if I sniped at you."

"Forget it. I'll see you in the morning."

"Sure you don't want some company tonight? I'm a little horny," Cynthia said, shifting into her best throaty voice.

"I'm really whipped."

"How about coming over some night this week. Thursday or Friday?"

"That's might work," Laura said.

"Good. See you tomorrow."

"Right." Laura punched off the phone and looked across the tub.

"Well?" Thorpe asked.

"Lot four's a vacant parcel owned by the hospital."

"And Kramer wants to convert it to cash?"
"Or maybe build on it. We don't know."
"Cynthia say anything else?"
"Wants me to visit. Says she's horny."
"Who isn't," he said. "Come here."

# FIVE

## MONDAY, MAY 10

Jacobi was still eating his poached eggs when he finished reading the document Father Cahill had given him that morning. It was a damning polemic against Clara Barton's policies in treating the underprivileged. Jacobi was surprised at the articulate, organized argument and the precise use of medical terminology. Cahill had always seemed a bit of a buffoon, but this was good stuff. If nothing else, the Jesuits knew their logic.

He had asked Cahill to e-mail a copy that he could edit, but right now he wasn't sure he'd change a word. It might make for a better strategy to present it as Cahill's work, then, depending on the committee's reaction, he could either claim co-parenthood or distance himself. The good Father would never know.

"Can I join you, Stan?"

Jacobi looked up to see Thorpe standing there in his scrubs.

"By all means, Peter," he said, sliding Cahill's report under a medical journal. "No breakfast, today?" he asked, nodding at Thorpe's empty tray.

"Saw you when I was in line. Wanted to make sure I caught you."

"What's on your mind?"

"I took a look at my post-op conference notes on Howard Schroeder this weekend," Thorpe said, naming the only truly questionable case he'd been able to find on Jacobi.

"You need to get a life, Peter. You striking out with the ladies?"

"I was asked to do it."

"By whom?"

"Schroeder's nephew from out of town called me," Thorpe said, using the lie he had devised. "Guy was very upset. Wanted to know why his uncle had died."

"Why didn't he phone me?"

"Said he wanted the truth. Asked if I could tell him what

really happened."

"What did you say?" Jacobi asked pleasantly.

"Naturally that I couldn't speak to the issue. But I was curious enough to read the file. Stan, it's possible Schroeder's sepsis could have been avoided."

"Then you should have said so during the conference. The sutures didn't hold, Peter. Sometimes the tissue's too far gone. You know that."

"You could have resected more of the colon."

"I could have. I didn't. What's your problem?"

"I don't have one, but it's not the kind of mistake you'd make if you were on top of your game."

Jacobi's eyes narrowed. "What's that supposed to mean? There was no mistake."

"Perhaps, but you've occasionally suffered from insomnia."

"So?"

"Well, we both know a sleeping pill sometimes leaves a person a little groggy in the morning."

"What are you insinuating, Peter?"

"Cool your jets, Stan. This is a friendly heads up, that's all. You could be facing a nasty lawsuit. And your insurance company won't like it if there's anything that might turn up."

Jacobi leaned back in his chair. "It so happens I haven't used sleeping pills for years. Anyway, since when are you so interested in my welfare?"

"It's my welfare too. We surgeons need to stand together."

"Sure you don't want your own premiums going up?"

Thorpe smiled, sensing it was time to move on. "There's that, but I also hear you're tossing your hat into a certain ring. I know a couple of the trustees fairly well."

"And could put in a good word."

"I could."

"This doesn't have anything to do with you moving up in the world, does it?"

Thorpe laughed. "Never crossed my mind, but if you win, we're going to need a new chief."

Jacobi smiled. "And you're interested, eh?"

"Of course. Just let me know if you'd like my help."

"I'll keep it in mind, Peter."

"That's all I ask," Thorpe said, getting to his feet. "How are the poached eggs today?"

"Over done. Oh, before you go, have you had a chance to look over the roster of candidates to replace Monroe?"

"As a matter of fact, I have. I thought Huber and Cottine were possibles."

Jacobi shook his head. "Huber's not available and Cottine turned me down. I already called them."

"You might have consulted me."

"Planned to if they would've come.  Just saving you time."

"I recall Cottine would give her right arm to come here."

Jacobi shrugged. "Changed her mind, I guess. Anyway, forget about her. How about Julia Vallance? She's trained with the best, and we know she's interested."

"She's pretty green."

"So were we, Peter. The file says her residency's just finishing up. So she can probably start immediately."

"Yes. I remember she applied a year early."

"Wanted to get her name in the queue. Smart cookie. She's eager."

"I can live with her," Thorpe said.

"Good. I'll shop her with the committee. Thanks for your input.  Mind dealing with this?" he said, placing his tray on top of Thorpe's and grabbing Cahill's folder and the journal.

"Not at all. Have a good day."

Thorpe watched Jacobi make his way toward the elevators.

Something he had said didn't quite ring true. He reached for his cell phone and punched in Laura's number.

"Administration. Prentice."

"It's me."

"Peter, where are you?"

"Downstairs. Do me a favor?"

"Name it."

"You have a set of the surgeon applications handy? Mine are at home."

"They're on Bob's desk. He's not in right now."

"Good. Get me the phone number for Sheila Cottine."

---

"No, Lydia, you spend enough time here," Vivian said to her housekeeper, caretaker.   She backed the Rover away from the dinner table. "Your children need their mother."

"You no mind, Miss Pershing? I made fruit salad for later."

"Fine. Now go home. I'll see you tomorrow."

"I clean up?"

"Scoot," Vivian said.  "The dishes can wait."

Having pushed Lydia out the door, Vivian was about to turn on CNN when the cell phone she kept in the Rover beeped. She hardly used her landline anymore.

"Hello," she said, not recognizing the number in the display.

"Vivian, Cynthia Ellis. Do you have a few minutes?"

"Depends what for," she said, irritated at the interruption.

"I won't be long. It's about one of your favorite topics. Money."

"Always high on my list."

"Bob Kramer sent me a note about your meeting with him in his office last month.  Looks like his confidence level for next year's budget has gone up thanks to you."

"He talks a good game."

"He is quite the optimist. But there was one thing I didn't understand. This business about money and lot four."

"Lot four didn't come up."

"You sure?"

"Yes, unless he was at a different meeting than I was."

"Hmm. Well, I might be misreading his writing."

"Better ask him."

"I tried him at home, but I guess it can wait till morning. Sorry to bother you."

"Sure. Good night."

They hung up, each wondering how much the other was lying.

## TUESDAY, MAY 11

"You disappoint me, Peter," Cynthia said after glancing through the file on Howard Schroeder's case.

They were strolling in the warm afternoon sun up the sloping path toward the new research wing adjoining Cabot Hall.

"There's nothing there, Cynthia. Even if you could arouse the Schroeder family, no ethical lawyer would touch it."

"Ethical?" she said, tucking it under the arm of her yellow blazer. "What about you putting this file together for me?"

"There's nothing in there Marcia Davis wouldn't get in discovery if she filed a complaint. What I'm saying is she shouldn't."

"I thought you wanted to help me."

"This isn't the way. I couldn't find anything to suggest Jacobi was compromised that morning. And when I implied he was, he didn't flinch."

She stopped, her eyes nearly on a level with his. "He's cocky. No one's taken him on for years. The charge itself would tarnish his image."

"Cynthia, doctors get sued all the time. That's why we have insurance. Plus, you're ignoring Kramer. He's still the CEO and carries a lot of support with the trustees."

"Which will evaporate when they see the year-end results."

"You know damn well he knows what's coming. He has to have a trick or two up his sleeve. You and Laura better find out what."

"We're working on it," Cynthia said, thinking about her phone call with Pershing the evening before. "But, look, I can't leave Jacobi untouched. So what do you suggest?"

"Let's keep walking. We look stupid standing here." They continued up the path and he glanced over to her. "If you insist on suing Jacobi, I might have stumbled onto another angle."

"It's about time."

"A sexual harassment case."

Cynthia gaped at him, then smiled. "Peter, that's brilliant. The trustees would go ballistic. Wait a second," she shook her head, "we need a plaintiff. He knows better than to mess with a woman who doesn't want to play."

"Don't be so sure. Our illustrious chief of surgery slipped up at the open house last year. I found out he groped an applicant for a surgical post, Sheila Cottine."

"Groped?"

"Her word."

"You talked to her? Would she sue?"

"I don't know. She's still upset enough that she turned down an offer to come here. Trouble is, she wasn't an employee, but maybe Jacobi's hit on someone on staff."

"Peter, you don't have to be an employee to sue. I'll talk to her. God, you really think he might have fondled others?"

"I leave that to you. You're a woman. It's nothing I can really pursue. Maybe someone's been afraid to talk, but would if they knew about Cottine."

"I'll get right on it," she said, as they reached the door of the research wing. "Peter, this is wonderful."

"Only if you find someone who'll follow through. Otherwise forget it."

"Marcia Davis can convince anyone to sign a complaint."

"Cynthia, you need a real case, otherwise it can backfire."

"Let me worry about that."

"Forget lawsuits a minute, will you? I've thought of another approach."

"You have been thinking. What is it?"

He told her while they strolled back down the path.

"I don't like it," she said. "It's half a loaf."

"But you'd be in place to be CEO when Jacobi retires. Plus it takes care of Kramer and I make chief. It's a good outcome."

"For you. I'd have to twiddle my thumbs."

"Only for a while," he said. "Better than putting all your money on some lawyer."

"I'll think about it, okay? Either way, I can still sue his ass."

"You want it both ways, don't you?"

"If I can have it," she clutched his arm. "And it's nice to know someone as shameless as me."

---

Kramer hesitated when he entered the solarium in the eighth floor VIP wing and saw Father Cahill sitting in one of the chaise lounges. He was tempted to turn and leave, but the priest looked up and waved a greeting. So much for a quiet break, Kramer thought.

"Afternoon, Father," Kramer took an adjoining chair. "Beautiful day."

"It is indeed, the Lord be praised," Cahill said, putting aside a magazine. "Glad to see you taking time to enjoy it. Soothes the soul."

"I should do it more often," Kramer said, striving to be agreeable.

"So should we all. Been too busy myself, lately."

"You spend a lot of time here, Father," Kramer said, pleased that Cahill wasn't in one of his moods. "I know the money doesn't begin to recompense you."

"There are other rewards, Mr. Kramer."

"Of course, but still you're as important to us as our medical staff."

"You're very kind. I only wish I had more time, but there are just so many hours in a day."

"Yes, and that reminds me, I've been meaning to call you about your last e-mail."

"Oh, yes. Thank you bringing it up, but in fact I solved that little problem."

"Did you?" Not a word of criticism, Kramer noted. "I hope Ms. Ellis was of some assistance," he smiled, probing.

"I talked to her once, but she was rather abrupt. A little off-putting in fact. She's not nearly as pleasant as Miss Prentice."

"Well, as you say, we've all been busy. I'm glad to hear things worked out."

"Yes. Dr. Jacobi was very helpful."

"Was he?" What's Jacobi up to, Kramer wondered.

"Yes, indeedy," Cahill smiled. "Took a real interest. He seems to have time for everything. We need more like him around here."

Kramer nodded. "Wish I had his energy. Might be able to come up here more often."

"You might be able to soon." Cahill gave him a small wink. "Well, enjoy your respite. Time to visit some patients." He pushed himself off the lounge and waddled off toward the corridor.

Kramer looked out the panoramic windows. The spire of the Episcopal National Cathedral could be seen in the far distance. *Jacobi's fingers were everywhere these days. And Laura seems to be currying everyone's favor. Time to find out if she was simply ambitious or carrying someone's water. It sure wasn't his.*

## WEDNESDAY, MAY 12

"Stan, wait up."

Jacobi turned to see Cynthia dodge around a volunteer who was pushing a patient in a wheelchair toward the cashier's office: the last stop on the way to freedom.

"Good morning, Cynthia," he said as she reached him, quite fetching in a red sheath, tied at the waist with a gold chain. She was one of the few women with whom he could talk without bending his head.

"Do you have a moment?"

"I'm due upstairs, but I have a few minutes. Your office?"

"No. I don't want Bob to walk in on us."

"Lock the door. I promise I won't bite," he said archly.

"I'd rather steer clear of the area."

"My loss," he smiled, then pointed. "Let's duck into the chapel."

"Fine."

He pulled the heavy glass door open so she could precede him into the dim quiet of the empty sanctuary.

"Do you require pew or altar?" he quipped.

"Bag the sarcasm, okay?"

"You're losing your sense of humor in your old age," he said, as they slipped into a pew.

"Maybe you're part of my problem."

"That's not very friendly."

"Try this. Stan, I want to deal."

"About what?"

"You know damn well."

"My crystal ball's not too clear in this light, Cynthia."

"Then listen up. I want us to stop working at cross purposes about Kramer's job."

"Good. Then you're not applying for it?"

"I didn't say that."

"Then why am I here?"

"Look, we both want to be CEO. But bad financials or not, if Kramer puts up a fight, he still has a lot of support, especially with the younger trustees."

"They're a minority of the board."

"Correct. So what would you think of making sure the majority picks one of us instead of him?"

"How? This isn't Rome. They don't keep burning ballots until we see white smoke."

"I'll endorse you. Getting Kramer out's the key."

"You'd let me win?"

"Only if Kramer is in the fight. If he resigns or is bounced and leaves a clear field, all bets are off. We both go for it and winner take all."

Jacobi said nothing for a moment, then, "What's in this for you? You're already chief of staff."

"Hell, Laura Prentice can handle human resources and government red tape. I'd want to share power with you. Consensus on policy and program, budget formulation and execution. And on all department head recommendations."

"Medical too?"

"Especially medical. Surgery, radiology, the works."

"Suppose we can't agree on a choice?"

"We let the relevant committee be tiebreaker and take it to the board."

"You want a partnership."

"You can call it that. I prefer chief operating officer, a whole new position. Then when you retire, I'm primed to step up."

"I may not retire soon."

"We can work that out in advance."

"How do you know I wouldn't renege?"

"Stan, you really are a cad. But so am I. Just to be on the safe side, we'd go to the trustees and present ourselves as a team with an outline of the deal. They'd love to avoid a conflict."

Jacobi nodded. "It's tempting. I could use someone like you helping me out. Let me mull it over."

"I'd need to know by the end of the month."

"That's fair. Look, Cynthia, I have my reasons but why are you so against Kramer? He jilt you?"

"The other way around."

Jacobi laughed. "I'd better go. It's almost eleven."

"Let me walk out first, alone. Can't be too careful."

He watched her stride up the aisle, hips swaying. He wouldn't mind seeing what was under that dress. Might happen yet, he thought as she disappeared through the doors. He followed shortly afterwards.

A few moments later, Father Cahill emerged from the alcove behind the altar where the hymnals were stored for Sunday services. He stared at the glass doors, shaking his head. Just as he thought. Jacobi was the kind of man Saint Paul wrote about in his epistle to the Romans: such people do not serve our Lord Christ but their own appetites, and by smooth talk and flattering words they deceive the hearts of the unsuspecting. Cahill would not be one of those.

# SIX

## THURSDAY, MAY 13

"How many patient discharges did we have today?" Vivian asked Connie as they made their way down the hallway after finishing their shift.

"Close to 20. I must have done six or seven, not to mention the flowers."

"You all were really scrambling. We never had a chance to talk and catch up. You have plans for lunch?"

"We could make some. How about my place?"

"That sounds--"

"Vivian! Perfect timing." Kramer suddenly appeared in the hallway a few feet ahead of them. The women halted as he approached.

"Afternoon, Bob," Vivian said. "Have you met Connie Vacarro, one of our new volunteers?"

"No, I'm embarrassed to say. Ms. Vacarro," Kramer smiled. "We're grateful for your help."

"It's my pleasure, Mr. Kramer."

"I'm glad." His eyes lingered on hers; then he turned. "Vivian do you have a few minutes? I know you've been on duty, but it's rather important."

"Ms. Vacarro and I were about to have lunch."

"I promise to let you go before you both starve."

"Connie, would you mind?"

"Not at all. I'll move my car near your van. Nice meeting you, Mr. Kramer."

"And you, Ms. Vacarro."

She gave him a brief smile.

"Lovely woman," he said to Vivian as they turned toward his office. "Unattached?"

"Forget it, Bob. She's had it with you Adonis types."

"Vivian, that's one of the nicest things you've said to me in a long time." He closed the door behind them.

"Don't let it go to your head," she said and steered the Rover to the front of his desk. "So what's on your mind? Usually, I have to fight your pretty bodyguard to get in here."

Kramer pulled over one of his desk chairs and sat beside her. "Vivian, I want your support for a new contract. And I know you're not inclined to give it in light of this year's results."

"I haven't made up my mind, but you know I'm not happy with the way things are going, Bob. You've had a full five years."

"I won't waste your time rehashing old arguments, but I have proposal in mind for the future that should interest you."

"Go ahead."

"I think it's time we developed lot four."

So Cynthia Ellis was onto something, Vivian thought. "Bob, we're already carrying debt for the research wing. If we're not careful some corporate pirate's going to come along with a merger deal and suck up this whole hospital."

"Vivian, if the trustees buy my plan, we'll have no trouble getting funding. Some of the endowment can get us started."

"Money's scarce."

"Not for this. I want us to build a combination senior residence and assisted living facility tied to a diagnostic and treatment center for Alzheimer's."

"How many units?"

"I'd say 120 or so residents and maybe 30 beds for the center."

"That's pretty ambitious."

"The population's skewing older every year, Vivian. But that's only half the project."

"Half," she repeated, shaking her head.

"Next to the residence I envision an office complex for our physicians to treat patients so they won't have to scurry back and forth between the hospital and their offices. They've been wanting their own building since before I got here."

"The doctors will love you. How many floors."

"I'd like five, with underground parking. And an annex."

"What's that for?"

"A rehab center for burns and spinal cord injuries. State of the art."

She smiled. "Bob Kramer, that borders on blackmail."

"The area needs it, Vivian. You know better than I the progress their making in those areas. And our research department would complement the facility beautifully."

"In a perfect world."

"No, an imperfect one. That's why we're here."

"I don't know, Bob. It sounds like pie in the sky. We simply can't afford it."

"Just a minute," he said going around to a desk drawer. "I've not shown this to anyone. It's all here, construction schedule, debt service, grants, staff recruitment plan, the works. I see us breaking ground next spring and opening the senior residence wing in 18 months."

"How much will all this add to the budget?"

"First year about 35 million, 40 plus in the second. My total projections come in at around 540 million."

"You've prepared a two-year package?"

"And a one-year budget without these plans. That's around 230 million. The trustees can take their pick."

"They may choose neither."

"That's their call. Al Jennings can always cobble something together for them."

She took the neatly bound folder and glanced through the pages, several of which had professionally drawn sketches. "Who paid for this?"

"I squeezed a few dollars out of my office fund, but most of it came from my own pocket. I intend to distribute it at the end of the month. I wanted you to see it first. You'll be my toughest sell."

"Listen, Bob, much of this may appeal to the board, but not at that price. And they still may want a new CEO."

"I'm aware of that, but if they like what they see, I'm banking they won't want Stan Jacobi or Cynthia Ellis taking it on."

"You don't think they can do the job?"

"Once it's up and running, maybe. But it's got to be paid for first. That's takes a top fundraiser. And that's where yours truly comes in. Neither one can touch me on that score and you know it."

"Yes, and that's what bothers me. You got us in the fix we're in now."

"Just keep an open mind till you look this over. I don't want a new contract at the price of a blood bath. If you sign up to this, I'll be here to nurse it through. If you don't, well, I'm prepared to move on if that's the decision."

She nodded. "Fair enough. I'll let you know."

"Good. And may I ask you to keep this just between us?  I don't want my competition to get wind of it."

"I'd like to run it by my accountant."

"No problem."

"I must say I'm impressed by your candor," she said, as they moved toward the door.

"That's two compliments in one afternoon," he smiled, opening the door for her. "Be sure to tell Ms. Vacarro."

She paused at the threshold. "Fooling around with the help doesn't pay, Bob. I thought you learned your lesson with Cynthia Ellis."

"I'm smarter now, Vivian.  No dating women who want my job."

## FRIDAY, MAY 14

"I've forgotten how beautiful you are," Laura said, kissing Cynthia's breast. They were lying together in bed.

"You need to visit more often. It's been too long."

"I plead guilty. What's my punishment?"

"I'll think of something." Cynthia reached up to stroke Laura's hair.

"I can't wait."

"You won't have to if you kiss me like that again."

Laura complied.

"Mmm, nice," Cynthia murmured.

"You seem real mellow, tonight. Is it me or the Chardonnay we had with dinner?"

"Mostly you, love, but I have had a good week.  My ploy

about Jacobi picking a successor got Peter moving. He finally came up with some good ideas."

Laura listened attentively to Cynthia's report even though Peter had already told it all to her.

"Anyway," Cynthia said, "if Jacobi decides to go his own way, so will I.  Marcia Davis is one tough lawyer."

"But what if he goes along? Would you really settle for  chief operating officer?"

"Maybe. Bob would be gone, and I'm twenty years younger than Jacobi. I'd set a timetable with him to take over as CEO."

"If you could stick to it and wait," Laura said. "I know how you think."

"I'll have a better fix after the budget committee meets. You still not picking up anything from Bob on what he's planning?"

"Not a word."

"Shoot. I used to have his computer password, but he changed it after we broke up."

"You sure?"

"Yeah, I checked. It was Sabres. Hockey team from when he worked up near Buffalo."

"Maybe it's Capitals now," Laura said.

"Tried it."

"Well, he could be working on the budget at home."

"I'd sneak in and find out, but it's not worth it."

"You can get into his house?"

"I know the alarm codes."

"He gave them to you?"

Cynthia giggled. "No, he was in the shower one night when I was looking for a match to light candles to set the mood. The owner's manual to the alarm system was in the bedside table. He wrote the codes inside the cover."

"And you copied them."

"Didn't have to. He uses the numbers of the hospital's address and his phone extension."

"You're really something," Laura smiled. "Why did you two break up anyway?  You would have been quite a pair."

"No elbow room.  He saw me as a competitor.  He was right.

Too bad. He was pretty good in the sack."

"In this very bed?"

"Used his usually. King size."

"This one's plenty big enough."

"Maybe not for what I have in mind," Cynthia smiled and reached for her. "Let's see."

## SUNDAY, MAY 16

A few minutes past six that morning the killer stood in the patients' bathroom in the cardiac care wing of Clara Barton. Having donned blue surgical scrubs, cap, mask, and shoe covers over street clothes, the killer fixed the mask in place and picked up the cardboard box that had once housed a Fisher hospital humidifier. It now contained a small pair of scissors and a stun gun inside a blue plastic shopping bag.

Opening the door, the killer moved into the corridor, through the lobby to the fire door and up the stairs to the fourth floor. There the killer crouched to one side of the fire door, glancing through the inset safety window into the lobby, waiting for a nurse to bring out a newborn for a feeding.

In a few minutes, the doors to the delivery suite swung open. A nurse pushing a bassinet emerged and passed by the killer who recognized Rita Morales. Good. Not a big woman. The killer reached for the stun gun, waited a beat, opened the door quietly and moved stealthily across the floor. As Morales reached the maternity wing door and was about to scan her plastic security card to open it, the killer clasped her mouth from behind, put the gun to her neck and pulled the trigger.

Instantly a high voltage, low amperage current with a pulse frequency shot into Morales and fused with her brain's electrical signals. The combination sent her muscles into overdrive, thereby depleting her blood sugar by converting it into lactic acid and interrupting the neurological impulses controlling her movements. Almost immediately, Morales became disoriented, confused and partially paralyzed. She slumped against the killer who lowered her to the floor. She would remain in that state for several minutes.

More than enough time.

Tucking the stun gun in the waistband of the scrubs, the killer lifted the infant from the bassinet and hurried back to the stairwell and the cardboard box. Seconds later the killer entered the first floor lobby, then walked across to a hallway, turned right and, after a few steps, placed the box on one of the sofas in the darkened waiting area where outpatient endoscopies were performed during the week.

The baby began to stir and whimper softly in her pink blanket. "Breakfast in a minute, sweetie," the killer said, lowering the mask, cut off the Baby Girl Thomas plastic ID bracelet, and then turned to stroll back up the hallway with the bracelet, scissors and stun gun now inside the blue plastic bag and tucked into the waistband of the scrubs. Then the public address system screamed into life announcing the abduction of an infant to the hospital community:

*Code Pink, Code Pink. This is not a drill.*
*Code Pink, Code Pink. This is not a drill.*

Faster than expected, the killer thought as the message blared a second time. In moments, all scanners on the maternity wing doors would shift to a another lock code, permitting only designated personnel with special cards to exit and enter; security and medical staff would block all exits to the hospital complex; and Second District police would be alerted and race toward the hospital.

The killer maintained an even pace, then paused in the lobby to watch three security guards exit the middle elevator and scatter in different directions. According to the latest criminal demographics, they'd especially be on the lookout for a woman with a backpack or a gym bag, both useful to carry a baby. But this was a case where a miss was as good as a mile. The killer headed to a lavatory to fold the scrubs into the plastic bag and wait for the all clear. Should anyone happen in to search beforehand, a toilet stall and familiar voice can cover a multitude of sins.

---

At twenty past one that afternoon Kramer stood next to an unmarked police car parked in the horseshoe driveway having final words with a young, freckle-faced detective named Jason Spence.

"Thanks again for the quick response, officer. We've been keeping you guys busy lately."

"How's that?" Spence said, jotting a last entry into his notebook.

"You know, two weeks ago, the shooting."

"Oh yeah, the doctor." Spence looked up. "Robbery caught that. The bad guys work weekends."

"They seem to. Uhm, did you and your partner learn much today?"

"Some," Spence said, leaning against the car. "The baby just happened to be the first one out this morning. And it doesn't appear the parents or their families are wealthy or famous. So I think we can rule out the baby was targeted."

"Then perhaps it won't be necessary to blow this out of proportion. I'd like to keep it as quiet as possible, you understand."

"Well, we have to do a little more checking, but I hear you. Probably just some nut wanting a kid or looking to sell it on the black market."

"What a world. That's why the doors are always locked in the maternity wings and the nursery. No one has access without a card unless they're let in."

"So the head nurse told me. And your alarms must have kicked in fast enough to scare off whoever did this. Still, you might beef up your security in the fourth floor lobby. Maybe a full-time guard."

"I'd hate to do that," Kramer said. "It's mainly a waiting room. Lots of people mill around there. They're already anxious enough."

"You could put him in plainclothes. Just a suggestion."

"How about this? We require that no babies be taken from the nursery unless accompanied by at least two nurses."

"Can't hurt," Spence said. "Might have prevented what happened."

"Ready to roll, Jason," a second officer said joining them.

"Yeah, okay," Spence said. He reached for the passenger
door handle. "Thanks for your cooperation, Mr. Kramer."

"Glad to help."

"Oh, there's one more thing."

"Yes?"

"Don't be surprised if the FBI pays you a visit."

"Will you have to notify them?"

"Routine.  But since the baby never got out of the
hospital...well, I'll see what I can do to downplay it."

"I'd appreciate it."

Spence grinned. "I don't think they'll make a Federal case
out of it. Meanwhile, I'll ask my sergeant if we can get a cruiser to
patrol the area for the next few days."

"Thank you." Kramer stepped aside and watched the police
car drive off.  He squared his shoulders and walked toward the
staff entrance, mentally composing a memo to the nursery staff as
he walked.  Cynthia would not be pleased.

# SEVEN

## MONDAY, MAY 17

Frank Stephens was reviewing the third draft of the remarks he intended to give at the upcoming police academy graduation when his intercom buzzed.

"Yes, Gerry," he said into the receiver.

"Captain, Gary Shapiro's on line one."

"Put him through!" Shapiro was Frank's old boss who had retired the year before. He was something of a legend, first in his class at the academy and promoted to captain faster than any member of the force ever.

"Frank?"

"Gary, how the hell are you?"

"Never better. How about you? Having fun yet?"

"Not as much as when you were here. But at least I get home most nights for dinner."

"That's no small thing. How's Sam doing?"

"Fine. Did you know Tawana's pregnant?"

"Is she? That's great. Keeping her with us was one of your best decisions."

"Thanks to you signing off. And the wedding was a hoot."

"They sent me a picture. Sorry I couldn't get up there."

"We missed you. How's Barbara doing?" Frank asked, referring to Gary's daughter who was fighting cancer.

"We think she's gonna beat it. All the scans are still clear."

"That's great. So you coming to the graduation?"

"I got the invitation, Frank, but I don't think so. It's a little too soon for me to show my face. Maybe next year."

"Can I pencil you in for the commencement speech?"

"Now for that I'd come."

"Pick out a new suit."

"I may have to. Not sure the old ones fit. Frank, have you heard about Tim Parnell?"

"Not since he left town."

"An old buddy from Philly called me. Seems Parnell got himself killed last month."

"No kidding. What was he doing, bank security or something?"

"He was sitting in his house having a beer. Looked like a heart attack, but the autopsy showed a drug killed him. Injection."

"Did he OD? Suicide?"

"No note and no needles around and he wasn't back trafficking. He was living quietly, running his mother's B&B."

"He being treated for anything?"

"Just a case of gout. Found his doctor's name in his address book."

"They thinking robbery?"

"Doesn't look like it."

"Argument with a guest maybe?"

"Hadn't had one in a few weeks according to the register and his ledger."

"Enemies or girlfriends?"

"He was seeing a few ladies. Nothing heavy and all accounted for. Folks up there are stymied. Ironic, huh?"

"Too bad he's not alive to solve it."

"Yeah, he was damn good. Ah well, takes all kinds. You'll let Sam know?"

"Of course. He'll want to follow up."

"I figured. Everything okay with Gail and the boys?"

"Thriving. They're getting big, Gary."

"Give them a hug for me."

"Will do."

"Oh, Frank, when's Tawana due?"

"September, I think."

"All right, I'll send them a gift. They still on McComb?"

"For the next few weeks. They've bought a house over in Palisades."

"Good for them. Send me the address. Have fun at the commencement. It's a neat thing to do."

"Regards to Louise. She okay?"

"Feisty as ever. Take care."

Frank hung up, thinking back to a long-ago summer when he and Sam and other young detectives were assigned to a special task force led by Parnell. They had tremendous success, putting over a dozen drug dealers behind bars and confiscating huge amounts of heroin and crack. But one noted dealer escaped punishment when critical evidence tied to him suddenly went missing. A few weeks later an informant told them the crack was back on the street and had caused the death of two teen-age girls. Sam was mystified and his curiosity made him delve into the case.

The department's internal affairs unit didn't seem interested, but Sam wouldn't let it go. Working on his own time with Frank's help, they double-checked property reports, files, and quietly interviewed other officers and snitches. After months of work they suspected Parnell was the thief and had resold the drugs. Sam and Frank brought their conclusions to Gary Shapiro, who had just made sergeant.

Frank could still picture the anger on Gary's face as he read their report. Then he looked at them with a tight smile. "Let's get this bastard. Come back when you have a plan." They did and the ensuing sting operation led to promotions for them and joined them at the hip, where they'd been ever since. Parnell's lawyer managed to orchestrate a mis-trial, but Parnell was forced to resign and left town.

Frank's intercom buzzed again. "Yes, Gerry."

"The chief on line two, Captain."

"Tell him you can't find me. I'll be in Sam's office."

---

Jacobi leaned against the hood of his black Lexus watching hospital employees hurry to their cars, eager to get home on such a pleasant afternoon, perhaps for a little gardening or an early season barbecue. Maybe I should buy a larger house when I become CEO, he thought. Kramer had a damn mansion. But then he also spent too much time commuting. No, I'll keep the townhouse on New Mexico. Minutes away from his office and the hospital, nice pool, and a comfortable bedroom for the ladies when the spirit moved him.

He spotted Laura crossing the driveway from the staff entrance. He began moving across the doctors' parking lot in her direction. She's really quite a fox, he noted, watching her legs swish through the slit in her light blue dress. Wonder if Kramer's sampling some of that. She might have much softer edges than Cynthia. He timed his approach to intercept her.

"Ms. Prentice?"

Laura turned. "Dr. Jacobi," she smiled. "What can I do for you?"

"I just happened to see you," he said, "and wonder if I might accompany you a minute."

Happened to see me, my foot. "Sure," she said and resumed walking.

"I was curious if you have any news on the budget we'll be considering next week."

"Yes. Mr. Kramer expects to release a draft Friday and the final package Monday or Tuesday."

"I see. Would there be any chance I might get something sooner? Of course, I understand it could change, but, well, I was thinking of taking Friday off. I'm sure Bob wouldn't mind."

"I'd like to help you out, but I don't have a copy myself. Perhaps you can ask Mr. Kramer in the morning."

"No, I don't want to bother him," Jacobi said. "We're all so busy right now."

"Except for this Friday, doctor?"

He smiled. "I heard you were smart."

"I must have a secret admirer," she said, taking her keys from her purse as they reached her car.

"Many, I'm sure. And that reminds me."

Here comes the other shoe. "Yes?"

"I guess you know there's a chance the CEO position might be up for grabs."

"I'm smart, remember?"

Another smile. "Then you also know I might offer my services."

How lucky for us. "Yes, I do," she said, leaning against the driver's door.

"Now I don't want you to compromise your present position in any way, but if I get the job, I'll need a good chief of staff. I've looked up your record. Impressive."

"What about Cynthia Ellis?"

"She's good of course, but I think I'd rather bring in my own team. Would you be interested? I warn you," he winked, "I'm a tough taskmaster."

"I'm flattered. Could I get back to you?"

"Absolutely. Not something to decide in a parking lot after a long day."

"I agree."

"And, I'd prefer if you could keep this to yourself."

"Certainly."

"That's settled then. Well, have a good evening."

"You do the same, doctor."

He gave her a small wave and turned.

"Oh, Dr. Jacobi?" she said, opening the door.

"Yes?"

"Why don't I call you if I can get a draft to you this week?"

"That would be wonderful, Ms. Prentice."

"My friends call me Laura."

## TUESDAY, MAY 18

"So how did you leave it with him?" Kramer said to Laura in his office that morning after she briefed him on her encounter with Jacobi.

"That I'd try to get him a copy of the draft ."

"Any thoughts?" he asked, wondering again what Laura's game was.

She leaned back in his side desk chair and smoothed the lapel of her short pink jacket. "Say no. It's common knowledge he's after your job. Why help him get it?"

Kramer saw an opening. "You're right, but perhaps you can gather some intelligence for me if you're willing to play spy."

"Spy?"

"No weapons other than that brain of yours," he said, unlocking his briefcase. "Show this to him but let him think I haven't authorized you to." He handed her a folder containing the current draft of the one-year budget.

"How does that help you?" she asked, glancing through the document.

"Don't let him keep it. Arrange to meet him. He can read it, take notes, ask you about it, whatever. Perhaps he'll say something useful."

She nodded. "Like how he might criticize it?"

"Precisely. Look, I know there are weak spots in that thing. I'm pretty much prepared for anything. But I'd love to know where he might attack."

"If he doesn't say anything, I could sort of prod him."

"Perfect. So you're willing?"

"You're my boss."

He pretended to study her a long moment. "This isn't in your job description, Laura."

She crossed her legs, modestly pulling down the hem of her light gray skirt. "Not yet, but you might find a way to make it worth my while."

"How so?"

"Jacobi mentioned my future if he became CEO. Thinks I might make a good chief of staff."

"He offer you the job?"

"A very strong hint."

"Well, he's right. You'd be excellent."

She was about to answer when the outer door burst open and Cynthia stormed in waving a sheet of paper. "What the hell is this, Bob?"

"It's customary to knock, Cynthia."

"And it's customary to go through channels before sending out crap like this," she snapped, tossing the paper on his desk.

"Perhaps you should excuse us, Laura," he said.

"No," Cynthia said. "She'll hear it soon enough. The whole OB-GYN nursing staff is pissed. Jenny Russo was in my office yelling for ten minutes."

"What's her problem?" he said mildly, leaning back in his chair.

"You know damn well what it is. You can't just order the nurses to double up moving babies around. You might as well ask them to unionize."

"Cynthia, we had an attempted kidnapping here Sunday."

"We didn't lose the baby did we? There are procedures to impose new rules like this."

"And if we wait to follow them, we might not be so lucky next time. The memo clearly states this is an interim step that the committee must ratify before it's permanent. Who's going to vote against it?"

"That's not the point. I'm taking all the heat. I don't need that."

"Perhaps you should resign."

She glared at him, then smiled. "You'd like that wouldn't you? You'd love to get me out of your hair. Well, forget it. I'm not going anywhere."

"Except out of this office. I have work to do."

Cynthia bit off a reply and marched out without closing the door. Laura went to shut it.

"She's right, you know," she said, coming back to the desk.

"Yeah, I should have run it by her, but I wanted the memo out ASAP. It'll keep the newborns safer."

"And give your competition a headache."

"Was it that obvious?" Kramer smiled.

"To me," she said. "Bob, perhaps I might let Cynthia look at a copy of this draft. A little more intelligence couldn't hurt."

Kramer considered a moment, then nodded. "All right, but I don't want any copies made. Use that one for Jacobi and then Cynthia if you have time before I circulate it Friday."

"All right."

He stood and came around the desk. "Thanks," he said, patting her arm. "I really appreciate your help."

"What are spies for? See you later," she said, waving the folder.

He watched her move toward her office door. There weren't any bombshells in that document, but this might produce dividends. If she was working for Jacobi or Cynthia, he expected she'd give him misinformation. He could deal with that. Her source was the key.

## WEDNESDAY, MAY 19

The Laughing Bull Bar & Grill was off Wisconsin Avenue in Georgetown. On weekends it catered to the university crowd, but during the week, local office workers and professionals would regularly stop in for happy hour and to chat with Connie Vacarro who was both easy on the eyes and generous pouring drinks.

It was past seven and Connie was in the process of turning matters over to Robin the night bartender when a voice called out from the doorway.

"Hey, do you validate parking?"

Connie looked over and was astonished to see the Rover motoring toward her. "Vivian!"

"I can't get on a stool," she said, "but perhaps you'd join me at a table."

"Of course, I was just closing out."

"Hah! I timed it right. How about that corner one?"

"Great. Would you like a drink?"

"You have to ask?"

A few minutes later Connie arrived at the table with two glasses. "This is wonderful. What brings you downtown?"

"Thought I'd like to see your playpen. Nice place. And that's some outfit you're wearing."

"Goes with the territory," Connie said, fingering the top of her low-cut peasant blouse. "You think it's too much?"

"Not if I was the one tipping you."

"Thank you."

Vivian smiled and took a long swallow. "God, that's good."

"Top shelf, and it's on me."

"I should have ordered a double. So what's new?"

"About what?"

"Don't be coy. Bob Kramer call you?"

"Sunday night," Connie said.

"Ask you out?"

"Lunch."

"And?"

"I said yes."

"Don't say I didn't warn you."

"Promise," Connie smiled.

"You say he called Sunday?"

"That's right."

"Interesting," Vivian said, twirling her glass. "Called me too."

"Budget?"

"No. Seems we had an attempted kidnapping of a baby that morning."

"No! What happened?"

Vivian told her what she knew. "So Bob phoned several trustees in case the papers got the story and blew it up. Luckily they didn't."

"Does this kind of thing happen often?"

"First time at Clara Barton, but these days stealing newborns is a cottage industry. All the hospitals have special precautions in place. Thank goodness ours worked."

"We were lucky he was scared off," Connie said.

"Or she. Women are more apt to do it."

"Jesus."

Vivian took a sip. "In any case this can't help your new boyfriend."

"He's not my boyfriend."

"But he's a charmer."

"Vivian, I'm a big girl."

"So I see by that blouse."

Connie laughed. "You're making me self-conscious."

"I just don't want to see you hurt," Vivian said seriously.

"I'll drink to that. How about a refill?"

"I'm driving, remember?"

"Then let's put something in your stomach. Why don't we have dinner? The food here's pretty good. My treat all the way."

"Now that's worth a parking ticket."

## FRIDAY, MAY 21

Thorpe was dozing in a sunny corner of the doctors' lounge when his cell phone went off. Automatically he reached to his belt for his pager. When it rang again and he realized his mistake. Fumbling in his jacket, he found the cell. It was Cynthia.

"You're late," he said. "I was about to give up."

"Jacobi didn't call till a few minutes ago."

"Well?"

"He likes the deal, but he's not ready to commit."

"Why's he stalling?"

"I sense he wants to wait till after next week's meeting. See how the wind's blowing."

"Smart."

"I don't like that he might make Laura chief of staff."

"Cynthia, you practically gave him the idea. Anyway, who better?"

"I want to be the one to control her."

"Relax. You'll have plenty of control over everything."

"Right now I'd settle for one uptight female Jacobi put the moves on."

"You won't need a lawsuit if he goes for the deal. Did he say anything about Kramer's budget?"

"Yeah, but pretty much what he told Laura when she leaked it to him."

"Well, good. He didn't have to tell you anything. At least he's being cooperative."

"Don't read too much into that," she said. "The budget's plain vanilla. A few increases here and there, mostly salary and benefits."

"You think Kramer's running scared?"

"Not sure. Laura said he didn't seem that interested when she reported Jacobi's reaction. I think he's up to something. This draft could be a red herring."

"Lulling you all over the weekend?"

"It's possible. I wish I could get into his computer. Maybe I should sneak into his house."

"Risky. And don't forget his brother Fred. It could all be on his computer."

"Yeah, you're right. Peter?"

"What?"

"You going home soon?"

"After I check on a couple of patients. No office appointments."

"Come over for dinner?"

Laura was expecting him. "Can't do it tonight," he said.

"Booked all weekend?"

"Tomorrow's open."

"I just closed it."

# EIGHT

## SATURDAY, MAY 22

The Sea Horse Inn was on MacArthur Boulevard in Potomac, Maryland a few miles west of D.C. Its sumptuous food had a loyal following among those who enjoyed fine dining. In winter its roaring fireplaces and private rooms provided cozy refuge for the affluent residents of the area. This time of year tourists in the know would have lunch on the spacious veranda overlooking the expanse of river below.

Today Kramer sat at his usual outside table waiting for Connie. He'd been delighted when she accepted his invitation, and was even more so now as he watched her climb the steps toward his table wearing a white dress that outlined her figure.

He stood and extended his hand. "You look wonderful. Remind me to have volunteers wear nothing but white in the spring."

"Some of the men might object," she said, taking the wicker chair across from his.

"They don't get a vote."

A waiter appeared instantly. "Would the lady care for a drink before lunch?"

"What's the gentleman having?" she asked, nodding to the bottle of wine in the chilled bucket next to the table.

"Mr. Kramer's decided on the Beaulieu Sauvignon Blanc. An excellent choice."

"Then I'll have the same."

"Very good," he said, and moved to fill her glass.

"Has the gentleman decided on lunch?" she smiled at Kramer.

"I recommend the spinach salad," he said. "It's the best around."

"Sounds fine."

"Two, Tony," Kramer said.

"Yes, sir. Your usual vinaigrette dressing?"

Kramer nodded.

"Honey Dijon for me," Connie said.

"Very good," Tony said and went off.

"Cheers," Kramer said, lifting his glass.

"To spring," she said as they clinked glasses.

"So, Ms. Vacarro, how did you come to volunteer at Clara Barton?"

"I did some in high school back in Ohio. Then this February I visited a friend and happened to pick up some literature about your program. My mornings are mostly free, so I decided to sign up."

"How fortunate for us."

For the next few minutes and into lunch they talked mostly about her. Whether it was the sun, the wine, or his easy smile, she found herself warming to him.  A definite danger signal, she knew.

She described growing up as Connie Riley, her mother leaving her father when he wouldn't give up drugs, and how he overdosed when she was nine. She told him about her wonderful stepfather Anthony Vacarro who adopted her and her brother and left his real estate fortune to her mother who passed it on to the kids. She talked about her decision to study art in New York and then to come to Washington where she now tended bar more for human contact than a need for money. Through it all, she omitted mention of any of her past romances.

"When did your mother die?" he asked.

"While I was in college. Seems she didn't quite turn off the burners on the kitchen stove. The police said it was an accident, but my brother swears it was suicide because it was so soon after my stepfather died. I just don't know."

"Lousy break either way."

She took a sip of wine, nodding. "Your parents still living?"

"Oh yes. The Kramers are notorious for their longevity. I don't know of a single relative who hasn't made it into their eighties."

"Any of them ever work in the medical field?"

"No. Mostly finance and law, and all wealthy. I'm the only one who took an interest in public health."

"Why did you?" she asked.

"Believe it or not, television. As a kid I loved all the shows about hospitals. I wanted to be a doctor, but didn't have the head for science. So I switched to business at Penn and went to Yale for graduate school."

"You sorry? About not being a doctor, I mean."

"A little, but I love what I do, and I think I'm good at it."

"There seems to be a difference of opinion," she said, her tone friendly.

"It's not an easy job. Lots of pressure, and never enough money for everyone's agenda." He smiled. "At least you volunteers don't ask for much."

"Not until now. What with Dr. Monroe and this kidnapping, some of us are worried about safety."

"So am I," he nodded. "Fact is, I've increased the outlays for security every year I've been here. But you can't have guards everywhere without turning the hospital into an airport checkpoint. Nobody wants that."

"Still, a more visible presence might be welcome," she said gently. "Perhaps you're trying to do too much in other areas."

"I see you've been talking to Vivian."

"She loves Clara Barton. It's her life."

"It's not mine, not yet anyway. I'm doing what I think best. I'll take whatever comes."

"Win, lose or draw?"

"Sure, but I don't like failure."

"How would you know? Child of privilege. Ivy League schools. Not many setbacks."

"There've been some," he said. "The worst was my marriage. Though it really wasn't my fault."

Oh-oh, here it comes. "She might say the same thing. What's your version?"

"Simple story. I met Roberta in Buffalo at the hospital where I was vice president. She was a surgeon. I learned a great deal from her about medicine. Problem was she knew some other things."

"Such as?"

"How to sleep around and shrug when she got caught."

"So you divorced her," Connie said.

"Yes. But the current boyfriend happened to be the son of the chairman of the board. Exit Bob Kramer."

"Nasty business."

"Call it a life lesson."

"So now you do the sleeping around."

"Is that what you've heard?"

"I've heard you have a lot of lady friends."

"You'd be surprised," he said, pouring the last of the wine into their glasses.

She was about to respond when the waiter appeared to clear their plates. "Will you be having dessert, today, Mr. Kramer?"

Kramer looked at Connie who shook her head. "I would like some coffee, though."

"Bring us a carafe, Tony."

"How often do you come here?" she asked watching Tony hurry off.

"Whenever I can. They have a wonderful dinner menu."

"Yes. I ate here last winter."

"Did you? Then there's at least one other man in your life who knows how to dine a lady."

"Did I say I was with a man?"

"Weren't you?"

"Yes, in fact. He was the friend I visited at the hospital a few days later."

"I hope we were able to help him."

She smiled. "No, but you helped me. It was Victor Devane."

"Devane?" Kramer exclaimed, then lowered his voice. "The guy they arrested outside the ICU?"

"The same."

"Did you know I helped set that up with the police?"

"Then I owe you special thanks."

Devane's arrest had been a media sensation. He was now awaiting trial for the murder and attempted murder of identical twins, one his wife and the other his mistress.

The coffee arrived. "Leave it, Tony," Kramer said. "We'll pour our own."

Tony looked puzzled, but dropped his hands. He had barely stepped away when Kramer leaned in closer.

"So you were there that night," he whispered.

Connie nodded. "In the hallway waiting with one of the detectives. I had evidence against him in my pocket."

"What evidence?" he asked, pouring their coffee.

"A gift to him from his mistress. I found it in his jacket in my condo. He was about to move in with me, or so he said."

"That was you? Then you're--"

"The unnamed other girlfriend." She took a sip of coffee and sat back. "I'll probably have to testify at his trial, though I'd rather not."

"Were you helping the police right along?"

"Oh, no. I never even talked to them until that afternoon. I became involved when a man named Nick Mercante visited me. He was working with them, warned me about Vic."

He shook his head. "No wonder Vivian said you've had it with men."

"She told me that. I had lunch with her the day she introduced us."

"That's right. So I guess she was wrong?"

"Not totally. She's a very wise woman."

"Maybe she'll put in a plug for me," he said.

"I doubt it. She knows I'm vulnerable to smooth talkers with a head on their shoulders."

"Ooops."

"Don't worry. I don't intend to stop living. But I'm going to keep my head in sync with my heart from now on. The irony is Vic did me a favor. For openers, no more married men."

"Score one for my side," Kramer said, as his cell phone went off. "Excuse me a second." He reached into his tan blazer, then glanced at the display before pressing the button.

"Vivian! You must be psychic. Because I'm having lunch with Connie Vacarro. You checking to see if I'm behaving myself? I see. What's the verdict?"

Kramer grimaced as he listened for several moments. "What's his reason? Vivian, it says that on page three. Yes, and there's a graph on that in the appendix. Very well. Let me think about what you've said. I'll call you first of the week. Yes, I will. So long."

He put away the phone. "Vivian says hello."

"She said more than that and you're not pleased."

"Looks like she won't support my budget proposal."

"What happens now?"

"I don't know. Listen, I hate to put a damper on this, but I'd better get back to work."

"No problem. I've had a nice time and we've been tying up this table for almost two hours."

He looked at his watch. "So we have. I hope we can do this again."

"Me too. I might even risk a dinner."

## SUNDAY, MAY 23

Jacobi had spent a half hour reviewing the latest MRI of David Cox whose bowel he would be resecting in the morning. Now, riding down the hospital elevator, he was looking forward to his date with Nancy Kwan. She intrigued him: close to six feet tall, and the combination of an Asian woman and former Olympic athlete promised adventure.

The elevator stopped on the third floor to let on an elderly couple when the public address system announced:

*Any Surgeon: 5080.*

*Any Surgeon: 5080.*

That's odd, Jacobi thought. That was the extension for the OR nurse managers and none of them was in today. The overhead speaker was repeating the message when the elevator arrived in the lobby. Jacobi let the couple precede him, then exited and turned down the corridor that led to the parking lot. Someone's bound to answer, he told himself. But no one had by the time he reached the glass doors and it sounded again.

"Damn," he swore, then stepped over to one of the many phone consoles that dotted the walls of the hospital. He punched in the number.

"Proctor," a harried voice said.

"Dr. Jacobi, Stephanie, what's up?"

"I think I've got a red hot appendix up here, doctor. Male Caucasian, about 14 and 120 pounds." Her answer provided Jacobi with important data.

"Who's the attending?"

"Isn't one. EMS brought him here straight from the street."

"No one examined in the ER?" he asked, irritated.

"I just work here, doctor," Proctor said. She was a veteran surgical nurse and a good one.

"All right, I'll be right up."

Jacobi took the stairs to the second floor and found Proctor bending over a boy on a gurney. His face was flushed and he was moaning, his head turning from side to side. Someone had opened the boy's trousers and shirt and his abdomen was hot to the touch as Jacobi palpated it gingerly, causing the boy to wince in pain. The appendix was ready to burst if it hadn't already. He looked up and nodded.

"You called it, Stephanie. What the hell are you doing here, anyway?

"Getting my ducks in a row. You seen tomorrow's board? Everybody scheduled Monday this week."

"Blame Dr. Thorpe. There an anesthesiologist around?"

"Your man McCoy," she said.

"Good," Jacobi said. Eugene McCoy would be working the Cox case with him in the morning and had probably stopped in to visit the patient. "I'll ask him in. Any surgical residents in the ER?"

"Booth, but he didn't answer my page, so he must be tied up. Vallance's pulling a shift too."

"In the ER? She's on staff and just got here."

"Then it's time she earned her stripes."

Jacobi smiled. "All right, have her paged. You'll have to help."

"No problem. Should I set up for a laparoscopy?"

He shook his head. "We'll go in open. Need more help and I don't like the scope when there's a risk of rupture."

"Very well. I'll scrounge up an orderly in the ICU."

"Then get this kid prepped.  See you inside."

The boy was already draped and in the supine position when Julia Vallance backed into OR 1 and turned to the side so the orderly could glove and gown her and then snap the gown closed in back. She nodded to the bespectacled face of Dr. McCoy behind his screen of sheets at the head of the table and took her place across from Proctor.

Suddenly the strains of soft, melodic music filled the room and Vallance looked up, searching for the source. "Tchaikovsky?" she asked from behind her mask.

"Sixth Symphony," Proctor  said. "Dr. Jacobi won't operate without it. He had the sound system installed when he was appointed chief.  The music means he's scrubbing."

Minutes later Jacobi entered and the orderly repeated the glove and gown procedure.

"Evening everyone," Jacobi said, moving into position.

"I've already induced him, Stan," McCoy said.

"Thank you, Gene. What's the weather report?" he asked, looking at the face of the boy, now serene in repose.

McCoy eyed his monitors that measured vital signs. "Heart 122, BP 141, Temp. 101.2."

"Not too bad. White count elevated?"

"And climbing."

"We'd better hurry. Tox screen, Dr. Vallance?" Jacobi's eyes stayed on the patient.

"Ordered, doctor.  Waiting on the ER."

"Terrific," Jacobi grumbled. "All right, Gene, it's your airplane."

McCoy placed a mask over the boy's face and proceeded to administer halothane to deepen the anesthesia he had already induced by intravenous drug.  A few moments passed, then "Ready, Stan."

"Betadine," Jacobi said.

Proctor quickly wiped the boy's exposed abdomen with the dark, sterile solution.

"A little more," Jacobi said. "Good. Okay, folks, I've got a dinner date." He reached out his hand and Proctor filled it with the grip of an electronic instrument. Modern surgical practice and the presence of HIV dictated increasing use of electrocautery instead of relying solely on scalpels.

Jacobi made an incision about one third of the way along a line from the boy's right hip to his navel--the McBurney point used to locate the appendix. He then began to cut through the subcutaneous tissue.

"Dr. Vallance, follow me in with suction and cauterize as I go."

"Yes, doctor," she said and leaned in with the two instruments, removing blood and closing off the bleeders as Jacobi cut deeper.

"Where did they find this kid?" Jacobi asked.

"EMS answered a 911," Proctor replied. "He was lying on the steps over at St. Benedict's. We were the closest hospital."

"He have a name?"

"No ID. Could be a runaway."

"Wonderful. How's he doing, Gene?"

"Pressure's up a bit, but holding."

"Good. Metzenbaums, please."

Proctor instantly had the scissors in his hand.

Jacobi cut the external oblique aponeurosis along the length of its fibers. "Dr. Vallance, what's keeping Dr. Booth so busy in the ER?"

"Accident on River Road," she said. "Two couples on their way to a party. Ran into a tree and totaled their SUV. Three DOA. He's working up the other one."

"They can't handle that without Booth?"

"They're down a team because it's Sunday," McCoy said.

"What does that have to do with it? Kellys, please."

Proctor handed him the clamps and Jacobi split the internal oblique and transverse abdominal muscles.

"It was in Kramer's latest memo," McCoy said. "He's experimenting with smaller staff in the ER on weekends. End of year cost cutting."

"That's nuts."

"Slow down a little, Stan," McCoy said, "I need to adjust the gas."

Jacobi paused. "Dr. Vallance, take the Kellys."

"Yes, doctor."

"Gene, how can Kramer downsize this time of year?" Jacobi fumed. "Kids are all over the roads with proms and all."

"Don't ask me," McCoy said.

"He's got to go," Jacobi said. "We can't have the ER sucking up residents and staff all summer."

"Full speed ahead, Stan," McCoy said.

"Two more Kellys," Jacobi demanded and Proctor complied.

Jacobi clamped and raised the peritoneum, the membrane lining the abdominal wall and enclosing the internal organs.

"Scalpel," he called, and, taking it from Proctor, sliced into the peritoneum. Immediately a foul odor erupted as pus oozed through the incision.

"Damn, she's already burst," Jacobi said.

"Need a culture?" Proctor asked.

"Don't bother. Gene?"

"Steady as she goes."

"Suction. Metzenbaums."

Vallance and Proctor responded, the surgeon removing the pus and blood mixture and the nurse handing Jacobi the scissors.

Jacobi completed the peritoneal incision. "There she blows," he said. "Babcocks please."

Jacobi took the clamps from Proctor and grasped the appendix, lifting it. "One more."

The team worked silently almost in time with the music, maneuvering, clamping, and dividing the mesoappendix in stages, suturing along the way.

"Clamping the base now," Jacobi said. "Dr. Vallance, another suture there. 0 chromic, I think. Gene?"

"You're fine."

"Okay. Ready to sever. Time for Excalibur."

Proctor slapped a shiny scalpel into Jacobi's hand, his personal knife since medical school. He deftly excised the appendix. "Present for you, Stephanie," he said. "Cauterize, please."

Vallance leaned in, stopped the bleeding on the base where

the appendix had been attached.

"Good," Jacobi said. "Okay, drain, please."

"Yes, doctor," Vallance said.

Jacobi watched her insert a small tube near where the appendix had been. "Nice touch," he said. "All right. Let's wash and get out."

Proctor began irrigating the boy's abdominal cavity with kanamycin solution.

Jacobi glanced at McCoy. "Gene, I'm going to call Kramer after we finish Cox's case tomorrow."

"I'll join if you'd like."

"I'd like," Jacobi said. "Ready to close, Dr. Vallance."

Vallance wiped a hair from her forehead and leaned in closer.

Proctor opened her mouth to speak when Jacobi shouted "Get out of there, Vallance!"

"Wh-what?" she sputtered, falling back as if pushed.

"You nearly contaminated the field. Get your ass out of here. And don't bother to rescrub. I'll close."

Jacobi began suturing the peritoneum, ignoring Vallance who stood there uncertain.

"Yes, doctor," she finally muttered moving past Proctor. "I'm sorry," she said and fled the room.

A few minutes later Jacobi finished suturing the incision and stapled the surrounding skin.

"Gene, thanks for stepping up," he said. "Stephanie, PACU's closed, so you'll have to set up recovery in the ICU. Antibiotics for the next 36 hours to deal with peritonitis and anything else."

"Yes, doctor. Ampicillin?"

"Right, 100 milligrams, and rotate it with 80 milligrams of Gentamicin. I'll sign the order before I go." He turned to leave.

"Doctor, I could have handled Dr. Vallance."

"I know that, Stephanie, and no doubt more gently. But she needs to learn it and not forget. She won't now. Have a good evening. I intend to."

# NINE

## MONDAY, MAY 24

Laura pulled into her driveway reflecting on the hastily arranged dinner with Peter at Caballeros. Their conversation had been dominated by Kramer's startling two-year budget package released late that afternoon. She wasn't sure whether it was an act of desperation or a brilliant tactic that would turn a bad year into an amazing victory. Peter was inclined to give Kramer credit.

"I told you he was tricky," he said as they returned to their cars. "Keep your antenna way up this week. I want to know how Cynthia and Jacobi are taking this."

"I'll call her when I get home," Laura said. "You want me to ring you later?"

"Not after ten, okay? I have surgery in the morning." They embraced briefly and he drove off.

Laura checked her phone messages as soon as she walked into her bedroom and saw that Cynthia had called twice, a half hour apart. She pressed Play.

"Where are you? We have to talk about this bullshit budget. Call me."

Laura dialed her number without bothering to listen to the other message. Busy. Cynthia really should get call waiting, she thought, undressing. She took the cordless into the bathroom and ran a hot bath. She had just settled in the water when the phone rang. Here we go.

"Hello, Cynthia."

"Where the hell have you been?"

"Shopping, if you must know. Called you a few minutes ago, but your line was busy."

"That was Jacobi. He's baffled and so am I. What the hell's your boss up to?"

"Beats me. It was a total surprise." It was true. There had been no further confidences from Bob since she had agreed to leak the draft one-year budget.

"You didn't have a clue this was in the works?"

"Nope."

"He puts together a glossy package like that right under your nose and you don't get a whiff of it?"

"Bob's like that. Hell, you know him better than I."

"Really? You sure you're not fucking him?"

Laura laughed. "I could be, but I'm not. Besides, I could say the same about you. That thing's full of salary and benefits for staff we don't even have. That's your bailiwick. He dream them up by his lonesome or did he have help?"

"Why the hell would I want to help him?"

"Maybe he offered you a deal like you offered Jacobi."

"That was Peter's idea."

"And it's a good one. Perhaps you went to school on it."

"Laura, sometimes I wonder where your head is. Jacobi's nearing retirement. Kramer will never leave unless he's kicked out."

"Then stop looking for ghosts and tell me what you plan to do. Jacobi have anything else to say?"

"He wants to carry the ball at Friday's meeting and let me handle questions about details."

"What to you think?"

"That he's setting me up. The committee probably won't like Kramer's stuff, so he'll be seen as the white knight."

Laura nodded into the phone. "I think so too. You shouldn't let him take the lead."

"Glad we're on the same page."

"We always have been."

"Yeah, I know. Sorry if I was bitchy."

Echoes of her former lover Allison's insults and apologies sounded in Laura's head and governed her reply. "It's not important."

"It is. I was trying to apologize."

"I accept. So what did you tell Jacobi?"

"I said I'd touch base in the morning. I want to check with Peter."

Laura glanced at her watch lying on the side of the tub. Not yet ten. "Good idea. You can tell him we've talked. I'm getting in early tomorrow. Stop by if you have a minute."

"You're not angry?"

"Just tired. See you mañana."

"All right."

Laura ran more hot water into the tub and began to soap her body. Let Cynthia and Peter work it out. She had other things to do.

## TUESDAY, MAY 25

Jacobi tossed aside the budget folder, nearly knocking over the glass of white wine on the patio table next to him. What the hell is Kramer thinking? Trying to bamboozle the board with this crap?

He stood and looked over the railing of his deck at the attractive derriere of Beverly Gorman watering her garden next door. She turned, saw him and waved. She'd been very friendly recently. Wonder what she sees in that mousy little husband of hers. Guy never seemed to be around.

He waved back and watched her bend over, apparently to adjust the hose's nozzle, which gave him even a better look at her backside stretched over her yellow shorts. It was a pleasant afternoon. Maybe he'd invite her over for a drink. But first things first.

He carried his glass inside for a refill, looked up Vivian's number and took his cordless phone back to the deck. Mrs. Gorman had moved closer to his hedges. "Your boxwood looks dry, doctor," she called to him. "Perhaps they could use a little bath. Should I?"

"I'd love it...Beverly."

"All right."

"Excuse me," he said, pointing to the phone.

She nodded and smiled.

He punched in Vivian's number.

"Hello, Stanley. Let me guess why you're calling."

"Vivian, does Kramer really intend to present this?"

"That's what he told me. Haven't you talked to him?"

"No, he'd already left when I stopped by his office today. Laura Prentice said some of the committee members don't even have this yet."

"They will by tomorrow," she said.

"They might be upset."

"Why?"

"Hell, Vivian, one budget's enough to deal with, but where does he get off proposing this monster for the meeting."

"He's within his rights."

Jacobi frowned. "You seem pretty calm. Did you know about this?"

"I had an inkling."

"Why didn't you tell me? I would have had the weekend to think about it."

"I had another commitment."

"What does that mean?"

"It means I had another commitment."

"Vivian, don't tell me Kramer's gotten to you with this nonsense about a spinal cord rehab center."

"Stanley, if you believe that, you're not as smart as I thought."

"I just don't like being sandbagged."

"Everybody will have the same papers you do."

Jacobi let the point drop. No need to antagonize her. "Well, I assume you're opposed to these excessive outlays."

"In their present form. But he's come up with some interesting ideas. Worthy of discussion."

"And where do we get the money to build an eldercare residence and a doctors' clinic?"

"That's only one of Kramer's problems."

"Well, I'm going to take him on."

"You should if that's how you feel. But a word to the wise. You'd better be prepared. He will be. He's put a lot of thought into this."

"I can handle him. I hope you weigh in on my side."

"I'm leaning that way."

"Good. Well, I'm going over this again. Can I call you if I

have any thoughts or questions?"

"Certainly."

"Thank you. I'll see you Friday."

"Wouldn't miss it. Bye, Stanley."

Jacobi took a sip of wine. Vivian was right. Kramer was a good salesman. He even seems to have scored some points with her. He should speak to Cynthia again. Make sure they coordinate their lines of attack.

"All done, doctor," Mrs. Gorman called out from below. She sounded very close.

Jacobi stepped over to the edge of the deck. She struck quite a pose, one hand on her hip, the hose dangling from the other, the water now a slow trickle against her leg.

"Thank you, Beverly. You deserve a reward. Do you like white wine?"

"Love it. Let me turn off my faucet."

"By all means. We don't want to run up your bill."

Cynthia could wait awhile.

## THURSDAY, MAY 27

Connie was returning to the information desk after delivering a bouquet of flowers when a fellow volunteer gave her the high sign.

"Vivian's on the line for you," Irene Stone said. "I'll transfer her to the nook."

Connie hurried toward the alcove where the volunteers had a separate phone and took coffee breaks. She picked up on the first ring.

"Hey stranger," Connie said, "are you okay?"

"In the pink. Miss my smiling face?"

"Of course. Why aren't you here?"

"I meant to call you. I need more time to prepare for tomorrow's meeting. Big day for your friend the CEO."

"He told me."

"Is he worried?" Vivian asked.

"Off the record?"

"Oh  my, aren't we getting protective after one lunch."

"That's unfair."

"Who said I was fair? Well?"

"Let's say he's not over confident," Connie said.

"Not surprised. I don't think his plan's going to fly.  Not the big one, anyway."

"Big one? What's that mean?"

Vivian briefed her.

"Why is he doing this?" Connie said. "It's not a good time for that kind of spending."

"Wish you were there to tell him six months ago."

"Six months ago I had my own problems."

"So you did," Vivian chuckled. "And don't get fooled again."

"You won't let me. Is this meeting public?"

"Sorry, kiddo. No sunshine law for the trustees."

"How do you think you'll vote?"

"Does off the record work both ways?"

"Of course," Connie said.

"I hope you won't be angry if I let your boy down."

"Don't be silly. You'll do what you have to."

"Atta girl. Let's have lunch Saturday and I'll tell you all the gruesome details. My digs?"

"Done."

"Good. Then you can tell me his side of the story. See you."

## FRIDAY, MAY 28

Father Cahill fingered his rosary as he waited outside the main conference room in Cabot Hall where the budget committee had been meeting for almost three hours. He had watched anxiously as people would appear, whisper earnestly, then return inside.  Cahill knew the committee's recommendation to the board would effectively set Clara Barton's budget for next year.

He was about to go to the restroom when the door opened and people began drifting out. Some were smiling and chatting, others were frowning.  Cahill spotted Vivian Pershing in animated conversation with Elmer Woodworth and a young man whose name Cahill had forgotten. As they passed where he was standing, she laughed and said, "Hell, I don't know, Woody. How about you as CEO?"

Will there really be a new CEO, Cahill wondered hopefully. A moment later Robert Kramer strode through the door, grim faced, eyes fixed on a yellow legal pad. Cahill maneuvered close to the door, looking for Dr. Jacobi. He was seated at the table head to head with Cynthia Ellis. That wasn't a good sign.

"Hello, Father, something I can help you with?"

Laura stood in the doorway, clutching a bundle of blue folders.

"Oh, hello, Miss Prentice," he said, taking a step back. "Ah, no, thank you, I'm waiting to speak with Dr. Jacobi. Is that the budget you're holding?"

"Could have been. Didn't pass. Nothing did. The committee couldn't agree, and some trustees had plans to get away for Memorial Day, so they adjourned."

"Then where are we?" he asked, confused.

"We'll have to wait till the full board meets next month. I'm to prepare a summary of what happened in there. You'll see it soon or perhaps Dr. Jacobi can fill you in. Have a good day," she smiled, the folders brushing against him as she went by.

Looking into the room again, he saw Cynthia get to her feet and head his way, then she moved past without a glance. Jacobi was still seated, making notes.

"Dr. Jacobi, may I intrude?" he asked, approaching.

Jacobi looked up, then grinned. "Father Cahill. Why am I not surprised?"

"Did you present our report?"

"Sorry, I didn't have the chance."

"But--"

"I was going to," Jacobi went on, "but the meeting was running long and Elmer Woodworth moved to adjourn. So I guess it'll have to wait until the board meets. See, the copies are still on that table."

"But you gave your word."

"Yes, and believe me, Father, I tried. Even said I had an item to present. Anyway, I can assure you the board will give it complete consideration next month."

"No they won't," Cahill shook his head. "They'll be too busy with the budget. You promised the committee would review the report today."

Jacobi decided on a convenient truth. "But I didn't know then that Bob Kramer was going to drop a bomb at this meeting."

"A bomb?"

"We spent most of the time debating some new harebrained scheme of his.  But I do have good news."

"Oh?" Cahill said, suspicious.

"Indeed. Several trustees balked at Kramer's ideas. He backpedaled, tried to save face, but I don't see how he can survive. He may go through the motions next month, but I'm almost sure his budget is dead."

"And that means what?"

"That he'll probably not even ask for a contract renewal."

"And you'll get the job?" Cahill asked, recalling Vivian Pershing's remarks a moment ago.

"Almost certainly."

"Almost?"

"I only have to keep some trustees in line."

"Like Vivian Pershing?"

Jacobi smiled. "She's critical, of course, but I think I can hold her. And don't forget, when I'm in, you'll have an ear at court."

"And I can get my report through?"

"If not next month, then as soon as I take office," Jacobi said standing. "I'm not Bob Kramer, you know."

He managed a thin smile. "A new man in charge."

"A whole new era. Now if you'll forgive me, Father, I have some matters to attend to. Oh, and would you mind holding on to those reports for me?"

Cahill watched Jacobi gather his papers and leave. He realized he was now alone in the room.

---

Cynthia was still in a foul mood even after two glasses of Chardonnay. She dialed Peter's number for the third time. When his answering machine again spoke in her ear, she slammed down the phone. "Shithead."

In the dining room, she checked the thermostat and turned on the air conditioner. "Eighty degrees in here and not even June." She took a cold shower and felt slightly better. Donning a yellow silk kimono, she went to her desk to review her notes.

Objectively, it hadn't been that bad a day. Kramer's ideas were intriguing but had received a cool reception. Jacobi had been smooth, but somewhat vague and repetitive. Meanwhile, she had done well taking the middle road, answering questions and making constructive suggestions without seeming to abandon Kramer or endorse Jacobi. And there was still the possible deal with him. If only Pershing hadn't been so damn inscrutable.

Carrying her glass into the bedroom, she stood before her bureau staring at the photo of her and her father taken at her college graduation. He was only in his 40s, yet he looked haggard and drawn. But it was his smile that always bothered her. She could never find any joy in it. It was the pasted-on grin of a manikin showing off the latest fashions. All those hours of his working to succeed and nothing positive ever coming back.

Like her today. This meeting could have been a tipping point for her--a step upward while Kramer's star waned and Jacobi's remained dark. But she felt hollow, as though she hadn't gained an inch. She gulped her wine. What the hell, she had plans in reserve.

The phone rang. Peter...finally. She grabbed the receiver without looking at the caller ID.

"At last."

"Cynthia, Stan Jacobi. We should talk."

---

After protracted but futile lovemaking, Thorpe quit trying.

"What's wrong?" Laura asked, looking up into those dark blue eyes.

"Everything," he said, rolling onto his side. "My mind's overruling my body. I'm still pinged up about the meeting."

They had avoided the topic during dinner, but Laura knew that wouldn't last. "I think things went well," she said, resting on her elbow. "Really. Cynthia's tone was just right. Measured, confident."

"Jacobi didn't steal the show?"

"Oh, he came on strong, but personality can do only so much. He wasn't very specific on what he'd propose."

"Is that you talking?"

"That's the gospel according to Kramer when I talked to him later."

"Well, I hear he made an impression."

"But he was floundering."

"You sure?"

"Peter, I was there. A few trustees were interested in his ideas, but not enough. Not after this year. I can't see that changing in a month."

"But no one seems to know where Pershing's head was."

"She's the wildcard," Laura nodded. "She asked Bob hard questions and really peppered Jacobi. She might be inclined toward Bob's one-year proposal, but I couldn't tell."

"Sounds like she's not ready to give up on him. You get the sense he'd settle for just his one-year?"

"He might try to hang in to fight another day. I would."

"Let's hope Jacobi sees it that way. I'd feel a lot better if he'd agree to Cynthia's deal."

She kissed him. "A positive thought at last. I'm thirsty," she said, slipping out of bed. "You want anything?"

"Just bring back that body of yours. Some parts of me are working."

"Then I'll hurry."

He watched her stride toward the doorway, appreciating her graceful movements. He'd had more exciting lovers, but this relationship had an ease, a feeling of comfort. He wasn't sure that was a good omen or a warning. Soon he'd have to decide. She was becoming impatient.

The bedside phone rang, but he ignored it, reaching over and taking a sip of the Couvosier that Laura always had on hand for him. Savoring the smooth taste, he heard her voice grow louder from downstairs. Her face was flushed when she returned.

"Your ex-husband pestering you?" he smiled.

"Worse. Cynthia. She's been calling you at home. Left you a bunch of messages."

"I'll call her later."

"You won't like it."

"Try me."

"Jacobi nixed the deal. He thinks he can win without Cynthia even if Kramer puts up a fight. She's going to call in Marcia Davis to sue him for sexual harassment."

"Damn it," he said, getting out of bed, brandy snifter in hand.

"Peter, you knew she might do this. You shouldn't have given her the idea."

"It was mainly to steer her away from a stupid malpractice suit. Did she say Julia Vallance was the plaintiff?"

"No. Why Vallance?"

"Because Jacobi threw her out of the OR."

"So?"

"So I don't understand it either."

"What do we do now?"

"I don't know," he said. "Let me think." He began to pace back and forth. "We've got to find a way to slow Jacobi down."

"Isn't this where I came in?"

Thorpe took a sip of brandy, then brightened, stopped near the bed. "Yes, it is, but now you can take the lead."

"I do what?"

"Listen, Jacobi sought you out, so let's use that. He's ripe."

"I don't think I'm going to like this."

"It's right up your alley. You tell him you're coming over to his side, that you're double-crossing Cynthia."

"Are you serious? Admit I've been working for her all along?"

"Yes. You say Cynthia promised to make you chief of staff,

but now she's told you he turned down her deal. You want to back a winner and you think he's it."

"Peter, even if I can sell Jacobi, what good does it do?"

"You learn what you can about his strategy. Which trustees he's targeting, why, how. We pass it all to Cynthia. Then we sabotage him."

"What if he thinks this is Cynthia's idea because she wants to get back at him?"

"Good point," he said and resumed pacing. "We need to make you credible."

She watched him a few moments. "Take your time, I've got all day."

He stopped and turned. "You tell him Marcia Davis is about to sue him."

"Cynthia'd go nuts."

"I'll work it all out with her when I get home. And I'll ask her to run it by you. So play ignorant when she calls."

"That won't be hard."

"Let's not wait on this. Jacobi might be in town this weekend. Call him tomorrow. It's the kind of thing he'd expect if you were switching sides. Maybe go to his house. He might even it on you like he did Sheila Cottine."

"What is it with you? First you want me to flirt with Bob. Now what? Am I supposed to go to bed with Jacobi?"

Thorpe grinned. "You wouldn't have much of a sexual harassment case if you did, now would you?"

Laura smiled and shook her head. "You sneaking s.o.b. So that's your ploy."

"Only half of it. We go after Jacobi from both directions. If Cynthia insists on going to court, we need a good plaintiff. I leave it to you to figure out how to get us there."

"You have that look in those eyes of yours."

"That's because I want a rematch."

# TEN

## SUNDAY, MAY 30

Laura was glad the Ford Escape had a good air conditioner. It was a ghastly, humid afternoon as she made the short trip from Brandywine to New Mexico Avenue. They had decided she'd drive over without calling ahead. "Take the offensive," Cynthia had said. "If Jacobi's home, he'll be sure to let you in."

Cynthia and Peter were very clever, and she enjoyed the intrigue of plotting together as a threesome and even more with Peter alone. She also had to admit she was enjoying her lovemaking with both of them. She had never had a concurrent bisexual relationship and it excited her. Maybe this is what she had always wanted.

Still, she had a few pangs about continuing to "cheat" on Cynthia. But that was one consequence of all her planning, wasn't it? Anyway, things were nearing resolution. She doubted Cynthia would turn on her the way Allison had. One stalker in her life was quite enough, thank you.

Laura drove past the intersection of New Mexico and Cathedral Avenue. Not much farther now. There, on the left. Wesley Heights Commons was a gated community, a mixture of lavish townhouses and smaller condominiums in low-slung buildings. She put on her blinker and turned into the driveway. She stopped at the gatehouse where she and the guard opened their respective windows.

"Laura Prentice for Dr. Jacobi," she said.

"He expecting you, ma'am?"

"Why don't you tell him I'm here?"

His window snapped closed and she rolled up hers, waiting. After a moment the gate rose and she drove in looking for 3804. She saw a sign with an arrow for the 3800 cluster and drove down a winding road, spotting his Lexus outside the third townhouse from the end. She parked alongside and stepped out of the car, the heat surging against her. She took the brick steps quickly and the door swung open.

"Laura, what a pleasant surprise."

Jacobi stood there in a colorful striped bathrobe and sandals. A fast change for her benefit? "Dr. Jacobi, thank you for seeing me."

"The pleasure's mine. Come in."

The living room furniture was glass, chrome and black leather. Nothing she'd ever choose but somehow soothing to the eye.

"Please take one of the club chairs. They're the most comfortable. May I offer you something?"

"Anything tall and cold."

"Diet Coke or Amstel Light?"

"Amstel. Never met a Dutchman I didn't like." That got the expected chuckle.

"Be right back."

After returning with a pair of frosted mugs and exchanging a few more pleasantries, Jacobi sat back in the other club chair and crossed his legs, making sure to exhibit his well-muscled calves. "So, what can I do for you?"

"Let me turn that around, doctor. I think we might help each other."

Ten minutes later Laura had finished making her pitch, surprised at how few questions Jacobi had asked.

Now he leaned forward. "So you've been playing Kramer for a sucker all these months."

She shrugged. "He's cagey. I've done what I could, but I'm not sure I've helped Cynthia very much. As I see it, she's stuck in third place."

"Perhaps you didn't try hard enough with Kramer," Jacobi said suggestively.

She let it pass.

He went on. "All right. What do you think you can you do for me you couldn't do for Cynthia?"

"I think you can use someone in the enemy camp."

"Not sure I need that."

"Listen, I was at the same meeting you were on Friday. I don't care what you told Cynthia. This is still a horse race and you know it."

He sat back again. "In that case, you could be a Trojan horse."

Laura smiled. "Then here's a gift with no strings. You're going to be hit with a lawsuit."

"Malpractice?" he asked, recalling Thorpe's warning about Howard Schroeder's nephew.

"I don't know, but plaintiff's counsel will be one Marcia Davis. Cynthia told me a couple of weeks ago."

"How would Cynthia know?"

"I think it's her idea. She and Davis are old friends."

"I see. Well, I've been sued before." Jacobi took a swallow of beer. "What makes you think you can work for me and still fool Cynthia?"

"I've fooled Kramer. He's a lot smarter."

"I wonder," Jacobi said, then smiled. "Laura, I'm delighted you came to me, but I'll need to think this over."

"Don't take too long. Kramer's not out of this thing, you know."

"You'd sell out Cynthia for him?"

"I want to be chief of staff, doctor."

He nodded. "Perhaps it's time you called me Stan, at least when we're alone."

Laura raised her mug. "Here's to solitude."

## MONDAY, MAY 31

For the fifth time in the past hour Connie wiped down the already immaculate bar at the Laughing Bull. Not much else to do. There had been few customers all afternoon, and only one surly woman now, nursing her third gin and tonic. I should have asked to work the evening shift, she thought. At least I might have seen a few familiar faces back in town from the beach. For a change the Memorial Day weekend had been sunny and hot. Great for Ocean City and Rehoboth; lousy for D.C. bartenders.

"Hey, Red," a voice yelled. "Can a guy get a beer around here?"

Connie turned to see Bob saunter in, wearing spiffy jeans, a white cotton shirt and a huge Panama hat. She was so nonplussed at his appearance she laughed out loud.

He put his hand on his hips. "Stop that cackling. Is that how you treat your customers?"

"Yeah, she's a real bitch," the gin and tonic yelled out. "Makes a lousy drink too."

Kramer bowed toward the woman. "Then by all means, my dear, you deserve a refill. Barkeep," he slammed his hand on a stool, "whatever the lady's having and a Beck's for me."

"Yes, sir," Connie gave a mock salute, then did as asked.

"Sorry, I didn't phone you this weekend," Kramer said softly moments later as she placed a bottle and glass before him. "I've been in a lousy mood."

"It's okay. Vivian told me about the meeting. I figured you were busy regrouping."

"Trying to," he said, taking a sip, "but it's not like me to break a promise."

"Where have I heard that before?" she said, teasing. "But you just made my day."

"Thanks. I thought the hat was a nice touch."

"Not that," she smiled. "No one's called me Red since my stepfather died."

"Really? Do you mind?"

"I insist."

"Consider it your new name. How was your weekend?"

"Quiet. Did some painting. A surprise for Vivian. Were you working today?"

"Oh yeah. And on the phone with my brother Fred picking his brain."

"He in finance?"

"He dabbles. He's a corporate attorney."

"So how do things look?"

"Uphill, but I'm not giving up."

"Vivian didn't think you would."

"Nice to hear, but I wish she'd been more supportive at the meeting."

"Were you surprised?"

"And disappointed. I thought she'd at least ask for a vote on the one-year plan. Sorry. You don't know what that means."

"I do now. Vivian's a wealth of information."

"Oh. Listen, Connie, I hope you don't think I'm trying to find out what you two talk about."

"Fat chance I'd tell you."

He took a long swallow. "What else do you know?"

"That you should watch your back. I'm not sure you can trust Laura Prentice. She's very friendly with Ellis."

"Vivian said that?" Kramer asked.

"I have eyes, Bob. They have a thing for each other. I picked up signals weeks ago and I've watched them. The way Laura looks at Cynthia, touches her."

He nodded. "I appreciate you telling me. I mean that."

"I'm glad," she said meeting his gaze.

"Look, Connie, I'm not here just to apologize. I'd like us to get off on the right foot, so I want to tell you up front that I'll be pretty busy for the next few weeks."

"You don't owe me any explanations."

"Shush up," he said, taking her hand. "I'll need to take an occasional breather, but I can't know exactly when. So I may ask you out on the fly. Like now. I'd love to take you to dinner next weekend but I'm not sure which night."

"I'll have to check with my social secretary, but I might be free."

"Can you handle The Sea Horse Inn or would that bring back bad memories?"

She grinned. "If that were a problem, I'd quit this job. Vic's office was right upstairs. He sat right where you are dozens of times."

"Geez, I'll switch seats."

"Bob, it's all right. He never called me Red."

## TUESDAY, JUNE 1

Lieutenant Sam Witkin occupied the same office Frank Stephens had before they were both recently promoted. Sam had added several touches that reflected his love for old furnishings, the latest being a roll-top desk that Tawana had given him as a wedding present. He had placed it against one wall so he could swivel toward the center of the room during meetings. He found organizing the little drawers and compartments wonderfully relaxing.

He was in the middle of transferring paper clips between drawers when the intercom buzzed. He pulled the phone toward him.

"Yes, Gerry."

"There's a Detective Neumann from Philadelphia on line one, Lieutenant."

"I'll take it," he said, tucking the receiver under his chin and pressing the button. "Johnny, how are you?"

"Overweight and 23 months from retirement."

"I thought you loved your work."

"You wouldn't say that if you were still a sergeant."

"Bull, I work harder than ever," Sam said, aligning four paper clips into a rough square.

"Sure you do. Listen, Perez told me you called about the Parnell thing when I was up at my kid's graduation."

"Patrick's finished at Syracuse?"

"Top ten percent. He's already landed an internship at a small radio station in Albany."

"Good for him. So why wait two more years to hang it up?" Sam started a second square next to the first.

"Tuition ain't cheap, Sam. We won't have the loans paid till then. Hey, I hear you're going to be a daddy. See what you have to look forward to?"

"Hell, by the time mine's ready for college, I'll be in the nursing home. Tawana will have to deal with it."

"Dream on, buddy. Anyhow, here's the skinny. Parnell died from an overdose of lidocaine."

"That some new street drug?"

"Not unless dealers are going to medical school. It's a heart drug, but not in the dose Parnell took. Fried his heart."

"You have anything at all?"

"Not much. Some mud on the rug, probably from the day before. A few prints, some stray hairs near the body and on his sheets upstairs. Didn't lead anywhere. That's about it."

"And no motive," Sam said, removing the middle clip and forming a large rectangle.

"Nope. Parnell kept pretty much to himself. No forced entry, apparently nothing taken and a fair amount of cash in his bedroom bureau."

"You still working it?"

"Yesterday's news, Sam."

"Understand. Well, thanks for the update, Johnny. Let me know if anything breaks."

"Sure. I know you loved the guy. Take care."

Sam hung up and pushed the paper clips away. He reached for the cigarette he always carried in his shirt pocket, but never lit anymore thanks to Tawana. He sat back and took a deep drag of air. Who'd want to murder Tim Parnell?

## WEDNESDAY, JUNE 2

Laura locked her car in the hospital lot and saw Cynthia approaching, her hands behind her back. What's this, she thought.

"Good morning," Laura said, shouldering her purse and admiring Cynthia's lavender pants suit. "Nice outfit. New?"

"Yes, and these are for you," she smiled, presenting a bouquet of six yellow roses.

"Cynthia, how lovely. What's the occasion?"

"Just a thank you. You did a great job getting to Jacobi."

"I'm not home free, and anyway it was Peter's idea."

"Last night wasn't. You were wonderful."

"So were you," she said as they walked toward the hospital. "But be careful, Jacobi may be watching."

"Unh-uh. He has surgery this morning. I checked."

"I should have guessed."

"And I've been thinking. How's this for your next move? Tell Jacobi you've learned the lawsuit will hit early next week. That will score a few points."

"Is Marcia ready?" Laura asked.

"Said she can be. That's good enough for me. Now here's what I need you to get from him, ASAP," she said, slipping a piece of paper into Laura's free hand.

They crossed the driveway and walked toward the staff entrance.

"I have to scoot," Cynthia said, squeezing her arm. "Call me later."

"Sure," Laura said, slowing and studying the note.

"Hello, Miss Prentice."

Laura looked up to see Cahill standing before her. "Good morning, Father. You seem to be everywhere I am these days."

"Purely my good fortune. Do you have a few minutes?"

"Sure. What's on your mind?"

"Ah, it's about the budget meeting last Friday."

"Oh yes. Did you ever talk to Dr. Jacobi?" she asked as they went through the doors.

"Briefly and, well, I thought you might clarify something for me."

"I'll try."

"At the meeting, did Dr. Jacobi mention a report he and I had worked on?"

"Report? Not that I recall. I may have missed it, of course. I did step out for a moment, but I'm certain my notes are complete."

"That's unfortunate. Well, I suppose I should pursue this with him."

"That might be best," she said, stopping outside her office door.

"Well, thank you for your time," Cahill said, turning away.

"Just a minute, Father. What was the report about?"

"Lapses in hospital security and incidents where we mistreated patients in the ER. Dr. Jacobi and I thought the trustees should know."

"Interesting. I assume you have a copy."

"Not with me."

"I'd love to see it."

"Really? I can bring you one this morning."

"Wonderful. Father, would you like a cup of coffee? I always make some when I get in."

"That would be very nice, Miss Prentice. I could use a pick me up. Just had my workout, you know."

"Good for you. Now, I take my coffee black, how about you?"

# ELEVEN

## THURSDAY, JUNE 3

Vivian was grinning as she drove the Rover down the corridor toward the volunteer office. She had come in a few minutes early to surprise Connie and help deliver the last of the newspapers.

Inside the volunteer office, she put on her blazer, signed in on the touch screen, then glanced at the message board. She was surprised to see a typewritten note with her name on it:

*Vivian--I'm in Cabot 4. I need to talk to you. W*

W. Woody? What's he doing here on a Thursday morning? Vivian stuffed the message into her blazer pocket, sped out of the office to the end of the hallway. No sign of Connie at the desk, she noted, as she turned right, and went past the elevators toward the archway leading to the ER and the corridor that connected the main hospital to Cabot Hall.

Passing the ER, Vivian continued along a hallway and made a right turn into a long, inclined corridor. The Rover now struggled to keep moving forward. I need to upgrade this thing, she thought. Needs more oomph. Finally, she reached the top where Cabot Hall began.

Crouched behind the slightly open door of Cabot conference room 1, the killer watched Vivian go by. Good, she was keeping to the right and would most likely do so on her return. The killer took a collapsible baton from a tote bag. It was a new police tool used for crowd control and street crime. It extended to a full 30 inches.

Vivian stopped at conference room 4, knocked and entered. Empty. She reached into her pocket and checked the message. Damn Woody, she thought. She backed out of the room, did a swift turn and drove back toward the corridor.

The Rover had large center wheels, designed to let the chair make sharp turns within a short distance. Unfortunately, the design was also vulnerable to ruts and uneven surfaces. Thus, when Vivian was passing conference room 1 and the killer snaked out the full length of the baton under the right center wheel as it rolled by, the chair lurched abruptly just as it started down the inclined corridor.

Losing control, Vivian panicked briefly as the Rover gained speed and careened left toward the panoramic glass windows. As the chair began to teeter, she applied the brakes sharply, exacerbating the problem. The chair crashed into the glass and Vivian's body was thrown out violently.

The killer stood and watched the drama unfold. Shouldn't drive so fast, Vivian. Collapsing the baton into the tote bag, the killer stepped into corridor and knelt next to her, searching her with latex-gloved hands and found the message that had summoned her. Perfect, no need to go retrieve it. The killer examined Vivian's neck. The vertebra seemed fine. She'd be sore, but there should be no permanent injury. The killer was about to make a more thorough check when the sound of voices floated up from the hallway around the corner. No time.

The killer walked rapidly back past the conference rooms, through a pair of swinging doors and ducked out the side door facing the back driveway. Striding past the gazebo between Cabot and the main building, the killer went through the doors leading to the ER. Once inside, the killer slowed and strolled toward the lobby and the elevators. Then the public address system sounded overhead.

### Code Blue, Cabot Conference 1
### Code Blue, Cabot Conference 1

That's fast, the killer thought. One of those voices in the hallway must have belonged to an employee familiar with the house phones. Medical personnel would soon appear and revive Vivian who would tell her tale. That was sufficient for now. After all, accidents happen even in hospitals. The elevator arrived and the killer headed down to the cafeteria, mentally reviewing the score sheet: Monroe, baby girl Thomas, Pershing. The groundwork had been laid.

Connie heard the Code Blue as she stepped out of the elevator on the first floor of Cabot Hall after delivering newspapers upstairs. Remembering her training, she hurried through the swinging doors and recognized the Rover lying on its side. Racing toward it, she saw two maintenance men near the chair. One of them was reaching out toward Vivian's face.

"Stop!" she shouted. "Don't move her head. Don't touch her at all."

## FRIDAY, JUNE 4

Father Cahill paused, took a breath, then knocked softly at the open door of room 518.

"Come in," Vivian called out.

"Good afternoon, Miss Pershing," Cahill said, stepping in, He was surprised to see her sitting up typing on a laptop. The only sign of her injury was a baby blue neck brace.

"Father Cahill! I was expecting the doctor. Have they listed me as a Catholic or something worse?"

"What? Oh. No, I just wanted to see how you were. I hear you had an awful crash."

"More like a blown tire, but never mind. Who told you about it?"

"It's all over the hospital."

"Are they saying I imagined the note or was just drunk? The police seem to think it was one or the other."

"I don't know. I mean--"

"Forget it. As you can see, I'm surviving. Haven't flipped a wheelchair in 24 hours, and my new one's right over there." She pointed toward the window.

"It looks very nice."

"It's a loaner, a Rover II. More power and more stable or so they tell me. We'll see. If I like it, I'll order one."

"Can you...drive it wearing that brace?"

"If I can't, Dr. Patterson will hear from me pronto."

"Oh."

She smiled. "Father, it was really was nice of you to come by, but I'm afraid I must concentrate on a budget problem right now."

"Yes, I can imagine. This may be of some help," he said and stepped toward the bed, placing a copy of his report next to her laptop.

"What's this?"

He told her.

She scanned a few pages. "You worked this up with Dr. Jacobi's approval?"

Cahill nodded. "He told me was going to hand it out last Friday, but he never did."

"Why not?"

"Uhm, I'm not really sure."

"So he asked you to give it to me now."

"No, Miss Prentice did. She thinks the trustees should have it before the next meeting and suggested I ask you what you thought."

"Laura Prentice said that? When?"

"A few minutes ago."

"Has she read it?"

"I suppose so. I gave her a copy the other day."

"Did you give one to Mr. Kramer as well?"

"She said she'd do that. I was going to give you a copy yesterday at the Information Desk, but, well, you...."

"I see," Vivian said thoughtfully.

"Do you think I should send it to the trustees, Miss Pershing?"

"Yes, Father. I think you should mail it off as soon as you can."

"Ah, I don't have all the addresses."

"Laura Prentice will. Now, Father, if you'll forgive me, I'd like to study this."

"Of course," he said and took a backward step. "And I'm glad you're feeling better."

Vivian nodded, but her eyes were fixed on the report. She waited until she was sure he was gone, then reached for the phone next to her on the bed and punched in a number.

"Hello?"

"Connie, its Vivian."

"You okay?"

"If you don't count being held prisoner."

"Sound's like you're fine."

"Or becoming paranoid. Listen, I'm supposed to be discharged late this afternoon. You working?"

"Yes, but I can switch with Robin if you need me."

"No, that's okay. How about breakfast at my apartment tomorrow around nine?"

"Deal. What's going on?"

"I'm not sure, but I'm beginning to think there are strange games being played around here."

## SATURDAY, JUNE 5

Connie eased her Saab 900 to the curb. The house numbers made no sense.  Then she checked the map. Oh, there's the problem. She was on Overlook Drive, not Overlook Court.  She went to the end of the block and turned left, driving up a long hill. 5300 was right in the middle of a cul-de-sac. A dark blue Camry was in the driveway.

She parked in the circle and turned off the engine, now reluctant to ring the bell.  She had wanted to call first, but couldn't get the number. Well, it's not like he doesn't know me.  She grabbed her purse and opened the driver's door only to see Nick walking toward her with a black and white Springer spaniel on a leash.

"Connie! How are you?"

"Hello, Nick. Sorry to drop by unannounced."

"Couldn't find me in the book, right?"

"Information didn't have a listing for you."

"Phone's under my wife's name, Kathy Stilmore.  I really should do something about that, but we get enough wacky calls as it is."

"And who's this?" Connie said, reaching down to pet the dog that was busily sniffing her loafers and blue jeans.

"Patches of Chevy Chase."

"Pardon?"

"It's a long story, but bottom line is we adopted her from a friend who lived over there.  One day some kids from her old neighborhood were visiting a few houses down the street. While I was walking her, they recognized her and started calling out 'Patches, Patches.' She's been Patches of Chevy Chase ever since."

"Look at her tail wagging. She seems to like the name."

"She might if she could hear it.  She's almost deaf now. So what brings you out here?"

"Would you believe I have another problem at Clara Barton?"

"Can't be as bad as the last one."

"I have my fingers crossed. Do you have a few minutes?"

"Sure. Kathy went to the quarry for gravel. That's even a longer story, so don't ask. I just made some coffee."

"Wonderful."

They were on their second cup sitting in Nick's living room when Connie finished telling him about the situation at Clara Barton, ending with her breakfast with Vivian that morning.

Nick leaned back and crossed his legs. "So Vivian thinks her fall wasn't an accident and somehow it's tied to this CEO/budget business."

"That's about it."

"Do you agree?" he asked, stealing a glance at how well Connie filled out her green cotton sweater.

"To a point. I believe she found that note and now it's disappeared. And I have to think she was pushed off that chair somehow."

"Connie, it's possible that when the chair crashed the note came out of her pocket and was overlooked."

"No, I was at the scene right afterwards.  There was no note and Vivian doesn't hallucinate."

"But she was moving fast and did hit her head."

"Nick, she tools around in that chair like a NASCAR driver. On the other hand," she shrugged, "does that mean the incident's tied to hospital politics?"

"She's a force on the board, isn't she?"

"Oh yes. She's a true leader."

"So, if she were incapacitated, it would create a power vacuum that someone who didn't have her support could exploit."

"I guess so."

"And if this someone pushed over her chair, it could be anybody, including your friend Bob Kramer."

Connie nodded.

"Or Dr. Jacobi," Nick said. "If he was holding back Father Cahill's report, he could release it now in Vivian's absence to pick up some votes for CEO."

"Vivian thought of that, but says he would have been ruled out of order unless he knew enough to circulate it to the board before the meeting."

"And if didn't, someone like Bob or Cynthia Ellis could challenge him."

"Not directly, but either of them could ask a trustee to do it. Vivian thinks Prentice wanted the report released now to undermine both Bob and Jacobi because she's friends with Ellis."

Nick smiled. "Well, Vivian either has a wild imagination or she could be onto something. Still, knocking over her wheelchair's a pretty extreme step."

"That's my feeling, but I'd like to make sure. Is there any way your friend Frank Stephens can have one of his people double check? Vivian insisted the police be called after she fell, but she says they hardly gave her the time of day, and no one questioned me."

"I can ask, but you know they're all in homicide."

"Will you try?"

"Sure. After all, you helped them out."

"Super," she said and put down her cup. "You know, I'm supposed to see Bob tomorrow night."

"And?"

"I intend to, but I'm debating how much to tell him about all this. I'm just starting to know him and I do like him, but I also have my loyalty to Vivian. She said it's up to me."

"What's your gut telling you?"

"To tell him everything. I hate deceit, especially after what Vic did to me."

"Well, I see no reason not to. There may be nothing to Vivian's concerns and he's probably heard about her version of the fall by now. Plus, he can add two and two the same way she and Prentice did about Jacobi and the Cahill report.

"Good, that makes me feel a lot better."

"Besides, if there is anything sinister going on, the police may find out and interview Bob and everyone else."

"Yeah, that's right," she sighed. "Boy, I can really pick 'em, can't I?"

"Connie, there's only one Victor Devane."

"Would you put that in writing?"

---

Jacobi slammed down the receiver. "What the hell's that idiot thinking?" he fumed at his image in the mirror that ran along the wall behind his bed. And that bitch Prentice. I knew she was up to something. I'm going give her a piece of my mind. He reached for his bedside phone book when the front door bell chimed.

"Not now!" he exploded. Beverly Gorman had hinted she might drop by for a drink around five. But he was in no mood for an early visit. He hurried down the stairs to get rid of her. Tightening his robe, he opened the door only to see Laura standing there in a bewitching white tennis dress.

"Don't you ever get dressed, Stan?"

Jacobi began to form a reply, then started over. "Laura, how nice. I was about to call you. We need to have a little chat."

"I agree," she said, swooping past him. "It's hot out here."

He watched her saunter over to the club chair she'd used before, placing her straw carryall on the floor. She turned to him and smiled. "Father Cahill reach you?"

"You're damn right he did. I just got off the phone. What the hell is this, Laura? I thought we had a deal."

"We do. That's why I suggested he speak to Pershing about releasing his report. I'd love a cold drink."

Jacobi loomed over her. "Not so fast. I was saving that report as the coup de grace to nail Kramer when the trustees voted on the budget."

"And he would have cleaned your clock. Stan, if you want to be CEO you'd better read the bylaws. The board isn't the committee. It can't consider any item that's not on the agenda at least 48 hours before it meets."

"What?"

"You heard me. Two full days."

"Why didn't you tell me that before you sent Cahill off to see Pershing?"

"I didn't read the report till Thursday," she lied, "and I seem to recall a certain Dr. Jacobi wasn't around yesterday."

"I was at a conference downtown."

"I trust you enjoyed it."

"Never mind. So what's the rush? The meeting's not for three weeks. I could have asked to put it on the agenda."

"I'll explain in a minute. Let's relax shall we? We've got some brainstorming to do before the trustees begin to read it."

"Cahill said he's already mailed out the copies."

"Not till this morning. I made sure of that. Now can I have one of your Amstels, or are you going to let me sit here and die of thirst."

"I'm all out."

"Then surprise me."

Jacobi hesitated, then shook his head and turned toward the hallway leading to the kitchen.

Laura watched him leave and relaxed. Peter and Cynthia had accurately gauged Jacobi's reaction, and so far she was handling her own part well. She opened the top button of her tennis dress.

A few moments later, he returned and handed her a glass of a chilled Mosel-Riesling. Beverly will just have to drink red wine, he thought.

He sat across from her, took a sip from his glass and crossed his legs. "Tell me, Laura, what would you have done with Cahill if Pershing had suffered more severe injuries or even died. I heard she took a very hard tumble."

"Sent him to Elmer Woodworth."

"Why bother sending him to anyone? You could have mailed them out yourself."

"No way. I needed cover. But Kramer can't object to my helping Cahill send out a possible agenda document when the chairman or vice chairman directs it be done.  You really need to study those bylaws, Stan."

He smiled. "You know, for a while I thought you and Bob might be having a little romance."

"Think again."

Jacobi said nothing for a moment. "All right, now why didn't we wait a couple weeks to release the report?"

"Because you need to use the time to show the board you can lead and not just carp at Kramer the way you did at the budget meeting."

"That's a bit harsh, but go on."

Laura leaned forward, noticing Jacobi's eyes shift to her bodice. "The trustees won't get the report until Monday or Tuesday. That gives you the chance to call Pershing and get ahead of the curve."

"How?"

"You tell her if she'll put the report on the agenda, you'll present specific plans to implement its recommendations in time for the trustees to vote."

"I don't have any plans."

She sat back and sipped her wine. "That's where I come in."

Jacobi studied her, then smiled. "I like it."

"I thought you would. And it will drive Kramer and Cynthia up the wall.  They won't have time to prepare a response."

"Can you really put together something convincing?"

"Oh yes, and even make it fit within Kramer's projections for next year. I know exactly what it will take to open the Clara Barton Community Outreach Center."

"You already have a name?"

"And more," she said and reached into the carryall. "Here are talking points to make with Pershing and a draft of your e-mail to the trustees if she goes along.  Marjorie Bannister doesn't have a computer, but you can personally deliver it to her. Schmooz her in the bargain.  I think she's loyal to Kramer. They talk all the time."

He read through the sheets of paper. "I might want to add a few thoughts, but this is really good."

"It's what I do. And that reminds me. I need something from

you."

"What is it?"

"A list of the trustees you want to cultivate the most. Who you think your weak links are.  It'll help me plan." And help Cynthia.

"You need them this minute? I'd like to look over the roster."

"No rush. I'm taking the rest of the weekend off. I worked on that draft last night and all morning."

"It shows. Care for more wine?"

"Keep it on ice," she smiled. She reached again into the carryall and pulled out a black bikini. "I was thinking of using your pool."

# TWELVE

## SUNDAY, JUNE 6

Vivian put the Aleve tablet in her mouth, then took a healthy swallow of coffee and made a face. She disliked taking any drugs, but the pills had helped the stiffness in her neck. Dr. Patterson said it was from the injury, but she thought it was the stupid brace he insisted she wear till her next appointment. Well, whether he likes it or not, she'd drive to his office and not depend on a van service.

She turned back to the *Post* Sunday crossword puzzle. She was baffled by a seven-letter word for "rates of tears, e.g." All she was had an "a" and "g" for the third and fourth letters. Niagras? No, that can't be right. As she took another sip of coffee, the phone rang. Saved by the bell.

She headed to the kitchen after putting her coffee in the cup holder that was built into the Rover II. She liked the pep and features of this new chair. She reached the phone on the third ring and saw that it was Jacobi. Well, well.

"Hello, Stanley."

"Vivian, how are you? I trust both your condition and spirits are improving."

"Coming along."

"Good. Dr. Patterson assures me you'll be back with us shortly. Meanwhile, if there's anything I can do to speed your recovery, please let me know."

"You can cut the crap and get to the point."

Jacobi chuckled. "Well, in fact there is something I'd like to run by you."

"Then do it."

"Vivian, I understand Father Cahill already gave you a copy of his report and that the other trustees will be receiving copies soon."

"That's right."

"Good.  I don't know if he told you, but I had encouraged him to complete the report and critiqued it at his request."

"He mentioned something about it."

"Problem is, I sort of let him down when I didn't hand it out on Friday."

"You had copies with you?"

"Oh yes. They were stacked over by the coffee alcove. But with Kramer's proposals, well, things heated up and we were running late, so I just thought better of it."

"Well, now he's done it for you."

"And I fully endorse his decision and, in your capacity as chair, I'd like you to place it on the agenda for the meeting on the 28th."

"Why should I?"

"Because I'd like the trustees to also consider plans I've been working on to implement the report's recommendations.  I hope to circulate a complete outline to the board in time for the meeting."

"What kind of plans?"

"Mainly to establish a community outreach center. Vivian, I want to change the direction of Clara Barton. To dramatically improve our level of services and standing in the community."

"How noble. Where do you get the money?"

"We have it. Unlike Kramer, I can do it and still meet our goal of fiscal restraint."

"You can?"

"You'll see. And if you'll agree to put both items on the agenda, I'd like to send a brief message to the rest of the trustees describing my intentions."

"Let me think about it."

"That's all I can ask."

"I'll call you tomorrow.  Tuesday at the latest.  I want to talk to a few people."

"Of course. And please let me know if you have any questions."

"You bet I will. 'Bye, Stanley."

What do you know, Vivian thought, hanging up. He's upping the ante.  She returned to the dining room, where she had left Cahill's report. She was looking over the notes she had jotted on the summary page when her cell phone buzzed. She recognized the number on the display. All of a sudden she'd become very popular.

"Morning, Bob."

"Vivian. How are you feeling?"

"Well enough. I see you're at the office. Working hard?"

"As always. Do you have a few minutes to chat?"

"What's on your mind?"

"This report from Father Cahill. Laura Prentice gave me a copy and told me you asked it be sent to all the trustees."

"Yes. What do you think of it?"

"I haven't studied it thoroughly, but I have some problems with the premise."

"Oh? Tell me more," she smiled into the phone. This is shaping up as a helluva meeting.

---

Cynthia took the last page from the printer and stapled the five sheets together. She glanced through them as she walked through her house to the deck where Peter was talking to Laura on the phone.

"Good," he said. "No, I wouldn't. Tuesday should be soon enough. No, Cynthia just printed out the draft. Okay, I'll talk to you later."

"She want to visit Jacobi again?" Cynthia asked, handing him the papers.

"No, follow up by phone. Doesn't want to scare him off. I think he got the message yesterday."

"Maybe he tried to get a something else from her."

"It'd do us a lot better than this lawsuit."

"Peter, just read it, will you?"

After a minute he looked up. "At least Davis writes well."

"She's the best. I'm sure she'll get Vallance to sign it."

Thorpe turned a page, then shook his head, "This won't fly, Cynthia. Jacobi may have fondled Sheila Cottine, but sniping at

Vallance in surgery has nothing to do with sexual harassment."

"Wrong, doctor. That's not what the courts say, and it's not what Clara Barton's policy statement says. Trust me, I know this stuff. Stephanie Proctor told me what happened in the OR. Jacobi clearly referred to Vallance's body. She has every right to file this in court or with the hospital EEO office."

"Not if she wants a career here."

"That's exactly the point. You don't get it because you're not a woman."

"I'll concede that much," he said, tossing the draft aside.

"Peter, I'm not dropping this."

"Look, now that Laura has Jacobi wrapping himself in Cahill's report, why don't you bide your time?"

"What for? I want to keep his feet to the fire. Anyway, he's expecting a lawsuit."

"Laura can tell him Davis isn't ready yet. We can wait till the budget meeting."

"Why?"

"Jacobi thinks he's home free with this community outreach crap. But when you hand out your rebuttal before the meeting he'll be thrown for a loop. Then Davis can hit him with this complaint."

"A one-two punch," she smiled.

"And maybe a knockout. Make the timing work for you."

"I'll mull it over," she said.

"Geez, you're stubborn. Will you at least tell Davis not to run to court unless she hears from you."

"Suppose Vallance gets hot to trot?"

"Tell Davis to lie like lawyers always do to their clients. Crowded court calendar, whatever."

"You really don't like lawyers do you?"

"Can't trust them."

"Do you trust anyone?"

"My mother, but I still make sure to call her once a week."

---

At first Connie was uncomfortable walking into The Sea

Horse Inn. She had decided on a light blue blazer and white pleated skirt, rather than an evening dress as she had with Vic four months before. But soon she wished she had worn something more alluring.

Bob had the foresight to reserve one of the private nooks where seating was limited to four small tables. And dinner had been very special, apart from the Lobster bisque and Maryland soft shell crabs. He was very attentive and charming, wanting to talk about her, especially her art training in New York. He seemed more relaxed than he had when he called to ask her to dinner on Tuesday.

Not quite ready to have him drive her home, she had suggested they drive separately to the restaurant. That had been before Vivian's "accident," and she had avoided the issue during dinner. But now, as they were walking back to their cars in the pleasantly cool evening, he brought it up.

"I spoke with Vivian this afternoon," he said.

She already knew that. "How did she seem?"

"Like her old self. Very grateful for your help, by the way. You know, she was lucky she hit the brakes before the chair struck the windows. She could have suffered some real damage if it had been traveling any faster."

"How do you know?" she asked, keeping her voice casual.

"Dr. Patterson and I discussed how it could have happened. I had already examined the hallway to make sure the floor wasn't wet or something. The hospital could have had some liability, you know."

"Except she insists her fall was no accident."

"Yes, but I'm not sure that puts us in the clear. Main thing is she's all right."

He sounded sincere. "What do you think of her story?"

"I don't know," he shrugged. "Vivian has a steel trap mind, and she believes something mysterious happened, so maybe it did."

Connie decided to probe. "It's hard to imagine anyone wanting to harm her."

"There's always money. Maybe someone owes her and can't pay or a relative named in her will's getting impatient."

"That hadn't occurred to me," she said truthfully.

"This is mine," he said, stopping next to a green Chrysler Sebring convertible. He had parked next to her Saab.

"I thought you drove a Lincoln."

"To work. This is my weekend toy."

"Nice," she said. "So, you think someone unconnected with the hospital could have written that note."

"Sure. Anyone who knows her schedule and about the message board."

Time to go for it, she decided. "On the other hand, someone might want her out of the way so she couldn't vote on the budget."

He actually smiled. "That's quite an indictment. Would you have anyone in mind?"

"There are a few around who might fit the bill."

"And of course I'm one of them."

"I'm sorry," she said softly.

"It's okay. I've thought of that angle myself. I was waiting for you to ask."

"You were?"

"You had to, Red."

"You're not angry?"

"No. You asked, I answered. Let's leave it there."

"All right, let's."

"Now," he said, "this is only our second official date, so I won't ask if you'd like to come to my place for a nightcap. But I make no promises about next time."

"You're promising a next time?"

He stepped forward and kissed her lightly on the lips. "Good night," he said.

"Thank you for a lovely evening. Call me?"

"How long is your drive?"

"Maybe 45 minutes."

"Till then."

## TUESDAY, JUNE 8

Kathy Stilmore pulled her pickup in behind Nick's Camry. Usually she drove his car to work except when he wanted to use it. She didn't mind; she loved driving the Mazda. Walking up the slate path to the kitchen door, she checked out the side hill. Getting overgrown, she thought, and this is only one spot. I've got a ton of weeding to do before the party.

She found Nick reading on the love seat in the living room with Patches asleep next to him.

"I'm jealous," she said.

"Don't be. I haven't made a pass at the dog all day."

"Moron," she said, kissing him on the forehead. "How was your day?"

"All errands completed and accounted for. Yours?"

"Not bad. Dex was in a good mood."

"Good. Let's celebrate. Did you happen to look in the fridge?"

"No."

"There are goodies galore. I'd get them but your pooch has her butt on my leg."

"Lucky dog. Don't go away."

A few minutes later she returned and placed a tray on the coffee table. "This is great. Creamed herring, Triscuits and cheddar cheese. Forget about dinner."

"Never crossed my mind. You forgot the beer."

"You said you wanted to cut back."

"I didn't say cut out. I've been looking forward to happy hour."

"I'm open to a bribe," she said, standing with her arms crossed.

"I'll tell you what Tawana told me about Vivian Pershing."

"Frank came through?"

"Do I get a beer?"

"No. You'd tell me anyway."

"Extortionist. What will it take?"

"Help me weed for the party," she said.

"Do you know how many weeds are out there?"

"That's why I'm asking. Watch out, Patches smells the cheese."

Nick pulled the tray away from the spaniel's nose. "How much weeding you talking about?"

"Every Saturday till the party."

"I can get the beer myself."

"You could."

"Do I have to weed all day?" he asked.

"Till noon. I know you tire easily."

"Not enough beer in my diet. Let's see, that's four Saturdays, twelve hours minimum."

"Where's my calculator?"

"I'll do it for one beer an hour. You have to fetch me twelve beers between now and the party. Starting now."

"Done."

"Really?"

"Sure," Kathy said. "It's a bargain. What's your pleasure?"

"I put Sierra Nevada Pale Ale in the fridge door."

"Had I known that, I wouldn't have given you such a hard time."

"Liar."

"Be right back and watch the dog."

"It's not my dog."

"It's my cheese."

By the time Kathy returned Nick had solved the Patches problem by balancing the tray on several books out of her reach.

"For weeding I deserve a glass," he said, taking a bottle from her.

"Not part of the deal. God, that's good," she said after taking a swallow from her own bottle.

"I shouldn't have negotiated. You'd have caved from thirst."

"Too late, sucker. How's Tawana feeling?"

"Didn't ask," he said.

"Figures. Did she RSVP for the party?"

"No, and I forgot to ask that too."

"God, you're helpless," Kathy shook her head. "Did she

mention the new house?"

"That she did. They close at the end of the week."

"That's my detective. All right," she said and sat back, munching a cracker. "Now tell me about Vivian Pershing."

"Sorry, that wasn't part of the deal."

"Nicky!"

"Twenty-four beers."

"No."

"Eighteen, and I get to pick the brand."

"All right, turkey. Now talk."

"There's not much. Tawana read the police report and spoke to one of the officers who interviewed Vivian. They were fairly thorough."

"Connie said they didn't question her."

"No, but they talked to the maintenance guys who got there first as well as Bob Kramer and Dr. Patterson."

"Vivian insists she was pushed or something."

"She does now. The officers spoke with her twice. When she first regained consciousness, she wasn't sure what happened, but when they went back Friday morning, she was definite it wasn't an accident."

"What about the note?"

"The police spoke to Elmer Woodworth. He denies writing it. And nobody else saw it."

"They check her clothes?"

"The admitting nurse and hospital security went through them. Nothing."

"Conclusion: accident."

"Yep. There's just no evidence of a crime."

"Connie Vacarro might like to hear that," she said.

"I know."

"You plan to tell her?"

"As much as I know, but Tawana said the file's open. Something still may turn up."

"And you'll just sit waiting."

"Well, I was thinking of visiting Vivian and then Kramer," he said.

"Why would he see you?" she asked.

"Connie could probably set it up.  She said they had a nice dinner this weekend."

"Oh? When did you talk to her?"

"She called this morning to see if I had any news."

"Too bad, I'm sure you were counting on another visit."

"You want more herring?"

"She is striking as I recall," Kathy said.

"That makes two of you. Herring or not?"

"Not, but thank you."

"Welcome. What do you think about my seeing Vivian?"

"Sure. When?"

"I was planning on Saturday morning."

"Not any more."

## WEDNESDAY, JUNE 9

"Fred, we've beefed up community outreach," Kramer said into his office phone. "Cahill would turn us into a public hospital." He watched a volunteer in the driveway help a patient out of a wheelchair into a taxi. "Exactly. The trustees can't want that. Good. I'll call you tonight after you look it over. Regards to Yvonne."

Kramer turned from the window and saw Laura standing in her office doorway.

"Sorry," she said. "I didn't mean to eavesdrop on you and your brother."

"It's okay. Just sharing some thoughts. I've asked him to review my new proposals."

"He making progress?"

"Some. How was the training?  Think I need to go?"

"No, I can show you the new steps. Software's changing too fast without improving very much."

"Hope I'm around when it does."

"The Cahill stuff getting to you?" she asked, sensing he might open up.

"More concerned about Jacobi's e-mail to the trustees."

"Won't you have time to shoot down anything he comes up

with?"

"Depends when I see it and how detailed it is. One problem is the trustees' attention span. Jacobi might blow so much smoke at them, they'll lose sight of the substance."

"I'll keep my ears open."

"Thanks. And don't forget about Cynthia. She's been very quiet lately. You hearing anything at all?"

"No. I'm afraid your spy's not doing so well."

"Well, do what you can, but I'd like you to focus on my own stuff."

"Oh? I get an advance peek this time?"

He smiled. "Sorry about that. Fred's a bit anal at times. Made me promise no one would see the big package."

"Brothers trump spies any day," she said.

"Not right now. The next ten days are critical. I want to get my revisions out to the trustees before Jacobi releases his plan."

"What can I do?"

"Read and react. I'll feed you drafts of each section of both budgets as Fred and I finish them. I'll need a quick turnaround. The first installment should be ready Friday. That means you might have to work over the weekend."

"No problem," she said.

"You sure? It's a lot to ask."

"I'll view it as an investment."

"You may be wasting your time."

"Bob, I believe in you, and I'm sure the trustees will. If I'm wrong, we'll lose together."

"Then let's not lose," he said, sure she was lying. He wondered if she had the same thought.

# THIRTEEN

## THURSDAY, JUNE 10

After rapping the knocker Nick prepared to wait, but the door opened almost instantly.

"Mr. Mercante, come right in," Vivian said and backed up her wheelchair. "I like a man who's on time."

"Thank you, Ms. Pershing." He stepped into the small foyer. "I told the woman at the front desk I was early, but she said it didn't matter."

"Unfortunately she's right. My day's wide open because of this," she said and fingered her neck brace. "I'm usually volunteering at this hour."

"In any case, I appreciate you seeing me."

"Glad to. Any friend of Connie's, as the saying goes. Please have a seat on the sofa. Would you like some coffee? There's a fresh pot."

"Sure. Black, please," he said and watched Vivian disappear into the adjoining kitchen. He picked up the *Post* magazine from the coffee table. Except for one corner, Vivian was close to completing last Sunday's crossword. He was studying the clues when Vivian returned.

"You do puzzles, Mr. Mercante?" Vivian asked.

"Sometimes. Thank you," he said, accepting the coffee.

"That last block has me stumped. Any idea what 'rates of tears' is an example of? I've about given up."

"I think the answer is 'anagram.' Rates of tears is one."

"That fits! You're very good, just like Connie said."

"She's a neat lady."

"Yes, and I personally want to thank you for helping her out of the mess she was in with Victor Devane."

"She was very brave," Nick said and sipped the coffee. "Mmm, this is wonderful.  You're not having any?"

"Mine's right here," she said, lifting her mug out of the Rover's cup holder. "Neat, huh? I love it. I can take my bourbon with me and not spill a drop. Except when I crash into hospital windows."

"They do creep up on you sometimes," he smiled.

"So, Mr. Mercante, have you heard anything from the police I haven't?"

"I'm afraid not. They're convinced your fall was an accident."

"Objectively, I can't disagree, but I did see that note and now it's gone."

"Ms. Pershing--"

"Vivian. May I call you Nick?"

"Please. Vivian, tell me your account of the fall. I haven't seen the police report, but I'm told you were inconsistent."

"I was. When I first woke up all I could remember was my chair veering and putting on the brakes. I probably said so. But the more I thought about it, I was sure my right wheel was jerked somehow."

"But you saw nothing or no one."

"Not that I can recall and believe me I've tried. Dr. Patterson thinks I had a minor concussion, and that might have affected my memory."

"But you don't agree."

"No. Oh, I confess I'm not as attentive in familiar places as I am on the street, but they didn't find anything in the hallway the chair might have hit. So who or what was it?"

"Vivian, it could have been an accident even if there was a note."

"Someone with the initial 'W' lures me to Cabot Hall on a whim and then I go ass over tea kettle? Strange coincidence, no?"

"Not if this 'W' person is too embarrassed to admit he or she wrote the note, given what happened to you."

"Then why the empty conference room?"

Nick had come to the same conclusion. "All right, Vivian, let's assume your story's 100 per cent true."

"It is."

"I understand you're fairly wealthy. May I ask if there's anyone who stands to inherit a good chunk of your estate?"

"There are some small legacies. Nothing worth killing for. I'm also leaving money to various charities but the bulk goes to Clara Barton's endowment."

"And you have no known enemies and no one owes you money."

"My maid owes me 35 bucks and unfortunately there's no jealous wife out there."

"So that leads you to someone who's afraid they won't get your vote."

"Yes."

"They must be pretty desperate."

"It's all that comes to mind."

"But you haven't announced whom you're supporting," Nick said.

"No."

"So why would a person do it unless they knew you were voting for someone else?"

"It would be too late after I vote, now wouldn't it?"

"Fair point," he nodded.

"Nick, the police may think I'm loony and perhaps I am, but would you be willing to question the candidates? I could pay you."

"I'm not in the business, Vivian, but I could take a shot at it. What can you tell me about them?"

For the next few minutes Vivian gave Nick a rundown on Ellis, Jacobi, and Kramer. "They're all smart, capable and ambitious," she concluded.

"What about Laura Prentice?" Nick asked. "Connie said she's tight with Cynthia Ellis."

"She is, but I suspect she's only Ellis's puppy dog."

"You never know. She could be holding her own leash."

"Careful, Nick, or you'll sound as nutty as me."

He smiled. "I've a detective friend who already thinks so."

"Then we start even. Now, there's no guarantee anyone will talk to you, but where would you start?"

"I think Connie could smooth the way with Bob Kramer, but, as you know, she's dating him."

"Better she find out now if he's a scoundrel. And, anyway, I like him too. That's why I pushed to hire him."

"But now you don't trust him."

"Let's just say this mishap has made me a little wary."

Nick finished his coffee. "Okay, I'll assume they're all hiding something."

"Good. Frisk them for my missing note."

---

There was a definite bounce in Father Cahill's step as he walked up the seventh floor corridor after visiting Mr. Mulchay that morning. He was about to recheck his copy of that day's religious census for other Catholic patients when he saw Jacobi come out of a room and head for the elevators. Quickening his pace, Cahill caught up with him.

"Dr. Jacobi, I've been trying to talk to you."

"Father, how are you? Yes, I got your messages. Forgive me for not getting back to you. Things have been hectic this week." Jacobi pressed the down button.

"I understand, but I wanted to thank you for your e-mail to the trustees. I'm so glad you're not still upset with me."

"On the contrary, Father," Jacobi smiled. "Upon reflection, I think you've done us a great service. I gather Ms. Pershing told you about the e-mail. I meant to send you a copy. Sorry."

"That's all right. Miss Ellis showed it to me." The elevator arrived.

"Did she now? And how's our favorite chief of staff?"

"Much more pleasant than usual," Cahill said, following Jacobi into the empty car. "She congratulated me on my report and asked a few questions."

"Our report, remember?" Jacobi pressed the first floor button. "What kind of questions?"

"About cost estimates, staffing, that kind of thing."

"What did you tell her?"

"I'm afraid I didn't know what to say. I said I'd check with you."

The elevator stopped on six, letting on a volunteer pushing a patient in a wheelchair.

"You never considered cost projections for the report, Father?"

"Goodness no, doctor. I wouldn't know where to begin."

"I see. How did Ellis react?"

"Well, she didn't seem surprised. She assured me things would work out. Even shook my hand when she left my office."

"Ellis came to your office?" Jacobi asked.

"Yes. I was very pleased. She'd never been there before."

"I see," Jacobi said, thinking I'd better tell Laura about this and make sure she's on top of it.

"Is there anything wrong, doctor?"

"Not at all. Ellis is absolutely right. Don't worry about this cost business. You leave everything to me."

The elevator reached the first floor, and Jacobi held the door as the volunteer backed out with the wheelchair.

"Thank you."

Jacobi nodded and stepped into the lobby, Cahill at his side. "Father, please keep me informed of all developments." He put his arm on the cleric's shoulder. "And I'll try to improve my phone courtesy. Have a good afternoon."

"You too, doctor."

Connie watched them as she pushed the wheelchair toward the cashier's office, debating whether to tell Vivian or Bob about the elevator conversation. Hell, I'll tell them both.

## FRIDAY, JUNE 11

The killer was confident walking toward the staff entrance shortly before midnight. After the unfortunate death of Ed Monroe, the abduction of baby girl Thomas and Vivian Pershing's "accident" had both gone off perfectly. If Parnell had been right about patterns, all three should eventually be seen as part of the whole.

And it was nearing time to decide whether the killing would begin. But first another decision had to be made.

After the conversation with Parnell, the killer had listed names of potential victims. There were both obvious and random choices, and the killer had methodically narrowed them down. But, as events had unfolded, one person had surfaced not only as a likely target but the perfect foil.

Using a security card to enter through the glass doors into the dimly lit hallway, the killer walked slowly in the familiar, soft silence. Hospitals are quiet at night, nurses speaking softly, the information and admitting desks dark, business offices empty, even the laundry chutes off limits until morning. Only the ER is often busy, but even there the noise is sporadic, the unit sometimes as hushed as the ICU.

Clara Barton's two medical records offices were also closed. Employees' files were kept in Cabot Hall, but those for patients were in the main building where the killer now paused, staring through the darkened glass of the office door into the domain of the luscious Nancy Kwan. She was still on the victims' list, but it now appeared she would be spared. It was time to make sure.

The locks on the doors and cabinets of both records offices were among the most secure in the hospital. The staffs were meticulous to control access to medical data, noting each time a file was removed or examined and by whom. These protections safeguarded both a person's privacy and, in the case of patients, the integrity of the information. After all, a worried doctor might wish to delete an embarrassing detail from a chart that could prove he or she had been negligent.

Despite these procedures, dozens of people, ranging from medical staff to volunteers to billing clerks, could potentially view a patient's chart at various times during the day. Ironically, employee records were more secure in this regard. Except from someone like the killer who could ignore the records offices, bypass all the procedures, and still obtain facts useful to committing murder.

In the information age, storage of medical data on computers was pervasive. And while altering an entry in a computer record was perhaps less difficult than making an erasure on a piece of paper, it still left tracks. However, simply viewing the data was easier than trying to pick a lock on a file cabinet. If one knew how, that is. And hospital administrators felt too many did. Due to the ease of retrieval and individual lapses in selecting or protecting passwords, unauthorized access to medical information was a serious concern. To the killer it was a Godsend.

Over the past several months the killer had discreetly learned the names and birth dates of the pets, spouse and children of a clerk in the employees' records office: information which ultimately translated into her computer password. After climbing an internal staircase to the fourth floor and entering the medical library, it took the killer only minutes at one of the computer terminals to open the medical files of two Clara Barton employees.

All personnel were required to have an annual physical and a PPD screening for tuberculosis. A personal physician could perform the tests, but Clara Barton also provided them free of charge. These tests were sometimes more perfunctory than those performed privately and the results often read by a harried staffer who might miss a new shadow on an image or a small but significant change in blood values.

The killer wanted to review the results for last three years, focusing on blood pressure, cholesterol, X-ray and electrocardiogram results, looking for predictors of future problems: abnormal values, trend lines, family history. Anything that might point to a proclivity for death from natural causes.

The killer wasn't optimistic about finding any such marker in Nancy Kwan's file. She was young, a trained athlete, and committed to vigorous exercise. Still, she could have an oversized heart that was literally a ticking time bomb. Hypertrophic cardiomyopathy was a common cause of sudden death for athletes under 35. Kwan's record was limited to the physical she had taken at the hospital when joining the staff several months before. And, after a careful review, the killer decided it contained nothing noteworthy. The heart data and shadows appeared normal. Lucky lady, the killer thought and turned to the second file. It proved to be a sign.

The employee's father had suffered a fatal heart attack. And while the first EKG readings were unremarkable, the most recent taken at the hospital showed slightly wider QRS complexes. These could suggest incipient ventricular tachycardia: a form of arrhythmia associated with structural heart disease. Cardiac failure might be on the horizon, not tomorrow, but likely some day without medical intervention. Moreover, there was nothing to indicate the employee had taken a stress test to identify this possibility or was taking any drugs to keep borderline hypertension from creeping into the danger zone. The killer smiled. Not a perfect scenario, but good enough.

# FOURTEEN

## SATURDAY, JUNE 12

After shaking hands all around the conference table, Sam and Tawana gathered the settlement documents into a folder and walked out of the bank lawyer's office into the bright sunshine. Before he had taken another step she was in his arms kissing him.

"Sammy, I'm so happy I could spit."

"Hey be careful," he said, easing her away. "You'll crush the baby."

"Don't be silly. Isn't it great? Our first house."

"Better be our last. I'd get writer's cramp if I had to sign my name this much again."

"Come on, grouch, smile." She took his hand and they started toward the parking lot. "No more rent. We have our own home."

"What we have is a $550,000 mortgage. Can you imagine that much money? Not to mention the interest."

"Can we go to the hardware store? I want to get paint for the baby's room."

"Sure. What color?"

"A nice bright yellow."

"You could go pink or blue after you take the test."

"I want yellow. That room only gets light in the morning."

"Oh." They reached Sam's Volvo. "You know, maybe I should get a newer car."

"You're worried about the mortgage and you want a car payment on top of it?"

"Doesn't seem like much more, considering. This thing's going to need some serious work soon and, well, look at the neighborhood we're going to."

"Sammy, Nick and Kathy are in an even nicer neighborhood, and she drives a used pickup."

"They can afford to be eccentric."

"Want me to tell her you said that?"

"I meant Mercante."

"Grow up. By the way, did I tell you nothing more's come in on that Pershing case?"

"Wonderful news." He unlocked the passenger side and held open the door. "Mercante strikes out."

"He was only doing Connie Vacarro a favor. He's not invested in the thing."

"Good. I'll sleep a lot better. I think we should try Home Depot for the paint. We'd get a better price."

"It may take too long. I want to be back before the movers show up. I intend to sleep in our own bedroom tonight."

---

Jacobi flipped on the dome light of his Lexus and checked the piece of paper for the address in the unfamiliar Bethesda neighborhood. Satisfied, he parked near a streetlight, locked the car with the remote and made his way down the block. The phone call had come as a surprise, but at this stage he was ready for anything.

Number 4319 turned out to be a small Victorian just before the corner. He climbed the steps and rang the bell. After a moment the door opened and Cynthia stood there silhouetted in a flowing translucent dress, a glass of wine in her hand.

"Perfect timing," she smiled. "You thirsty?"

"What's this all about, Cynthia?"

"The price of poker just went up, Stan. I've just been talking to an attorney friend of mine. Come on in."

---

Thorpe relaxed with his eyes closed listening to the soft classical music on his BMW's sound system while waiting for Laura. He had decided on a surprise night out as a way to mollify her if she was even more antsy than he suspected. Things were moving along and he was pleased he'd been able to handle both these women so far. He just had to keep tight reins on Cynthia before she did something to jeopardize their plans.

Chief of surgery at Clara Barton Memorial. Mom would have been so happy for him if she were able to understand. He knew what his father might have said. "Well, son, why stop there? Why not shoot for Johns Hopkins?"

"Hey, day dreamer, aren't you going to kiss me?" Laura's face was suddenly next to his.

Startled, he shook his head. "Sorry, must have dozed off to the music."

"Mozart'll do that," she said, closing her door. "Want me to drive?"

"I'm fine." He started the engine and pulled into traffic.

"What a treat, dinner out and not Caballeros. So where did you pick?"

"Hunter Mill Cafe."

"Never heard of it."

"It's in Reston," he said, turning onto Wisconsin Avenue.

"That's the end of the world."

"It's 20 miles. When's the last time you were out there?"

"Hell, I don't know. Maybe when I was still in boarding school. I think Reagan was President."

"A lot's changed. It's a real town now."

"How come you know so much about it?" she asked.

"I know a nurse who lives there."

"What a surprise. Aren't you afraid she'll see us?"

"She's on vacation," he smiled at her.

"God, you're just like Cynthia," she said, putting her head back and closing her eyes.

"So how's the CEO treating you?"

"Good. Sent me home early."

"He that far ahead of schedule?" Thorpe asked.

"Oh no. He wants me to come in tomorrow.'

"And you said yes."

"Yep. Don't forget, he's my boss."

"You're not getting soft on him are you?"

"As much as I am on Jacobi."

"That's an interesting answer," he said, turning onto

Western Avenue.

"I'm an interesting person. Aren't you taking the Beltway?"

"No way. Going down to cross Chain Bridge. So is Kramer making headway?"

"With me or his proposals?"

"Whichever."

"He seems to be going with an eight percent reduction across the board for the big budget."

"But he's still sticking with the eldercare and medical buildings."

"As far as I can tell. I'll know more tomorrow. His stuff is better, but I still can't see him carrying it off unless the trustees do a 180."

"Don't sell him short. Pershing sponsored him once and could do it again. She can sway a lot of votes."

"For Jacobi too."

"Don't remind me. Let's hope you and Cynthia can bring him down."

"At least with him we're in control of the papers. Which is exactly where we want to be."

He reached over and rubbed her thigh. "You've been a great teammate, you know."

She moved his hand higher. "Do they have motels in Reston now?"

---

Connie lived in a large two-bedroom condominium on the 4100 block of Connecticut Avenue. It was not far from downtown where she and Kramer had had dinner after she finished her shift at the Laughing Bull. Now, she flipped on the living room light as they entered her foyer.

Following her inside, he toured the room, nodding appreciatively at the handsome decor. "This is very nice. Hey," he pointed to a wall, "a Monet and a Picasso lithograph?"

"The Monet's a copy. My mother gave it to me. I bought the Picasso out of my inheritance when she died. Also paid for this apartment."

"Money well spent."

"Would you like a nightcap?" she asked, taking his hand.

"After that wine, I'd better not. Don't want to weave my way along River Road and get a ticket."

She stepped closer. "You don't have to go, you know. This is our third date."

They kissed long and deeply.

"Oh my," she said, shaking her head and stepping back. "You see, that's my problem."

"What is?"

"The first real kiss. It can just be magic for me."

He smiled and kissed her again, on the forehead. "And I don't mean to reject such a wonderful offer--"

"But you are."

"No, I'm accepting it conditionally. I fully intend to make love to you, but not tonight."

"And just what's wrong with here and now?" she asked, pretending to pout.

"Because I don't want leave right afterwards. I never want to do that, Red."

"That's very nice to hear," she said. "But why would you have to?"

"I still have work to do to get ready for tomorrow. Laura and I will be working most of the day."

"On a Sunday? Should I be jealous?"

"What do you think? I'm watching my back, remember?"

"That's a question not an answer. Now, how long must I wait to spend a night with you?"

"How does next Saturday sound?"

"Like seven days. My lucky number."

## MONDAY, JUNE 14

Cynthia was watering her plants when Thorpe barged into her office that morning. "Are you nuts?" he shouted.

"I see you got my voice-mail," she said calmly. "You really should keep your cell phone on."

"How could you offer to support Jacobi after he turned you down?"

"Stop screaming," she demanded. "It was worth a shot. And since when do I need your permission?"

He lowered his voice, barely. "Look, we have a plan, we've made adjustments, we don't freelance."

She leaned back against her desk, crossing her long legs at the ankle. "I wasn't freelancing. In fact, I improved on your idea."

"Improved? You'd give up your chance to win and get rid of him now?"

"He'd be gone in four years. That's a firm number, unlike your plan."

"Cynthia, you were supposed to work that out with him. Hell, he's 57. He'd probably leave when he's 60."

"I must have missed that paragraph in your memo. My way was better."

"Sure. He'd agree to negotiate with Davis just to keep Vallance from suing."

"Peter, I had to do something to keep my lawsuit alive. Vallance has cold feet and Laura hasn't made Jacobi even tell a dirty joke. And we wouldn't sue him now. Isn't that what you wanted?"

"Looks like you misjudged him, doesn't it?"

"It took him till this morning to say no. And if he'd gone along, you'd have jumped on it in a heartbeat. Admit it."

"Regardless, you shouldn't have offered the deal without clearing it with me. And what about Vallance? Negotiations would force her hand and put her career in jeopardy."

"Since when are you worried about Miss Butter Ball? You putting the moves on her?"

"Come on, Cynthia."

"You come on," she said, then smiled. "Give me some credit, Peter. I never referred to Vallance by name. I wouldn't have unless he'd said yes to the deal. No harm, no foul."

"And what did Marcia Davis say?"

"She wasn't there. Jacobi kept babbling about malpractice and I strung him along. Thanks to you, I'm sure he thinks Marcia represents the Schroeder family."

Thorpe walked to the window and looked at the patients coming and going. "Did you mention the budget meeting?"

"I tried, but he didn't want to talk about it. His highness thinks he's got a lock on the thing. You should have heard him on the phone this morning."

He turned toward her. "Good. That's the whole point of getting Laura inside his guard."

"You're putting too much faith in knocking down the Cahill report. Some of the trustees are talking it up."

"Listen, we're damn lucky it fell into our lap. The numbers are the key to beating Kramer, remember? Same with Jacobi. Not some trumped-up lawsuit."

"The sexual harassment card will work, Peter."

"We'll play it if we have to. In the meantime you and Laura better finish the rebuttal to Jacobi's plan. I want him spinning."

"Relax, for God's sake. We're picking apart our own stuff."

"Okay," he nodded and stepped forward. "I'm sorry if I yelled. I'm a little tense."

"I could fix that," she said, moving closer to him. "Say the word and I lock the door."

"I have a meeting," he said.

"Like hell."

He patted her arm and started toward the door.

She followed him. "If Vallance won't budge, I'd still like to have something else in reserve besides facts and figures."

"So would I, but I've scoped Jacobi from every angle. He's clean."

"You still have two weeks. We're so close, Peter."

He turned the knob. "One last look. But no more surprises."

"Promise. Unless you skip that meeting."

"Take a cold shower."

# FIFTEEN

## WEDNESDAY, JUNE 16

"Go right through there," Laura said to Nick. "Mr. Kramer's on the phone, but said to send you in the moment you arrived."

"Thank you," Nick said and moved toward the door.

Who is this guy? Laura wondered, following Nick with her eyes. A friend of a friend was all Bob had said. Must be a heavyweight, waltzing in here without an appointment.

Nick knocked once and entered. Kramer was standing with his back to the door facing the window, a phone held to his ear. Nick wasn't sure he'd heard the knock and was about to try again when Kramer turned and waved him to a chair.

"The figures look good," he said. "Will you be home tonight? No, that's fine. I'll call you on my cell driving in tomorrow. It'll give me a chance to sleep on it. You too."

Kramer hung up. "Budget talk with my brother Fred," he smiled, reaching across the desk. "Mr. Mercante, we meet at last."

"Mr. Kramer, I know how busy you are now and I appreciate you taking time to see me."

"Frankly, I can use the break." Kramer removed his glasses and rubbed his eyes. "I'm not sure what's more tiring, this job or talking to the police. Vivian makes three times this year."

"You counting Victor Devane in February?"

"Oh, right," he said, "that makes it four. That was your production, wasn't it?"

"Only in part."

"Well, regardless, it turned out well for Connie. She's quite a fan of yours."

"I hope she didn't twist your arm too hard to get me in here."

"I can't say no to the lady. Besides, if I can help Vivian, I'm more than willing."

"I understand you're not certain her fall was an accident."

"No, but I'm leaning that way," Kramer said. "It appears she simply lost control of her chair. She saw no one and the hallway floor was dry and clear."

"And the note?"

"Oh, I think Vivian saw something, but what? She took a blow to the head. Perhaps she's forgetting exactly what the note said or if she tossed it after she read it."

"But let's suppose for a minute that someone pushed her over."

"All right."

"Could it be one of those worried about getting her support with the trustees?"

"No," Kramer said without hesitating, "and that includes me. I've considered the notion, but I can't see anyone harming Vivian."

"People have done worse things for power."

"Of course, but I'm not sure anyone knows where Vivian's coming from. So unless you knew she was against you, why risk it?"

Nick smiled at the echo of his own thought. "Maybe they're hedging their bets."

Kramer shook his head. "Then they're lousy gamblers."

"Meaning?"

"They failed. Look, if I wanted Vivian out of the way, I'd do it right. No fall in a corridor that she might survive."

"Any ideas how you'd go about it?" Nick asked deadpan.

"Haven't thought about it."

"Care to try?"

For the first time Kramer paused. "Why not," he smiled and leaned back in his chair. "Let's see. Okay. Unless I could arrange an alibi, I'd want to be as sure as possible my competition didn't have one either."

So would I, Nick thought. "And?"

"Cynthia Ellis and Stan Jacobi both live alone like me. So I'd do it at night during the week. Say around eleven."

"Less likely they'd be with someone."

"Right. And everyone knows Vivian's a gadabout. So I'd

pick a night I knew she was going out. The theater, whatever. I'd stake out her building and wait for her to drive off."

"And then?"

"I'd wait in her garage. When she returned and parked her van, well, she's an easy target for all sorts of mischief and probably wouldn't be missed till the morning."

"Not bad," Nick said. "Weapon of choice?"

Kramer laughed. "Hell, I don't know. Pistols at dawn."

Nick's grin was genuine. "That's enough for me," he said. He started to rise, then paused. "By the way, you seemed upbeat on the phone a moment ago. Are you?"

"Getting there, but it won't be a landslide."

"If your budget fails, can't the trustees still renew your contract?"

"Yes," Kramer nodded, "but I'm not sure my heart would be in it. I might move on."

"Really? That would leave the field clear for Jacobi or Ellis to take your job."

"On an interim basis. Though if they chose Jacobi, I doubt they'd hire someone else later."

"You think they'd pick him over Ellis?"

"I do, but he has to beat me on the 28th first."

Nick stood. "So he does. I'll be on my way."

"I'll show you out," Kramer said. "You can use this other door."

"All right. Good luck with your budget. I know Connie's rooting for you."

"I wish she had a vote."

Kramer opened the door and they shook hands. "Thanks again for your time," Nick said.

"My pleasure. I hope I was of some help."

"I think so."

"Good. Regards to Vivian when you speak to her."

"Sure thing."

Very engaging guy, Nick thought, walking toward the exit. He could see why Connie and Vivian liked him. He could also see that Jacobi and Ellis better be prepared.

## THURSDAY, JUNE 17

At 9:30 Connie left the information desk to take a break with a cup of the complimentary coffee the hospital provided in the lobby. She decided it wasn't too early to phone Nick and went to the volunteers' alcove.

He answered on the second ring.

"Nick, it's Connie."

"Good morning."

"Sorry I didn't get back to you yesterday, but I pulled a double shift and got home late."

"Where are you? I don't recognize the number."

"At the hospital."

"Click. Of course, it's Thursday morning. Boy, you must be dragging."

"I'm fine. You enjoy meeting Bob?"

"That's why I called. He's very impressive. Candid too."

"I'm glad. He thought you were, shall I say, a tad pushy."

"I guess that's good."

"May I ask if you learned much?"

"Let me put it this way. He had some interesting things to say."

"Uhm, he wonders if you're planning to meet with Ellis and Jacobi."

"I've tried making appointments, but no luck so far. I'll ask Vivian if she can help."

"There aren't many doors she can't open."

"That's what I figured. Is she there?"

"Not due back till next week. You can reach her at home."

"Okay. I'll keep you posted."

"Nick?"

"Yes?"

"I'm seeing Bob again Saturday. Things are starting to get serious."

"You thought they might."

"And I'm a little gun shy, you know? I mean, well...never mind. I'm not sure what I'm saying or how you can help."

"Connie, I can't tell you what to do, but look, if I find out anything that you should take as a warning, I'll let you know. Promise."

"Thanks. That's very kind."

"Where do I send my bill?"

"I'll fix you and Kathy dinner. I'm actually a helluva cook. Make a mean la sagne."

"For that, I'll take ten percent off. Talk to you soon."

---

Jacobi turned his Lexus into the circular driveway of Vivian Pershing's condominium in the 7300 block of Woodmont Avenue in Bethesda. Spotting the "No Parking or Standing" sign, he flipped down the visor where he had mounted a bright red on white placard with the Clara Barton logo and "Doctor On Call" in bold-faced letters.

Grabbing a folder from the front seat, Jacobi bounced out of the car without bothering to lock it. Stepping into the vestibule, he was about to press Vivian's button when a couple opened the glass door on their way out. They smiled their way past as he held the door.

No one was at the security desk so he went straight to the elevators. A car was standing empty and he pressed the button for the fifth floor. As the doors closed, he took one more look at the document in the folder.

Laura had done a bang-up job. This will blow Vivian away. He smiled as he recalled Kramer's St. Patrick's Day party when Vivian coaxed him to get involved if he wanted to be CEO. If she only knew the groundwork he'd laid before that night. And since then, he'd become more certain he would win. Still, he had to admit Father Cahill's and Laura's unexpected help had been a bonus.

The elevator reached five. Jacobi hurried down the hallway to 515 and rapped on the door with the knocker.

"Who is it?"

"Stan Jacobi, Vivian."

"I gave at the office, Stanley," Vivian said, opening the door.

"But come on in."

"Thank you," he said, stepping into the foyer. "You're looking well."

"Rounding into form."

"Good. Well, here it is," Jacobi said, handing her the folder. "A cogent and fiscally responsible program for the Outreach Center and all the rest. Some cuts had to be made, but this is all based on the assumptions in Kramer's one-year budget."

"Stanley, you continue to astound me. I never figured you for a numbers geek."

"I'm really not, but Father Cahill set me to thinking. Vivian, Clara Barton simply has to provide better medical care to the community. That's why we're a hospital and why I took my oath. We need a doctor to lead the way and I'm the man."

"That's quite a speech," she said. "You should save it for the board. How about some coffee?"

"Thanks, but I can't stay. Oh, and you should know I'm not circulating this to the other trustees until Tuesday. I wanted you to have an advance copy."

"I'm honored."

"You deserve it. Now, I'm taking tomorrow off and I'll be home all weekend if you have any questions. But take your time. Except for surgery Wednesday and Friday, I've cleared the decks for next week. I want to be prepared for the meeting."

"Sounds like you're itching for a fight."

"I'm not lukewarm anymore, Vivian. I took your advice and the amazing thing is, I haven't enjoyed myself so much in years. I hope I can count on your support."

"I've backed late bloomers before, Stanley, but usually they're three-year-olds with four legs. But I promise I'll read this closely. I'll see you next Friday."

"Be well. I'll let myself out."

She watched him leave. She opened the folder and glanced through the document. This seems very well done. Something she'd expect from Bob Kramer, not a surgeon. How many hats does Dr. Jacobi have?

## FRIDAY, JUNE 18

Sleep usually came easily for Father Cahill, but not in the last several weeks. After months of prayerful reflection, his decision to take the initiative had reaped positive results, a few setbacks, but overall progress. Still, he found it increasingly difficult to relax after dinner, anxious for the morning so he could return to the hospital to pursue his mission. And his anxiety held its own torment.

Some evenings he felt ashamed because he was proud of what he'd accomplished, other times inadequate because he'd not done enough, and sometimes, like tonight, despairing because, despite his worthy cause, he knew his methods were not in keeping with the Lord's teachings.

He switched on the bedside lamp in his Spartan bedroom and reached for his Bible. Inside was a folded sheet with an Easter prayer he had found years before while a seminarian. The words always seemed to console him and tonight they seemed particularly appropriate:

*God of all worlds and all time, we voice thanks for this season of Resurrection.*

*Yet like the disciples and all those who have followed you, we, too, are sporadic in our faithfulness.*

*You command us to love one another, yet so often we act out of malice and enmity.*

*You call us to works of mercy and reconciliation,*

*yet so often we retaliate, unwilling to forgive and be reconciled to our brothers and sisters.*

*You show us the path of righteousness, yet so often we stray into the ways of Satan, caught in the obsessions of the wicked.*

*Wash over us, seep into us, refresh and cleanse us.*

*Dissolve the prejudices that cling to us, the anger that permeates our memory.*

*Help us let go of the obsessions of the past, in order to see your future for us.*

*Forgive us of all our sins and bid us, O God,*

*to dare to journey on the sea of the Holy Spirit.*

*For we ask these things in the name of the Risen Lord. Amen.*

As he finished,  Cahill's eyes became heavy.  Praying for grace and continued guidance, he turned out the light. Tomorrow he would hear confessions at the hospital, on Sunday he would celebrate Mass in the chapel and then he would go about the business of the Lord.

## SATURDAY, JUNE 19

"You were quiet at dinner," Connie said, looking at Kramer's profile in the soft light of the dashboard as he started the Chrysler in the parking lot of The Sea Horse Inn.

He reached over and patted her knee. "I'm sorry, Red. It's been an up-and-down week. I'm just preoccupied."

"Nick Mercante couldn't have been that bad."

"Wasn't him. I was really looking forward to tonight, but maybe I should just drive you home."

"I'd understand if you did, but I'm a good listener if you'd like to talk about it."

He looked at her and nodded, wanting to trust her, but wary. "It might do me some good," he said, flipping on the car's AC. Leaving the engine idling, he began to talk.

Connie said nothing until he was done. "So you've thought Laura's been playing you for awhile."

"I'm sure of it," he said, "but I don't know if she's simply trying to get ahead or working for someone."

"It has to be Cynthia."

"Well, that fits, of course, but then again this outreach program Jacobi's promised is exactly the kind of thing Laura would be helpful on."

"Can you find out which one it is?"

"I doubt it. I'm using the ploy I tried before, only this time I'm showing Laura both budgets and more details. But, I've overstated capital outlays and debt service and some construction costs in the drafts she's seen."

"You want her to pass on misinformation."

"Yes, and if Cynthia or Jacobi prepares a response based on those figures, they'll be caught flat-footed when I release the real numbers. So regardless of whom Laura's in with, I should come out ahead."

"And both your proposals have improved?"

"Yes. The board should be pleased if not impressed."

"How can you be so sure?"

"I planned it that way."

"I'm sorry?"

He'd gone too far. "Never mind. Just tell Vivian to sharpen her pencil. What with Jacobi's plan, the trustees will have a lot to digest."

"Will Cynthia pitch something of her own?"

"I dunno. She'd have to give it to Vivian soon under the rules. If I know her, she's up to something."

"I hear you know her pretty well."

Another pat on her knee. "Ancient history."

"How long did you date her?"

"Not as long as I hope to be seeing you." He leaned over and kissed her. "I'm feeling better for talking. Thank you."

"Do you have a prediction for Friday's meeting?"

"That's easy. I win if I can turn Vivian's head."

"See? Maybe someone really didn't want her at the meeting."

"You've bought into her conspiracy theory."

"I'm a realist," Connie said. "Perhaps Laura's accomplice is behind it."

"If they want my job that badly, they can have it. Let's go," he said, putting the car in gear.

"Taking me home?"

"I have a better idea."

"Yes?"

"Have you ever seen the Potomac at night?"

"Never," she fibbed.

"There's a lovely view from my balcony."

"I'm afraid of heights."

"I'll hold your hand."

---

Cynthia locked her front door and wearily tossed her purse

onto the bench in the foyer. She carried her briefcase into the living room. It was jammed full and its contents accounted for her exhaustion. Thirty-five copies of a critique of her and Laura's own draft of Stan Jacobi's Community Outreach Center and Security Action Program. They had also assessed Kramer's drafts and spotted their weak points. But did she now have enough to win? Peter seemed to think so, but none of it was the magic bullet she'd wanted.

Tired and depressed, she poured a half tumbler of dry sherry and went into the bedroom to check her messages. Neither Peter nor Marcia Davis had phoned. Undressing, she looked at the picture of her father. His smile seemed even more artificial tonight. She felt her eyes welling up.

In the bathroom she turned on the faucet, wishing Peter would call to reassure her. Stepping into the hot spray, she reached for the shampoo and began soaping her hair, not hearing the phone ringing in the bedroom.

Emerging from the shower, she didn't notice the blinking light of the answering machine until she had finished toweling off and putting on a robe. Hurrying over to the end table, she saw that Marcia had called. Taking a swallow of sherry, she pressed the play button.

"Cindy, it's me. No go with Vallance. She's a savvy kid and wants to keep her powder dry. Thinks Godzilla's either going to stay head of surgery or be the next CEO. Either way, she doesn't want to take him on. And get this, she now says she was wrong in the OR and knows it. Sorry, hon, I tried my best. Call me."

Cynthia stood there fighting back the tears, then reached for the phone.

---

"Here's to the next chief of staff," Thorpe said, extending his brandy snifter across Laura's dining room table.

"And next chief surgeon," Laura responded, clinking her glass against his. "I'll be glad when it's over. Cynthia was still uptight when I left today."

"She'll be fine. And so will you. Congratulations."

She allowed herself a smile. "Chances look good, I'll admit."

"Better than I thought they would."

"I think Jacobi will be speechless."

"Let's hope," Thorpe said. "You're not worried he'll come after you when the meeting's over?"

"He's bound to, but Cynthia and I came up with a good story: the truth. I'll discover I entered a wrong digit in the memory control and it screwed up everything right down the line. I'll lay it all out for him, plead time pressure. Just an unfortunate mistake."

"Couldn't happen to a nicer guy. He'll never talk to you again.

"But Cynthia's no shoo-in, Peter. Bob has time to improve on what I've seen and he's very persuasive.  The trustees still may decide to go with the devil they know."

Thorpe laughed and reached for the brandy decanter.

"I say something funny?"

"Sort of. You and I'll be fine even if Kramer does somehow manage to hang on. He'll probably fire Cynthia the minute he gets a new contract."

"But Jacobi would still be chief surgeon."

Thorpe held the snifter up to the light. "I don't think so. I'm pretty sure Kramer will make Jacobi's life as miserable as Cynthia would."

"Why?"

"He and I had a few drinks one night a couple of weeks ago. He told me about his ex-wife and how he got bounced from his last hospital. I won't bore you with the details, but trust me, he'll never give Jacobi a chance to go after his job again. I'm next in line and I have you to put in a good word with him."

"If he promotes me."

"Don't worry. He hired you. You're a shoo-in unless he finds out you've been working for Cynthia."

"How could he?"

"Who knows? Maybe she'll tell him. She might become vindictive if he fires her."

Laura shook her head. "She's no reason to do that. I've been nothing but supportive."

"Is that what they call it now?" he smiled. "Which reminds me, I'd better call to see if she's heard from Marcia Davis."

He went to the closet and took his cell phone from his jacket. Turning it on, he scrolled through the display and saw Cynthia had been calling. He keyed in her number.

"Sorry, my phone's been off," he said when she picked up. "What? Well, I'm not surprised. She was always a question mark. No, everything's okay. Would you relax? Look, I don't make predictions like that." He looked across the room to where Laura was watching him. "All right, I'll work on it." He closed the phone.

"Vallance, won't sue," he said, returning to the table. "Cynthia wants me to come over. I probably should."

"She's fretting."

"More like hyperventilating. She's been calling every ten minutes."

"Will you come back?"

"Depends how long this takes. If not, I'll drop by tomorrow afternoon. You'll be done with Jacobi by then?"

She came into his arms. "Mm-hmm. He just wants to go over a few points."

"Good. We're almost there, babe. Only six days to go."

"Try and convince Cynthia of that, will you? I don't want any hitches this week."

"I'll give her some Valium to calm her down."

"No, we need her to stay sharp. Try Diphenhydramine if you have some. Less apt to muck up the old brain cells."

Thorpe lifted her chin. "You study pharmacology at Ohio State?"

She smiled. "I'm a vet's daughter, remember? We used the stuff all the time to settle old dogs at night."

"I won't tell Cynthia you said that."

# SIXTEEN

## SUNDAY, JUNE 20

For 15 years Ramon Vargas had run the gift shop at Clara Barton on Thursday through Saturday and every other Sunday. The shop's prices were fairly steep, but it had always turned a tidy profit. The store's owner--who split the money with the hospital--attributed this to a superb inventory.

Which was only partly true. Much of the success was due to Ramon who knew exactly which flower arrangement, card, toy or trinket was suitable for a patient. While some transactions occurred by phone, most were face to face and this was where Ramon was at his best. He was handsome, flirtatious, savvy and a charmer: the ingredients of a good salesman and a womanizer. Ramon was both.

His reputation was, of course, widely known among the hospital staff who sought his advice on all sorts of issues. The men were especially interested in picking up a few pointers from the master. But Ramon lived for the encounters with the women who would drop by to talk about their lives.

He would listen attentively to the lady's problems, offer a few words of wisdom, and occasionally parlay the chat into an after-hours drink. This in turn could lead to a dalliance, nothing more permanent than that, and the inevitable parting of the ways--usually but not always amicable. This made him a perfect target for the killer who had decided the world wouldn't miss one more reprobate.

Tonight, as usual, Ramon turned off the ceiling lights in the shop a few minutes after visiting hours were over and put up the Closed sign. He went to the counter to empty the cash register for the bank deposit he would drop off on the way home. Reaching into a drawer behind him for a deposit slip, he felt something odd. He saw it was an envelope addressed to "Ramon." Inside were a plastic vial of gel caps and a typed note:

*A gift for your advice the other day. These really work. I get them on the Internet. They're called Spanish Fly so you probably know all about them. Ha ha. I take just one and in no time I can go like a bull. Have fun.*

Ramon read the note twice, then shrugged. He couldn't keep track of every dude he talked to. He'd heard of this stuff. Supposed to be magic. He'd be home in an hour and Marie was supposed to drop by. What the hell, he thought and popped a pill in his mouth. Putting the vial and note in his pocket, he took a Diet Coke from the wall cooler and swallowed the capsule in two gulps. He returned to the register to start counting the cash, now in a hurry.

Some minutes later, the killer wandered by, saw that a few lights were still on and casually leaned against the door. It was unlocked. This is too good to be true. Ramon must have taken a pill right away. Looking around at the empty lobby, the killer donned latex gloves, entered the shop and called out. Silence. Ramon was on the floor behind the counter. The killer knelt and checked Ramon's pulse. Very thin and thready. Predictably, he had vomited blood. Respiratory failure would soon follow and any coma would be brief. He'd be dead soon.

The best possible outcome: a body on the premises. The killer turned off all the lights. Don't need anyone to get curious, and Ramon would have had enough time to turn them off. The killer turned to leave then, as a precaution, nudged the phone off its cradle. Any caller would get a busy signal. That would buy a few more minutes if someone was getting impatient.

The killer headed out of the building. The note would tell the medical examiner what to look for and the autopsy would show the severe internal damage associated with Cantharidin. Unless the police were really stupid, they would conclude the writer of the note was no friend of Ramon. But even if they were dumb enough to think otherwise, a corpse in the gift shop was sure to have them swarming all over the hospital, making everyone antsy even sooner than planned. Not that it really mattered now. The next murder was just around the corner.

## MONDAY, JUNE 21

It wasn't until seven that Frank Stephens returned Nick's call. "Monday's are hell around here. What's on your mind? I only have a minute."

"Ramon Vargas and Clara Barton," Nick said. "I saw the news."

"They playing it up?"

"Of course. They're suggesting it wasn't natural causes. Something about a note. Suicide?"

"There was a note, but it wasn't his. Seems to be from someone he knew."

"Any connection with the Vivian Pershing matter?"

Frank smiled into the phone. "You sound like Gail. Nothing ties the two together."

"Another note at the hospital."

"First one we've seen, and this was printed on a computer. Look, Nick, I have to run. Give Kathy my best."

"Can I stay in touch?"

"Could I stop you?"

## WEDNESDAY, JUNE 23

Detective Michael Avery hurried down the hall toward Sam's office. A burly five-seven, his short legs seemed to churn rather than stride. He had spent the last two days interviewing friends and family of Ramon Vargas while Tawana and Larry Foster had concentrated on the hospital. This morning Sam wanted a progress report and Avery was glad to take a break from driving around Olney, Maryland where Vargas had lived.

As he neared Sam's office he saw Foster's lanky frame heading his way.

"Last one in has to make the coffee," Avery said, knocking on the door.

"Come in," Sam called.

"I'd rather do it than drink yours," Foster said, adjusting his thick, tortoise shell glasses and following Avery inside.

Sam was in his swivel chair at the roll top desk talking on the phone and Tawana was flipping through her notebook at the conference table. Avery plopped his muscular physique in the chair next to her while Foster went to the coffee maker.

"I just made some, Larry," Tawana called to him.

"You look a little tired," Avery said, studying her with his kind, dark brown eyes. "Feet holding up?"

"I'm okay, thanks. It's not the walking, it's the damn unpacking at night."

"You guys haven't finished yet?"

"Not even close. We really only had the first Sunday. My mother visited this weekend."

"Say no more. Maybe you should take a few days off."

"That's what I keep telling her," Sam said, approaching them looking at a sheet of paper.

Tawana shook her head. "You just want me to work through the boxes while you play around here."

"Yeah, this place is a real circus," he said, taking a chair. "So make me laugh. Larry, whatcha got?"

"A crime with no motive," Foster said, joining them with his coffee. "People think Vargas was a pretty cool guy. And I can't see this as an accident. If Vargas's pen pal had taken one of those pills he'd probably be dead too."

"Maybe they're from a bad batch," Avery said.

"Yeah, but nobody's fessing up."

"Fat chance they would," Sam said. "Tawana?"

"Vargas was a bit of a rogue, but everyone knew that. A couple of the women he bedded down felt a little used, but no serious grudges or jealous boyfriends."

"Nobody who might want to pay him back?"

"I didn't get that sense, but it's early. Everybody's being cooperative so far, though."

"Same here," Foster said, readjusting his glasses.

"Nobody's jumpy or tense?" Sam asked.

"Actually," Foster said, "the whole place is pretty calm, as though nothing's happened. It's kinda weird, like the gift shop's not part of the hospital and Vargas was from another world."

"How about the shop's owner? He check out?"

"She, Lieutenant," Tawana said, using his rank as she always did at work. "Ann Duffy. She was really shook up. Doesn't know how she'll replace him."

"They were good friends," Avery said. "Vargas even had her and husband and kids over for barbecues."

"You get anything else?" Sam asked, turning to him.

"Yeah, a surprise. Vargas's sister says he was a saint. Helped support her and her daughter, big contributor to his church, you name it."

"Any steady girlfriends?"

"Some. Latest squeeze was a Marie Santoro. Been seeing her a few months. Nothing heavy. She's a very popular lady, as his sister put it. I'll talk to her."

"Jealous husbands or enemies?"

Avery shrugged. "If there is one, he's not local. Vargas didn't seem to fool around with married women. Folks all seemed to like him, but his next-door neighbor said he was a pain in the ass. Always ran his lawnmower early on the weekend."

"That would piss me off too," Sam said, "but I wouldn't kill over it."

"Right," Avery said. "And I didn't see a computer around the guy's house for the note and he claims he doesn't know how to use one."

"Wouldn't have to be a neighbor or an employee," Tawana said, turning a page in her notebook. "Lots of regulars go to that gift shop. There are a bunch of suppliers. Some cabbies stop in for a soda and a chat. Bus drivers too. Clara Barton's the first and last stop."

"And maybe someone has lots of sick friends," Avery cracked.

Sam picked up the sheet of paper. "Well, it looks like Larry's right. That was ME on the phone. Whoever wrote the note probably wanted Vargas dead. Those pills were almost 100 percent toxic. Something called Cantharidin. Virtually burned away the guy's insides."

"And that's the stuff in Spanish fly?" Avery asked.

"Yeah, that's a name for the green beetle where they get it." Sam looked again at the paper. "Doctors once used it to form blisters on people's skin. Idea was to reduce inflammation of internal tissues."

"Sounds barbaric," Tawana said.

"Not a hundred years ago."

"I thought it was for sex," Avery said. "I read it's--what do you call it--an aphrodisiac."

"Ever try it?" Foster smiled.

"I might with the right lady."

"Save your money," Sam said. " The ME said that's never been proven.  You can buy it on the Web but not the pills that killed Vargas unless someone's selling pure poison."

"So we're definitely dealing with a murderer," Avery said.

"Or a fool who got hold of some very deadly stuff," Tawana said.

"But where would you get it?" Foster asked. "It's not a street drug."

"Why not at the hospital?" Avery said.

Sam shook his head. "Don't use it medically any more."

"Clara Barton has a new research department," Tawana said. "Maybe they're diddling with it."

"Where'd you find that out?"

"Nick told me after he met with Vivian Pershing."

"Small world.  He call you about Vargas?"

"No."

"He will." Sam leaned back in his chair. "Already called the Captain. Asked if this is linked to Pershing's accident."

"Might be," Foster said. "Somebody using notes to set up victims at the hospital."

"Only one note we know of for sure," Avery said.

"Pershing was pretty emphatic on that point, Mike," Tawana said.

"She also gave different versions of how she fell."

"Well, if there's a connection," Sam said, "it's not Mercante's idea about the battle of the budget."

"It's not his idea," Tawana said.

"Oh-oh," Avery said. "The fair Tawana may risk her throne to save the good knight Mercante from evil King Witkin."

Sam laughed along with everyone else. "All right, let's keep at it. Tawana, focus on the women at the hospital and take another look at the Pershing file just in case. Find out if she knew Vargas. And see if we should interview her again. "

"Yes, sir."

"Larry, interview the vendors and anyone else we can tie to the gift shop. And see if they're doing work with Cantharidin over there. Call their headman, what's his name, Kramer. He's a good guy and can tell you who to contact."

"I talked to him today," Foster nodded. "He remembers you from the night we set up Devane."

"What about me, Lieutenant?" Avery said. "I'm about done checking out Vargas's neighborhood and there's only the Santoro dame."

"Check with the priest at his church to see what he knows about the guy. Then work with Larry. Contact the local hospitals, research facilities and pharmacies to see if there's been any usual activity or thefts involving Cantharidin."

"How do you spell it?"

"Here, make a copy of my notes. Okay, any questions?"

No one spoke, and they began to edge toward the door. Sam got to his feet. "Tawana, I'm going to leave early to do some unpacking. I can take a cab if you're not back by five."

"No, take the Lumina. We've been using Larry's car. He can drop me off at home."

"Yeah, Lieutenant, I'd like to see your new digs," Foster said.

"Good. Plan to stay awhile. I've got an extra box cutter."

## THURSDAY, JUNE 24

I need glasses, Vivian thought, rubbing her eyes. Can't concentrate on numbers the way I used to. Maybe those drug store magnifiers would help. She reached for her coffee and took a swallow. Cold. Backing the Rover away from the dining room table, she went to the kitchen and poured a fresh mug. Bob's new two-year proposal was more realistic, tempting, but still too ambitious. Too bad he hadn't done more work improving the annual budget.

She returned to the dining room and shuffled through her papers looking for Jacobi's folder. While he had begun to grate on her, his plan was interesting. If we scaled it back a bit and folded it into the bulk of Bob's plans for his one-year budget, it might be the perfect compromise. And it might keep Bob around. That is, if the trustees didn't somehow blame him for what happened to Ramon Vargas, which really wasn't a security issue. What to do.

She leafed through Jacobi's document one more time. Father Cahill's ideas were appealing and Jacobi's figures very persuasive. The more she thought about it, the more attractive a combined package became. Satisfied, she began writing her argument when her cell phone rang. It was her accountant. Perfect, she thought and pressed the talk button.

"Right on time, Morty."

"That's why I charge you so much, Viv."

"You're a prince. How do they look?"

"Kramer's big package is thoughtful, clever. But unless you increase your fees across the board, he'd better be a helluva fund raiser."

"Suppose he is?"

"Then it might fly. Barely."

"Only might?"

"Even money, that's as high as I go."

"And his one-year?"

"It's doable if he can hold the line on salaries and benefits through next spring and the research department stops bleeding money. Otherwise, he's into the hospital endowment again."

Not what she wanted to hear. "How about Jacobi's outreach program?"

"It's a non-starter."

"You're kidding."

"Sorry, Viv. Superficially it's good, but there's a glitch. Takes a crosscheck to catch it."

"Is it in the cost estimates?" she asked, recalling Connie's report on Jacobi's elevator conversation with Father Cahill.

"You got it. They're okay for the most part, but remember what I said a moment ago about salary and benefits?"

"Yes."

"Well, they're around 58% of both Kramer's one-year budget and Jacobi's substitute, but his assumes different staffing requirements: shifting employees, re-training, specialized new hires and forced attrition."

"That makes sense."

"No argument. Trouble is he undercounts the money needed to do all this. If you go through the footnotes for each department, the same error occurs in every entry."

"By how much?"

"I make it about 9 percent. Just under 12 million."

"How can he be so far off?"

"A simple mistake. If you set the your calculator wrong, it happens each time you punch the memory for a given factor. Of course he could have done it deliberately."

"You kidding?"

"Vivian, I've never seen books that couldn't be cooked. Look, I'll e-mail you my figures and conclusions. Call me if you need to."

"Sure, Morty. Thanks."

"Take care, doll."

She hung up. What the hell's Jacobi up to? I might have missed this, but not Bob or Cynthia or some trustees. She sipped her coffee. Now what? Call Jacobi? No. I need to keep this inside the board. She picked up the phone and began to key in Woody's number, then started over. Father Cahill at least deserved a warning and could keep his mouth shut.

---

After squatting twice without success, Patches looked up at Nick with the closest thing there was to a canine shrug.

"Dumb pooch, why did you want to come out?" he said, trying to communicate his irritation with his tone and glare.

Patches struggled out of the high grass onto the flagstone path and turned toward the kitchen door, Nick following, leash in hand.

"Fine, but you'd better not poop inside."

Letting the dog into the house, Nick gave her a handful of kibble and went upstairs to the bedroom. Maggie, his old white domestic shorthair, was snoozing on the bed, and Puffer, the feisty little calico, was perched on the window sill gazing out the screen at her corner of the world.

Nick checked the answering machine. Nothing. It was almost 12:30, and he had an idea. After checking the number, he picked up the cordless and dialed.

"Clara Barton patient information," a female answered.

"Is Connie Vacarro still there? This is Nick Mercante, a friend of hers."

"Hold on."

Puffer leaped gracefully to the floor and strolled across the room.

"Nick, are you at home?"

"Yes."

"We're changing shifts. Let me switch you to the other phone."

"Sure," he said and waited, watching Puffer bounce onto the bed and creep toward Maggie, her tail low.

"Hi," she said a moment later. "What's up?"

"You're on site, you tell me. What's the latest on Ramon Vargas?"

"Everyone's saying how strange it is not to see him around. I thought he was a bit of a sleeze, but there's no doubt the gift shop won't be the same without him."

"Is it open for business?" Nick asked as Puffer crouched, tail now twitching back and forth.

"Yes. I think the owner's in there. Except for that, it seems like any other Thursday. Bob's been going around, visiting staff, trying to keep things normal."

"That's smart," he said and smiled as Puffer pounced, batted Maggie's rump twice with her paw and darted off.

"But I know the police are here because I recognized that black detective Lieutenant Witkin introduced me to last winter. What's her name, Brooks?"

"Tawana Briggs."

"Nick, one of the volunteers heard Vargas was murdered. Is that why Briggs's here?"

Tawana had briefed him and he could share some information. "Well, they know Vargas died from a strange poison that the hospital research department has in its inventory."

"No! Then someone here killed him?"

"Too soon to say. Other hospitals are working with it. And it's possible this was an accident. Some idiot might have thought he was giving Vargas something harmless."

"Does Bob know all this?"

"Since yesterday."

"He must be a basket case. This couldn't happen at a worse time. He released his new budgets this week."

"The trustees' meeting still on for tomorrow?"

"According to Vivian."

"What's her take on Vargas?"

"She's mystified like all of us. Nick, I need to talk to Bob. Please let me know if you learn anything more."

"You do the same."

"Deal. And I haven't forgotten about the la sagne. Keep in touch."

Connie tried Kramer's private line but it was busy. After waving to members of the new shift, she went to the volunteer office to hang up her blazer and sign out. When she came out Bob was waiting in the hallway. He was in shirtsleeves, tie askew, and looked tired.

"Ms. Vacarro. Do you have a minute? An issue's come up about the newspapers."

"Certainly, Mr. Kramer," she said. They had yet to reveal they were dating to anyone at the hospital except Vivian.

"Follow me, would you?" He didn't speak as they went toward his office. She slowed, but he took her elbow. "Outside," he whispered. "The walls might have ears."

They went through the glass doors and strolled toward Cabot Hall.

"How are you?" she asked softly after a few moments, resisting the urge to take his hand.

"Better for seeing you," he said. "Things are quiet. Thank goodness not all police wear uniforms."

"The press hasn't been too bad. Just the piece Tuesday."

"Not much to report," he shrugged.

"Bob, I know about the poison that killed Vargas. This wasn't an accident, was it?"

He glanced at her. "Nick Mercante?"

"Yes."

"Couldn't keep a secret from you if I tried."

"Do you want to?"

"Never, but I didn't want to upset you. What did Mercante say?"

She told him.

"He has it right," he nodded. "A detective asked me for the name of the head of research. When I checked over there later, I found out we've got the damn stuff right on the premises."

"Do you think this is connected to Vivian's fall?"

"I'm haven't the vaguest idea. Let's sit," he said when they reached the gazebo which was empty of smokers.

They sat close and he let the back of his hand rest lightly on the side of her thigh.

"You know, Red," he said, his eyes sweeping the grounds, "I almost wish Ellis or Jacobi were behind this. Be one less lunatic to worry about."

"This must awful for you, and those two are probably gloating."

"Jacobi may not be for long. I read over his proposal last night. Some of the numbers don't seem quite right."

"Are you sure?"

"I didn't have time to flyspeck it. Fred's doing that for me, but Jacobi could be in trouble."

"Maybe Laura Prentice let him down."

"She's too good to make that kind of mistake."

"Unless she did it on purpose for Cynthia."

He turned to her with a smile. "You talk to Mercante too much. But to tell the truth, I am worried what Cynthia might do tomorrow."

"Can you find out?"

"Not likely, but I still have a decent chance if the trustees don't hold me accountable for what happened to Vargas. Want to lay any money on that?"

"No, I just want to hold you. Can you come over tonight?"

"Sorry. Have to caucus with Fred. And I'm here at the crack of dawn."

"Come for a little while. You could use a break."

"This has been a nice one," he said, squeezing her knee before he stood up. "Anyway, you're working."

"Robin owes me one," she said standing. "I can get her to sub. I'll fix a quick dinner and you can be on your way."

He hesitated, then shook his head. "I'd better not. There's just too much on my plate. Is that okay?"

"You know where to find me."

---

Thorpe spotted Cynthia sitting on the patio outside the nearly empty cafeteria. At his hour, it was officially closed, lunch having ended and dinner not to be served until six. But one could always get a drink or snack from the vending machines or just sit and relax, which was what Cynthia appeared to be doing as he went through the doors.

"Laura thought you might be down here," he said, sitting across from her.

"Needed to escape. The police finally left."

"Tough day?"

"More like the whole week, with them nosing around and interfering with everyone's work."

"Medical staff's been pestered too. Cops have any ideas who did this?"

"How should I know? They're just a pain in my butt."

"Nice butt," he smiled. "You don't seem too frazzled."

"Coddling the staff's what I do best," she said. She glanced around, then reached across the table and touched his hand. "You were nice to come over Saturday. I needed a boost."

"You deserved it. The rebuttal you guys prepared is really good. You should crucify Jacobi. By the way, have you seen him around? I haven't laid eyes on him all week."

"He's hibernating with his papers. Called Laura today, wants her to come over for a drink tonight."

"She going?"

"Why not? She's doing better getting info from him than from Bob. The stuff he was feeding her was not quite the real deal."

"We knew he was shrewd."

"A snake you mean. And we thought he trusted her."

"Confirms my view of the world. Laura thinks his new plan's pretty good. I'm worried about Pershing."

"It doesn't matter. He's toast. Vargas couldn't have died at a better time."

"Cynthia, he didn't just die. I'm hearing someone fed him poison."

"Bottom line's the same isn't it?"

"I'm glad you're on my side," he said. "Laura says you two aren't doing a final prep."

"Not unless she tells me Jacobi comes up with a new idea over cocktails."

"Good. You're just where I'd hoped. Kramer's reeling, Jacobi will be a laughing stock, and you'll walk away with the prize."

"I want two, Peter. CEO and you."

"Laudable goals both," he smiled, glancing at his watch. "I've got to visit a patient."

"I'll call you tonight if I need encouragement," she said as he stood.

"Not too late. I want you get a good night's sleep. Big day tomorrow," he said and moved off.

Tomorrow, she thought, watching his back. Her day to

claim victory. She knew she was ready, but will it happen? Peter trusted no one. That's why he was so confident and assured. Laura was still naive, and so could be fooled by the likes of Kramer. And what about me? Somewhere in the middle, but every inch her father's daughter, planning, worrying, sweating the details. Had she overlooked anything? No. Everything was in place, the smallest item accounted for. Too bad about Vallance, but Peter can relax. She'd sleep well.

---

Father Cahill sat in the front pew in the darkened chapel, clutching his rosary, his lips reciting the eighth Hail Mary of the Third Luminous Mystery: Jesus' Proclamation of the Kingdom of God. As he prayed, he meditated on the Mystery, which imparted the Lord's directions to obtain salvation. It had always appealed to him as he worked through his own struggles to receive grace.

"Love your enemies," Jesus had told the world. "Pray for those who persecute you." And He had held to that belief to the very end. Dying on the cross, He sought absolution for those who had crucified Him--"Father, forgive them; for they know not what they do."

Cahill began another Hail Mary. If only he could live his own life that way, but he was weak. Perhaps he might forgive the ignorant, but not the indifferent who cared little for the unprotected and needy. And certainly not those who had given him false assurances. Deceivers whom it now appeared he had been right to distrust. Vivian Pershing had told him the possibility was very real Jacobi had been deceitful and would fail tomorrow.

He must do something to save his program. Failure was not an option. He had come too far, worked too hard. The Lord would help his plans succeed. Completing the tenth Hail Mary, Cahill began the Gloria, the final prayer of the Mystery. He wept as he recalled the Lord's words: "I have come to call sinners, not the just."

---

Jacobi's rule was never to have alcohol after nine on the
night before surgery. Tonight he broke it by a full hour, finishing by
himself the bottle of the Mosel-Riesling he and Laura had started at
poolside that evening. Premature celebration, perhaps, but he was
feeling good.

He looked at his image in the huge mirror, admiring his lean
body. Climbing into bed, he switched off the light and closed his
eyes, hoping sleep would come swiftly. He couldn't wait for
tomorrow's meeting. Once that was over, he'd make the moves
necessary to secure his position. He smiled at the thought that
Laura had leapfrogged to the top of his list.

---

Laura was on the edge of her bed applying nail polish to her
toes when Peter called a few minutes after ten.

"How'd it go with Jacobi?" he asked.

"Piece of cake," she said, tucking the phone between her
chin and shoulder. "Thinks I hung the moon. Quote 'Chief of Staff
isn't enough. I want to pick your brain every day' End quote."

"Perhaps he's finally decided he wants a little night action
too."

She picked up the bottle and applicator. "He's had his
chances. And you should have seen the bikini I was wearing
today."

"He still didn't question the cost figures?"

"Not a peep," she said, brushing her little toe. "The numbers
add up. That's all he cares about. He's so cocky, he was describing
how he'd redecorate Kramer's office."

"So Bob's not a threat anymore."

"Not since Vargas swallowed poison," she said, painting the
next toe.

"You hear from Cynthia?"

"Not a word, thank God."

"Huh. I was half expecting her to call me. You think she's
okay?"

Laura moved on to the next toe. "You want to run over and

hold her hand again?"

"Come on, Laura, it's important."

"Peter, we've done what we can. She's ready. If there's one thing she can do, it's whine when she's upset. Let her be. I intend to."

"Meeting starts at ten?"

"On the dot. They're bringing in lunch for the siege. Should be quite a show."

"Prediction?"

"Three way tie," she said, starting on the big toe.

Thorpe chuckled. "Maybe I should come over and hold your hand."

"Door's open."

"Celebrate tomorrow night?"

"I'll be here."

# SEVENTEEN

## FRIDAY, JUNE 25

Dr. Bruce Mallory was nearing the end of his residency and this might be his last time assisting Dr. Jacobi. This morning's colectomy was not complicated even though a fairly large tumor was to be removed from Mrs. Goodwin's colon. Nevertheless, knowing Jacobi's reputation, Mallory had thoroughly reviewed the procedure. He was confident he would do a good job, which, incidentally, couldn't hurt his chances to make the staff at Clara Barton.

Mallory was on his way to the scrub sinks when he heard his name called. He turned to see Jacobi coming toward him.

"How are you feeling today, Dr. Mallory?"

"Fine, sir," he answered, somewhat uneasy.

"That's what I like to hear. You have any last minute questions about this case?"

"None, sir," he said, relaxing. "I'm looking forward to working with you again."

"Fine. Now, I'd like you to pay particular attention during anastomosis."

"Of course. You anticipating a problem with the tissue during resection?"

"Not at all, but I'd value your opinion. I don't want any crap at conference like in the Schroeder case. Do I make myself clear?"

"Perfectly," Mallory nodded. "I appreciate your confidence."

Jacobi patted him on the shoulder. "And I'm sure it's well-placed. I'll see you inside."

That takes care of that, Jacobi thought, entering the locker room. Mallory was a suck-up so he knew he could count on him to deflect any criticism. He wanted no roadblocks after today.

Many athletes have pre-game rituals and would readily admit to being superstitious. Surgeons might not be as candid, but a fair number also follow strict routines before they operate. It was well known that Stanley Jacobi was one of them.

Standing before his locker, Jacobi first hung up his jacket and pants, placing his pager and cell phone side by side on the top shelf, then he removed his tie and shirt and finally his Rolex and class ring. Next he put on scrubs, trousers first, then top. At the door leading to the sinks, he picked out a cap and mask from the right-hand pile and slipped on a pair of shoe covers.

Being lead surgeon on a case had its privileges, one of which was to be the last person to scrub. And, as chief of surgery, Jacobi had decreed that the sink closest to the locker room was the exclusive province of surgeons--no other personnel allowed. The OR staff often ignored the rule, but on days when he was operating, no orderly, technician or nurse would dare use "Jacobi's Jacuzzi" until after he had left the floor.

Even if you were a surgeon and permitted to use Jacobi's sink, you were not allowed to touch the special Bose sound system he had installed on a table next to the storage cabinet. Continuing his routine, Jacobi checked to make sure Tchaikovsky's Sixth Symphony was in the CD player. Satisfied, he pressed the power and play buttons. Nothing happened.

Frowning, Jacobi pressed the buttons again with the same result. He examined the wires behind the unit only to find they were all properly attached. Bending down, he peered under the table and saw that the power cord was slightly unplugged from the socket.

"What the hell," he swore.

Squatting, Jacobi reached to push in the plug. He didn't notice the thin strip of sharpened metal the killer had fastened across the underside of the table exactly twelve inches from the wall. Thus, as Jacobi stretched, he scraped the skin of his forearm below the sleeve of his scrub top.

"Damn it," he exclaimed, pulling back his arm. A slight amount of blood oozed from the wound. At least it's not my hand, he thought. He shook his head, vowing to have Maintenance fire the idiot responsible for this. He looked back under the table, changed the angle of his approach and inserted the plug.

Standing, Jacobi re-pressed the buttons and the comforting music began to play. Savoring his small triumph, he reached into the cabinet above his head and selected a bottle of iodine. He turned and leaned over the sink, its electronic eye turning on the water. He washed and rinsed the wound, dried it with a paper towel, applied the iodine and covered it with an adhesive bandage.

Back on track, Jacobi turned to the shelf and took a fresh scrub brush, one of the newer type already filled on the sponge side with liquid soap.  After soaking with the sponge, he began scrubbing with the bristle side, first his fingers, then wrists and arms several inches below where he had placed the bandage.

As he scrubbed, Jacobi looked through the window into OR 1, his personal domain.  He saw that the surgical team was already assembled--the techs, nurses, anesthesiologist, and Mallory who was hunched over Mrs. Goodwin preparing her abdomen.

Several minutes later, Jacobi backed into the OR and stepped over to the table, where he turned so the assistant could glove and gown him.

"Dr. Volmer?" he asked the anesthesiologist.

"She's under and values steady."

"Good. All set, everyone?"

A series of nods.

"All right. Let's begin. Cautery, please."

The unit was slapped into his hand and Mallory moved in closer to Mrs. Goodwin.

Jacobi then stepped back. "Just a moment."

The team paused and looked at him in silence.  Finally, Dr. Volmer peered around her screen. "You all right, Stan?"

"Just a little cramp, Mary. I'll be fine in a minute." Jacobi took a deep breath. "Okay. Let's go," he said and collapsed.

Two floors below, the killer heard the public address system:

**Code Blue, OR  1**
**Code Blue, OR  1**

The big fish was down.  The minnow would follow.

---

Vivian was on her way out the door when the kitchen phone

rang. Don't have time for this, she thought, tempted to let it ring, then gave in.

"Hello," she snapped into the receiver.

"Vivian, it's Woody."

"Woody, I'm running late. You need a lift or something?"

"No, I'm already at the hospital."

"You forget something?"

"Bob Kramer asked me to call you. He's canceled the meeting."

"Canceled? Why? Let me speak to him."

"He's in with the police."

The police. "What's happened, Woody?"

"Dr. Jacobi's dead."

---

Shortly after five that afternoon, Dr. Eugene McCoy knocked on the door of Father Cahill's tiny office on the first floor of the hospital.

"Come." Cahill's voice was barely audible through the wood.

The anesthesiologist had to blink to adjust his eyes to the dark as he entered. Father Cahill was at his desk, holding a penlight flash over a small book.

"Father?"

Cahill looked up squinting. "Did you know Dr. Jacobi gave me this flashlight? It's perfect for carrying in a pocket."

"I'm sorry about what happened, Father," McCoy said, sitting. "Are you all right? Laura Prentice asked me to stop by."

"Oh, yes. She visited earlier. Were you...with him?"

"No, Dr. Volmer was. She said it was very fast. She thinks it might have been a cardiac incident."

"Incident. Such a nice, clean word."

"Yes, it's, uhm...somewhat general."

"There was so much we were going to do. But he got it all wrong."

"Wrong?"

"The money.  There isn't enough money.  Why didn't he tell me the plan couldn't work?"

"What plan, Father?"

"The trustees would have defeated him. He must have known."

"Father, would you like to pray with me?"

"Oh, that's right. You're Catholic."

"Yes. Would you like to pray?"

"Pray? No, no, but thank you. I have things to do. But you go ahead.  Would you like to borrow my New Testament?" he asked and lifted the book.

"I have one, Father," McCoy said, standing. "Let me know if you need anything, all right?"

"We need money from somewhere."

"The Lord be with you, Father."

"Yes. Thank you, doctor. And with you."

## SATURDAY, JUNE 26

A few minutes past seven Connie unlocked her door and rushed to her bedroom. The answering machine's red light was blinking and she eagerly pressed Play, but the message was from her bank offering a low interest credit line. In a way she was relieved. Since speaking with Bob the night before, she'd been unable to shake a growing feeling of dread that she knew was the ghost of Victor Devane.

Physically and mentally drained, she decided a long bubble bath might revive her spirits.  Leaning back in the crested foam, she closed her eyes, replaying the past 32 hours.

She had been at home painting when Vivian called with the news of Jacobi's death. Stunned, she frantically tried to reach Bob, but was forced to leave messages. Then her shift at the Laughing Bull seemed to last forever while she called several more times without success. He didn't phone until she was getting ready for bed.

"I'm exhausted," he said. "It was a madhouse today. Jacobi was healthy as a horse. And now there's talk among the staff this wasn't a heart attack."

"What else could it be?"

"I've no idea and the police aren't saying anything except asking questions. They're coming back tomorrow. I'll be there first thing. Look, Red, I've been up since five and need sleep. I'll buzz you in the morning."

The morning came, but Bob never called. Instead Nick phoned around noon.

"Things have gone from bad to worse," he said. "The police think Jacobi was poisoned."

"My God, another one. They're sure?"

"I think so. They expect to announce something later today. You're not to say anything until you hear about it, okay?"

"All right, sure....Nick, do they have any idea who might have done this?"

"That's all I know, Connie, honest."

She again spent anxious hours at home, then at the Laughing Bull, with one eye on the phone, waiting for further word from Bob, from anybody.

Now, stepping from the tub, she was tempted to call Nick, but told herself he'd contact her if he had any information. Donning a nightgown, she went to the living room, lit candles, and sipped a glass of wine in the flickering light, the phone next to her on the sofa. Finally, she could take the silence no longer and decided to call Vivian. The phone rang just as she reached for it. Startled, she gripped it firmly.

"Hello?" she said, a twinge in her stomach.

"Hey, Red, it's me. I finally came up for air."

"Are you all right?"

"Been better. Listen, I'm sorry, but it looks like I was right about Jacobi."

She was about to mention Nick's call, but held back.

"It wasn't a heart attack," he went on. "Some kind of poison."

"Yes," she said, the twinge stronger.

"Oh, then you saw the evening news. Well, now I have to come up with a statement for the staff. Main thing is to make sure they don't get hysterical. Thank God it's the weekend and they're not all here."

"Do you...have any details?" she asked, her eyes squeezed shut to concentrate on his voice.

"All they're saying is it's a probable homicide. Wonderful, huh?  Maybe two in one week. The press will eat this up. Who'll want to come to Clara Barton now?"

"I don't know," she said softly, eyes still closed. It seemed to help her stomach.

"What's wrong, Connie?"

"I--I'm upset...for you. That you're going through this." Her words seemed to come from far away.

"Ah, what the hell. Won't be my problem much longer. I've spent the last two hours on the phone with trustees.  They want answers and I don't have any. Have you spoken to Vivian?"

"Not today," she said.

"Yeah, she's probably been working the phones too. She told me she wants to vote on the budget right away. That's shorthand for making yours truly walk the plank."

"What's going to happen?"

"If I were you, I'd back the other guy."

"Cynthia Ellis?"

"ABK, anybody but Kramer."

She heard the rueful humor in his voice, but knew she couldn't match it. She took a breath, struggled to reach out. "Do you want...would you like to see me?"

"I'd love to, but I have to work on this statement, and Fred's calling later."

"I see," she said, the twinge subsiding. Another breath. "Tomorrow?  I could make us dinner."

"Wonderful, but let's keep it loose."

"All right," she said, her eyes fluttered open. "Will you call me?"

"I'll do my best. God, I miss you, Red, I hope you know that."

"Yes...I do," was all she could manage.

A pause. "Okay, then. Sleep well."

"And you." She heard him click off and listened to the dead

air, totally miserable.

## SUNDAY, JUNE 27

Laura and Thorpe watched Cynthia pace around her living room that afternoon waving a glass of wine. "That sonofabitch Kramer has to be behind this. He couldn't beat us fair and square so he gets rid of Jacobi."

"We weren't exactly playing by the rules, Cynthia," Laura said. She was curled up on the couch, legs tucked beneath her.

"But we didn't kill anybody," Cynthia said, eyes blazing. "And, by the way, you don't seem particularly upset. He already talk to you about replacing me?"

"Of course not."

"How could he?" Thorpe said, legs crossed in an easy chair. "He's worse off than before. Vargas is dead, the numbers are bad and Jacobi's probably been murdered. The trustees have to turn to you."

"Wishful thinking, Dr. Thorpe. But what do you care, you come out smelling like a rose either way, don't you?" She raised her glass. "A toast to the next chief of surgery."

"What's with you?" Laura asked. "I thought you asked us here to plan, not for a pity party."

"Screw you. I'm hanging out to dry here."

"Will you cool it?" Thorpe said. "You're in good shape. This is happening on Kramer's watch."

"It's mine too, isn't it?" Cynthia fumed. "Thanks for nothing."

"She has a point, Peter," Laura said.

"Hey, I'm not exactly out of the woods here. Jacobi being dead doesn't hurt my career. People might get curious. But we'll all get through this if we keep our heads. Cynthia, when will the board meet?"

"Who knows?" she answered, still pouting and plopping into a chair. "Depends on the Czarina, but she's pushing."

"So we may have some time," Thorpe said. "The thing to do is keep the pressure on Kramer. You know, tsk-tsk all the woes of the hospital under his leadership. Finances, the Cahill report,

Vargas and now Jacobi."

"Right," Laura said. "And don't forget Ed Monroe. There were lots of complaints about security again on Friday."

"Sounds wonderful," Cynthia said, refilling her glass. "Just like all Peter's plans. Great on paper, lousy execution."

"I've had enough of this," Laura said, sitting up straight. "I'm going home."

"I'm sorry," Cynthia said. "Please don't go."

"Only if you stop carping."

"Promise."

"All right, then," Laura said. "Now pour me some of that wine and let's get down to business."

Soon they agreed on a strategy: Laura would discreetly undercut Kramer with the admin staff and any trustees that phoned or dropped by; Thorpe would do the same among the medical staff; and Cynthia would be very visible and take the high road, concentrating on a business-as-usual approach to display her steady competence.

After exchanging goodbyes with Cynthia, Thorpe and Laura walked to their cars.

"You think she really has a chance?" Laura asked, stopping next to her SUV.

"If she sticks to the script. I'd say at least 60-40 right now. And it should improve if we work hard with the time we have."

"Let's hope Pershing doesn't convene the board too soon."

"She can't wait too long without a budget. We're at the end of the fiscal year.

"That's not a problem," Laura said. "The charter provides for spending at current levels until the new budget passes."

"Good. Okay, I'll see you in about ten minutes. Want me to stop off for carry out?" he asked and rubbed her arm.

"No, I've thawed some steaks. And be careful with those hands. She might be able to see us."

In fact, Cynthia had been observing them from her upstairs window. Now, as they drove off, she watched until their taillights disappeared. She turned and nodded at her father's picture.

---

"I haven't heard from Bob today," Connie said across Vivian's dining table where they were finishing the chef's salad Lydia had prepared after Connie had invited herself over for dinner.

"I'm not surprised. He was on the phone lobbying me this morning, then he was going off to his brother's. But I'll bet he called other trustees from his car driving out there."

"How did he sound to you?"

"Surprisingly good. Asked me to keep an open mind on the budget. He might have a new wrinkle to present."

"That's comforting. I was afraid I might have upset him. I wasn't very warm to him last night."

"You can always pick up the phone, you know. Want some coffee?"

"No, but I'll make you some."

"Rather a bourbon. Fix us a couple will you? And just leave the dishes in the sink for Lydia. I'm going to the john."

Connie began clearing the dishes as Vivian curled the Rover around the table and zoomed toward her bedroom.

"You heard from Nick?" Vivian asked minutes later, sipping her drink as Connie settled on the sofa.

"Not yet. I'm not sure they've told him anything."

"Well, they sure haven't told me. I've called that Tawana Briggs four times since Friday. Not a word."

"Maybe she's not on the investigation."

"Wanna bet? She called me about Ramon Vargas and the *Post* is already tying his death to Jacobi's."

"Vivian, what's going on? I'm really worried."

"Well, I'm beginning to think there's a nut out there. What would killing Ramon have to do with me or the budget?"

"It's like the hospital's under siege," Connie said.

"Yes, and we have to calm the waters and not overreact. So regardless of what kind of budget we pass, I'm going to support Bob for the near term. Work out a short contract extension."

"Did you tell him?"

"Not yet. I've not told anyone and you're not to say a word to him. I want to check with Woody and some other trustees this week after the dust settles a bit."

"Won't there be pressure for Ellis?"

"There could, but Bob's got the experience and he's worked with the police before. For the moment I think that's more important than profit and loss statements."

"I suppose you're right."

"You don't sound particularly thrilled."

"I'm...well, confused."

"Perhaps I have more faith in him than you do. Would you rather I suggest he leave?"

"No...I don't think so."

"It might let him off the hook. If he walks away gracefully, no one could accuse him of being power hungry."

"Except the police."

"There. You said it. Feel better?"

"No."

"That should tell you something," Vivian said, handing Connie her phone. "Call his cell and say hello. But refill my glass first."

# EIGHTEEN

## TUESDAY, JUNE 29

Jacobi's death coming only days after Ramon Vargas's caused a predictable flap in the media, punctuated by speculation that the killings were the work of the same person. Rumors weren't facts, however, and few new details had been reported. Nick had a call into Tawana and was surprised when Frank called after dinner.

"We've learned Jacobi and Vargas are linked," Frank said shortly into the conversation.

"Somebody send Jacobi a note?"

"Not exactly. He died from another weird poison the hospital researchers are playing with."

"What's this one?"

"Batrachotoxin. Has potential for developing treatments for the nervous system. That's how it kills you, by the way, shuts it down."

"Potent as Spanish Fly?"

"Less than .02 milligrams can take you out."

"Wow. Where does it come from?"

"Believe it or not, a frog. ME showed us a picture. Hold on a sec...here it is. Phylobates Terribilis. Lives in Central and South America. Colorful little thing. Tribes in Colombia have used it in poison darts forever."

"Darts? Did Jacobi run into the point of a scalpel?"

"Might as well have," Frank said. "The poison won't permeate the skin, but if it comes in contact with an open wound watch out."

"He was operating with an open wound?"

"Bandaged. On his arm. The table where he scrubbed had sharp metal underneath that caused the cut. We found traces of blood and skin on it."

"What was Jacobi doing under the table?"

"We figure he was plugging in his CD player. Always operated to music."

"And the poison was on the metal?" Nick asked.

"No. In the iodine and the Neosporin ointment in the medicine cabinet. Jacobi must have scraped his arm, put on iodine and a bandage. Then a few minutes later, boom."

"That took some planning."

"Not the first time. That's why I'm calling you. Looks like you stumbled into another one."

"Another what? I've never even talked to Jacobi."

"But guess what we found in the corner of the cabinet near the iodine bottle?"

"My name and phone number," Nick said.

"Close. The note Vivian Pershing reported finding in the volunteer office."

"You're kidding."

"Not today, amigo."

"Just as she described?"

"To the letter. Typed on the same message blank the volunteers use. Looks like it was their office typewriter."

"No prints on this note either?" Nick asked.

"Folded once but clean."

"But Vivian must have handled it. What the hell's going on here?"

"That's what we want to know. We're brainstorming in Sam's office tomorrow. I'll ask Tawana to call you when we have anything more."

"I'd love to be there."

"I'm sure, but Sam nixed it. And, Nick, keep this close. No chatting with Pershing or Vacarro. We're not telling anyone about the Batrachotoxin or the note except Kramer."

"But isn't he a suspect? Jacobi wanted his job."

"Sure, but if he did it, he already knows what we know. Better we play along."

"Can't you at least tell Vivian about the note?"

"We don't want the media making more of this than they already have."

"Come on, Frank, she won't talk. You can take her into your confidence."

"I'll run it by Sam, but it's his case."

"Tell him I'll have extra Killian's Ale for him at the garden party."

"You're bribing a cop? I'm appalled. Can Gail and I bring anything by the way?"

"I think you guys are down for a dessert, so maybe a pie."

"My kind of party. See you then."

## THURSDAY, JULY 1

Unlike the last meeting in Cabot Hall, Father Cahill waited little more than an hour before he heard clapping and people began filing out of the conference room. Everyone seemed in good spirits except Cynthia Ellis who appeared bewildered. Then Cahill spotted Robert Kramer smiling at the side of Vivian Pershing's wheelchair. Cahill watched as they went by, deep in conversation. Kramer's pleased? After all that's happened? What went on in there?

Laura Prentice could tell him, he thought, searching the crowd for her. He then checked the room, but didn't see her. He started down the inclined corridor toward the main building when he saw her nearing the bottom. He called her name and caught up with her.

"Hello, Father." She, too, was smiling.

"Miss Prentice, good morning. Have they...did the meeting go well?"

"I think so."

"Then there's a new budget?"

"In a way. Mr. Kramer surprised everyone."

"Surprised?"

"He offered to resign."

"What?"

"That's right," she nodded, "but the board refused when Ms. Pershing said she'd also resign if the trustees let him step down."

"But what about his new projects, the eldercare facility an

all?"

"He had another surprise. He conceded they might appear too costly, so he asked the trustees to adopt his one-year budget but only for six months. Meantime he'll work without a contract."

"Then what happens?"

"Well, if results improve during that time, he said he'll request the board to renew his contract and to approve the second six months of the budget along with funds for preliminary plans for the new projects. Full funding would come up for a vote next year."

"And the board went along?"

"It wasn't even close. And he had very nice words for you and Dr. Jacobi."

"Me?"

"Yes. He said Dr. Jacobi's plan was flawed, but because of your efforts, he asked the board to adopt the ideas in principle pending a feasibility study by the budget committee."

Cahill stared at her. "He never said a word to me."

"Father, I work for the man, and I didn't know this was coming. Now, you have a good day. I've got a staff advisory to draft."

Cahill watched her walk swiftly down the hall past the ER. He followed at a more leisurely pace, pondering what he'd just been told.

"Congratulations, Father," Dr. McCoy said, walking by on his left. "I just heard the news. Looks like you may get your money after all."

"Yes, yes it does. Praise the Lord."

---

"Bob set us up," Cynthia ranted at Laura in the first floor rest room. "Feeding you those phony drafts, releasing that hopeless budget and then walking away from it."

"Quiet down," Laura said, nodding toward the door.

"I don't care who hears us. I'm telling you, he's been playing us for chumps."

"And where were you today? Why didn't you speak up, at

least critique Jacobi's plan the way he did?"

"After the Czarina shot down his resignation, I'd have looked like a fool. I'm sure she cooked this up with him."

"That can't be right. Kramer couldn't have pulled off this stunt if Jacobi were still in the running."

"I rest my case. He takes out Jacobi, piggy backs on Cahill, lifts Pershing into the saddle, then rides away in the sunset."

Laura shook her head. "You really think Bob's a killer?"

"Or the luckiest guy alive. He even had the nerve to ask me to stay on with some continuity-good-for-the-hospital crap."

"He said the same kind of thing to Peter."

"Oh, you've heard from the brilliant Dr. Thorpe?"

"Just before you pulled me out of my office. Bob's asked him to become acting chief of surgery till the credentials committee meets to decide."

"Oh, that clever s.o.b. I suppose Peter said yes."

"Of course," Laura said.

"Well, if I were you, baby doll, I wouldn't make any plans for Christmas. The way he and Pershing are manipulating the board, you and I are history."

"It doesn't sound that way."

"Just watch," Cynthia said.

"All right, then, what do you suggest we do?"

"Well, I'm sure not going to rely on Peter. I'll figure this out myself. Of course, I'd love your help."

"I'll do what I can."

"Then come over tonight and we'll caucus. Just the two of us this time."

---

Connie stepped out of the elevator that evening and was startled to see Bob standing outside her apartment.

"Hey, Red," he smiled and stepped toward her.

"Bob!" She found herself running into his arms. "How did you get in?" she asked after they'd kissed.

"I bribed your doorman."

"He can be fired for that."

"I'm kidding. I slipped past him when I helped a woman carry in some groceries. Well, why are we standing here? Aren't you going to ask me in?"

"Of course," she smiled, reaching for her keys. Forty minutes later they had reconnected as lovers do and Connie was delighted at the seamless transition they made from the last time they were together.

Now he was stroking her hair, her head resting in his lap. "I wanted to have lunch with you today, but people kept coming by my office."

"No wonder. I heard what happened. You really wowed them."

"Couldn't have done it without Vivian's support."

"I knew she would back you if she could. When did you find out?"

"Tuesday night. She didn't tell you about our conversation?"

"Not in any detail. And she missed her shift today, of course, and didn't answer when I tried her from the Bull."

"Well, it really started when Jacobi announced he'd include an outreach program as part of an alternative budget. My brother Fred and I thought we needed a response, so we worked out today's scenario as a fallback: the six-month plan, Cahill feasibility study, the works."

"Very smart."

"We thought so too. But after Jacobi's death, I figured I was on real thin ice, so we decided to present the fallback as our own substitute."

"And you told Vivian when she called you."

"Yes, but then I talked to Fred afterwards, and came up with the resignation idea because we didn't want Vivian to have egg on her face if the board really wanted me out."

"Did you warn her?" Connie asked.

"Oh sure. Called her right away. Then she had the idea of resigning if I did."

"Boy, you two are like Batman and Robin."

"She's as savvy as they come. And she never stops. Now she

wants to press the police on the investigation."

"Any news about that?"

"No, I've really been out of pocket this week. What's your friend Mercante telling you?"

"Hardly anything. He says the police aren't sharing much."

"They've given me some details confidentially. They sort of have to since I run the place. But I'm sure they think I could be involved."

She kissed his hand. "So did I for a time. I'm so sorry."

"Hey, it's okay. It was a no-brainer. And it doesn't stop with me. Cynthia has as much a motive as I do."

"You don't think she did it?"

"No. This isn't the work of a rational person. There's a psychopath on the loose."

"Who also killed Ramon Vargas?"

"Makes no sense, right? That's why it has to be a nutcase. Look, let's change the subject. I've brought you a present," he said, lifting her head. "It's in my jacket."

"I don't deserve a present," she said, sitting up.

"Not your decision. Here we are." He handed her a square jewelry box.

Connie stared, remembering the box with the ID bracelet she had found in Vic's pocket. His mistress had inscribed to him with love. The discovery had shattered her dreams.

"Well, don't you want to open it?"

"This is really for me?"

"Your name's Connie, right?"

She lifted the lid. Inside was a gold heart-shaped pendant with a gem in the middle.

"It's a ruby," he said. "Not quite your color red, but I thought you wouldn't mind."

"Bob, it's beautiful. But I can't accept this. It's too expensive."

"I can afford it, remember? Don't say no--you'll break my winning streak. Hey, where are you going?" he said as she hurried toward her bedroom. "Are you all right?"

"Shut up. I have a gold chain that will go with this perfectly."

---

It was close to midnight when Laura called Thorpe.

"Well?" he asked.

"Cynthia's royally pissed at the world. If she had a gun, I think she'd have used it on me."

"You have any wounds?" he laughed into the phone.

"Peter, it's not funny. She's worried Kramer's going to fire her. Maybe all of us. She thinks he knew about our plans all along and outfoxed us."

"He is a crafty one. But he could have just been lucky."

"Or homicidal."

"You singing her song now? Laura, for all we know she killed Jacobi herself to set up Kramer."

"That's crazy."

"Is it?"

"Well, then, it backfired. The chips have all fallen, and Kramer's the one standing tall."

"For six months anyway. You two come up with any thoughts on what to do?"

"No, she was too upset to think straight. Peter, I'm afraid she may do something stupid. We need a plan."

"She doesn't want my ideas.  You should have heard the voice-mail she left me today."

"Let her get a night's sleep."

"I don't have much choice."

"You have to do something."

"I suppose I could drop by this weekend. She in town over the Fourth?"

"Far as I know. You'll be here for dinner Sunday?"

"Sure."

"Peter, when will you tell her about us?"

"Soon, I promise. Let her calm down and let me settle in as acting chief."

"There never seems to be a good time. I'm tired of the delay. I'm getting pressure from my parents."

"Give me a week or so, okay?"

"All right, but no longer."

"Laura, I don't need an ultimatum."

"Make it happen, Peter."

## SATURDAY, JULY 3

Kathy's garden party had been a huge success. To frustrate the deer, she had placed netting over the flowerbeds and so had dozens of varieties of daylilies on display when she removed them that morning. Now, it was after dark and the guests had left except for Frank and Gail and Sam and Tawana who were relaxing with their hosts on their glass-enclosed porch.

"Pot luck's a great way to give a party," Gail said to Kathy.

"It really works with 40 or 50 people like we had today. Everyone brings their favorite appetizer, salad or dessert and so we all get great variety and the best of everything."

"And easy on the pocketbook," added Nick. "All we do is supply the drinks and the main dish."

"You cooked all that fried chicken yourself?" Frank asked.

"Of course. Slaved all morning at the Safeway deli."

"You two have it down to a science," Sam said.

"Thank you," Kathy said. "Now if science could only come up with a deer repellant to protect my lilies."

"I'd love to grow them," Tawana said. "Could you show me how?"

"Sure, it's easy if you have good soil and sun. They maintain themselves."

"I love this one." Tawana pointed to the vase next to her.

"Isn't that a lovely shade of yellow? A friend from church gave me that. It's called Ascending Hymn."

"Spelled H-I-M," Nick said, then took a bow at the laughter. "I'll be here all week. Who needs anything?"

Frank raised a hand. "Gail's driving so I can go for one more Sam Adams."

"I'll join you."

"I'll take a bottled water if there's any left," Tawana said. "I'm a real fun date since I got pregnant."

"I wouldn't have guessed," Kathy said. "You're hardly showing."

"Doesn't she look great?" Sam said.

"Will you really work till September?" Gail asked.

"If I can. Depends how things go."

"Be glad you're in homicide," Nick said, handing her the water. "No wild car chases."

"I'd take one right now. Not much doing at Clara Barton."

"That's right, Nick," Frank said. "We need one of your famous hunches."

"I'm running on empty," he said, opening the beers.

"Come on, Mercante, help us out," Sam said. "If Jacobi didn't cause Pershing's fall, who planted the note in his locker?"

"Oh, that one's easy. The crazy who killed Vargas or the person who wants us to thinks so. I'd arrest them both."

"No fair. You have to make a pick. Kramer or Ellis?"

"I pass."

"There are others," Gail said. "Lots of the staff didn't like Jacobi."

"Yeah, like Dr. Peter Thorpe," Sam said.

"Who's he?" Nick asked.

"Male model type. Kramer just named him acting chief surgeon. There's your motive."

"Sam, Dr. Thorpe's an excellent surgeon," Gail said. "Besides, he couldn't count on Bob picking him."

"He was on the short list as near as we can tell. All he needed was the vacancy."

"Care if I talk to him?" Nick asked.

"Go ahead," Sam shrugged.

"Well, I for one don't think it's Kramer," Kathy said. "From what I know, he doesn't need that job. He's very wealthy."

"Money isn't everything," Sam said. "At his last hospital he was involved in a little power play with the head of the trustees."

"Vivian told me he had his reasons," Nick said "Besides, I thought you liked him."

"Things can change. I didn't much care for you once."

"Hear that?" Nick turned to the group. "You're all

witnesses."

"I agree with Kathy," Gail said. "Bob Kramer wants Clara Barton to be number one. This doesn't help the hospital."

"But it makes people forget about negative cash flow," Frank said. "You said the staff's getting real edgy."

"They must be," Kathy said. "And I'm surprised there hasn't been more press and TV coverage. Even Tom Carter's been fairly quiet."

"Thank Joe Cornell for that," Sam said, referring to the department's PR chief. "The party line is we're treating Jacobi's death as a homicide but Ramon Vargas was killed accidentally by a misguided friend."

"And so far we've managed to keep the Pershing note out of play," Frank said.

"I still think she deserves to know you found it," Nick said. "She'd keep it quiet."

"Nick's right," Gail said. "She'd do anything for the hospital."

"With all due respect to my hubby, I agree," Tawana said. "I don't see much downside. I've talked to her."

"They're ganging up on us, Sam," Frank said.

"I suppose you want us to tell Connie Vacarro too," Sam said to Nick.

"You know you can trust her. She'll do whatever Vivian asks."

"All right," Sam said. "You can tell Pershing we have the note but nothing about what killed Jacobi. We've only told Kramer."

"You sure he won't tell Connie?"

"No, but he's agreed not to."

"Fair enough," Nick said and sipped his beer. "You know, Kramer had an interesting comment about Vivian's fall."

"What was that?" Frank asked.

"He said if he had wanted her out of the picture, he'd make sure she was, wouldn't have taken a chance she'd survive an accident. Then we get Vargas and Jacobi. No way they live."

"Which makes you think Kramer did them?"

"He could have, but my point is perhaps whoever pushed Vivian off her chair wanted her alive. Otherwise, they could have easily strangled her in that empty conference room."

"So where does that take you?" Sam asked.

"I'm not sure. But if we're not dealing with a screwball, maybe the killer's got a more complicated plan than we think."

"Murder's enough for me, thank you," Gail said.

"Amen," Kathy nodded.

"On that note, I think we should go," Tawana said, standing. "Thank you both again for a wonderful time."

"Yes," Gail said. "Thanks so much."

"Tawana, if you'll wait a minute, I'll give you one of my favorite day lilies for your yard. It's a lovely yellow and purple called Tune the Harp."

"Another churchy name," Sam said, getting to his feet. "What we need is a Jewish day lily."

"There are plenty of those," Kathy said.

"You're kidding."

"No. How about Leonard Bernstein? It's a beautiful bright coral. I have it in front. I can dig one up for you."

"Is this a great country or what?" Sam grinned.

# NINETEEN

## SUNDAY, JULY 4

"You can see the fireworks from here," Cynthia said, leaning on the railing of her deck that afternoon.

"All the way from the Capitol?" Thorpe asked.

"No, up there at Strathmore Park. Beats fighting half a million people on the Mall."

Thorpe followed her finger with his eyes. "You know, back home we always had a town picnic on the Fourth. My Dad made sure to go in case someone ate too much or got burned by the fireworks."

"You don't talk about your Dad much. Were you close to him?"

"Oh yes. My brother Bill and I idolized him. Dad always said he was the best doctor in town, then he'd wink and remind us there were only two others. Bunceton wasn't very big even then. Only 300 or so live there now."

"You're not in Missouri any more, Dorothy."

Thorpe smiled. "Glad you're back in a good mood."

"You being here helps," she said, moving closer to him, her hip touching his. "I know you can't stay, but it is nice to see you."

"Same here. You had me going there for a while."

She nodded. "I think I was in shock Thursday. Kramer blindsided me. Us. But you've come out looking pretty good."

"I haven't lost perspective. I'm aware this might be temporary. He could cement his position and change his mind. Or he could get booted in six months and a new guy come in if they don't pick you."

"They could show Kramer the door, but he's already pulled one rabbit out of his hat. So I don't think we have much time before the ax falls."

"How long you suppose?"

"Couple months maybe. He has to show the trustees he's not standing still. I think he'll fire me and Al Jennings first. Bring in a new financial guy and chief of staff."

"Laura?"

Cynthia shook her head. "She can't last. I don't think he trusts her."

"And me?"

She put her hand on his arm. "Stay away from us and you could hang in for the duration."

"Then I should walk out of here this minute."

"You could," she said, "but if you listen a moment, you could still prove your loyalty."

"Go ahead."

"I have a new weapon. The Czarina."

"Pershing?"

"She's in Kramer's corner right now. The trick is to turn her against him."

"Not Marcia Davis again."

"Father Cahill."

Thorpe looked at her, then nodded. "He already dislikes Kramer."

"But he loves the fair Laura. We'll make that work for us."

He frowned. "How? She sabotages the feasibility study of Cahill's ideas?"

"You're getting warm, but Kramer will do that. He doesn't care anymore about outreach than I do. Plus he knows Jacobi's numbers are nonsense. He was just blowing smoke at the tree huggers on the board."

"What then?"

"We have Kramer admit the study's a fraud."

"Oh, I get it. I buy a Colt 45 and hold it to his head."

Cynthia smiled. "Effective but messy. No, we draft a letter for him. He'll summarize the flaws in Jacobi's plan, then confess the study was just a ploy that he'll scrap in a few months to make the board think he's fully considered it."

"Even if Kramer felt that way, he'd never put it in writing."

"He would for his brother Fred as a recap. He's been Kramer's guru in all of this. You know how it is with brothers." She instantly raised her hand to her mouth. "Oh God, Peter, I'm sorry. I didn't mean--"

"It's okay. That was a long time ago."

"But--."

"I said forget it. Lots of brothers have died in the Gulf since '91." He patted her arm. "So you compose this letter, then what?"

"Then Laura discovers a copy and brings it to Cahill and Pershing."

"Wonderful. Whom do we hire to forge Kramer's signature?"

"No one. He signs it."

"We're going in circles here. Why would he do that?"

"He's asked me to stay on. So I'll be Miss Happy Face for the sake of the hospital. Then one afternoon, I'll slip the letter in with some routine correspondence and purchase orders. I'll stand and wait while he signs them."

"Boy, that's risky."

"I've done it before, but just to make sure, here's where you come in. If he and Pershing can stage a set piece, so can we."

"Go on."

"We time it. I go in, stand there while he signs the first couple of letters and in walks the acting chief of surgery with some minor medical crisis. I start to leave, but you sit and say it can wait while he's done with me. That'll prod him to finish signing everything. Then off I go with the magic letter in my hand."

"Cynthia, you're an absolute genius."

"Tell me something I don't know, Peter."

## MONDAY, JULY 5

Frank studied the Scrabble board shaking his head. "I hate this game. You always get the best letters. Lucky stiff."

"It's not luck," Gail said across the coffee table. "You should do more crossword puzzles."

"You're better at those too. The hell with it. I'm turning in this bunch of crap."

"You'll lose your turn."

"I don't care."

"Save your best letters."

"They all stink," he said and placed his tiles face down, mixed the pile and picked seven others. "That's better. Watch out for me now."

"After this," she smiled and carefully added "juxta" to the left of the word "pose."

"Geez," he groaned, "that has to put you over 100 already. I knew I shouldn't have taken the day off."

"108 to be exact. Your turn, sour puss," she said as the phone rang in the kitchen.

"A reprieve," he said, getting up. "You want anything from the fridge?"

"I could use a Coke," she said, picking up the *Post* Metro section. She was deep into an article about telecommuting by single mothers when he returned.

"Frank, did you know there are more computers in today's cars than in the first lunar module that landed on the moon?"

"Big deal. My Mustang still stalls in cold weather. Here's your soda."

"Who was on the phone?"

"Mike Avery. Got a call from one of Jacobi's neighbors this morning. Woman named Beverly Gorman. Seems we've got a possible romance in the case."

"Goodie. What'd she say?"

"She's seen an attractive woman at Jacobi's place a few times recently. She gave us the license number of the lady's car. Guess who?"

"Cynthia Ellis."

"Laura Prentice."

"Bob Kramer's assistant?"

"The same," he said.

"Let's see. You're thinking he and Prentice were playing around and then he dumped her. Motive."

Frank smiled and picked up two Scrabble tiles. "Not bad."

"Did Mike talk to her?"

"Tawana caught up with her at home. Prentice says it was all business. Claims she was helping Jacobi work on some presentation to the trustees."

"Helping Jacobi? Does Bob Kramer know that?"

"Prentice didn't say, and he's not mentioned it to us."

"What ever happened to employee loyalty?"

"Went south when companies started hiring part-timers and cutting benefits and pensions. Mike also found out Prentice has some medical training."

"So do I. So do most people who work there."

"But you don't have a motive." He put the letters back in his rack.

"Even if she does, it doesn't mean she's a killer. Still most likely some psychopath."

"Enough. I'm getting a headache."

"You're looking for an excuse to stop the game."

"Right again. I'd rather play something else. And don't say you have a headache."

## WEDNESDAY, JULY 7

Nick entered the doctors' lounge on the first floor of Clara Barton just before eleven. Three men and a woman were reading or talking on cell phones, but it wasn't hard to spot Thorpe by the window. Male model, Sam had said.

"Dr. Thorpe?" Nick said, approaching.

"That's right. Mr. Mercante, I assume."

"Correct." They shook hands. "Thanks for taking time to see me."

"No problem," Thorpe said, resuming his seat. "I'm usually free mornings after surgery. Just hang around to hear from PACU."

"PACU?"

"Post anesthesia recovery unit, a holding area where patients are monitored after they leave the OR."

"Do they call you often?"

"No, but they will today."

"Problem?"

"A little bump in the road. My patient had low potassium values during surgery. So I ordered a post-op IV to get his numbers up."

"That happen a lot?"

"No, and his pre-op screening was fine. We're not sure what caused it."

"Is he at risk?"

"You interested in medicine, Mr. Mercante?"

"I'm the curious type."

"So I hear. Well, there could be cardiac implications unless we get his levels to at least 3.5 meq's. He was at 2.4 in the OR. Now, do want to hear about meq's?"

"I think I'll skip it."

"Just as well. Anyway, PACU should let me know how it's going soon. Unless I'm needed, I'll head over to my office once we're done here."

"I thought the chief of surgery had an office upstairs."

"Not for seeing patients. None of us do. Besides, I haven't finished moving into Dr. Jacobi's office.  That's why we're meeting here. If you're hungry, we can go down to the cafeteria."

"No, this is fine."

"So, you wanted to talk about Dr. Jacobi. Homicide finally bringing in the first team?"

"Doctor?"

"Come now, Mr. Mercante. Let's not be modest. I've read all about your exploits. What can I tell you I haven't already told them?"

"Perhaps nothing, but I understand you didn't get along with Dr. Jacobi."

"I wouldn't go that far. We certainly had our issues, but I didn't kill him, may he rest in peace."

"Any idea who did?"

"No, but from what I understand, it's someone who knows this hospital and the habits of his victims very well." Thorpe smiled. "Someone well-versed in drugs and medicine."

"That could be you."

"Except I'm not a lunatic," Thorpe said, crossing his legs.

"What makes you say that?"

"What reason would anyone have to kill Stan Jacobi and

Ramon Vargas?"

"So you think the same person killed them?"

"Helluva coincidence if not."

"But assuming there was a motive, who'd want to see Dr. Jacobi dead?"

"I don't know about dead, but there're plenty of people who won't miss him, me included. He didn't have many fans."

"How did he become chief surgeon?"

"By running a smear campaign against the man he ousted ten years ago. Plus he was very good, though I personally think he was slipping lately."

"I'm told he was angling to become CEO. If he wasn't popular, do you think the trustees would have chosen him?"

"Very possibly," Thorpe nodded. "Jacobi still had a good reputation. And he could be a prince charming if you didn't have to work with him. Ask the surgical nurses. He was a bully in the OR."

"Would you have become chief of surgery if Jacobi became CEO?"

"Not if he had anything to say about it, and he would have. The CEO can carry a lot of weight around here in medical staffing."

"What did Jacobi have against you?" Nick asked.

"I'm all the things he isn't. Sorry. Wasn't. I'm younger, a better surgeon, and well-liked and respected among the staff."

"And like me, modest."

Thorpe grinned.

"What do you think of Robert Kramer?" Nick continued.

"Good man. Get along with him well, and I commend his judgment picking me to replace Stan."

"Think you'll become permanent chief?"

"I'm fairly optimistic," Thorpe replied. "The surgical staff seems pleased and if Kramer survives with the trustees, I'm well-positioned even if they do a search."

"Things suddenly looking up for you."

"Right place, right time. I deserve it."

"And Kramer's long-term prospects?"

Thorpe shrugged. "Might have bitten off more than he can chew, but I love his idea to build a physicians' building next door.

In any case, he's better than Jacobi ever would have been."

"Kramer one of those who won't miss him?"

"At the top of the list."

"Cynthia Ellis too?"

"Do the math," Thorpe said. "She and Jacobi were rivals for Kramer's job and she's ambitious. But she's not stupid enough to kill him."

"Why stupid?"

"No point. She'll be CEO someday. If not at Clara Barton, another hospital."

"How would it affect you if it was here?"

For the first time Thorpe paused a moment before answering. "Shouldn't be a problem. I like her and vice versa."

"You ever date her?"

Thorpe tilted his head. "My reputation precede me, Mr. Mercante?"

"Hers too. I'm told she had a relationship with Kramer, but he ended it."

"I heard it differently. Ellis broke it off after she'd picked his brains. Her ambition got in the way of romance."

"That made her available for you," Nick said.

"She still is, but I've never made a play. Might someday, but then I can't help her career."

"Do you know Kramer's assistant, Laura Prentice?"

"Of course."

"Was she a fan of Dr. Jacobi?"

"I'm not sure she had an opinion," Thorpe said after a moment. "I do know she's a fan of Kramer, if that affects the equation."

"Are you sure? Someone mentioned she wants to be chief of staff. Wouldn't that be easier if Kramer left and Cynthia Ellis became CEO?"

Thorpe shook his head. "Not necessarily. As I said, Cynthia may move on and Kramer might well pick Laura to replace her. After all, he hired her."

Thorpe's pager went off. "Excuse me," he said, reaching to his waist. He read the display, took out his cell phone and fingered in a number.

"What's it look like, Jenna? Only 2.8? Hmm. Oh, you talked to him? He did what? I'll be damned. Okay, double the dosage per unit of saline. He experiencing any pain from the drip? All right, slow the rate a bit and try an ice pack. Listen, I'm going over to my office. Let me know his values in two hours. We can switch to oral if need be. Sure. Thanks."

"How's he doing?" Nick asked.

"Improving but not as fast as I'd like. But I think we've solved the potassium mystery. Standard pre-op protocol had him on a liquid diet yesterday and to take an enema before bedtime."

"I've heard about no solid food, but why the enema?"

"The last thing we wanted was a distended colon for his procedure. Makes everybody's job more difficult. Anyway, his wife took the instructions to the drugstore, found the right type enema, but purchased a twin pack because it was the only one on the shelf. He took them both."

"Mistake?"

"Apparently. An enema reduces the body's electrolytes. Two must have knocked the hell out his potassium levels." Thorpe looked at his watch. "We almost done, here, Mr. Mercante?"

"Just a few more questions. If Jacobi had become CEO, would he have made Laura Prentice chief of staff?"

"You know, he might have at that," Thorpe said, thinking this guy must be in the loop. Briggs talked to Laura only yesterday.

"Any reason?"

"Jacobi could have been planning to get rid of Cynthia. Clean sweep at the top, if you will."

"Do you think Prentice might have suggested that to him?"

"Now that would be Machiavellian wouldn't it? Where's this going, Mr. Mercante?"

"Maybe Jacobi disappointed her."

"Then I suggest you ask her."

"I intend to," Nick said. "One final question. Vivian Pershing claims someone interfered with her wheelchair to make her fall. In view of what's happened here since, what do you think?"

"Then that's how it happened," Thorpe said, standing. "I

would never take issue with her. She could cause me more problems than two Stan Jacobis."

## THURSDAY, JULY 8

Vivian was already in bed when Connie called that evening.

"Hey, stranger," Connie said. "We missed you today. I'm beginning to think you're avoiding us."

"Blame your beau. Second briefing for the trustees this week."

"My beau. I haven't heard that word in years. You're dating yourself, Viv."

"I'm entitled. I'm also tired. I've never seen Bob so energized.  He's like that bunny with the battery."

"How's he doing?"

"Has his hands full, but he's keeping us current on the police investigation as best he can. Juggling that, the PR and a very restless staff. Not bad under the circumstances."

"I'm still worried."

"Did something happen?"

"Nick stopped by the information desk before I left."

"I assume he wasn't there to donate blood."

"Hardly. He had a lunch date with Laura Prentice, but she canceled."

"She was in my meeting. Nick say why he was seeing her?"

"He sort of fudged."

"Well if Nick's interested in her, so are the police."

"That's what bothers me. He wouldn't give me any details."

"And of course you think it involves Bob. Did Nick ask you not to tell Bob?"

"No."

"And he's promised to give any bad news, right?"

"Yes."

"Then stop being paranoid. Listen, I can't keep my eyes open. Can we talk more over lunch Saturday?"

"Love to. Sweet dreams."

Vivian turned off the light and fluffed her pillow. Connie's experience with Victor Devane made her rightfully cautious. But she was also the type who fell hard for a guy. And that made her vulnerable. Just as I was with Andrew before the car accident. So help me, if Bob hurts Connie, I'll personally cut off his balls. Damn these men....

---

At that moment the killer also lay in bed, eyes closed, reviewing the past three months, content. To be sure, there had been some twists and turns along the way, but the contingency planning had kept things moving forward. Parnell had confirmed that preparation was everything: you foresee the risks and build in defenses. The thought of Parnell brought a smile to the killer's face. It was time for the dead man to tell his tale.

## SATURDAY, JULY 10

Nick had never been to Caballeros, but he knew its reputation. This morning it seemed justified. Although it was only 10:30 as he stepped onto the veranda, most of the tables were already occupied.

"Mr. Mercante, over here."

Laura Prentice was at a back corner table tucked next to the porch railing. He negotiated around several tables to join her.

"Good morning," he said. "You didn't say you'd be wearing sunglasses."

"That better?" she said, removing them to reveal her blue eyes.

"Keep them on if you like, but you'd be cheating the world."

She put them into her purse. "There. Now no one will be disappointed."

"Thank you," Nick smiled and picked up a menu. "Quite an array of dishes."

"That's only breakfast. Everything's good, but the eggs are wonderful."

"Ready to order now, ma'am?" a painfully thin waitress

asked.

"Mr. Mercante?" Laura asked.

"I've already eaten, thanks. Just coffee."

Laura turned to the waitress. "I'll have the Huevos Rancheros and coffee."

She watched the waitress go off, then sat back. "So, Mr. Mercante, I've already talked to detective Briggs about Dr. Jacobi. What can I add?"

"Something useful, I hope. I'd hate to waste part of your Saturday."

"Actually, I'm more comfortable talking here than at the hospital. Less obvious, if you understand."

"Of course," Nick said, studying her.

"You seem transfixed, Mr. Mercante. Are my eyes that remarkable?"

"They're stunning. I don't mean to stare, but I understand you received your master's degree about five years ago. No offense, but I expected you to be a bit younger."

She shrugged. "I had a detour after college, couple of jobs, two failed relationships and too much overpriced therapy. But I'm in a good place now."

"Emotionally or career-wise?"

"Both," she said. "Clara Barton's working out. I'm gaining experience and should move up in the organization if things break for me."

"Expect that to happen?"

"I'm hopeful. And I watch for openings."

"Like chief of staff?"

She winked. "I must have missed the vacancy sign."

"I hear Dr. Jacobi might have found room for you."

"A little bird talking behind my back?"

"Maybe more than one."

"Whatever. Look, Dr. Jacobi asked me to help him work up a proposal and I did. But I wasn't sleeping with him. I told Briggs that."

The eggs and coffee arrived, and Laura attacked both with gusto.

"You remind me of my wife, Ms. Prentice."

She paused with a forkful of eggs halfway to her mouth. "She have blue eyes too?"

"More toward the gray side, but she puts hot sauce on everything as you did to those eggs."

Laura smiled. "A wise woman."

Nick sipped his coffee. "Did you tell Mr. Kramer you went to Dr. Jacobi's home to assist him?"

"No, and I told Briggs that too."

"Shouldn't you have?"

"Didn't have to. It was part of my job."

"What?"

"Bob asked me to keep an eye on what Jacobi and Cynthia were doing. I was his spy."

This was new. "When did he do that?"

"Oh gosh. A couple months ago."

"Did you give him any information?" Nick asked.

"If I thought he could use it."

"So you didn't tell him everything."

"I made some judgment calls," Laura said.

"But never against the home team, right?"

"I'm not stupid, Mr. Mercante."

"So you had cover with your boss just in case, but you could also make inroads with Jacobi."

"I told you I have ground to make up. If I can shorten the road, I will."

"Is Cynthia Ellis helping you pave the way?"

"Exactly what does that mean?" Laura put down her fork.

"Well, she wants to move up too. You could support each other. I hear you're somewhat close."

"Close?" Laura asked pleasantly.

"You're friendly at work. Eat together."

"I'm doing that with you this moment."

"Once does not a twosome make," Nick said.

"Now that's an interesting word."

"Yes."

"I admit I'm fond of Cynthia. She's helped get me adjusted

to Clara Barton. She's very smart and will make a great CEO someday. That enough of a twosome for you?"

"That will do nicely, thanks."

The conversation drifted to other things for a few minutes when the waitress reappeared. "Will there be anything else?"

"Mr. Mercante?"

"No, thank you. How much do I owe for the coffee?"

"My treat," Laura said quickly.

"Thank you."

"Certainly." Laura turned to the waitress and handed her a couple of bills. "I'll have a refill, but keep the change."

"Yes ma'am," she said, actually managing a smile.

"Enjoy the rest of your weekend, Mr. Mercante."

Nick took the hint. "You do the same."

She watched him stroll off. After a moment she took her cell phone from her purse and keyed in Peter's number.

"How did it go?" he asked.

"Fine. Did you know my eyes are stunning?"

# TWENTY

## SUNDAY, JULY 11

On Sundays Father Cahill had a regular schedule at the hospital. A quick workout, ten o'clock services in the chapel, lunch in the cafeteria, then visits to patients.

Today was no different except that when Cahill entered the basement fitness room, the killer was on one of the treadmills, walking slowly, wearing earphones plugged into an IPOD. Cahill nodded and went into the male locker room.

Removing the earphones, the killer stepped off the treadmill, reached into the gym bag on the floor and took out a Closed For Repairs sign, placed it on the outside of the fitness room door, then locked it from the inside. Other than Cahill, staff rarely used the gym at this hour on a Sunday, but you never know.

Reaching again into the gym bag, the killer removed a hypodermic syringe filled with 1500 mg. of a quinidine solution, nearly four times the usual initial dose for a man Cahill's size. The drug was used to control ventricular tachycardia--the abnormal heart rhythms the killer had seen in Cahill's future. But high doses had the nasty side effect of pushing the arrhythmia into cardiac fibrillation where the ventricular muscles twitch so rapidly and erratically that normal coordinated heart contractions cannot occur.

Raising the syringe to the light, the killer pressed the plunger until a few drops of the solution squirted out, then returned the syringe to the bag and started stretching exercises. From the floor the killer watched Cahill emerge from the locker room, take the adjoining treadmill and set it at a leisurely pace. The killer waited a moment, then stepped back on the other treadmill, setting it to nearly five miles per hour. "Got to get the pump moving," the killer said.

Cahill took the bait and increased the rate on his own machine. After nearly ten minutes, the top half of Cahill's Notre Dame sweatshirt was drenched. After a few more minutes, the killer upped the speed again. "Time for a strong finish."

Cahill didn't try to go faster, and in fact began to slow down. "Can't go like I used to," he huffed. "May have overdone it today."

"You are a bit red in the face, Father," the killer said, also slowing. "Why don't you sit down and put your head between your legs. Take some deep breaths. I'll get some water."

"Good idea." Cahill stopped the treadmill and went over to the nearby weight bench.

The killer followed, grabbing the gym bag and putting on latex gloves on the way. "How are you feeling?"

"Lightheaded," Cahill said from between his legs.

"That's to be expected. I've got a nice cold towel here."

"But I thought--"

"This is better. Lean over a bit more. That's it." The killer pressed Cahill's head down while rubbing his neck with an alcohol cloth, then plunged the syringe into his jugular vein on the front left side.

"What are you doing?" Cahill said, squirming.

"Killing you, Father. In a moment your heart rate should be around 150 or so. Then, with another dose of my tonic here, it should zoom way up. After that, I'm afraid it won't be so high. But you won't be in pain for long. And just think--you'll receive your salvation ahead of schedule."

Cahill slumped to the floor, gasping. The killer took a stethoscope from the gym bag and placed it on Cahill's chest. Over 160 and climbing. Hell, I might not need the second syringe.

The killer took the gym bag into the locker room and placed a folded piece of paper in Cahill's shirt pocket. A few minutes later, after changing, the killer returned to examine Cahill. Dead.

They'll think it was a heart attack, the killer thought, wiping down the treadmill, then did the same to the doorknob, closed the door, removed the sign and walked briskly down the hall. Then they'll find the message in Cahill's pocket and the quinidine in the blood. It would cause a major stir. It was time the cops started doing their job.

## MONDAY, JULY 12

Detective John Neumann was pouring his first coffee of the morning when Sam Witkin's call from Washington came in.

"Hey Sam, what's up?"

"I've got a firestorm down here, Johnny. Three killings in two weeks, all at Clara Barton Hospital."

Neumann made an immediate connection to their last conversation. "Lidocaine?"

"No, but I'm sure our guy knows about it." Sam described how Vargas, Jacobi and Cahill had died.

"Geez, he's a walking laboratory," Neumann said.

"And he might have known Tim Parnell."

"Talk to me."

"There was a blank page from Parnell's B&B guest book in the priest's pocket. You still have it around?"

"Think it's still in the evidence room somewhere."

"As far as we know, none of the victims had any connections to Philly, but they might have visited Parnell's place. Wasn't he killed around Easter?"

"Lemme see. Hold on. Here we go. April 4. Palm Sunday."

"Then Cahill was probably here doing his thing, but check this year's entries in the book for his name and the others. Last year, too, if it's in there."

"You got a lead?"

"A few. Your investigation ever go anyplace?"

"You know where."

"Gotcha. Johnny, did you run any DNA tests on the hairs you found in Parnell's place?"

"Yeah, we sent them and the prints to the Bureau, but it was a dry hole. Most of the prints were smudges anyway."

"Could you get me copies of the DNA readouts?"

"Sure," Neumann said. "I'll FedEx a set right down. You find something to match against?

"That's what we'll tell people. We'll ask everyone at the hospital who has access to the ORs or uses the fitness room to provide a DNA sample."

"That's gotta be a bunch of people."

"Try a ton," Sam said.

"Good luck. What if they don't cooperate? You don't have enough to get a warrant to force them, do you?"

"No, but that'll give us something to play with."

"Sure," Neumann said. "Keep me up to speed, Sam."

"Want your name in the paper next to mine?"

"Ask me after you make the arrest."

"Count on it. Thanks, Johnny. Have a good day."

"Mine'll be better than yours."

## TUESDAY, JULY 13

For close to four minutes Tom Carter's earnest good looks had been beamed into thousands of living rooms that evening. Now he stared gravely into the studio camera at the end of his special report.

"And so Washington is left with only questions. Is the death of Ramon Vargas connected to those of Dr. Stanley Jacobi and Father Brian Cahill or was it an isolated event? Will there be more victims? And what of Vivian Pershing? Was her fall an accident or attempted murder? All we know is that there's an fatal epidemic spreading at Clara Barton Hospital, and it's not a disease the police seem able to cure. News 4 will continue, right after this message."

Nick used the remote to mute the sound, then turned to Kathy sitting next to him on the bed. "What did you think of all that?"

"Could have been worse. The interviews with Bob Kramer and Vivian seemed fair."

"She sure made it clear she's not scared to volunteer at the hospital this week."

"And she never even hinted the police had her note. Sam ought to thank you."

"He's not Frank. If he were, he'd have agreed to be interviewed."

"This is just crazy. Who'd want to kill a priest?"

"Cahill and Jacobi worked on that report. Didn't paint a nice picture of Kramer's leadership."

"He's innocent," she said, poking him with her elbow. "Besides, it's too obvious. He must be smarter than that."

"Sam would say that's what he'd want you to think."

"Don't you say it. Which reminds me, how's Connie doing?"

"Amazing. She's totally behind Kramer now. So, my dear, if it's not him, who is it?"

"I'd pick Cynthia Ellis except she's playing a losing hand so far."

"Yeah, but I'd still love to talk to her. No shortage of motives in this case. And now we have to deal with Parnell."

"Will Sam release any information about him?" Kathy asked.

"I wouldn't. Just make people more nervous."

"I wonder what connection he has to all this," Kathy said watching Maggie pull her bulk onto the foot of the bed and start a bath.

"I've been thinking drugs. Frank said that's what got him in trouble in the first place, and drugs killed him and Father Cahill."

"But not Jacobi and Vargas," Kathy said.

"Poison's kind of a drug."

"Not really, and besides Vargas wasn't involved in hospital politics."

"Yeah, it always comes back to that." Nick reached down to pet Maggie who glared at the interruption. "Frank said Parnell was a brilliant detective. Told me about his trial back in the '80s. I don't remember it, do you?"

"Sorry, chum, I was busy raising the girls."

"Shoot, that's right. You were still with Steve. I can hardly remember a time without you."

"You had a life before me?"

"Wasn't as much fun," he said, caressing her arm.

"For me either."

"An Italian does make a difference."

"I know," she winked. "Anthony Bellino was my first."

"Bellino? You never mentioned him."

"Sure I did. Sixth grade teacher. Taught me all about the Seven Hills of Rome."

"He teach you anything else?"

"God, do you ever have a clean thought?"

"No," he kissed her shoulder. "Want to watch anymore of the news?"

"You have something in mind beside dinner?"

"Another geography lesson about Italy."

---

"I saw your interview with Tom Carter," Connie said into her bedroom phone.

"You're watching TV at work?" Kramer asked.

"Bartenders' rules. You were great."

"You're prejudiced."

"No, really," she said, fingering the ruby pendant which she had not taken off since he gave it to her. "Your point about patients being safe was important."

"Vivian said it better. She was a real trooper getting there for the taping. Carter would have interviewed her at home, but she insisted."

"He was really grim."

"That's his job. He's not paid for good news."

"The police getting anywhere?"

"Unclear. They've been pulling staff files and talking to fitness room fanatics. Cynthia's been coordinating most of it."

"So she's agreed to stay," Connie said.

"For now. I'm toying with keeping her permanently if I'm still here in six months."

"Are you serious?"

"Who better? But I doubt she'll want to. She really should be running a hospital."

"She's that good?"

"Very. I'm also wondering what to do about Laura. If Cynthia goes, she'd make a good chief of staff."

"Bob, she's a double crosser."

"Perhaps I can salvage the situation."

"And here I thought you were tough. My head says don't do it."

"You're not saying that just because she's pretty?"

"I'm not worried," Connie said.

"You sound cocky."

"I am. Can we have lunch Thursday?"

"Let's try. I have to go to Father Cahill's funeral in the morning. I can't wait to see you."

"That's the idea."

## WEDNESDAY, JULY 14

"This place is finally beginning to feel like home," Sam said, coming out of the bathroom after his shower that evening.

"Why's that?" Tawana was stretched out on floor doing leg exercises.

"I can turn off the hot water without looking for the faucet."

"Wonderful. Now if you can only make it to the john in the middle of the night without turning on the light."

"Does that bother you?"

"Only when I'm trying to sleep."

He sat on the edge of the bed. "I can get you eyeshades."

"I hate those things. They make me sweat."

"You're sweating now."

"I want to," she said, glancing up at him, "and you're not supposed to notice."

"When you're naked and doing those sexy things with your legs?"

"I'm getting fat."

"You're supposed to get fat."

"My mother actually lost weight carrying me."

"That can happen? Your belly doesn't grow?"

"Sure, but you can still lose weight." She stopped kicking. "It's complicated."

"Well, I'd rather you stick to tradition."

"Like when I married you, honky?" she smiled.

"You know what I mean."

"Sammy, I think the baby just moved."

He reached down and felt her stomach. "Where?"

"Here." She moved his hand higher. "There, you feel that?"

"No. Maybe it's upset about your exercising so hard."

"That wasn't hard," She felt her abdomen a few moments. "Anyway, I'm done for now. I'm going to take a bath."

"Must you?" he said. "I love sweaty women."

"I'll be right back and we'll play."

"Then you'll get all sweaty again."

She disappeared into the bathroom and he went down to the kitchen for a beer. He was on his way back up the stairs when he heard his cell phone ring. Hurrying into the bedroom, he grabbed it from the bedside table, recognizing the number.

"What's up, Frank?"

"Pringle at the Bureau just called me. They have a DNA match with our samples and the hair from Parnell's rug."

"Wow. Who?"

"Peter Thorpe."

"I'll be damned."

"Want to pick him up?" Frank asked.

"No, I don't think he's going anywhere, but I'll send a cruiser over to keep an eye on him. I'm more concerned he's destroyed evidence since he gave us his DNA."

"He raise a fuss about it?"

"Tawana said he didn't even quibble."

"We can go for a warrant in the morning," Frank said.

"Yeah, let's do that. I'll phone one of the Assistant U.S. Attorneys tonight. Give them a heads up so they can call their Maryland contacts first thing."

"Will you call Philly?"

"Yeah, I've got Johnny Neumann's home number. I'll see if we can take the first crack at Thorpe."

They talked a few more minutes before hanging up. Sam took his beer into the bathroom and briefed Tawana.

"What's your plan?" she asked, toweling off.

"If I can get Neumann to agree, I want you and Mike to visit

Thorpe at home tomorrow.  Question him and see if he'll submit to a search of his house."

"He might have surgery scheduled."

"There must be a duty nurse or someone we can call."

"I'll find out and phone Mike while you're calling the AUSA and Neumann."

"Good. And call the airlines and Amtrak to see if Thorpe traveled to Philly the weekend Parnell was killed. Greyhound too. Oh, and check the Marc train. He could have switched to Amtrak in Baltimore."

"What about hotels up there?"

"I wouldn't think Thorpe would stay over, but I'll ask Neumann to check. And he could find out if any taxi's had fares to Parnell's house." He turned, stopped. "And then we can play."

She put her arms around him. "Would you mind if I got on top?"

"It may be late. Think you can find me in the dark?"

"If you can find the john."

# TWENTY-ONE

## THURSDAY, JULY 15

Thorpe was reviewing patient files over a cup of coffee when Tawana and Mike Avery rang the front door bell of his Chevy Chase townhouse. At the window he saw a gray Lumina parked next to his BMW. Whose car is that? he wondered.

"Good morning, doctor," Tawana said when he opened the door. She was wearing a maternity dress for the first time.

"Oh, hello. Briggs, isn't it?"

"You have a good memory, and this is Detective Mike Avery. Do you have a few minutes?"

"Sure. Come on in. I just made coffee, if you'd like some."

"I'll have a cup," Avery said.

"How do you take it?" Thorpe said as they moved toward the living room.

"Black."

"Okay. Please have a seat."

Tawana chose the sofa, as Avery walked around the room, stopping to admire the black and white desert photographs that adorned one wall. "If Thorpe took these, he's good. Look like Ansel Adams."

"I didn't know you were into photography, Mike."

"Not me. A lady friend of mine."

"You're dating?"

"Shh. Yeah, but don't tell Larry."

"Why?"

"He'll rag me," Avery said, now examining the medical bag in the bookcase. "You know how he is. Anyway, it's only been a few weeks."

"Well, I think--."

"Please don't touch that, detective," Thorpe said, entering the room. "It belonged to my father."

"Sorry," Avery said.

"That's all right," Thorpe said, handing him a mug. "It's just that's it's very old."

"I understand. Those are wonderful photos. You take them?"

"My brother did. They're of the Saudi desert. He was in the Gulf in '91 just after the war."

"He a professional?" Avery asked, sipping the coffee.

"Could have been, but he was a surgeon like me. Died in an accident right after he took those."

"Gee, that's tough."

"Yes. Now what brings you here?" he asked, sitting in his chair.

"It's about your DNA, doctor," Tawana said.

"Don't tell me you need another sample," Thorpe smiled, leaning back.

"No, you did a good job," Avery said, taking the remaining chair. "We matched you."

"With what?" Thorpe asked pleasantly.

"Your hair," Tawana said. "Can you tell us where you were on April 4 of this year?"

"Detective Briggs, without checking my calendar, I can't even tell you where I was last Thursday."

"It was Palm Sunday, doctor."

"Well, I can assure you I wasn't in church."

"That's too bad," Avery said, taking out a notebook. "Someone might have seen you. Were you with anyone that day, doctor?"

"That's my business, detective. What makes it yours?"

"Timothy Parnell," Tawana said, looking for a reaction. "Who's he?"

"A retired D.C. policeman," Avery said. "Remember the name?"

"Should I? Was he a patient at Clara Barton?"

"No," Tawana said.

"Then what does he have to with me? And, please, stop playing which-detective-gets-to-ask-the-next-question. My neck's getting tired and I'm not impressed."

"Parnell was murdered on April 4." Tawana said.

Thorpe shook his head. "That was three months ago, detective. I thought you're investigating the deaths of Stan Jacobi and Father Cahill."

"Parnell died by injection of a drug."

Thorpe crossed his legs and smiled. "Administered by a surgeon no doubt."

"A strand of your hair was found at the murder scene," she said."

The smile left Thorpe's face.

"Now will you tell us where you were that day?"

"I really don't remember, but my guess is I was here reading the Sunday paper. I may have gone out to dinner with someone. I really will have to look at my calendar."

"Did you make any long distance or cell phone calls?"

"I probably called my mother. I usually do on Sundays."

"What time was that?" Avery asked.

"I don't know for sure. Around seven in the evening. Our time. She lives in Missouri. If I was out, I would have used my cell."

Tawana glanced at Avery who nodded. "Parnell was killed in Philadelphia," she said.

Thorpe relaxed. "Well, I certainly didn't spend Palm Sunday touring the Liberty Bell. But tell me, why are you concerned with a killing up there?"

"We've linked Parnell to the hospital."

"You're full of clues today, detective. How did you do that? More of my hair?"

"We can't say."

"You'd better if you try to tie me to this nonsense. I know the law."

"So you deny being in Philadelphia that day?" Avery asked.

"I haven't been there in years."

"You could have driven there and back in five or six hours."

"So could whoever killed this Parnell with my hair in his hand."

"Who might that be?" Tawana asked.

"That's your job to find out, isn't it?" Thorpe said, standing.

"Now, unless you have something more, I have work to do."

Avery got to his feet. "We'd like to take a look around if you don't mind. Your office and car too."

"Would you now. Then I suggest you get a search warrant."

Tawana grabbed her purse. "Thanks for your time, doctor. We'd appreciate you keeping our talk to yourself."

"No such luck, Ms. Briggs. I fully intend to inform your chief and Bob Kramer about your tactics. The hospital's one thing. Pestering people at home is sheer harassment. Now, you both know where the door is."

---

"So where is Peter?" Laura asked Cynthia who had summoned her.

"On his way in, and he's furious with your boss."

"Why?"

"Thinks he's too cozy with the cops. Peter's finally beginning to see the light. I told you this is Kramer's doing."

"Bob's no killer," Laura said.

"Somebody is. Why not him?"

"Why would he try to implicate Peter after appointing him acting chief?"

"Will you wake up? Peter had as much a motive to kill Jacobi as anyone. Kramer would frame me if he could. We've got to go on the offensive pronto."

"I'm working on the letter to his brother."

"That's not enough. You need to do another search of his office. Massive this time. If he's playing games with evidence, he may have more around."

"What do I look for?"

"Anything related to these killings and this dead cop. Check his files, desk, computer, lamps, wall plugs, under the carpet, the works. But be super careful. We don't want to tip him off."

"I'll need time for that. Saturday maybe. See if I can figure out his password. You know his birthday?"

"October 17th, 1965. Wait till late afternoon or evening. He's less likely to drop in."

"What should I do if I find something?"

"Leave it. Just tell me where and what it is. We'll get the info to the police."

"How?" Laura asked.

"Through your brunch buddy, Nick Mercante. I've got an idea that might work."

"And what will you be doing while I'm giving up my weekend?"

"Coming down with the flu so I can call in sick Monday. While Kramer's here, I'll be searching his mansion for evidence."

"He might have changed the alarm codes since your bedroom days."

Cynthia smiled. "I rechecked the manual during the St. Patrick's Day party. Some times it's better to have good old-fashioned keys and locks."

"Or be careful who you sleep with."

"I'll take that as a compliment."

---

When Kathy stopped for the light at MacArthur Boulevard that evening, she reached for her cell phone and dialed home.

"Where are you?" Nick asked.

"Right down the street. I left early, so kick the bimbo out of bed."

"She couldn't make it, but Cynthia Ellis called. Wants to meet with me. She never got back to me about Vivian's fall and then today, boom, there she is."

"Why'd she change her mind?"

"Says it about the investigation. Of course I said yes."

"What a surprise. The light's changing. I'm stopping at the drug store. We need anything?"

"We're covered. See you soon."

When she walked into the kitchen, she found Nick frowning into the phone. She busied herself greeting Patches as she listened to his conversation wind down.

"No, I won't tell Vivian or Connie. Thanks for the update. Have a good weekend."

"Tawana?" Kathy asked when he hung up.

"Yeah. Good news and bad news."

"Bad news is they don't want you meeting with Cynthia Ellis."

"I didn't even raise it." He gave her a brief hug. "You hungry?"

"Always."

"I've made a tomato salad and there's still some frozen fried chicken left from the party. I can zap it and tell you the good news."

"I'd love it."

As Nick put the leftovers in the microwave and Kathy washed up, he told her about Thorpe's DNA and the interview Tawana and Mike Avery had with him that morning.

"How about some wine?" he asked, carrying the chicken and salad into the cafe adjoining the kitchen.

"Wouldn't turn down a glass."

"Grab the opener," he said and pulled a bottle of Cabernet-Sauvignon from the rack next to the table.

"Here you go," she said. "So, did they get a warrant?"

"That's the bad news," he said, wrestling with the cork. "The AUSA wouldn't even phone the Maryland State's Attorney."

"You're joking."

"Wish I were." He poured the wine into their pair of pewter goblets. "Cheers," he said, handing her one.

"Cheers. But what happened? They have Thorpe's hair at Parnell's house."

"Wrong house. The AUSA said there's no factual connection between Thorpe's residence and Parnell's murder. Or with any other crime. Sam's furious. You know how much he loves lawyers."

"What more evidence do they need?"

"Something to convince the AUSA and a judge, I guess. They're so focused on Thorpe, I felt foolish mentioning a meeting with Ellis."

"Well, at least it's a plus for Connie," Kathy said, nibbling on a chicken wing. "But if Thorpe's guilty, why would he put a page from Parnell's guest book in Father Cahill's pocket?"

"Kathy, all these clues have to be diversions, some kind of mind game."

"But that piece of paper leads right to him."

"Only because of his DNA. He couldn't know he'd leave a strand of hair behind."

"Suppose the hair is another mind game and was planted by someone else?"

"That's what he claims, and that takes us right back to Kramer and--."

"Cynthia Ellis. You'd better be careful there, Nicky. Remember what I said about her."

He took a sip of wine. "I suppose I should tell Frank she's asked to meet with me."

Kathy smiled. "Afraid to call Tawana back in case Sam answers?"

"I'm not pushing my luck, if that's what you mean. You want that leg?"

"No, go ahead."

"So," he said, after taking a bite, "Thorpe's a real suspect, Prentice could be, Ellis is rearing her head and Kramer's riding high with the trustees."

"That's because he's innocent."

"He's something, anyway. And getting great press even after all these killings."

"And the Thomas kidnapping," she said.

"Apples and oranges. That never made the papers. Besides, it didn't succeed and no clue was left behind or has showed up since. "

"Nobody played up Vivian's accident at first either. Was that an apple or an orange?"

"A banana," Nick smiled. He was about to take another bite of the chicken leg, then put it down. "You know something? They could all be bananas."

"What?"

"Remember I told Sam the killer might have a complicated plan?"

"Yeah...Oh, I get it. This is all one big scheme."

"Parnell was killed early April, right?"

"If that was Palm Sunday."

"And Dr. Monroe was shot in April too."

"Come on, Nicky. That is apples and oranges. A murder in Philadelphia and a holdup in D.C.?"

"It happened in Clara Barton's parking lot."

"You're making too much of that."

"Am I? Why can't Monroe be the second murder? And maybe the Thomas baby isn't just a coincidence."

"Does that explain Ramon Vargas?"

"Yes, because then you don't need to connect him to Jacobi or Cahill. The hospital's the key."

"Boy, you're reaching. Why would anybody go to all that trouble?"

"To hide your real goal with a bunch of smoke."

"What's the real goal? Kramer keeping his job, Ellis getting it, Prentice wanting hers, or Thorpe becoming chief surgeon. You're right back where you started."

"But at least it all makes sense," Nick said.

"Not Parnell. Why go to Philadelphia to kill somebody and plant evidence? Why not simply drive across the bridge into Alexandria?"

"Parnell worked in this town. He could have some connection to Clara Barton."

"He moved away in the '80s and now he gets murdered for his trouble?"

"Maybe he knows something about the killer."

Kathy shook her head. "Unless I'm mistaken, the only people who go that far back are Jacobi and Cahill and they're both dead. Vargas, too, come to think of it."

"The killer had to want Parnell dead for some reason."

"Sounds like you're still sitting on square one," she grinned. "I don't blame you for not wanting to talk to Sam."

"Maybe I will."

"Suddenly you have courage?"

"He could use a laugh tonight."

## FRIDAY, JULY 16

"Mr. Mercante, right on time," Cynthia said, after opening her office door. "Somehow I knew you would be. Let's sit by the window, shall we?"

"Sure." Nick followed her leggy stride across the room.

"Forgive the mess," she said, gesturing to a cluttered conference table, "but the police keep asking me to pull files, and I'm behind putting them back."

"They tell me you've been very helpful," Nick said. He took a chair as Ellis sat on the sofa.

"Good, then you're still working with them," she said, crossing those legs, her pink skirt riding up her leg.

"We've shared some information."

"Perhaps you can tell them they're spinning their wheels. All they're accomplishing is disrupting the staff."

"It's a big hospital, Ms. Ellis and, so far as I know, Mr. Kramer hasn't complained."

"Why would he? He's kept his job. In fact, there's someone in his office from the Northwest Current interviewing him as we speak. Not bad for a murderer."

Nick hid his surprise. "If you really mean that, why are you still his chief of staff?"

"Because I'll get his job when he gets caught."

"By the police spinning their wheels?"

"Look, Kramer's leading them around by the nose. This DNA testing's just the latest example."

"Is it? You provided a sample, Miss Ellis."

"Of course," she winked. "Didn't even have to pee in a bottle."

Nick smiled. "I hear it's less intrusive than that."

"Just a little saliva, and I'm sure dear Mr. Kramer gave some, too."

He had, Nick knew. "How can you be certain?"

"Because it won't prove anything. His DNA's all over this hospital. So's mine."

"But the police found another person's DNA on one of the victims," Nick said, echoing Sam's justification for the testing.

"That's BS and you know it. What took them so long? Vargas and Jacobi have been dead over two weeks."

"Not Father Cahill."

She laughed. "Mr. Mercante, I know how the maintenance crew works around here. The fitness room's not cleaned as well as the public areas, and it's a DNA swamp to begin with. There's more hair, sweat and skin in that place than in a police lab."

"You're a wealth of information, Ms. Ellis. Why exactly did you call me?"

She extended an arm across the back of the sofa, accentuating her breasts in the process. "Because I can look in places the police can't. Not without a search warrant."

"What places?"

"Where it might do some good, and that doesn't mean Dr. Thorpe's house."

"Dr. Thorpe?"

"Let's not waste each other's time. I heard all about the interview with him yesterday. How convenient, finding his hair with some dead cop in Philadelphia."

"Have you ever dated Dr. Thorpe, Ms. Ellis?"

She didn't blink. "No. I was too busy screwing Bob Kramer. My mistake, but it paid off. I happen to know the alarm codes to his house, and I'll bet there's real evidence there."

"He gave you his codes?"

"A lady has her ways."

They smiled at each other, then Nick sat up straighter. "Look, Ms. Ellis, if you know where there's relevant evidence, you should tell the police."

"Except I'm not certain and I don't want my name associated with Kramer's downfall. The trustees will think I'm on a vendetta. I'd like to give anything I find to you."

"Me? But you can't avoid becoming involved, testifying and so on. "

"That depends on the kind of evidence, doesn't it? It's not like I'm a witness. Anyhow, any trial's way down the road. By then

I'll be CEO.  I just want you to keep my name out of it for now."

Nick remembered his promise to Connie if he suspected Kramer were guilty. If Ellis really could...then he shook his head. "No sale. I'd have to tell the police about you."

"But why? I'll tell you right away if I locate anything useful. Then you go to them and they can get a warrant based on that.  My name doesn't have to come up."

"I can't guarantee you that, Ms. Ellis. And I'm not sure the police would consider it a legal search. Plus any defense attorney will want your name."

She leaned forward. "I'm not concerned about legalities or lawyers right now. All I ask is you ask your police cronies."

"Let me think about it. Understand, I may have to give them your name."

"Could they agree not to divulge it publicly?"

"They have in some cases," he said, thinking of the deal they'd cut for Connie with Devane. "But here?" He shrugged.

She hesitated, then nodded. "All right.  How long will it take before you can let me know?"

"I'll call you tomorrow morning at the latest. Maybe tonight."

"Great. The police have my home number." Cynthia stood and he followed. "I look forward to hearing from you." She moved close to him, her breast grazing his arm. "I'll walk you out."

"No need."

"Indulge me."

## SATURDAY, JULY 17

Connie squared her body and waited for Bob's second serve. She was breathing rapidly and her legs felt heavy.  It had been a long time since she'd played tennis and it showed. She had managed to win only one game and this was set point. Bob smiled at her across the court, bounced the ball twice and tossed it in the air. The ball flew over the net toward her backhand. Damn, she thought, surprised. She lunged but was late.  Her return wobbled weakly out of bounds.

"I surrender," she yelled, trotting up to the net. "Give a girl a break."

"I'll do better than that," he said, reaching for her hand. "I'll make lunch and Bloody Marys while you take a shower."

"Don't rub it in," she said, kissing him. "You haven't even worked up a sweat."

"Then how about a rematch?" he said, as they walked hand in hand toward the house.

"Another time, thank you. I want to be able to walk tomorrow."

To her delight, he had called her yesterday to suggest an early tennis match. When he had picked her up this morning, he was as relaxed as she'd ever seen him. This was the first time they were spending an entire day and night together and she had packed an overnight bag with great anticipation. So far she wasn't disappointed.

Connie showered in the huge master bathroom, luxuriating in the plush appointments. She could get used to this kind of life, she smiled to herself, then shook her head. Get real, Vacarro. Sure, they were having fun now but this man can have any woman he wants. But he's dating me, she answered herself, touching her pendant. Put away the yellow flag and enjoy the day.

"You look terrific," he said a few minutes later when she joined him on the back veranda overlooking the pool and tennis court.

"You weren't so nice with a racket in your hand. My self-esteem's shattered."

"Not permanently, I trust. See if this helps you recover." He handed her a chilled glass. "Be careful, it's potent."

She took a swallow and nearly gagged. "My God, what did you put in this thing?"

"My secret ingredient. Green horseradish."

"If I served that downtown, they'd fire me."

"Like hell. They'd give you a raise and your tips would double. Have some of these eggs to wash it down."

She eyed them carefully. "You put horseradish in them?"

He laughed. "Just a wee bit of pepper, honest."

They bantered their way through lunch and finished the entire pan of eggs and home fries.

"I must say you're in a great mood," she said, watching him pour coffee from a silver carafe.

"It's being with you. Takes my mind off the hospital."

"That's the first time you've mentioned it all day."

"See? Actually, yesterday wasn't so bad. Felt almost normal."

"The police finally leave?" she asked.

"For the time being. Turns out only seven people refused to give their DNA."

"Anyone significant?"

"A security guard, three nurses, two doctors and the general counsel."

"The hospital's lawyer?"

"You know attorneys. Everything the police do is unconstitutional. Oh, and Tawana Briggs called me in the afternoon. They have a lead."

"Bob! Why didn't you tell me?"

"Wanted to surprise you over lunch."

"Did she say who?"

"No. I have an idea, but I'd rather not say. Anyway it is good news."

"It's wonderful. And speaking about getting back to normal, I've been talking to Vivian. She thinks you have to get rid of either Cynthia or Laura. Can't keep them both. They're too chummy and can only spell trouble for you."

"Suppose one of them doesn't want to leave?"

She reached across the table and touched his hand. "Life's full of hard choices, Mr. Kramer."

---

Cynthia had been waiting over an hour before her bedside phone finally rang. She looked at the incoming number and grabbed the receiver.

"About time," she said to Laura.

"Cynthia, I'm in Bob's office."

"I know. Any luck?"

"You won't believe it. I found directions to a Philadelphia address in his computer."

"I knew it! It has to be that cop's house. So you cracked his password?"

"Didn't have to. Not all the files are protected. He has one he's named Trips. Routes to places up and down the coast. Philadelphia was right there."

"Son of a gun. You find anything else?"

"No, but I still have the cabinets to go through."

"All right. Keep at it and call me if you turn up something more."

"I will," Laura said. "Do you want to call Peter with the news?"

"He's still at that conference in Baltimore."

"Oh, that's right. I'll call him tonight from home."

"Call me too. I want to know everything you have before I go to Kramer's house. Now I'm sure I'll find something. Then I'll call Mercante."

"You think you can trust him?"

"Who knows? But he's our best bet right now to nail Kramer."

"All right. Talk to you later."

Cynthia hung up and smiled at Thorpe next to her.

"What did she find?" he asked.

She told him.

Thorpe shook his head. "I'll never doubt you again."

She pressed her body against his. "Now, I want my reward."

# TWENTY-TWO

## SUNDAY, JULY 18

"Okay, Sam, see you in the morning." Frank closed his cell phone and watched Gail give their sons Chris and Mark one last hug, which they seemed to tolerate rather than enjoy. Then the boys ran off and joined their friends who were laughing and shoving at the end of the line waiting to board the bus for camp.

Gail waved at them and started slowly back toward where Frank leaned against his Mustang. She had promised the boys she wouldn't wait until the bus took off, but she glanced over her shoulder as she approached him. "The line's moving," she said.

"I can see. You're not supposed to be looking."

"Think they noticed?"

"You kidding? They don't know we exist."

They climbed into the car and sat there.

"We're supposed to go," he said.

"Let's."

He started the engine, backed up and drove slowly out of the lot, as Gail took one last look at the bus.

"I called Sam," he said, as they pulled into traffic.

"Any word?"

"Mike and Tawana have been through all the reports. Nothing suggests Monroe's death and the Thomas abduction are connected to the murders. No notes, no exotic weapon, nada."

"So Nick's idea doesn't fly."

"No, but nothing rules it out either. They all do involve the hospital."

"Conclusion?"

"None, other than Nick's scenario is the kind Parnell might have come up with. Gary Shapiro too. They both had this knack to put odd things together. Remember the Fitzpatrick murders?"

"How could I forget? You were on stakeout for a week during the worst snow of the year."

"Yeah, but Parnell had this feeling the daughter's story about the stolen jewelry was just too perfect and if we watched her long enough, she'd give it away."

"Homicide 101."

"You can say that now, but give Parnell credit. Kids weren't much into killing their parents back then."

"Maybe there wasn't as much child abuse as now."

"Gimme a break, Gail. Nowadays any discipline is called abuse. You've heard Chris and Mark accuse me of it when I dog them about their chores or homework."

"They really don't mean anything by it."

"How do you know? That's all they hear at school and on TV. I swear the world's going to hell."

"You're just missing them already."

"Aren't you?"

"Of course, but camp's only three weeks. We'll have most of August with them."

"Until school starts and we become irrelevant again."

"They have to grow up, Frank."

"It's too damn fast. Seems like they were just born."

"It'll be worse when they go off to college. That's true empty nest, but then I can go on a regular shift, so we'll have more time together. Are you ready for that?"

"Yeah, I can't wait to play you in Scrabble."

## TUESDAY, JULY 20

"It's Cynthia Ellis," Kathy said sleepily, handing Nick the phone. "At this hour and not even an apology."

"I told her never to call till you left for work."

Kathy stuck out her tongue and sank back on her pillow.

"Good morning, Ms. Ellis," Nick said. "You're up early."

"Been sitting in my office watching the clock since six. I left you a message last night."

"My wife and I got home very late. I was going to call you this--."

"Mr. Mercante, I was right. I have information about Kramer. Do you have a pencil and paper?"

"Can I call you back? I don't function very well without coffee."

"Very well, but please hurry.  You have the number?"

"Yes. Give me half an hour," he said and hung up before she could protest. "Talk about hot to trot."

"What she want?" Kathy murmured.

"I think maybe she found something."

"Bully for her. Could you find the coffee?"

About an hour later, Nick watched Kathy back the Camry out of the driveway and punched in Cynthia's number on the kitchen phone.

"Mr. Mercante, where have you been?"

"Waking my wife and walking my dog. You said you had information."

"Do I ever. Kramer has driving directions on his office computer to 121 Van Dyke Street in Philadelphia."

Nick squinted into the phone. "Should that mean something to me?"

"I don't care, but I'll bet the police are familiar with the address."

"This was on Mr. Kramer's computer?" he asked, reaching for a pencil.

"Yes, please pay attention. I also found some curious items in his bedroom."

"So you did go to his house."

"Do I have to spell it out for you?"

"Not to me, but the police will want to know."

"I'm sure. Anyway, I left everything exactly where it was. Very interesting."

"Interesting?"

"Vivian Pershing would think so. How about an owner's manual for a Rover electric wheelchair? Last time I looked, Kramer had two working legs."

No thanks to you, Nick thought. "Where was this manual?"

"In his bedside table. And there's more."

"I'm sure you'll tell me."

"Get this. There was a hypodermic syringe and ampules of lidocaine between the towels in the bottom of the bathroom cabinet."

Nick knew what had killed Parnell, but didn't let on. "What's lidocaine?"

"A cardiac drug. Doesn't that look suspicious? What's Kramer doing playing doctor?"

"I don't know."

"You need a blueprint? So when will you call the police? I'm sure they've had their coffee by now."

"As soon as we hang up," he said. "But remember, I can't promise to keep you out of this."

"Do what you can, Mr. Mercante, but just do it."

---

"Detectives Briggs and Avery to see you," Laura's voice said over the intercom.

"What now?" Kramer asked.

"They didn't say."

He glanced at his desk calendar. "Okay, I have nothing until the ethics committee meeting. Send them in."

"Thank you for seeing us, Mr. Kramer," Tawana said, coming through the door. "This is my colleague, Michael Avery."

"Mr. Kramer."

"Hello, I think I've seen you around. What can I do for you, Ms. Briggs?" he asked as she and Avery took desk chairs.

"We received a phone call this morning relevant to our investigation."

"I trust it was helpful."

"That's what we're trying to find out. Mr. Kramer, do you store travel directions on that computer?" Tawana asked, pointing at his monitor.

"Yes. I often drive up north."

"Like to Philadelphia?" Avery asked.

"No, I don't go there often. Tell me, does this concern what

Dr. Thorpe called me about last week?"

"Would you show us the file, Mr. Kramer?" Tawana asked.

He hesitated, then, "Sure." He fingered the computer mouse and clicked several times. "There," he said, pointing.

"Don't open it," Avery said, going to Kramer's side. "It was last modified on March 31. That sound right to you?"

"No, in fact. I don't recall making any changes since the fall when I drove up to my cottage."

"Where's that?" Tawana asked.

"Maine. Cape Elizabeth."

"You often make changes?" Avery asked.

"It depends. You know, they're always tearing up the highways. So I check the internet for problems before each trip."

"And then save the directions in the file?" Tawana asked.

"After I print them out."

"All right," Avery said. "Would you open it now?"

Kramer complied. "There. Potomac, Maryland, where I live, to Orchard Park, New York. My ex-wife's house."

"Show me the others."

"All right," Kramer said and scrolled down.

"Stop right there," Avery said and nodded at Tawana. "Van Dyke Street."

"I've never seen that entry," Kramer said. "Someone inserted it into this file."

"The same someone who placed things in your home?" Avery said.

"My home?"

"Yes, sir."

Kramer looked at Tawana. "Who called you this morning, Ms. Briggs?"

"Mr. Kramer, we're told you have certain items in your house that bear on our investigation."

"Such as?"

"A quantity of lidocaine."

"Lidocaine's involved in your investigation?"

"Mr. Kramer, we'd like permission to search your house and automobile."

"And this office," Avery said.

Kramer drummed his fingers on his desk. "I think this is where I call my lawyer, right?"

"You're not in custody, but that's your privilege, sir," Tawana said.

Kramer smiled. "Suppose I call my brother instead? Would you excuse me a moment? I promise not to run out the side door."

"Certainly," Tawana said, nodding to Avery. "We'll wait outside."

Laura looked up as Tawana and Avery returned to her office. They went over to the hallway door, talking quietly. Several minutes later, Kramer appeared, briefcase in hand.

"Laura, would you ask Cynthia to cover the ethics meeting? I'm leaving for the day. And lock both doors to my office. No one's to go in until further notice, including you."

"Yes, Mr. Kramer," Laura said.

He turned to Tawana. "Will that suffice for the moment?"

The detectives exchanged glances. "Okay," Avery said.

"Then, let's go, shall we? I'd like to see what other surprises you have for me."

---

Nick had just returned from walking Patches that evening when Connie called him from the Laughing Bull.

"Nick, what's happening with Bob?"

"He hasn't called you?"

"No. Vivian heard the police came to his office and he left with them."

"That's right. He let them search his house."

"Why?"

"The police received a tip." Nick told Connie about Cynthia's information without naming her.

"I can't believe this. Nick, I was in that bedroom last weekend, took showers in the bathroom."

"Did you happen to look in the bedside table or the towel cabinet?"

"No, but I could have. Why would Bob hide something where it was so easy to find?"

"Connie, I don't know what to say."

"Say something!"

"I already have."

A pause. "Why didn't you call me today?"

"I wanted to, but...I couldn't. Look, the police say they've found other things. Bob says none of it belongs to him, but he's clearly in trouble."

"But where is he? I can't reach him."

"He's gone to see an attorney."

"His brother?"

"Is he a criminal lawyer?"

"Criminal," she repeated softly. "Nick, what should I do?"

"Wait for him to get in touch."

"Like I waited for Vic?"

"Connie, I don't like this any more than you do. Bob claims he's being set up. You'll have to decide whether you believe him."

Another pause. "Will you call if you hear anything more?"

"If they...If I can. All right?"

"Yeah, sure. Such a deal."

---

When Kramer checked his answering machine that evening, there were several messages from Connie and one from Vivian. Connie's probably on her way home from work, he thought, tossing his jacket on the bed. He punched the call back button for Vivian's number.

"Hello, Bob."

"Vivian. I just got in."

"Laura Prentice told me what happened today. Have you talked to Connie? She's been calling me all day."

"How is she?"

"Climbing the walls."

"Yeah, well I've been either closeted with my lawyer or on the phone with my brother. I'll call her later. Vivian, I'm under the gun."

"I can imagine."

"I need to take a leave of absence. I can't devote time to the hospital right now."

"I see. Well, I'm sorry to hear that. How long do you think you'll need to...resolve this?"

"As long as it takes for the police to get it right. Meanwhile, Cynthia can hold down the fort."

"You're willing to let her?"

"It's up to you all. I have to protect myself. I don't know when or where the next arrow's coming from."

"It could come from Ellis. Why would I want her running the show?"

"Does it really matter what desk she's sitting at? Look, there's already been a leak. Laura told my brother she got a call from the *Post* asking if I'm a suspect. You and the other trustees shouldn't have to answer those questions."

"But that leaves you out on a limb."

"That's as good place as any to figure out my strategy. Can you make it in tomorrow afternoon to meet with Cynthia and me? I'll call her tonight."

"Certainly, but I'd like you to consider staying on at least as a consultant. Bury yourself in your office if you have to, just be there. I don't want Ellis to be seen as totally in charge."

"All right, I'll go in a few hours a day if you insist."

"I insist. You should be there when they catch the s.o.b."

## TWENTY-THREE

## WEDNESDAY, JULY 21

Just after six that morning the killer ducked into a lavatory on the second floor of Cabot Hall. Nodding to the person at the sink, the killer went into the last stall and waited until outer door opened and there was silence.

Immediately, the killer stood on the seat and used a nail file to loosen the screws of the vent high up on the wall. Reaching behind the grate, the killer removed the large envelope put there months before, then replaced the grate.

A few minutes later the killer stepped into the empty office in the main hospital and went quickly to the desk. Donning latex gloves, the killer emptied the contents of the envelope into the center drawer, arranged two of the items, returned the rest to the envelope, closed the drawer and left.

---

It was past ten when Frank entered Sam's office and found the detectives huddled around the conference table. "Sorry I'm late, but the Chief wanted to talk old times."

"Always does before vacation," Sam said.

"You've noticed. Okay, what do we have?" he asked, squeezing into a chair.

"A large inventory and a very cranky lawyer," Sam answered.

"His or ours?" Frank grunted.

"His. Linda Barringer."

Frank nodded. "Nothing but the best. Give me a run down."

"Kramer's office is clean except for the directions to Philadelphia," Tawana said. "We found the wheelchair manual under some papers in a bedside table and the syringe and lidocaine in plastic envelopes between towels in a bathroom cabinet."

"There were also metal strips in a tool bench drawer in the garage," Mike Avery said. "Looks like the same type as the one screwed under the table where Jacobi cut his arm."

"And there was a stun gun in a tool box," Larry Foster said. "The report in the Thomas abduction suggests one could have been used on the nurse."

Frank glanced at Sam. "Could be Nick was right."

Sam shrugged. "He seems smarter today."

"Any sign of Spanish Fly or that frog poison?" Frank asked.

"Negative," Avery said, "but you should see that garage. Sinks, machine tools, electronics, ovens, name it. You could build anything in there. Hardly enough room for the cars."

"Anything else?"

"Yes," Tawana said. "A parking stub in the glove compartment of Kramer's Chrysler. From a garage in Philly."

"Stub have a date?" Frank asked.

"April 4. Day Parnell was killed. 11:37 a.m. in, 1:19 p.m. out."

"How nice. Prints on any of the stuff?"

"No, sir," Tawana said.

"You get Kramer's?"

"Gave us a full set before the search."

Frank rubbed his jaw. "Okay. What's his story?"

"Not talking since he called Barringer," Sam said. "Before that, he swore he never saw any of what we found."

"So it was all put there by someone else, like Thorpe said about his hair."

"Yup," Sam said.

"What does Barringer say?"

"Same script. Kramer hosts two big parties a year. Claims anybody could go to his bedroom and steal the alarm codes to get into the house. And she wants to know if Cynthia Ellis tipped us off."

"We'll have to tell her if we push on this. Why'd she single out Ellis?"

"Ellis had regular access to the bedroom when she was dating Kramer."

"You speak to her?" Frank asked.

"This morning," Tawana said. "She admitted that's where she found the codes and how she got into the house. But swears she didn't go near the garage, only the bedroom."

"Hell," Frank said, "she could have planted everything. You believe her?"

"Wouldn't turn my back on her," Avery said, "but she was convincing. Willing to take a polygraph."

"Who isn't these days?" Frank grumbled. "Do we know if Kramer throws big parties?"

"Yes, sir," Tawana said. "Ellis confirmed that. There were over 100 people from the hospital staff there for a St. Patrick's Day party in March."

"Yeah, a leprechaun stole the alarm codes and car keys," Avery snickered, "then sneaked back three weeks later to plant the parking stub in the glove compartment."

"A guest could have done that," Tawana said. "Maybe the car keys were on his dresser. Someone could have made an impression at the party and had a key made at a hardware store. It's tricky, but it can be done."

"Could even have made the impression at the hospital if Kramer carries the keys in his jacket," Foster said, wiping his glasses. "Or you can copy the vehicle ID number through the windshield and get a dealer to make a duplicate key."

"That won't work on some newer cars," Avery said. "The keys have microchips. You have to get the car to the dealer to program the new key to the ignition."

"Is that right?" Frank asked.

"Yeah. Dorsey over at robbery told me. Otherwise, the key will only open the doors. Won't start the engine."

"Don't need the engine for the glove compartment," Sam said. "All right, guys, what's your take?"

"Kramer's our man," Avery said. "He plants Thorpe's hair in Philadelphia, sticks Pershing's note next to the iodine and the page from Parnell's guest book in Cahill's pocket."

"How does he get Thorpe's hair?" Tawana asked.

"Easy. From the back of a chair, or a paper towel in the men's room. Or like Larry said about the keys, from Thorpe's jacket."

"Motive?" asked Foster.

"He was afraid Jacobi would get his job. He's the real target. The rest is misdirection. Kramer knows he's in trouble, visits Parnell, comes up with a plan, does the victims, then offers to quit for the good of the hospital. My hero."

"Where would he have heard of Parnell?" Tawana asked.

"Who knows?" Avery said. "From an old timer around the hospital. Vargas maybe. Or he's a closet cop and likes police history. If I wanted a guru, I'd pick Parnell too."

Tawana shook her head. "What am I missing? Why would Kramer commit murder to keep a job he doesn't need? He got bounced from that hospital in New York but didn't kill anyone."

"And it's been bugging him ever since," Avery said. "He doesn't want it to happen again. The evidence points to him."

"Mike, the parking stub bothers me," Foster said. "Why would Kramer save it? Even if he tossed it in the glove compartment, why wipe off his prints?"

"Wake up, Larry, he could have been wearing driving gloves."

"But if he's guilty," Tawana said, "why keep evidence at home and invite us in to find it?"

"You're forgetting Ellis," Avery said. "Kramer couldn't know she had the alarm codes. But when he watches us find the driving directions and hears we have a tip about his house, he decides to play innocent victim instead of hardball. Then he hires the best attorney in town. He's smart as hell."

"But Thorpe or Ellis could be guilty," Foster said. "They're both smart and have motives to get rid of Jacobi."

"Fine," Avery said, "then I'll ask you Tawana's question. Why would Thorpe leave a hair behind and point a finger at himself?"

"Maybe he didn't," Foster said. "Maybe the hair just fell out."

"And we happened to get lucky," Avery smiled.

"Right," Foster said.

"Except Ellis tipped us, not Thorpe."

"Maybe they're a team," Tawana said.

"Then why wait so long to knock off Jacobi?" Avery said. "If Ellis wanted to be CEO that bad, she'd have offed Jacobi and set up Kramer before the trustees' meeting. The lady's is running awfully late."

"I don't have an answer," she said. "All three seem plausible. And we're leaving out Laura Prentice."

"Forget her," Avery said. "I don't buy the romance angle with Jacobi. She only started going to his pad in June. Three week's a pretty short time to get all torqued off because he won't play house."

"But she could be working with Ellis," Tawana said. "They both move up if Kramer's out and Jacobi's dead."

"Right," Foster said. "And Vacarro told Mercante they might be a couple."

"Ellis must have quite a social life," Avery laughed.

Tawana rolled her eyes. "Mike, do you know anything about women? I'm not saying Nick's right, but he could be."

"And I still say Ellis should buy a watch. I'm telling you Kramer's the guy."

"You'd take that to the lawyers?" Frank asked.

"Say the word, Captain," Avery nodded.

Frank smiled. "Sam?"

"I'm with Mike, but there's a bit too much reasonable doubt for a jury, especially with Barringer on the other side. We haven't nailed him yet."

"I agree, but let's tell the AUSA where we are. Meanwhile, we keep sniffing and watching. See if Ellis will let us search her house, and let's put her and Kramer under surveillance. Thorpe and Prentice, too. All of a sudden I'm getting itchy."

---

Shortly after two that afternoon, Laura looked up from her desk to see Cynthia emerge from Kramer's office with a broad smile on her face.

"Well?" Laura asked.

"Show time, sweetie," Cynthia said. "You're looking at the

acting CEO come Monday."

"It's done?"

"Just about. The Czarina still needs to canvass the trustees, but that's a formality. She spoke to Woodworth while I was in there. Naturally, I agreed to the deal."

"Congratulations."

"You may kiss my ring, among other things, but first, I propose a celebratory libation. Come sneak away for a few minutes."

Laura glanced toward Kramer's door. "How long will Pershing be in there?"

"Who knows? They're still huddling. Why? You need a hall pass?"

"Let's go," Laura said, standing.

They moved into the corridor and turned toward Cynthia's office.

"Does this mean you'll be permanent CEO?" Laura asked.

"It should. As soon as Bob resigns or they put him in the slammer, whichever comes first. Would you believe the turkey's going to hang around as a consultant? That's Pershing's idea. No matter. It won't be long."

"We should call Peter," Laura said as they reached Ellis's door.

"I told him I would. He's at his office." Cynthia walked over to a small credenza. "I have sherry and Scotch."

"Dewars for me," Laura said, following her.

"You've been peeking."

"You're just predictable."

Cynthia half-filled two paper cups. "Here's to me."

They each took a sip.

"So," Cynthia smiled, "you ready to become acting chief of staff?"

"You can do that?"

"They'll have to stop me. You're it on Monday. You can start by reading those personnel evaluations on my desk this weekend."

"Wow. Sure."

"We'll worry about a new office for you down the road."

"You're not taking Bob's?"

"Not till he leaves, but I'll set someone up in the small conference room to handle calls. I know a clerk in Human Resources who'd love to work over here."

Cynthia moved to the sofa and picked up the phone on the side table. "I'm calling Peter. Get on the other phone. I don't want to use the speaker."

"Okay." Laura went to the desk and picked up the receiver.

After two rings, a pleasant voice answered. "Dr. Thorpe's office."

"Anita, it's Cynthia Ellis and Laura Prentice from Clara Barton. Is Peter free?"

"He's in with a patient. Is this urgent?"

Cynthia hesitated. "No, just ask him to call me when he's through."

"I'll do that, Ms. Ellis."

"Thanks." She hung up and took another sip of Scotch. "Let's work on a memo to the staff."

"Now? I thought this wasn't happening till Monday."

"I want it ready to go as soon as the trustees vote. And I want to party this weekend if you're free."

Laura smiled. "You just gave me work to do. Do I get a raise?"

"Depends if you do a good job," Cynthia winked. "Grab a legal pad from the desk and come over here."

"All right, but I can't stay too much longer."

"Don't worry about the lame duck, for God's sake."

"Cynthia, what's this?" Laura was staring into the drawer.

"What's what?"

"Come here."

Cynthia went to Laura's side. Dr. Edward Monroe's ID bracelet rested on top of what appeared to be a printout of driving directions.

"That double-crossing son of a bitch," Ellis swore. "No, don't touch anything," she said, pulling back Laura's arm. She picked up the phone.

"You calling the police?"

"Who else?"

---

Thorpe was driving home when Cynthia reached him on his cell phone.

"I got your machine when I called you back," he said. "Where were you?"

"Probably walking to the police to their car."

"The police are back? What's going on?"

Cynthia told him about Laura's discovery.

"You sure it was Monroe's bracelet?" Thorpe asked, turning onto Massachusetts Avenue.

"I can read, Peter."

"How do you suppose it got there?"

"How do you think? Kramer figured out I tipped the police. He plays nice with me in front of Pershing, then sandbags me behind my back."

"So you had the meeting with him and Pershing?"

"Right on schedule." Cynthia told him about becoming acting CEO and making Laura acting chief of staff.

Thorpe stopped for a light. "Was Laura there when you talked to the police?"

"Of course."

"Who'd they send?"

"The Briggs woman and that muscle-bound guy. They listened, took the bracelet and the printout, snooped around, then left. They weren't there that long."

"You're right," Thorpe said. "Kramer must be getting desperate. The police are bound to see it."

"I think they have. Briggs told me not to mention anything to him. Glad they did, I would have probably slugged him."

"Ouch," he smiled into the phone. "Sounds like you handled everything just right." The light changed and he moved forward.

"Peter, I want to celebrate this weekend. The three of us."

"Why not?" he said. "Dinner at Lardiere's Saturday. On me."

"You'd better make a reservation."

"No problem. I'll get any table I want. I've spent enough over there."

"Will I get to see you alone?"

"Let me work on that."

"Work hard. Call me later."

"Sure."

He ended the call. He should call Laura. How to play it? Can't keep juggling both these women much longer. It's time to fish or cut bait . But which one?

---

Nick closed his case folder and leaned back in his chair on the enclosed porch, gazing out at Kathy's flowerbeds. The evidence against Kramer was very damaging. Cynthia Ellis might not have seen it happen, but she'd pointed a finger directly at Kramer toppling Vivian's wheelchair.

He stood and stretched. Hell, Ellis could have done it herself. Or Thorpe or Laura Prentice. Or someone else. Vivian's the only witness. If only she could remember more about her fall. Yeah, and if only there was a wonder drug for concussions that screw up your memory.

Time for lunch, he thought. He had reached the kitchen when he stopped. Wait a second. He hurried back to the study where he looked up a phone number in his Rolodex. The receptionist answered on the second ring.

"Dr. Sawyer's office."

"Hilda, it's Nick Mercante. Is Erica free?"

"Just a minute, Mr. Mercante."

He reached for a pad, picturing in his mind's eye the attractive psychotherapist who'd been so helpful in the past.

"Hello, Nick," Sawyer said, coming on the line. "Somebody die? This can't be a social call."

"Foiled again," he smiled. "Do you have a few minutes?"

"I get paid by the hour. Can you afford me?"

"No."

"Didn't think so. What's on your mind?"

He told her about the case, some of which she was familiar with from news coverage.

"Well," she said, "at least none of my patients is involved this time. So why are you calling?"

"You're an expert with hypnosis and amnesia. Can you hypnotize Vivian Pershing to learn more about how she was shoved off her wheelchair?"

"Slow down, Nick. You're assuming she has some form of amnesia."

"Don't you suffer memory loss from a concussion?"

"Not always. Pershing may already remember everything she experienced. From what you've said, she has a pretty clear picture of what happened."

"But could she remember additional details?"

"I have no idea without examining her. Has she avoided going back to the hospital or talking about the incident?"

"Just the opposite," Nick said.

"Is she exhibiting any anxiety about the fall? Any flashbacks or nightmares?"

"Not that I know of."

"Well, all that would seem to rule out post-traumatic stress disorder."

"Does that include amnesia?" he asked.

"At times. People often avoid reminders of the original trauma. For example, they won't go swimming if they've witnessed a drowning or almost drowned themselves. This aversion can present as amnesia."

"So if Vivian had this, she wouldn't return to the hospital."

"Possibly not. The disorder can be particularly acute if the person revisits the site of the event or is exposed to a similar situation. On the other hand, it can occur without warning."

"Can you treat it with hypnosis?" Nick asked.

"Psychotherapy's the real answer because of the patient's anxiety, but hypnosis and/or drugs can be useful adjuncts in some cases."

"Would the killer be aware of all this?"

A pause. "There's a good chance. It's well-known in the

literature and from what you've said, your suspects are all medically trained or have been close to those who are."

"Erica, you've been terrific as always. May I call you again if I have more questions?"

"Sure, but next time it'll cost you lunch."

## THURSDAY, JULY 22

"It feels like I haven't seen you for weeks," Connie said as she and Kramer placed their lunch trays on a rear table in the hospital cafeteria. "Was it only last Saturday?"

"We left my house Sunday morning, remember? I guess the overnight didn't make an impression."

"Too much of one. I might become addicted."

"See that you do," he said, openly patting her hand. "You're what I need right now."

"That why you're spending so much time with Linda Barringer?"

He pointed his soupspoon toward the crowded room. "But I reserved this quality time for you."

"It's Thursday, so it must be Connie," she smiled, cutting into her meat loaf.

"Oh yeah? Well, starting Monday, I'll have lots of time on my hands. We can have lunch any day you're free."

"I'd rather you keep your job."

"I hope to be back soon, so you better get me while you can."

"Is Barringer really that good?"

"That's the word," he nodded, grabbing his hamburger. "She seems very smart."

"Why'd you pick her?"

"She's a classmate of my brother Fred. And here's a coincidence. She was defense counsel in another case your friend Mercante was involved with. The church killings."

"You're lucky she had time."

"She loves high profile litigation. Anyway, I'm comfortable with her even though she chewed Fred and me out for letting the police search the house without forcing them to get a warrant."

"Why did you?"

"I had nothing to hide. Was that a mistake? I don't know. If I had come across that hypodermic, I'd have called the police myself."

"And you think Cynthia Ellis sneaked all those things into your house and called the police?"

"She had a golden opportunity, but lots of people could have snooped around upstairs to find those codes."

"Ah yes, all those lovely ladies next to your bedside table."

"Not by invitation. Only you and Cynthia since the new alarm system was installed."

"Should I believe that?"

He squeezed her hand. "I'd take a lie detector test, but Barringer won't let me."

His cell phone rang. "Hold on," he said and reached inside his jacket, checking the display. "Linda, hi. Just talking about you. No, I haven't heard from them." He frowned. "I have no idea, I swear. Of course. All right. Sure. Thanks."

"What is it?"

"Cynthia called the police yesterday. Said she found a printout of those driving directions in her desk along with Ed Monroe's ID bracelet."

"Dr. Monroe? My God! But, wait, that's good news, isn't it?"

"Except my fingerprints are on the paper."

---

Kathy leaned over and kissed Nick's forehead. His eyes flickered open.

"Hi," he said. "Trick or treat?"

"Trick. I'll give you a treat later."

"What time is it?"

"After seven."

"Damn," he said, sitting up. "I must have dozed off. I want to call Connie and Vivian. Hand me the phone."

"Something going on?"

"Plenty. I called you three times."

"I saw, but Dex held one of his meetings. You know how he gets before a launch. What have I missed?"

"Everything." He told her about the items discovered in Cynthia Ellis's desk.

"And they found Kramer's fingerprints?"

"Yeah," he said. "They figure he felt trapped and wanted to divert attention from himself onto Ellis."

"I hate to say it, but it makes sense."

"Not to me. There hasn't been one fingerprint in this case. Now suddenly his show up. And here's Ellis finding evidence again."

"Bob could have gotten careless."

"All of a sudden? And where did he come up with the bracelet? They've searched his office, house and cars and he hasn't gone near his safe deposit box since then. They've been watching him."

"Nicky, they've watched Ellis too."

"Haven't been in her house. And if she's guilty, it's the perfect way to put the last nail in Kramer's coffin."

"You've got Ellis on the brain."

"Yes, and why not?"

"So what happens now?

"They may arrest Bob any minute. I just hope they haven't already."

"Poor Connie. Does she know?"

"I suppose," Nick said. "I didn't call her at work because I need a good chunk of her time to run an idea by her. Vivian, too."

"Care to let me in on it?"

"You'd already know if you'd take my calls."

"I'm here now."

"I called Erica Sawyer again today."

"Why do you keep bothering her? She's already said Vivian may not have amnesia."

"We don't know for sure. And I've come up with an idea to catch the killer. Erica thinks it might work. Listen to this."

She did. "Clever," she said when he was done.

"It's inspired."

"Connie and Vivian may not go along. It could bring Bob down for good."

"You all think he's innocent. So let's see. Do you have to go in tomorrow for the launch?"

"I should."

"Can you skip this one?"

"If Elaine can square it with Dex."

"She's good at that. How about Monday?"

"I may have to say pretty please," Kathy said.

"And you're good at that. I'd like you to help."

"How?"

"First hand me the phone."

# TWENTY-FOUR

## FRIDAY, JULY 23

To accommodate Vivian, the detectives had agreed to come to her apartment where she and Nick outlined the plan while Kathy and Connie listened. After some lively, then heated, discussion and a few barbs between Nick and Sam, Frank held up his hand.

"All right, hold it," he said from his armchair. "We're not here to score debating points. Let's step back and review." He turned to Vivian who had parked the Rover next to his chair. "Ms. Pershing, you're confident Dr. Patterson will agree to this?"

"Captain, he's been after me to check in for an updated MRI. If this is what it takes, he'll be delighted."

"But wouldn't he rush you in if you really had bumped your head again?"

"He'd wait till Monday if I insist. After all, in theory he'd have examined me."

"And he'd even confirm you had a flashback of your fall?" Sam asked from his perch on the corner of the sofa.

"Once he hears the plan. Erica Sawyer's name carries a great deal of weight in this town."

"Why should he lie for you?" asked Mike Avery, who stood next to the sliding glass door that led to the balcony.

"Because he's been my friend as well as my doctor for over 20 years."

"What about hospital procedures?" Frank asked.

"We should be fine. Dr. Patterson signs the orders for the MRI and arranges for me to stay over to see Dr. Sawyer Tuesday morning. That's it."

"Won't Kramer and Ellis know something's up?" Sam asked. "Or Thorpe or Prentice?"

"Not even if they read my chart. They'll know nothing more than what Dr. Patterson wants them to. And whatever you convince Tom Carter to say on television. I leave that to you."

"What about other hospital personnel?" Tawana asked, taking notes at the dining table where she sat with Nick and Larry Foster.

Vivian smiled. "Accidents at home are fairly routine with people my age. And there won't be anything out of the ordinary until late Monday afternoon. By then Kathy takes over."

Avery looked at Frank. "With all due respect, Captain, I say we arrest Kramer right now."

"You have nothing to lose by waiting," Nick said. "And if Kramer's the one who falls for this, you'll have a stronger case."

"What if Kramer or whoever doesn't bite?" Foster asked.

"Then do what you have to do."

Frank looked across to where Connie was seated on the sofa next to Kathy. "Ms. Vacarro, we appreciate you advising us you're seeing Mr. Kramer. Are you certain you'll be able to keep this from him?"

"I'm not entirely comfortable with the notion, Captain, but I want to find the real killer. And I owe Clara Barton this one."

"Kathy?" Frank asked.

"I have the easy job, assuming you make sure I'm not killed."

"Sam?"

"I can live with it but not for long. The AUSA's ready to move against Kramer. I don't want to delay so she'll change her mind."

"What about that, Nick?" Frank asked.

"If you get Tom Carter to air the story, it'll be all over the hospital before Vivian's admitted on Monday. If I'm right, the killer has to act that evening. He can't risk having Vivian see Erica Sawyer."

"All right, enough for now," Frank said, standing. "I'll let you know. Thank you for inviting us, Ms. Pershing. We can make our way out."

"Thanks for coming, Captain. Have a good day."

The detectives left and didn't talk about the meeting until they piled into the Lumina Tawana had driven over.

Sam turned to Frank who was in the back seat. "We can't pull this off without Carter, but if we issue any kind of statement, the killer will know it's a trap."

"Why don't we ask Carter to fudge something?" Foster said. "He's cooperated with us before."

Frank shook his head. "He has too much integrity to lie on camera even if I asked him to."

"What about the other networks?" Foster said. "Fox walks close to the edge."

"No," Frank said. "NBC's got a larger audience and Carter's already interviewed Pershing. He's perfect for this."

"Captain," Tawana said, "why don't we have one of our PR guys leak a little bait, then let Carter run with it."

"He might if it were juicy and sounded legit. Any ideas?"

"Suppose we say a friend of Vivian called us about her hitting her head and having a flashback?"

"Who? Mercante?" Sam asked.

"No, Connie. She knows us."

"It's asking a lot of her," Frank said. "You think she'd let us do it?"

"If Pershing backs us up. I can ask Nick to work on it. We can also say Connie told us Dr. Patterson is scheduling her for an MRI. Technically, that's true so we wouldn't be leaking a lie to Carter."

"That could work," Foster said. "But we'd have to make sure Pershing and the doc get their story straight if Carter contacts them."

"From what I heard today, that shouldn't be a problem," Sam said. "Patterson wouldn't reveal much about Pershing's condition anyway."

Frank nodded. "Carter will call me to corroborate, and when he does, I'll neither confirm nor deny. God, he'll be ticked off when he finds out."

"By then he'll have made it his story," Sam said. "You can buy him a beer and tell him how you protected his damn integrity."

"I like it," Frank said, rubbing his hands together. "Wait, doesn't Pershing have a housekeeper?"

"Lydia Montez," Tawana said.

"Better have her clued in case she picks up the phone if Carter calls. In fact, we should pretend Pershing's condition won't let her take any calls."

"There's a language problem, Captain," Tawana said. "I recall the housekeeper's English isn't so hot."

"Then let's have Vacarro get on the phone," Sam said. "That'll close the loop to the leak."

"Good idea," Frank said, then nudged Avery next to him. "You still unhappy, Mike?

"Yeah, but I'll survive as long as we get to arrest Kramer."

Sam winked. "I'll let you do it personally on Monday."

## SATURDAY, JULY 24

Kramer stood in front of his bedroom mirror that afternoon, adjusting the lapels on his light blue blazer. Satisfied, he pocketed his keys and turned toward the door when the bedside phone rang. He saw it was Connie.

"Hi, Red, I was just leaving."

"Glad I caught you," Connie said. "Vivian's housekeeper Lydia just called me. Vivian's had an accident."

"What happened?"

"Some kind of seizure in her garage on the way to do an errand. Hit her head. Made it back upstairs, though."

"She call Dr. Patterson?"

"Lydia did. He's on his way over. Lydia asked if she should call the police."

"Why the police?" Kramer asked, rubbing his jaw.

Connie looked at the notes in her lap. "Vivian mumbled something about Vivian having a flashback of her fall from the wheelchair."

"A flashback?"

"I'm not sure I understood Lydia clearly. I told her not to call the police until the doctor sees her."

"Good thinking."

"Bob, Lydia said Vivian wants me to come over right away."

"Oh? What did you tell her?"

"That I'd call her back. I wanted to talk to you first because of our date."

Kramer hesitated. "Well, of course I want to see you, but I think you should go over there first. I'll cancel our reservation. You want to try for a late dinner?"

"Let me see what's happening. Do you mind terribly?"

"Yeah, but I'll get over it."

"I'll miss you. I'll try to call later, but it depends."

"Let me know what's going on. And give Vivian my best, okay?"

"I will. Bye." Connie tossed her notes aside and dialed Vivian's number. She picked up on the first ring.

"How did it go?"

"Perfectly and I feel like a total fraud."

"Connie, he wants to catch the killer too. Down the road, he'll thank you. I'm sure of it."

"I'm don't know, Vivian. He gave me my pendant when I doubted him. I wouldn't blame him now if he asked for it back."

"Listen, I'll take some of the flak with you. You'd better call Nick to start the PR machine before you come over."

"I will. I've already packed a bag."

"Good. I'll bet Tom Carter will call here before five. I haven't had this much fun on a Saturday in years."

---

Cynthia's dinner celebration with Laura and Thorpe had begun in Lardiere's lounge where they had drinks and watched Tom Carter's special report on Vivian Pershing. Now, back at her house, Cynthia snapped off the TV half way through the ten o'clock Fox news.

"Nothing about Pershing," she said, turning to Laura and Thorpe seated on her sofa. "Glad we stayed for dessert."

"Maybe Carter will have an update at eleven," Thorpe said.

"I doubt it. Too late in the day."

"Patterson's smart having Pershing in for an MRI," Laura said.

Thorpe nodded. "Absolutely. Never know about a blow to the head."

"If she really had one," Cynthia said. "This could be a ploy the Czarina cooked up to take the heat off Kramer."

"The paranoia continues," Thorpe smiled.

"Screw you, doctor," Cynthia snapped.

"Cynthia has a point, Peter. It does seem a long time from the accident to have a flashback now."

"Not at all," he said, shaking his head.

"The hell with it," Cynthia said, standing. "I for one am not done celebrating.  Who'd like a night cap?"

"I pass, and so should you," Laura said. "You've been guzzling all night."

"I'll take a small brandy," Thorpe said.

"Laura, you're becoming a baby," Cynthia said, going to her credenza.

"I have to drive."

"So? I'm reviewing files all day tomorrow."

"CEO's never sleep."

"Ain't it the truth, and I intend to hit the ground running Monday without consulting Mr. Kramer."

"I still can't figure why Pershing wants him to hang around," Thorpe said.

Cynthia handed him a brandy snifter. "Can't admit her fair-haired boy's guilty."

"She'll have to when the police arrest him," he said.

"They should have already," she responded, returning to her chair. "They have enough evidence."

"Maybe they're confused," Laura said. "After all, they've got Peter's hair in Philadelphia and Dr. Monroe's bracelet in your desk."

"But they have to blind not to see its Kramer's doing."

"For once you're right," Thorpe said. "With the stuff you found in his house, I think he's had it. It's just a matter of time."

"Amen. And to think, I once slept with a murderer."

"We all have to start somewhere," Thorpe smiled.

"Very funny," Cynthia said and gulped her brandy. "Come on Laura, join the party."

"Not tonight," Laura said, standing and slinging her purse over her shoulder. "The acting chief of staff needs her beauty sleep. I may have to fire someone on Monday. Walk me to my car, Peter?"

"I'm still working on this," he said, raising his glass.

"My loss," she said, "and thanks again for dinner." She went over to Cynthia, bent and embraced her. "Go easy on that stuff. Wouldn't do for the CEO to show up hung over."

"Don't worry, my dear, you can't fire me."

"Not yet. 'Night, guys," she waved and headed for the front door.

Cynthia waited till she heard the door close. "I'm glad you're not going after her."

Thorpe looked at her over the rim of his glass. "It's over, Cynthia."

"It's about time," she smiled and put down her glass. She came toward him. "Have you told her?"

He shook his head and watched her approach. She framed his face with her hands and kissed him. "When will you?"

He removed her hands. "I said it's over."

She recoiled. "What are you saying?"

"You need it in writing? We're finished."

"What do you mean? We're a team."

"And a good one. Let's take our championship rings and leave it there."

"Leave it? After a year, all my planning?"

"We planned it together, remember?"

She put her hands on her hips. "I dumped Kramer for you."

"Bull. He was blocking you. That's why you came to me."

"I could have gone to Jacobi."

"Like hell," he said. "And I know you tried."

She stared at him. "How long have you known that?"

He smiled. "Not till this minute."

"You bastard."

"What's with you, Cynthia? I never promised you anything."

"You said I was special."

"You are."

"You freakin' liar. You've been using me."

"Come off it," he said, standing. "We used each other. Just like we used Laura."

She nodded slowly. "I get it. You've fallen for the little twit. I hand her to you on a silver platter and now she's got you by the pecker."

He pushed a strand of black hair from her forehead. "Actually, you're better in bed. But let's be clear. You didn't hand me a thing. I had to work like hell to make her unwind."

"That's crap. I softened her up in the hot tub."

"It's different for a woman."

"Yeah, the woman who mucked up her car after that thunderstorm so you could play Sir Galahad."

"Look, Cynthia, neither of us is an angel, but we have what we want, so let's enjoy it."

"You're not permanent chief yet, Peter. When I take over for good, I'll see you never get appointed."

He pointed a finger at her. "You try anything with the staff or trustees and I'll blow the whistle on the whole plan. How long do you think you'd last?"

"Long enough."

"I'll risk it. You want the job too much."

"I want you."

He laughed. "What you want is to be CEO at NYU Medical Center so you'll be worthy of being Daddy's little girl."

"Go to hell. Now I suppose you're running off to her bed?"

He took her by the shoulders and kissed her forehead. "I'm going home. I haven't decided what to do about her."

"Get out."

"On my way," he said and moved toward the foyer.

"I'll tell her everything, Peter. Then where will you be?"

He turned with a smile. "Why should she believe you? She'll think you're being like her old lover Allison."

"I should never have told you about her."

"But you did."

She hurled the brandy snifter at him but was well off the mark as he dodged and disappeared through the door. She picked up the bottle and took another swallow, then hurried to the phone, lurching and almost losing her balance. Drank too much, she thought, dialing Laura's home. The answering machine came on and she hung up and dialed her cell and was sent to voice mail. Damn.

Taking the bottle with her she walked carefully up the stairs to her bedroom. She shed her clothes and left them on the floor. Climbing into bed she redialed Laura's home. When the machine clicked on, she left a message.

"Your human vibrator just left, sweetie.  Call me in the morning."

# TWENTY-FIVE

## SUNDAY, JULY 25

Kramer was on his veranda scanning the Metro section and sipping tomato juice. There was nothing in the paper about Vivian. The *Post* is way behind Tom Carter, he thought. The guy has sources everywhere, and once he latches on to a story he doesn't let go. On the other hand, his report raised more questions than answers. What I need is real information.

He glanced at his watch. Connie should have called by now. He'd wait till ten and then try her. A few minutes later the cordless phone next to him rang. Vivian's number, he noted and pressed Talk.

"Hello?"

"Bob, good morning. Sorry I didn't check in last night."

"That's okay. I see you're at Vivian's. How is she?"

"Hard to say. Did you see Tom Carter's report?"

"Uh-huh. I gather you were the friend who called the police."

"Yes. Vivian asked me to after I got here, but Dr. Patterson showed up before I could."

"What's his opinion?" he asked, sitting back, his eyes resting on the swimming pool.

"Doesn't think it's anything serious, but he's admitting her for an MRI tomorrow as a precaution."

"Really? I'm surprised he hasn't had her in already."

"Vivian didn't want to ruin her weekend and you know she usually gets her way."

Kramer gazed at the cloudless blue sky. "Sounds like she's acting herself. She tell Carter any more than I saw on TV?"

"Actually, she was napping when he called. By then I'd already spoken with Tawana Briggs."

"What did you tell her?" he asked.

"I'm not allowed to say."

Kramer frowned. "You won't tell me what you told her? Whose side are you on?"

"Yours, of course."

"Well, then, if Vivian has a clue who pushed her chair over, I need to know. It could helpful to my case."

"I'm sorry, Bob. Briggs was very clear. Vivian's information could affect their investigation."

"Maybe so, but Carter said Vivian saw herself back in her wheelchair going down the hallway. You didn't tell me that."

"He didn't get that from me."

"He got it from someone."

"You don't have to yell, Bob."

He backed off. "Look, Linda Barringer's already called me and the police for details, but you're shutting me out."

"It doesn't really matter if I tell you, does it? I mean, aren't the police supposed to give her any information that helps you?"

"But I'd like to hear it from you. They're not in my corner. I thought you were."

"Bob, I want to do the right thing. Look, I have to call Dr. Patterson and Briggs. Vivian just had another flashback. And I shouldn't even be telling you that much."

He tightened his grip on the phone. "I know what this is about--it's Victor Devane, isn't it? You're still not past him."

"I am," she insisted. "It's just that--"

"Please, Connie, I don't mean to be difficult, but this is important. So far Linda's been able to keep the police off my back."

"Let me think it over, and I should ask Vivian."

"You need her permission?"

"Did I say that?"

He took a breath. "No. No, you didn't. Perhaps you can have her call me directly."

"I'll see, but she'll do whatever she wants."

"Just ask her, all right?" He was squeezing the phone now.

"Bob, I said I'll see." Anger in her voice now.

"Please do what you can," he said, trying to sound pleasant. "Will you be accompanying Vivian to the hospital tomorrow?"

"Yes. I'm going home for a change of clothes later this morning."

"Would you like to meet for lunch?"

"I can't. Lydia has to go soon and I don't want to leave Vivian alone for long."

"Call me later?"

"When I can. Bye."

He hung up, staring at the tennis court.

---

The ringing phone jarred Cynthia awake. She sat up too quickly, and pain knifed into her forehead. She managed to focus on the caller ID. It was Laura.

"What time is it?" she croaked into the receiver.

"Around eleven. I could barely understand your voice-mail last night, so I thought I'd let you sleep in. You still sound awful."

"You should be inside my head."

"You wanted to talk."

"Yes. No, wait. Can you come over?"

"I've got a ton of work as you well know."

"I give you a dispensation," Cynthia said. "I don't want to do this on the phone."

"All right, I'll be right there."

"Give me a few minutes to put myself together."

"Take your time."

Cynthia stumbled into the bathroom for a hot shower. After coffee and two aspirins, she was close to feeling herself. She had just finished dressing when Laura rang the doorbell.

"Welcome to the world of the living," Laura said, standing in the doorway. "You still don't look so hot."

"No lectures. Not yet, anyway. Let's go to the deck."

"It's your meeting," Laura said, following her.

"I have a confession to make," Cynthia said, as they took adjoining chairs.

"Let me guess," Laura smiled. "You've known about Peter and me for awhile."

"You figured it out?"

"No, you basically told me in your message last night, remember?"

"No, but that's not the point. Listen, Peter's been seeing you because I asked him to."

"What?"

"It was my idea. Most of it anyway. From when you and I made love in the hot tub."

"Peter knew about that?"

"Yes. After that day, I approached him. We began to plan. He had the idea to rig your car so he could drive you home. I'm the one who did it. The storm was a bonus."

Silence, then, "I guess I should thank you."

"Don't. I want--wanted him for myself."

"Ahh, that pass you made at him."

"No. Telling you about that was part of the plan. There were plenty of others."

"Oh," Laura said, her voice suddenly small. "Did he...ever make love to you?"

"Not often. He said he didn't want to risk you finding out."

Laura closed her eyes. "Why are you telling me this?"

"Because he doesn't want me. He said so after you left last night. He was supposed to tell you about the whole plan, then be with me."

The eyes opened. "Cynthia, back up the tape, will you? What exactly is this plan?"

"You know parts of it. I wanted to be CEO, Peter wanted to be chief of surgery. We recruited you to keep an eye on Kramer while we tried to get rid of him and Jacobi. It wasn't a hard sell. You made clear you wouldn't mind having my job."

"Fine, but why have Peter come on to me?"

"I could tell you were looking to reconnect with a guy and I wasn't sure I could trust you. I figured Peter would keep you in check. Turns out I shouldn't have trusted him."

"Then his making love to me has been a lie from the beginning."

"I thought so, but now I don't know. Maybe he's played us

both for suckers. Maybe just me."

"So it's been just a game? Peter pretended we were fooling you?"

Cynthia gave her a tight smile. "We let you think so. We were keeping you in the dark all along."

"And I thought you were my friend."

"Laura, I'm truly sorry. I was really was trying to help you, but I guess I wanted to help myself more. I'm not proud of what I did."

Laura picked up her purse and stood over her. "Why not? Because you lost, you bitch?"

"I deserve that," Cynthia said and looked away. "What will you do now?"

"Pay Peter a visit. He was coming over tonight. Or did you already know that?"

"Sure. It's Sunday."

---

Laura found Thorpe sitting on a chaise lounge in his backyard reading the *Post*, a glass in one hand, and a tray table beside him with a cell phone, ice bucket and bottle of wine.

"Thought you'd be out here when you didn't answer the door," she said, striding across the grass toward him.

"What a treat," he said and put down the paper. "I thought you were going to call."

"And I thought doctors were supposed to stay out of the sun." She pulled over a lawn chair.

"All kinds of vices are permitted on a weekend," he said and took a sip. "Care to join me? I can get you a glass."

"I can't stay. I have files to read."

"Ah yes. You want to fire someone tomorrow."

"I'm starting today with you."

He looked at her and smiled. "You've talked to Cynthia."

"You lied to me, Peter."

He shrugged. "Nothing serious."

"What would be serious?"

"If I said I loved you and didn't mean it."

She laughed. "You're such a bullshitter. So conspiring with Cynthia against me isn't a big deal."

"Get off the soap box, Laura. You were happy enough conspiring against Cynthia."

"That was different."

"Why? Because you were in on it?"

"No, because it was for you and me. You weren't supposed to be fucking her on the side."

"Once or twice," Thorpe said.

"One too many."

"Laura, she was getting nervous. You saw that. I wanted to keep her happy and on board."

"And all the secrecy about us? Was that to keep Cynthia on board?"

"Think it through, will you? We wouldn't have succeeded otherwise. Kramer would have frozen you out. So would Jacobi. Or have you forgotten flirting with him."

"I didn't screw him, Peter."

He refilled his glass. "How do I know that?"

"Stop trying to twist this. This is about you lying about our future."

"I wasn't lying."

"Show me. Pick up that phone and make your weekly call to ma-mah and introduce me as your fiancée."

"I can't do that," he said, shaking his head.

"You can't because she's never heard of me, has she?"

"Of course she has. I told her about you on Mother's Day."

"Then pick up the phone."

"Now's not a good time."

"Where have I heard that before," she said, standing.

"Laura, don't leave like this. I want us to be together."

"You didn't tell Cynthia that last night."

"What difference does it make what I say to her? It's you I care about."

"And now I should believe you?"

"Laura, some day you're going to have to trust someone

again."

She turned away. "It won't be you, Dr. Thorpe."

---

Nick made a note on the large sheet of paper spread on the desk in his study. "And Larry's the last one," he said into the phone. "All right, Tawana, I think that covers it. I'll see you tomorrow." He hung up and went to the living room where Kathy was knitting on the love seat.

"Here you go," he said, placing the sheet on the coffee table. "The full schematic of the eighth floor VIP wing at Clara Barton, compliments of hospital security."

"So that's why you went over there after church."

"Man has to have some secrets," he said, sitting beside her. "I just reviewed the layout with Tawana."

"The rooms seem huge," Kathy said, studying the L-shaped blueprint.

"They are," he said, over her shoulder. "Much larger than the standard ones. Very plush and very pricey. The wing's rarely full."

"So who uses it?"

"Wealthy donors, celebrities who demand total privacy, and the aging beauty in for a face lift who wants no one to know."

"Total privacy in a hospital?"

"As much as you can get. Limited visitation, no nametags on the doors, and controlled access via closed circuit TV and card scanners. Without a card, you have to press a buzzer and identify yourself to the nurse inside before she'll open the doors. Come Monday afternoon, that'll be you."

"Who has cards?"

"Security personnel and medical staff assigned to the wing."

Kathy looked over the names Nick had penciled in on the diagram. Sam was in room 826, the last one on the left before the corridor turned right to form the L. Vivian was across the hall from Sam in 828. Frank, Nick and Connie were in the solarium at the beginning of the L. Kathy glanced up. "Connie will be there?"

"Vivian insisted."

Kathy's eyes returned to the sheet. "Why is Mike Avery in Vivian's bathroom?"

"See how it sits in the far corner? When Mike opens the bathroom door a crack, he has a perfect view of the whole room and the doorway. And Sam's right across the hall."

Kathy pointed to her own name at the nurses' station midway up the corridor. "Nicky, shouldn't I be closer to Vivian's room if I'm supposed to be her private nurse?"

"She'll be the only patient in the wing. This way you can double as gatekeeper and stay away from the action. Things could get crowded."

"You mean dangerous."

"Not likely, but possible. You're better off down the hall."

"But the murderer could get antsy when he walks in if he thinks I'll remember his face."

"He shouldn't care about you unless he's already harmed Vivian and that won't happen."

"Unless he takes his victims in the order he sees them."

"Relax. Tawana's right across the hall from you in room 810 and we'll hear everything the killer says to you over the mikes."

"Easy for you to say, you're a mile away."

"Kathy, trust me, we've thought of everything."

"What do they say about the best laid plans?" She leaned back. "All right, Einstein, what time do I show up?"

"Around four. You'll relieve the regular nurse. Patterson's arranged for that."

"And I won't have to worry about phone calls or visitors?"

"No. Patterson will post orders to make sure Vivian's not to be disturbed. We'll set up dinner for her, but that's it."

"So if someone comes to the wing by mistake, they have to ring the buzzer to get in and I can turn them away."

"Right. And if they give you a rough time, Tawana will deal with them."

"When does Vivian arrive?" Kathy asked.

"She checks in at noon with Connie and goes directly to radiology for the MRI. After that, she'll go to her room."

"Couldn't the killer try something while she's in radiology?"

"Too many people around, but we've got it covered just in case. Two detectives will pose as medical personnel and drive the ambulance, then accompany Vivian every minute until she goes to her room."

"Why not use them for backup in the wing?"

"Because they return to the ambulance to cover the exits and tape record everything we say."

"Hangs together nicely," Kathy said.

"Thank you. Have you checked out your uniform?"

"It's tight."

"No pasta tonight."

"I'll skip dessert."

"You don't eat dessert."

"I might want it tonight for courage."

He rubbed the back of her neck. "You really having second thoughts? We can always get a detective to be at the desk."

"Oh no. If Vivian can do this so can I."

"I knew you were tough," he said and folded the diagram in half.

"One last question. Aside from the buzzer, do I get any warning if the killer heads my way?"

"What do mean if? You doubt the ace detective?"

"Answer the question."

"Larry Foster will be on a bench across from the first floor elevators and stairs. He'll be able to spot Kramer and the others if they head upstairs."

"Won't they recognize him?"

"He'll wear sunglasses and a baseball cap and keep his face in a newspaper."

"But Thorpe won't be traveling from the first floor."

"There's no way to cover him close," Nick said. "Besides, any of them can take the elevator down to the cafeteria and then switch elevators or take the stairs. Plus, the killer could put on a disguise to avoid being seen going to or from the wing."

"How comforting. So I'm left with the buzzer."

"Best we can do. Less of a warning but not a surprise either."

"And I suppose Tawana and the rest of you with familiar

faces will also be wearing sunglasses?"

"Think I'd look good in them?" he smiled.

"Could be an improvement. Seriously, how do you get in?"

"We arrive in a van while Vivian's having the MRI. Security lets us in through the loading dock area, then we take the freight elevator to the seventh floor and the stairs to eight."

"And wait for a killer to pay Vivian a visit."

"That's the idea," he said.

"What weapon do you think he'll use?"

"We're ready for anything, needles, pills, whatever. We've even given Vivian a Kevlar vest."

"You don't think he'd use a gun."

"Not really. We expect him to go in close. And the first threatening move he makes, Mike will step out and arrest him."

"Suppose he resists?" Kathy said. "Can Mike risk a shot with Vivian nearby?"

"He's very good."

"I thought Tawana was their best."

"She is, and that's another reason we want her in the hallway. The sightlines are longer from there and she's better at hitting a target in a crowd."

Kathy shook her head. "Whatever happened to pregnant women staying at home?"

"Ever hear of women's liberation?"

"Shut up."

"Or glass ceilings and role reversal?"

"I said shut up."

"Suppose I make us some pasta?"

---

The killer lay back against the headboard, reflecting on the weekend, the sound of the NBC evening news tuned low in the background. Things had turned sour, but if it hadn't happened now, it probably would have eventually. A permanent relationship just wasn't in the cards. Not now, not here. Still, the feeling of loss was disturbing. Perhaps I need to end it more cleanly, on my terms.

Suddenly there was a bright flash and the crack of thunder, followed by the downpour of a classic summer squall. The killer picked up the wine glass from the bedside table and raised the volume on the remote when the weather map disappeared and the pretty face of Stacy Remington filled the screen.

"Those storms look fierce, Scottie. Let's hope things quiet down before tomorrow's rush hour. And now, as promised, here's Tom Carter with an update on a story he's been following about those killings at Clara Barton Hospital."

The camera panned back to show Carter and Remington then focused tight on Carter.

"Thanks Stacy," he said, looking straight ahead. "Tonight, as the police investigation continues with no arrests imminent, we've learned what could prove to be a significant development.

"In my exclusive interview two weeks ago with Vivian Pershing, chairman of Clara Barton's board, she claimed she was pushed from her wheelchair while at the hospital. And, as I reported last evening, Ms. Pershing experienced a flashback of her fall after suffering a blow to the head at her home yesterday morning. It now appears she has had additional flashbacks today accompanied by details of the attack.

"This afternoon, we contacted Ms. Pershing's doctor, Donald Patterson, who told us she's resting comfortably. He would not confirm, however, our information that, after undergoing an MRI tomorrow, she will spend the night at Clara Barton. We have also learned that Ms. Pershing is to meet with Dr. Erica Sawyer at the hospital on Tuesday morning. Dr. Sawyer is a noted Washington psychotherapist who specializes in post-traumatic stress disorder, hypnosis and amnesia."

"Tom," Remington said on cue as the camera view widened to include her, "does that mean Ms. Pershing might be able to identify her attacker?"

"We're not sure, Stacy. Dr. Patterson refused to speculate and Dr. Sawyer did not return our calls. As soon as we have further information, we'll bring it to you."

"Wow, thanks. We'll be here waiting. Now for the day in sports, we--."

The killer turned off the TV and began pacing. Erica Sawyer? Hypnosis? Could Pershing actually remember anything? She never got a look at my face, and her eyes were closed when I examined her. Was she faking? Or perhaps regained consciousness and saw me as I was leaving. Hold it. This all could be a trap. Still, if it's true, Pershing could pose a problem.

Assume it's true. After the MRI, she'll be monitored because of the flashbacks. Probably not in the ICU, but where? It all depends on Patterson's orders. If she's meeting with Sawyer, he'll probably have her take a sedative to make sure she has a good night's sleep.

After a few minutes, the killer refilled the wine glass and took a sip. There was a way to deal with this. For someone Vivian's size, it wouldn't take much and needed minimal preparation. And if the cops were around, a cautious approach would lure them out of hiding with no risk. Parnell would have been pleased.

# TWENTY-SIX

## MONDAY, JULY 26

Thorpe was putting on his tie in the surgical locker room when Dr. Julia Vallance walked in. He stepped over to her. "Thanks for your help with Mrs. Cummings's bleeder."

"My privilege," she said, removing her surgical cap. "Especially on a Monday."

He smiled. "I see you've heard of my lecture."

"My first week. And this is already my second time working with the chief of surgery. Has to be a record."

"That's right. I guess number one wasn't very pleasant for you."

"No, but I screwed up. Dr. Jacobi was right to throw me out."

"Perhaps, but he never was much for diplomacy."

"Thanks," she said. "I was upset at first. I even considered complaining to the EEO office."

"You were probably wise not to."

She shrugged. "Still, I feel bad. I never got the chance to apologize to him properly."

She had wonderful light brown eyes. "Listen, I've got the whole day stretching ahead until the post-op conference. How about a cup of coffee or an early lunch? We really haven't talked since you joined us."

"I'd like that. Give me a minute to run a comb through my hair."

"It looks fine to me, but whatever you say. I'll meet you by the elevators."

"Okay."

Vallance disappeared into the lavatory. She could stand to lose a few pounds, he thought, but had real promise. Especially since Laura was unlikely to relent. Smiling, he whistled his way down the hall.

---

Kramer watched Cynthia shut the door as she left his office. He'd been irritated by her visit. With no meetings scheduled, he was using the time to review his next move when she'd blustered in.  Could he possibly meet with her later on a budget matter? Might be after six, but it would only take a few minutes. She'd drop the file off later. Nothing could be so important at that hour, he'd thought.  She just wants to show she's in charge. Fine, let her have her fun. Sure, he'd said to her.

He returned his attention to his computer, glancing at his watch. Linda should be reporting in soon. She had called the night before for a strategy session after Tom Carter's news report. She told him she would demand to be present when Erica Sawyer interviewed Vivian. Just in case Pershing revealed anything exculpatory, she said. It was a fool's errand she knew; the police would stonewall for sure. But she wanted to go on record. That way they couldn't accuse her of not playing fair when--. His intercom beeped. He grabbed the receiver.

"Yes?"

"Ms. Vacarro for you, Mr. Kramer."

"Oh. Thank you, Ms..."

"Conrad."

"Right, Conrad. Put her through, please."

"Yes, sir."

"Bob?"

"Hello, Connie."

"Who answered your phone?"

"Someone Cynthia sent in to handle calls."

"Oh, that's right, she took over today."

"I see you remember some things," he said.

"Pardon?"

"You were supposed to call last night."

"I said I'd try. I'm sorry, but Vivian was...very needy. The thunderstorms really upset her."

"She have more flashbacks or should I ask Tom Carter?"

"Bob, I said I was sorry. In fact she did have one after the storms. Look, I only have a minute. We're about to go down to the ambulance."

"I see," he said and pulled a pad closer. "What time's Vivian supposed to get here?"

"Noon. She's running late."

"Is she really spending the night? There's nothing in the computer."

"You checked?"

"She's my friend too, Connie."

"Yes, well, Dr. Patterson's putting her in the VIP wing."

"You have a room number?"

"He wants her near the solarium. She's to meet in there with Dr. Sawyer tomorrow."

He made a note. "Was it Patterson's idea to bring in Sawyer?"

"That's right. He's worked with her before. He's hopeful she can help trigger Vivian's memory with hypnosis."

"I'm surprised. Patterson's old school."

"So?"

"Hypnosis is hardly mainstream medicine. Maybe your friend Tawana Briggs suggested it. But of course you can't say."

"I can see you're still upset. I just wanted to say I miss you. I'd like to make up for this past weekend."

"We'll talk about it. You need to go and I'm expecting a call from Linda."

"Will you phone me tonight?"

"Where will you be?"

"Home. Dr. Patterson wants Vivian to get to sleep early."

"It may be late. I have things to do here, then some legal points to go over with Fred and Linda."

"Call anytime. Bob?"

"Yes?"

"Nothing. I'll be waiting to hear from you."

He hung up and looked at his notes. The VIP wing. Good location. Quiet and isolated.

---

Cynthia knocked on Laura's door and stuck her head in. "Afternoon."

"Hello," Laura said coolly.

"A civil greeting. That's better than a flying paperweight. May I come in?"

"You never asked before."

"Is that a yes?"

"I suppose."

Cynthia entered, sporting a new tan pinstriped suit and silk blouse, and took a seat on the sofa. "How's your day?"

"I'm muddling through, thank you."

"Fire anyone yet?"

"I'm working up to it. Some of these personnel evaluations are awful. Why haven't you acted on them?"

"If you recall, I've been kind of distracted. So, do you hate me?"

Laura shrugged and sat back. "Yes and no. I'm happy for the promotion but I still think you're a shit."

"Guilty."

"But I'm no better, am I?"

"No."

"And Peter's just as bad."

"We all deserve each other," Cynthia said. "How was your visit?"

"Predictable. He tried to lie his way out of it."

"But you'll miss him for a time."

Laura hesitated. "I already do."

"Get over it."

"Have you?"

"I'm a realist. Guys like him are always a long shot."

"Don't you feel anything for him?"

"Not since I walked in this morning," Cynthia said. "It's been a real trip. Calls from well-wishers on the staff, though I know some of them are covering their ass and hoping Kramer survives."

"You're amazing. Peter gives you the shaft, and you shrug and move on."

"Oh, he hasn't heard the last of me. He'll never be appointed chief if I can help it."

"What can you do?"

"Plenty. He's not going anywhere without Pershing's vote. I intend to make sure she knows what a conniver he is."

"She'll listen to you?" Laura asked.

"Not to worry. Once Kramer's gone, I'll find a way to win her over."

"Bob's not giving up, Cynthia. He's got a good lawyer and this Dr. Sawyer may muddy the waters. I assume you saw Carter's report."

"Oh yes, but I wouldn't put it past the Czarina to lie for Kramer. She'd concoct an epiphany to save him. I'm not falling for that and neither will the police."

Laura laughed and shook her head. "That's my girl. It really is all about power, isn't it?"

"Nothing like it," she said, standing and moving toward the desk. "Wait till you've been sitting in that chair a while. You'll be after my job in no time."

"I'm not like that."

"Listen, honey bunch, I've seen you put that body and brain in gear to con Stan Jacobi."

"That's not the same. I did that for all of us."

"Sure you did." Cynthia leaned over and stroked Laura's cheek. "For which I'll be forever in your debt. See you later," she winked and left the room.

---

By two that afternoon, anyone with top level access to Clara Barton's Affinity computer program could have learned Vivian's MRI was completed, her room assignment, that she was not allowed calls or visitors, would have a private nurse after four and a light dinner at six.

All good omens, the killer thought. Patterson would probably have left drug orders by now. They were very methodical in the pharmacy and would have entered everything in the computer. The killer pulled up their database. Access to patient information was theoretically restricted by a special password given to authorized personnel but in fact was known by many more.

The orders for Vivian Pershing appeared on the screen. If this was a trap, the police had done their homework. An Ambien sleeping pill at eight. Breakfast tomorrow at seven, but no coffee or tea. Then at nine, a maximum of 600 mg of sodium amytal in a 10 per cent solution was to be administered via IV drip.

Used with hypnosis, sodium amytal alleviated a patient's anxiety. This in turn facilitated unlocking the memory of an earlier trauma or increasing the accuracy of the recall. The protocol was often employed where memory was not spontaneous or there was some urgency involved. In Vivian's case, the hospital setting would have the dual benefit of monitoring any complications while returning her to the site of the original event: so-called exposure therapy.

Very well, the killer thought, if this is real, Pershing must not talk to Sawyer. When to act? The police are sure to be hovering around tomorrow. Late tonight would be perfect. Well after visiting hours when the hospital would be quiet and Vivian asleep. But if this were a trap, that's exactly when the police would expect an attack. So the time to go in was before dinner. When they might be a tad off guard.

---

As the afternoon wore on, Laura grew restless, no longer tolerant of loose ends in her life. Cynthia's visit had confirmed her sense that she couldn't leave things as they were with Peter. Perhaps their relationship had been doomed from the start, was all a mirage, but he had said they could still have a future. Was that simply another lie? Sure, he'd been exposed yesterday, but did that mean he could never be truthful to her? One clue would be if he really had told his mother about them; if I called and she knew who I was.

Peter's personnel jacket with his mother's address was in Cynthia's office, but Laura didn't want her to know what she was about to do. Instead, she dialed his office.

His receptionist answered immediately. "Dr. Thorpe's office."

"Anita, hi, it's Laura Prentice from Clara Barton. Is Peter available?" she asked, knowing he wasn't.

"It's his late day, Laura. My schedule has him over there until the post-op conference, then he sees a patient here at 6:30."

"Darn, sorry to bother you. Oh, wait a second. Do you happen to have his mother's phone number in Missouri? I'm working on a press release, but my file seems to have a gap."

"Sorry. Even if I did, I wouldn't be able to give it to you. Our office policy's even stricter than HIPPA. I'm not telling anybody much of anything these days."

"I know how it is," she said. "Well, I'll see if I can track him down. Thanks."

"Sure thing."

She found the area code on the Internet, then dialed Information and worked the touch-tone menu to reach an operator.

"Business or residence?" a voice answered.

"Residence. Number please for Eleanor Thorpe in Bunceton."

"One moment....Ma'am, I don't show any such listing."

"Are you sure? It could be an unlisted number."

"Sorry, no, ma'am."

"Operator, I'm calling from a hospital in Washington, D.C. Mrs. Thorpe's the mother of one of our surgeons. It's important I reach her."

"I'm sure it is, ma'am, but there isn't a number for the name. Perhaps if you called the local hospital or one of the doctors."

"Yes, fine, give me the hospital number."

"One moment....Ma'am?"

"Yes," Laura said.

"There's no hospital in Bunceton, and only two doctors listed."

"I'll take them both, thank you," Laura said and wrote down the numbers the operator provided. Then she dialed the first.

"Dr. Eldridge's office."

"Hello, this is Laura Prentice. I'm calling from Clara Barton Memorial Hospital in Washington, D.C. I'm trying to reach Mrs. Eleanor Thorpe. She's the mother of one of our doctors."

"Peter Thorpe?"

"Yes, you know him?"

"Ever since he was a little boy. Dr. Eldridge was a good friend of Peter's father. My Lord, I haven't laid eyes on Peter since they buried his dad. Poor family's had so much troubles. I hope Peter's all right."

"He's fine but unreachable right now. I have to call his mother to get some background for a press release we're doing, but the phone company doesn't have her number there."

"Of course they don't. Eleanor doesn't live here anymore."

"She doesn't?"

"Heavens, no. She's been in a nursing home since her husband died. Nice place up near St. Louis. But you won't get much information from her, I'm afraid."

"Oh? Why not?"

"No one can. Poor woman has Alzheimer's."

"Alzheimer's?"

"For years. 'Course, she wasn't too swift even before her husband's stroke. Not sure she knows to this day that her son Bill's dead too."

"I see," Laura said, perplexed. "Well, perhaps she's better off. Sons shouldn't be killed in war."

"War? Bill died at the ocean."

"What? But there was an explosion in Dubai. A truck with mines from the Gulf War."

"You have some bad information in that file, Ms. Prentice. Bill died in a fire at a beach cottage on Cape Cod the summer the war ended."

"Cape Cod?"

"That's right. Big obituary in the *Post-Dispatch*. I remember showing it to Dr. Eldridge. Very sad situation. We don't talk about it much here. Listen, a patient just came in. I can give you the number of Eleanor's nursing home. Maybe they can help you."

"No, that won't be necessary. I--I'll just have to wait till Dr.

Thorpe returns."

"All right then. And tell Peter that Thanet Sherman asked after him will you?"

"Yes, of course. Thank you."

Laura hung up, confused. Was Peter too embarrassed to tell the truth about his mother? And what about his brother? Could this Thanet Sherman be mistaken? She pulled her computer keyboard closer and began hunting for the *St. Louis Post-Dispatch*.

---

"Thank you, Dr. Lyman," Thorpe said. "Perhaps you should switch to duct tape as your suture of choice."

Lyman laughed along with most of the surgeons assembled in conference room 4 in Cabot Hall.

"Seriously, Ann," Thorpe continued, "I appreciate you being such a good sport. We've all had those little surprises and I totally agree with your response to this one." That prompted several nods and a smattering of applause.

"All right, then," he continued. "Unless anyone has any other thoughts, I think that covers today's agenda." He waited two beats. "See you all next time."

Thorpe lingered at the head of the long table as the doctors filed out. Julia Vallance rose from her seat against the wall and came over to him. "Thank you for inviting me, Dr. Thorpe. I learned so much just listening."

"By all means come again if you have the time. And bring one or two of the new residents when they show up. After all, I wouldn't want to be accused of favoritism." He winked and took her elbow and guiding her toward the door.

"Oh, no, I understand," she said quickly.

"But just between us, I really enjoyed out time together today."

"So did I."

They started down the hallway toward the main building. "There's no reason we couldn't meet again to chat. That is, if you'd like."

"Anytime," she said.

"Wonderful. I'm on my way to see a patient right now, but let me check my calendar and give you a call. Perhaps we could have something other than cafeteria food."

"That would be a welcome change," she smiled.

"Good," he said and slowed his pace. "Now, tell me why you decided on surgery."

---

Kathy exited the elevator and stepped across the eighth floor lobby to the entrance of the VIP wing. She was about to press the buzzer when the door clicked and swung open.

"Florence Nightingale, I presume," Nick said.

"Sorry if I'm late," she said.

"You'll never work here again," he said, as they started down the hall.

"How long were you standing there waiting for me?"

"Since the detectives in the ambulance saw you drive into the parking lot."

"Gee, I never noticed it."

"You weren't supposed to."

"Where's Tawana?"

"Right here," she said, coming out from behind the nurses' station. "Just checking the setup one last time. Kathy, you missed your calling. You're perfect in that outfit."

"Thanks. How're you feeling?"

"Fine, but the baby's kicking today."

"Better get used to it," she smiled.

"That's where you sit," Nick said, pointing.

Kathy stepped behind the first computer station. "The regular nurse leave?"

"Right after we told her you'd arrived," Tawana said.

"She know enough to keep all this to herself?"

"Not a problem. Gail already talked to her."

Kathy looked at the small TV monitor next to the computer. The screen showed the lobby side of the doors leading into the wing. "Perfect," she said. "I can see anyone who wants in."

"The system has a two-way speaker," Tawana said. "The mike's set in the base of the monitor. Just talk at the screen and the person at the door will hear you. The buzzer to open the doors is that red button."

"What're those?" Kathy asked, pointing to small objects resting on the computer keyboard.

"Your earplug so you can hear us. You talk to us with that lapel mike pin. We all have them except Nick and Connie. They only have the earplugs."

"They won't let me talk," he said.

"That's a first," Kathy said, settling in behind the desk. She looped the earplug around one ear, then picked up the pin. "Things quiet?"

"Very," Tawana said. "So far everyone's invisible except for Thorpe. Larry Foster saw him get on the elevator a few minutes ago with a woman, probably another doctor. You have your notes?"

"Right here," she said and took a sheet from her purse. "I've almost memorized them."

"Good," Tawana said, "but don't be afraid to consult them. Any private nurse might do that."

"Okay. How's Vivian?"

"An impatient patient," Nick grinned.

Kathy rolled her eyes. "Give it up, Seinfeld."

"Heads up," Foster said in their ears. "Kramer's come into the lobby carrying a plastic bag. He's turned toward the elevators."

"Battle stations," Tawana said, but Nick was already hurrying down the hall.

---

At that moment Cynthia knocked on Kramer's door. Getting no response, she entered, carrying the budget file she'd mentioned to him. She lay it on his desk then noticed the memo pad next to the phone. She turned it around to read his note.

*V--another flshbk. Rm 826-28, 30-32?--Patt knows Swyr. V may rmber fall.*

She stared at the words. Pershing's telling the truth?  Where was Kramer?  Was he going up there?  She couldn't afford to wait to find out.  She ran for the door and didn't bother closing it behind her.

---

Frank was adjusting his lapel mike when Nick entered the solarium. "Any news?" he asked.

"You're hearing what I am," Frank said, covering his lapel mike so no one else would hear.

"Can't we do something?" Connie asked, wringing her hands and pacing in a small circle.

"Stay calm and wait," Frank said. "That's why we're here."

"Keep the faith," Nick whispered to her.

"Kramer's gone to the information desk," Foster said in their ears. "He's talking to one of the volunteers. She's pointing toward the front entrance. Hey, he's leaving the building."

A moment later Sam stepped into the room, hand covering his lapel mike. "Ms. Vacarro, does he usually go off in the afternoon?"

"Sometimes," she said. "But the front doors lead to the main driveway. His car's in the lot. He'd use the staff entrance unless someone's picking him up."

Sam removed his hand. "Larry, can you see what Kramer's doing out there and still keep an eye on the elevators?"

"Negative," Foster said. "Can't see around the corner to the elevators."

"Okay, get back in position. Calvin," Sam called to one of the men in the ambulance, "get over to the main entrance. See what's Kramer's up to."

"On my way."

"Guys, Ellis just showed up," Foster spoke in their ears.

"Where's she headed?" Sam asked.

"Hold on. She pressed the button for an up elevator."

"Hear that, Kathy?" Tawana's voice said.

"Yes, I'm all set."

"Ready here," Avery chimed in from Vivian's room.

"Ellis is on her way," Foster said.

No one spoke for several moments. "Calvin, what's happening outside?" Sam said, now back in room 826.

"Kramer's walked over a white van parked across the circle. The driver's handing him a small package and he's signing for it. He's opening it, but I can't see what it is. They're talking."

"There's a woman at the door," Kathy spoke into her mike.

"Here we go," Nick said.

---

It didn't take long for Laura to find the *Post-Dispatch* Web site and establish an account with her credit card to gain access to its archives. It took only slightly longer to find the obituary for Dr. William Thorpe in the August 28, 1991 issue. Just as Thanet Sherman had said, he had died on Cape Cod.

She shook her head as more new truths emerged about Peter's brother. He had died in a propane gas explosion along with Congressman Patrick Devlin and his wife. It soon turned out both men were implicated in a criminal investigation of Medicare fraud. The police thought it possible that the apparent accident was in fact murder. Murder, Laura repeated to herself as she stared at the screen in disbelief.

---

"Who's there?" Kathy asked when Cynthia rang the buzzer.

"Cynthia Ellis," she said and waved her ID badge at the scanner she knew was there.

"Can I help you?"

"I doubt it. I'm the CEO around here in case you haven't heard. Open the damn door."

"Just a minute."

Kathy's finger was still on the button when Cynthia pushed through the door. "Who are you?" she snapped at Kathy, striding toward at the desk.

"Ms. Pershing's nurse."

"Is she alone?"

"She's asleep."

"Has anyone been up here?" Cynthia asked.

"She's not allowed visitors."

"I want to see her."

"I'm sorry. Doctor's orders."

"I don't give a damn about your orders," Cynthia said, leaning over and placing her palms on the desk. "You either let me by or I'll pick up that phone and call Don Patterson right now. He's not going to like what I'll have to say and you won't either."

Kathy shrugged. "I'll let you pass, but I must make a note about this."

"You do that, honey," Cynthia said over her shoulder as she marched off.

"You ready in there, Mike?" Frank asked.

"All set."

"Calvin," Sam whispered, "what's with Kramer?"

"Still talking to the van driver."

Vivian was in the bed with her back to the open doorway as Cynthia entered the darkened room.

"Vivian?" she called.

Vivian said nothing, but took deep, regular breaths.

Cynthia walked around the bed toward the head, Avery watching every move. "Vivian?"

No response.

"Lieutenant," Calvin said in their ears, "the van's leaving. Kramer's headed back to the front entrance still carrying the bag."

"Roger that," Sam said softly. "Stay put and cover those doors."

Cynthia stepped closer to the bed. Her hand reached out, moving toward Vivian's neck.

"Police. Freeze," Avery said, stepping from the bathroom.

Cynthia jumped back. "What the hell are you doing in here? What is this?"

"Your unlucky day."

"Hello, Cynthia," Vivian said, sitting up.

"Vivian! You're okay. I was worried."

"Why is that, Ms. Ellis?" Sam said from the doorway.

"Who are you?"

"Lieutenant Sam Witkin, D.C. Homicide."

"Do you people always hold conventions in hospital rooms?"

"I'll ask the questions. Why are you here?"

"I thought Ms. Pershing might be in danger."

"Why?"

"I read a note on Bob Kramer's desk. He's afraid Dr. Sawyer will help Vivian identify him. Check it out."

"Is that why you were reaching for her neck?" Avery said.

"Listen, muscle brain, I was trying to wake her up to warn her. I wouldn't have to if you jerks had arrested Kramer before now."

"Mind if we search you, Ms. Ellis?" Sam asked.

"You're damn right I would. You better arrest me first and read me my rights and then get ready to defend my lawsuit."

"Kramer's back in the lobby," Foster said in their ears. "He's taking something out of the bag. Looks like a wall clock."

"A clock?" Sam said.

"Come again?" Cynthia asked.

"Yeah, you know," Foster said, "one of those office clocks. Round, white face and black numbers. He's looking at the back of it."

"Is it about a foot wide with a black casing?" Sam asked, looking at the wall clock hanging across from Vivian's bed.

"That's it. Hold on, he's gone into the gift shop. He's pointing at something on the shelf behind the counter."

"Move in closer. See what it is."

"Wait a sec," Foster said. "Batteries. He's buying a pack of batteries, the square ones, nine volt. Now the clerk is reaching into a drawer. Taking out something with a red cross on it. I think it's a roll of gauze. No, check that, adhesive tape."

"Tape," Sam repeated.

"I'm moving back, Lieutenant, he's coming out. Going around the corner now. Looks like he's headed back to his office."

"Ms. Ellis," Sam said and pointed at the wall, "are there many of those clocks around the hospital?"

"They're all over the place if you must know."

"What kind of batteries do they take?"

"How would I know?"

"Check it, Mike. See if it's a nine volt."

Avery lifted the clock from the wall. "Double A, Lieutenant."

"I'll be damned," Sam said.

"You thinking what I am?" Frank said in their ears.

"No doubt," Sam said. "Mike, get back in the bathroom. Ms. Pershing, back to sleep. Ms. Ellis, please come with me to the solarium."

"Go to hell."

"Look, I can arrest you right here, but if you really think Kramer's guilty, move it."

She hesitated, then nodded. "All right."

Sam stepped out and followed Cynthia into the solarium. "Ms. Ellis, meet Captain Frank Stephens and Connie Vacarro. I think you know Nick Mercante."

"What is this?" Cynthia said.

"Time for you to sit down and shut up," Frank said. "Please do so."

---

Laura angrily turned off her computer. The bastard's an inveterate liar. How much else has he fabricated? She looked at her watch. The post-op conference should be over. She unlocked her desk drawer where they kept the set of master keys reserved for use in emergencies. I'll finish this face-to-face, she thought, putting the key for the sixth floor in her purse. Then give Vivian Pershing an earful.

"Heads up," Foster said moments later. "Laura Prentice is in the lobby headed toward the elevators. She's pressing Up."

"Gonna get crowded around here," Sam said and headed

back to 826.

Laura got off on six, tried the door to Thorpe's office, but it was locked. Not wanting to be seen waiting in the hallway, she used the master key and entered disorganized chaos. Boxes were stacked in corners, files were jammed on chairs and mountains of paper sat on the desk.

She paced the room, rehearsing what she'd say to him and looking at her watch. The conference never lasts past five. She stepped over to the closet. His jacket wasn't there. Maybe he'd gone directly to his office. She didn't want to confront him in front of Anita or a patient. Best to deal with him on her own turf.

Returning to the desk, she opened her purse and ripped a page from her Day timer. She'd leave him a message in case he was still in the hospital. She paused, took a deep breath, and began to write:

*Peter--I must talk to you. I know about your mother and brother. Please come over tonight. Call me so I know you received this. Laura*

There. If he didn't call, she'd phone him. She looked around for a place to leave the note. He'll never find it in this mess. She decided to put it in an envelope and tape it outside the door. Then she spotted his father's medical bag on a shelf behind the desk. So he must still be in the hospital.

She moved the bag to the top of the mound of paper on the center of his desk. Working the clasp, she opened the bag, intending to lodge the note just inside so it would peek out after she closed it. She never finished.

---

Nick and Connie crisscrossed each other as they paced the solarium, the minutes dragging by with no sign of Laura or Kramer.

"What's happening, Larry?" Sam asked from inside 826.

"Lobby's quiet, Lieutenant."

"Emilio?" Sam asked the second detective in the ambulance who had a view of the side entrance.

"Nothing, sir."

"Buzzer," Kathy suddenly said in their ears. "We've got company and it's a man."

"Christ, how did Kramer get up here?" Sam said. "Get set, everyone."

"Who is it?" Kathy asked the handsome face in the screen.

"Dr. Peter Thorpe, chief of surgery."

"Terrific," Sam said. "Let him in, Kathy."

Kathy pressed the button, and Thorpe entered and walked toward her.

"Hi, there," he smiled, "thanks for buzzing me in."

"You're welcome, doctor," Kathy said. "Can I help you?"

"I was wondering how Vivian Pershing's doing."

"She's asleep."

"Good, good. We're all rooting for her. I'd like to look at her chart if I may. Which room?"

"Let him pass," Sam whispered, "I want the hallway clear."

"Very well, doctor," Kathy said. "She's in 828, but she's not to be disturbed."

"I understand. I won't be long."

Thorpe walked slowly to the end of the hall, paused at the Carsten wall unit that hung outside a patient's rooms. He pulled the cover down and scanned Vivian's chart. Dr. Patterson was very thorough. Replacing the cover, he ducked into Vivian's room.

"Thorpe came in," Mike whispered.

"Roger that," Sam said. "Kathy, if Kramer or Prentice show up, stall them."

"Do my best."

Thorpe went around the bed to Vivian's side and studied her breathing, then checked the Datascope vital signs monitor to which she was attached. "Good evening, Vivian. Can you hear me?"

"Answer him, Ms. Pershing," Sam said from the doorway.

Vivian sat up. "Hello, Dr. Thorpe."

"All right, doctor, outside, please," Sam said.

Thorpe didn't move. "Who are you?"

"Lieutenant Sam Witkin. D.C. Homicide. Outside. Now."

"May I ask why?"

"Do as he says, Thorpe," Avery said, emerging from the bathroom.

"Well, well, the detective who likes photography," Thorpe said, but began moving toward the door. "Now I'm doubly curious."

"Back to business, Mike," Sam said, "I'll take it from here. What are you doing in here, Dr. Thorpe?"

"I could ask you that, Lieutenant."

"Keep walking to the solarium."

Thorpe shrugged, but complied and entered the large room. "Mr. Mercante," he said, "and Cynthia. Is this your doing?" She didn't respond. He turned to Frank. "And you are..."

"Captain Frank Stephens, D.C. Homicide."

"Another one," he smiled.

"Exactly what brought you to Ms. Pershing's room, doctor?" Frank asked.

"Just checking on her condition."

"She's not your patient," Sam said. "You could have called Dr. Patterson."

"I had a few minutes. Vivian's very important to this hospital and I've always been quite fond of her."

"She's never told me that," Connie said. "Maybe you were worried she'd remember you upsetting her wheelchair."

Thorpe turned. "Forgive me. Seems I've overlooked someone. Who are you?"

"A good friend of Vivian's. I volunteer at the hospital."

"Really? I don't recall the face. I must be slipping."

"Maybe the lady has a point, doctor," Frank said.

"Captain, I'm not sure I was even at the hospital that day."

"You were," Connie said. "I saw you walk through the lobby when I arrived that morning."

Thorpe smiled. "Well, then, thanks for reminding me."

"Would you mind if we searched you, doctor?" Frank asked.

"Feel free," he said pleasantly.

"You weren't so cooperative when we visited your house," Sam said, stepping over to him.

"This isn't my home, Lieutenant."

"What's this?" Sam asked, lifting a cellophane-wrapped object from Thorpe's lab coat.

"Huh, I forgot that was in there. It's a 30 milliliter hypodermic. To aspirate fluid from the body."

"It can be used for other things," Sam said.

"Of course, but that's what I use it for."

"Maybe you kill people with it," Connie said.

"Ms. Vacarro, please be quiet," Frank said.

"Thank you, Captain," Thorpe said. "As you can see, Lieutenant, the syringe is empty and harmless."

"Maybe not," Cynthia said. "Check and see if he has a needle on him that fits it."

"I'll save you the trouble," Thorpe said. "There're probably several and some alcohol swaps in the same pocket."

Sam pulled a packaged needle from Thorpe's pocket. "What can he do with this, Ms. Ellis?"

"What about that, Cynthia?" Thorpe said. "Perhaps I have a vial of poison in my shoe."

"Too obvious," Cynthia said. "But you could inject Pershing with air."

"Air?" Frank repeated.

"That's right, Captain. Pinch the right nerves to stun a person and inject enough air into their veins and they'll die in minutes of an embolism."

"How do you know that?" Sam asked.

"I'm a trained nurse for God's sakes. And correct me if I'm wrong, Dr. Thorpe, but isn't an embolism almost impossible to detect because the air bubble escapes during an autopsy?"

Thorpe shook his head. "Cynthia, you never cease to amaze me. You're quite right, of course. Trouble is, your imagination's going wild again. Last week Bob Kramer was your villain of choice."

"But you're here," Sam said, "and he's not."

"Look, Lieutenant, I identified myself to the nurse down the hall, and you just saw me in Vivian's room. I simply spoke to her and made no threatening gesture of any kind. Besides, I have absolutely no motive to harm the lady."

"Unless Dr. Sawyer can help her identify you," Cynthia said.

"But she's not due till tomorrow, now is she? Why don't you call me when she shows up? Somehow, though, I think I'll skip your little charade."

"Smart ass."

"I love you too. You're much more entertaining when you go after the real killer."

Foster spoke into their ears from the lobby. "Kramer's on the move with the plastic bag. He's headed toward the stairwell."

"Copy that," Sam said.

"You know, doctor," Nick said, "I think you're the killer. You drugged Parnell and planted your own hair in Philadelphia."

"Another country heard from," Thorpe said. "Mr. Mercante, if you want real evidence, I understand Ms. Ellis and Bob Kramer have plenty in their possession."

"Except for one piece. You were a little careless putting that paper in Father Cahill's pocket."

"What paper is that?"

"You know damn well," Nick said.

"I suggest you tell me."

"We took another look in the fitness room and found your thumbprint on the edge of Cahill's locker door."

Thorpe opened his mouth to speak, then smiled. "I've had enough games for one day. Captain, Lieutenant, if you don't mind, I'll be leaving. I have a patient waiting."

Sam hesitated, then nodded. "You can go. The sooner the better."

"As you wish." Thorpe turned away with a wave.

"You're just going to let go?" Nick protested to Sam after Thorpe left.

"I don't have a choice, Mercante. What do I arrest him for, his good looks?"

"You saw him. He almost admitted he was in Cahill's locker."

"I don't take 'almosts' to court."

"What about that hypodermic?"

"He's a doctor, Nick," Frank said.

"He's a devious s.o.b." Cynthia said.

"She's right," Connie said. "He lied about Vivian. She hardly knows him."

"That's not a crime, Ms. Vacarro," Sam said.

"This is ridiculous," Connie fumed.

"It really is," Nick said. "We set this up and you're letting him skate."

Sam turned away. "Your gambit didn't work, Mercante. Get over it."

"So now what?" Nick asked.

"We wait for Prentice and Kramer," Frank said. "It shouldn't be long if either of them is coming."

"And see what's in his bag," Sam said.

"What bag?" Ellis asked.

"Bob's carrying a plastic bag," Nick said.

"With a clock inside, Lieutenant?" Cynthia asked.

"I'd rather not say, Ms. Ellis."

"It's a bomb, isn't it? You think he's using the clock to make a bomb."

"He's not!" Connie shouted at Cynthia.

"Shut up, fancy pants."

"Ms. Ellis, why don't you just sit down," Frank said.

Cynthia shrugged and no one spoke as Connie resumed her pacing.

"Where the hell is he?" Sam said.

"Probably went to the cafeteria for a cup of coffee." Connie said. "I'm telling you he's not your man."

"This is nuts. Mike?" Sam said into his mike.

"Yes, Lieutenant."

"I'm heading back to 826. If--."

"GUNSHOT!" Tawana screamed. "Kathy, hit that button when I reach the door. Second shot!"

"I'm moving," Avery shouted as Sam and Frank bolted to the door, drawing their Glock 19 police specials and brushing Connie aside. "Everyone stay put," Sam called over his shoulder.

Tawana burst through the lobby doors, Glock 19 in hand.

"Freeze, Kramer! Drop that gun! Now move away from them."

Kramer stepped away as Tawana kept him covered and moved swiftly to the fallen bodies of Thorpe and Prentice, trying to avoid the blood spatters and human tissue on the carpet.

Avery was next into the lobby, followed by Sam and Frank.

"Prentice's unconscious but seems okay," Tawana said, looking up, "but Thorpe's taken a head shot. We need a doctor here."

Vivian heard Tawana's words in her earplug and was already on the phone as Connie hurried into her room. "This is Vivian Pershing in 828. Dr. Thorpe's been shot in the lobby up here. Call a Code!"

"Put down the bag, Kramer," Avery said, pointing his gun. "Nice and easy."

Kramer placed the bag on the carpet very slowly as the overhead speakers bellowed.

> **Code Blue, Lobby 8**
> **Code Blue, Lobby 8**

"Good," Avery said, then glanced at Thorpe. "Let's see Linda Barringer get you out of this one."

"She will. I didn't pull the trigger. And that's not Peter Thorpe."

# TWENTY-SEVEN

## TUESDAY, JULY 27

The bullet that slammed into Thorpe's forehead was a probable death sentence. True, the slug lost momentum when it hit bone and penetrated his skull, but this left only the brain to cope with the residual energy. It is ill equipped to do so.

Like a human embryo, the brain exists inside a membrane filled with fluid. Any severe trauma causes it to swell. If the pressure is not relieved, death almost always follows because the brain stem, which controls vital life systems, is virtually squeezed through the bottom of the skull.

These principles took over as the bullet careened through Thorpe's brain and exited on the right side of his head before he crumpled to the lobby floor. Fortunately for him, he was only an elevator ride away from Clara Barton's surgical floor and Dr. Ann Lyman and a staff neurosurgeon, both of whom had lingered in the hospital after the post-op conference.

Within minutes, the doctors used drugs to stimulate diuresis, the removal of water from the body through urine, thereby reducing Thorpe's blood pressure as well as the swelling in his brain. After that, they dealt with the injury to the brain itself. That took over six hours. It was after midnight when Thorpe was wheeled into recovery.

---

Some eight hours later, Sam started the coffee brewing in his new kitchen and began telephoning. By the time Tawana came downstairs, he had a fairly complete report from Frank, the hospital medical staff, and the surveillance team assigned to Laura Prentice.

"Long night," she said kissing his forehead.

"You look pretty fresh considering."

"I'll look better after some coffee," she said, reaching for her mug. "What's the word?"

He handed her the fax Frank had sent over. It was the press release they were issuing.

*Peter Thorpe, acting chief surgeon of Clara Barton Hospital, is in critical condition this morning, after being wounded last evening when a gun discharged during an apparent argument in the lobby of a private wing of the hospital.*

Tawana looked up. "We're still going with him as Peter?"

"Till we know for sure otherwise."

She continued reading, sipping her coffee.

*The incident is being investigated by Metro homicide detectives who were nearby at the time interviewing Vivian Pershing, chair of Clara Barton's board of trustees, as part of their inquiry into recent killings at the hospital. Ms. Pershing was scheduled to be examined this morning by Dr. Erica Sawyer about the details of a fall she suffered last June that might be linked to the case. That examination has been postponed.*

*Police have yet to determine whether the altercation involving Dr. Thorpe is connected to their investigation or when they will be able to speak with him.*

"Nice and tidy," Tawana said.

"Frank let Pershing and Ellis have some input. They're trying to keep things calm at the hospital.  Works for us, too."

"Thorpe going to make it?"

"Long odds. They did what they call a craniotomy. Drilled holes near the wound with something called a Gaggle wire saw, then opened the skull to work on the brain. They saved as much bone as possible to use to close the skull."

"They really use saws?" she asked.

"Yeah, and get this. The nurse said the Gaggle was invented by an Italian gynecologist in the 19th century to cut through a woman's pelvic bone."

"Thanks for sharing that."

"You're welcome," he smiled. "Anyhow, Thorpe lost lots of brain tissue from the bullet and the operation. Even if he lives, he's probably going to be a vegetable. Could wind up in a wheelchair for life."

"Geez, how ironic. That means we can't prosecute him for any of this."

"If he's guilty," Sam said. "That depends on Kramer and Prentice and what evidence we find."

"The Thomas baby's ID bracelet in his medical bag's a good start."

"If he put it there."

"Too bad you can't ask him," she said and took a long swallow. "But I'll bet the bullet that hit Thorpe and the one we took out of the ceiling match the one that killed Dr. Monroe."

"No bet. But we still need to get inside his house. Frank said the AUSA's meeting with the Maryland State's Attorney to get a warrant."

"About time she got off her butt. Is Prentice still sedated?"

"No, she's awake and seems fine. Would you believe Ellis stayed with her overnight?"

"Right now I'd believe in the tooth fairy. Prentice say anything? I'd love to hear her version of what happened."

"Not a word, and I don't think she will."

"Why?"

"Frank's already been called by her lawyer, a woman named Marcia Davis who's a friend of Ellis. She's demanding a copy of the note Prentice wrote to Thorpe we found near the medical bag."

"Ellis has more moves than Elvis."

"Kramer's no slouch either. Whatcha think of his story?"

"It rings true to me. He was holding the gun pointed down with only two fingers. He could have picked it up that way. And he was damn eager to take the gunpowder test."

"And the results are in. He's not the shooter."

"So Prentice argued with Thorpe like Kramer said."

"Looking that way."

"What about the radio taped to the clock?"

"It's not a bomb, but we're not sure what Kramer was doing with it. Linda Barringer's put a muzzle on him since last night. We've had to let him go."

"She's really good isn't she?"

"I'd hire her."

Tawana swallowed more coffee. "Have you called Massachusetts?"

"I'll do it when we get in. I don't know anybody up there to roust at home. Want some eggs?"

"I want more sleep," she said, holding out her mug. "Pour."

"You can stay home, you know."

"No way. This is the fun part."

---

For the third night running Connie had stayed at Vivian's apartment. They had slept late and had an early lunch and Connie was now pouring the last of the tomato juice.

"Let's move to the balcony," Vivian said, placing her glass in the Rover. "I need a sunshine fix."

"Want me to get you a hat?" Connie asked. "It's pretty strong today."

"You can use one of mine, if you'd like, but skin cancer's the least of my worries at my age."

"Then I'll be daring, too. Let me open the door."

They moved outside. "Such a lovely day," Vivian said, as she raised her face to the sun, then looked at Connie leaning against the railing. "You don't agree."

"No, it's beautiful."

"But you've hardly said a word since you got up. Are you feeling all right?"

"I'm fine."

"Look, if it'll help, I'll lift the embargo. Let's talk about Bob."

"I don't need to do that."

"Then let me. Now, let's see. He hardly spoke to you before he left with the police last night because his lawyer said he couldn't. Right so far?"

"Yes."

"And you've had a night to sleep on it and you're still upset."

She nodded. "Barringer never told him that before."

"He was never caught standing over someone who'd just been shot before."

"And he has to be angry with me for working with the police. You should have seen his face when he saw me walk into the lobby. I just wish he'd call so I could explain."

"Look, he'll understand when he hears the whole story. If it doesn't, he's not the man I think and not worthy of you."

"Yes, but..."

"But what?"

"Well, he was holding the gun."

"Come on, you've crossed that bridge. And besides, how could he make Prentice pass out on cue?"

"I don't know. But, there he was and I can't talk to him. And there's that plastic bag."

Vivian's cell phone rang. She took it from the Rover and glanced at the display. She shrugged and pressed Send.

"Hello? Bob! I'm fine. Yes, she's here. Good. I thought so. Tomorrow? I guess that would work. Fine. Wait, why don't you tell her yourself. Hold on." Vivian offered the phone. "He's calling from Barringer's office."

Connie stepped over and took the phone. "Hi. No, that's okay. Thank goodness! Yes, lunch's fine with me. What? Who's she? Oh. Okay. Me too." She hung up beaming. "He's not angry."

"How about that. Did he happen to mention the police confirmed he didn't fire the gun?"

"Of course he did," she smiled.

"Not good news for Laura Prentice. He told you about Marcia Davis?"

"Yes. He might like Nick to join us to talk about it tomorrow at lunch. Says he'll call me later."

"Fine, but let's not hang around waiting. Know any good bars downtown?"

---

Nick stepped onto the enclosed porch where Kathy sat stroking Patches's ears.

"That was Tawana," he said.

"The blooms are almost all gone now," she said, gazing at the day lily bed that was half in shadow.

He heard the sadness in her voice. "I saw some yellow ones in front today."

"That's Sandra Elizabeth. Won't be many after her. Fall Farewell will be the last one in that bed."

"Until May when Esperanza and Stella Doro show up."

She turned to him and smiled. "I'm impressed."

"Don't be. I memorize prices too. Want to know what Melba toast's going for today?"

"No, that's your deal."

"Sourdough bread?"

"Stop it. Who'd you say was on the phone?"

"Tawana. They got the search warrant. There's a team heading to Thorpe's house."

"Why'd it take all day?"

"No emergency involved, I guess. Thorpe's not exactly a flight risk."

"So how come the AUSA went along this time? The shooting?"

"For one thing. And Laura's note and baby girl Thomas's ID bracelet linked the medical bag to his house."

"So Thorpe gave them a roadmap," she said. "Did you tell Tawana about lunch tomorrow?"

"Yeah. She said there's no reason not to go. Thinks I should hear Kramer's ideas now that they've released him."

"I hate to say I told you so, so I won't."

"And I was also wrong about the gun powder test. Tawana set me straight."

"They didn't check his hands?"

"Yeah, but they don't use paraffin anymore."

"I can see you're dying to tell me."

"They have all kinds of tests. Neutron activation analysis, whatever that is, or chemicals like diluted hydrochloric or nitric acid. They swabbed Kramer with one of those."

"Whatever. Now can you tell me who Dr. Thorpe is?"

"We're getting close," Nick said. "The police up in Springfield Mass. faxed down William Thorpe's photo. Tawana says it looks something like our Thorpe but the hair seems lighter and the nose's different."

"We know what the real Peter looks like?"

"They're backtracking to find out. Missouri's the first stop. Ellis said that's where Peter and William were raised and went to medical school. Their mother still lives there."

"Nothing more recent?"

"Fort Collins, Colorado, where Peter practiced."

"Laura Prentice still isn't talking?"

"Only to her lawyer," Nick said.

"What about this congressman Bob said Laura named when she was arguing with Thorpe?"

"He's real. In the summer of 1991 a congressman named Devlin and his wife were burned to death in an explosion in his beach cottage along with one Dr. William Thorpe."

"Questionable circumstances like Bob said?" Kathy asked.

"Very. Devlin was a target in a Medicare fraud investigation involving some shady characters. Seems Thorpe was part of the scam."

"But we don't know if it was William or Peter who died with the Devlins."

"Or even if they did. DNA testing doesn't work on ashes. But Sam's going to match our Dr. Thorpe's fingerprints against whatever birth records he can find for him and his brother."

"What a mess," Kathy sighed. "Could Thorpe really kill his own brother?"

"You always ask the tough questions."

"I thought you were a master detective."

"Office is closed.  Want some dinner?"

"What are you offering?"

"Got to start from scratch," Nick said.

"No chili in inventory?"

"Chili in July?"

"It's not like oysters, is it? I'd eat your chili anytime."

"I've got some ground turkey.  I can whip some up. Can you

wait an hour or so?"

"Sure. I'll wait ten months for my day lilies."

---

Cynthia was leaning on her railing watching the sun dip toward the horizon when the phone rang behind her. She hurried across the deck, hoping it might be Laura, but the display said it was the infamous "Unknown Caller."

"Who is this?" she snapped, prepared to do battle with a telemarketer.

"It's me, Cindy," her brother answered.

"Rick! You got my message. They wouldn't tell me where you were."

"It's classified, but we're about to wrap it up. So they caught your killer?"

"Looks that way."

"Bob Kramer like you thought?"

"No, I guess not. Could be one of our doctors. A...friend of mine."

"Does friend mean what I think it does?"

"Probably," she said.

"Boy, you're case is more juicy than mine. But you're still not certain?"

"Not totally. Laura Prentice's in the middle of it, so I called in Marcia Davis to represent her and now nobody's talking to me."

"Marcia, my old flame?" he asked.

"The very one."

"Why does Laura need counsel?"

"It's all mixed up. They're still sorting everything out. When will you be back in town?"

"Tomorrow. I'm on the shut--. Ooops. You didn't hear that. Can we have dinner?"

"God, yes. I need someone to talk to. I'm really at sea right now."

"Afraid you'll be dethroned after only one week?"

She paused. "You know, Rick, I thought that would really

bother me, but it hasn't. I'm more upset that my judgment's been so screwed up. About Bob...about everything. What do you suppose that's all about?"

"Ask me tomorrow. My boss just walked in. I have to run. Love you, Cindy."

"Me too, bro."

---

Gail arrived home close to nine and found Frank in the bedroom on his cell phone. She kissed him on the cheek and headed straight for a hot bath. He was still talking when she reappeared. Putting on a bright yellow robe, she went to the bed to glance at the mail and saw the postcard from the boys that Frank had propped up against her pillow.

"Not the longest note in the world," he said to her closing his phone.

"They say they miss us," she grinned.

"They miss their computers."

"The camp has plenty. At least they sent us a card."

"Only took them three weeks. They're home Saturday."

"Don't be such a grouch. You miss them, too."

"Miss what? They're hardly ever here."

She went to his side of the bed and kissed him. "I am."

He put his arms around her. "So you are, but that robe's hiding some of you."

"I can fix that, but first tell me what's going on. Everyone's talking about Dr. Thorpe."

"It's just beginning. He's our killer. Mike called in a couple of hours ago. More evidence in Thorpe's basement than we need. Files on Parnell, reports from the hospital's research department on that poisonous frog, and your drug of choice: lidocaine, quinidine, and Spanish fly."

"Cantharidin," she corrected.

"Thank you. Oh, and a few more items that belonged to Dr. Monroe, wallet, cell phone and the like."

"No possibility of any of it being planted?"

Frank shook his head. "He had written on some of the documents. No, Thorpe's our man, all right. The irony is, his notes make clear he only wanted to rob Monroe, never intended to kill him."

"Good God," she said, shaking her head. "Frank, this is going to be a huge black eye for the hospital. I hope it can recover."

"It's got a better chance he does. By the way, he's William Thorpe, not Peter."

"You're sure?

"Ninety-five per cent. The hospital in Colorado where Peter practiced sent us his photo and Springfield PD sent us William's. And we have pictures of them from medical school."

"How can this be? Our credentials office does background checks on all the medical staff. Education, experience, any litigation, complaints with regulatory agencies, the works, including photos."

"Sure, and William knew you would," Frank said, stretching out on the bed. "So he made adjustments."

"How?"

"Peter's hair was long and black, William's was short and graying. We think he grew it out and dyed it and also had his nose shortened into a pug more like Peter's. Result? The face in the Colorado photo and the one in Clara Barton's file are very similar, but definitely different."

"And William would know his brother's background and experience and could give it to us when he applied."

"Bingo. He becomes Peter and no one's the wiser. But we'll pin it down for sure when we check his prints against his birth records."

"Maybe we should start checking fingerprints at the hospital."

"Wouldn't hurt, but hell, Gail, you know those can be faked. DNA's the only certain test."

"So Bob Kramer's telling the truth."

"He's batting a thousand so far. He passed the gun shot residue test. Prentice had to be the shooter."

"Will you arrest her?" she asked.

"We want to talk to her first, but her lawyer's playing

hardball.  She wants to get Kramer's story before she'll let us talk to her client."

"Do you care?"

"Not really, but we're all jockeying for position. We'll work it out. In fact, Nick's having lunch with Kramer tomorrow. We might learn something."

She stroked his arm. "You don't look as tired as you used to after a day like today."

"Hell, Sam and the guys have been doing all the work. I've just directed traffic. Now about that robe."

"Yes?" she asked.

"Well?"

"You see a stop sign, officer?"

## WEDNESDAY, JULY 28

Connie had suggested lunch at Vivian's to make it easier for her and Nick and Kramer agreed. She prepared gazpacho and a salmon salad with sliced vine-ripened tomatoes garnished with olive oil and fresh basil. The meal kept the tone of the conversation light for a while, but it soon turned to the events of the last two days.

Once they adjourned to the living room where Connie served coffee, Kramer proposed a meeting he and Linda Barringer wanted to have with the police, Laura and Marcia Davis.

"What's the point, Bob?" Vivian asked. "You've already told the police your story."

"I have another piece of the puzzle that hasn't surfaced that could wrap up this whole thing if I can get Laura to go along."

"All the murders?" Nick asked.

"Everything."

"What do you have?"

"I'm not at liberty to say till Linda let's me.  We're saving it for the meeting. She'll reveal some of it to
Davis in advance to sweeten the pie."

"So you don't want Laura to talk to the police?" Connie asked.

"That's up to her, of course, but I'd rather not do this piecemeal. I want everyone present, including Cynthia and you three. Your wife too, Nick, if she can make it."

"Why Cynthia?" he asked.

"It's critical," Kramer said. "She called me late last night. I was on the phone with her for almost an hour."

"She can't have you back," Connie said.

"Don't think she wants me, Red, but she was very apologetic about the last few months."

"Did she confess she was out to get you?" Vivian asked.

"More or less, but she also had quite a tale to tell about Thorpe and Laura. Did you know Cynthia had a romance going with him at the same time he was seeing Laura?"

"Wait a second," Nick said, "Thorpe was dating Cynthia and Laura Prentice?"

"Told you it was some story. Seems Laura only found out about Thorpe's affair with Cynthia this past weekend."

"That's a motive for her to shoot him," Nick said.

"Yes, but I'm certain that's not why she did. Anyway, I called Cynthia back this morning and she's agreed to come to the meeting if I can set it up."

"Why do you want the three of us there?" Vivian asked.

Kramer smiled. "Connie gave me the details of your plan. You were the star performer, you have to be there."

"It was Nick's idea," she said.

"Perhaps, but you can make sure the police handle the story with the right tone. Cynthia told me you two helped on that press release."

"A few jots and tittles."

"You're not getting off that easy. I'll need your ideas for damage control. I--we have to handle the public long term. And frankly, Vivian, that's well beyond the next six months."

"I'll start canvassing the trustees this afternoon. Perhaps we can work out a longer extension if not a new contract. Give you more breathing room."

"I promise you my best shot, but it's going to be a tougher job than ever."

"No argument," she nodded.

"Anything I can do to facilitate things for the meeting?" Nick asked.

Kramer paused. "I don't think so. Linda will be the stalking horse, but if I can count on you if needed, great."

"I can't see why the police wouldn't cooperate," Connie said.

"Neither can I." He looked at his watch. "I'd better check in with Linda. Excuse me a minute." He stepped toward the kitchen working his cell phone.

"He's right," Vivian said. "I don't know if he can pull this off."

"Will the trustees let him try?" Connie asked.

"After all that's happened this week, they may be hard to convince."

Nick smiled. "They should deal with Sam Witkin."

---

Kathy was in her office that afternoon when Nick phoned.

"How was lunch?" she asked and reached for her Coke, being careful to turn away from her computer keyboard in case of a spill.

"Fascinating." He briefed her on what had been said.

"Wow, Thorpe two-timing Prentice puts a new slant on things."

"Yeah, I told Frank. He really wants to interview her now."

"Will he wait for this meeting Kramer wants?"

"He'll check with Sam, but I sense he didn't have a problem with it. Depends on how free they are to ask questions."

"You have any clue what Kramer has up his sleeve?"

"Nope, but it sounds favorable to Laura," Nick said.

"She'll need all the help she can get."

"So will Kramer if he manages to stay on as CEO."

"It may be time to change horses, Nicky. I think he should resign."

"I thought you backed him."

"He's still not totally in the clear and now Thorpe and

Prentice are in the news. He's right about the public perception. They have to be losing confidence in the hospital and its staff."

"Yeah, Vivian has the same concern."

"See? You can't put the toothpaste back in the tube. Listen, want me to pick up anything on the way home?...Nicky? Did you hear me?"

"Hmm?"

"I said do we need anything from the store?"

"No, no. We're okay. Oh, I think we could stand some Merlot."

"All right. I'll see you after six, maybe closer to seven."

"Take your time. You just gave me an idea."

"I did?"

"Toothpaste."

"I thought we had plenty," she said.

"Listen, I'm turning on my cell phone in case you want to reach me before you get home."

"You'll be online?"

"No, on the phone with Kramer."

---

"Your boy Mercante's up to it again," Sam said to Tawana as she climbed into his Volvo.

"You're my boy, Sammy," she said, placing the shopping bag between her legs. "They were all out of my shampoo, can you believe it?"

"Want to try a CVS?"

"No, I have enough for awhile. What's going on with Nick?"

"I just talked to Frank on my cell," Sam said, pulling into traffic. "Mercante's working with Kramer on some kind of plan for this meeting that may require our cooperation."

"About the case?"

"Quote--the media aftermath."

"What's that mean?"

"Who knows? We're supposed to take it on faith until the meeting. Which, by the way, Barringer now wants to move to

Friday morning."

"She said tomorrow afternoon."

"Kramer needs to work on some details. You know how it goes when Mercante gets involved."

Tawana smiled. "What'd you tell Frank?"

"That I'd think about it, but I don't see the harm. Hell, we've already agreed to the sit down."

"Kramer wants more people there?"

"Barringer didn't say anything about that."

"Good. Everybody in one room's going to be complicated enough."

"You're preaching to the choir."

She poked him. "What do you know about choirs, my Jewish friend?"

"One sang at my wedding, remember?"

# TWENTY-EIGHT

## FRIDAY, JULY 30

Just before ten o'clock, Nick, Connie and Vivian entered Frank's office where the detectives had already assembled.

"Kathy sends her regrets," Nick said to Frank, "but she couldn't spare another day off."

"Understand. We working stiffs have to put food on the table."

A few minutes later Cynthia, Laura and Marcia Davis arrived. The lawyer was conservatively dressed in a light gray blazer and skirt. She was a smaller version of Cynthia but with brown eyes and her black hair was cropped severely short.

Kramer and Linda Barringer showed up last. "Am I holding up matters, Captain?" she asked, breezing in, a tall auburn-haired woman in a shocking pink pants suit set off by fashionable glasses with red titanium frames.

"Wouldn't start without you, counselor," Frank said.

"You know better, right?" she smiled. "Morning, Lieutenant, good to see you again."

"Let's hope so," Sam said.

"Morning, Marcia," Barringer waved.

"Linda."

Barringer looked around the room. "All present and accounted for. Ready when you are, Captain."

"First, let me review the ground rules," Frank said. "We are free to ask any questions related to our investigations. Counsel may advise clients to invoke the Fifth Amendment, but anything disclosed here may be used by the Department and by the U.S. Attorney's office in any judicial proceeding, correct?"

Barringer nodded, reaching into her briefcase for a pad.

"And by defense counsel, if exculpatory," Davis said.

"Agreed. All right, Mr. Kramer, we're here at your request. You have the floor."

"First, let me express my thanks for you indulging all of us, Captain. If I may, I'd like Cynthia to get the ball rolling, and then Laura."

"Ms. Ellis?" Frank gestured to her.

"Yes?" Cynthia said, seemingly startled. "Oh. Okay."

She spoke haltingly at first, at times glancing at Kramer and Laura, once or twice with a small smile. She took them through it all from the beginning: the initial contact with Thorpe, recruiting Laura, the planning, the strategy to oust Kramer and fool Jacobi, the jousting with the police, finding the items in Kramer's house, her romance with Thorpe, and its unraveling the weekend before the shooting.

"So what you're telling us," Sam said, "is that you three were deceiving Kramer, Jacobi, Father Cahill and God knows who else, while you and Thorpe were lying to Laura Prentice and he was double-crossing both of you."

"Yes, except I'm not sure we ever fooled Bob, at least I didn't."

"Your nasty little trio thought of everything," Sam went on. "You sure homicide was never in your plans?"

"Not in mine, Lieutenant," Cynthia said firmly. "Or in Laura's either."

"How about planting evidence?" Mike Avery asked.

"Sorry, detective. I looked, that's all."

"You have anything to add, Ms. Prentice?" Sam asked.

Laura opened her mouth, closed it, then, "Cynthia has it right, and I want to be clear. I went along with everything. I'm as much at fault here as anyone."

"More if you count shooting Thorpe," Avery said.

"That's out of order," Davis glared at him.

"Is it? She shot him didn't she?"

Davis turned to Sam. "Can you rein in your Cossack, Lieutenant?"

"Seems like a fair question to me, Ms. Davis. In fact, I have one myself. Ms. Prentice, did you go to Thorpe's house to confront him the Sunday before the shooting as Ms. Ellis has said?"

"Ellis didn't say confront," Davis objected.

"It's okay, Marcia," Laura said. "That's right, Lieutenant."

"And you left angry?"

"Yes."

"And were you still angry the next day?"

"Can we stop this, Captain?" Davis asked, impatient.

"Marcia, please," Laura said. "Yes, I was angry, but I still had hopes about our relationship."

"That's right," Cynthia nodded. "Laura told me on Monday she still had feelings for Thorpe."

"Doesn't prove a thing," Sam said, "but I'll leave it there for now."

"Good of you," Davis snarled.

"Thank you," Sam smiled. "Well, Ms. Prentice, I guess we've arrived at Monday afternoon. Care to tell us what happened?"

Laura began with her idea to speak with Peter's mother to test him. Her voice was strong as she recounted her phone call with Thanet Sherman, learning about Eleanor Thorpe and Cape Cod, and then finding William Thorpe's obituary in the *Post-Dispatch*.

"That's when I learned the Dr. Thorpe who died with this congressman was possibly a criminal. But it was the photograph in the paper that got me. The more I looked at it, the more I knew it was Peter, at least the man I knew as Peter."

"How could you sure?" Sam asked. "We probably have the same photo. Thorpe's nose and hair are different."

"I know those eyes, Lieutenant. I once asked Peter, excuse me, William, why he didn't have any pictures of Bill around. He said his brother hated to be photographed because his eyelids made him look half asleep. Of course, he was talking about Peter's eyes. I guess he told half the truth for once."

"All right, continue."

"Yes, well, I was livid when I realized Peter--William--had lied to me, to all of us, about everything. Cynthia wanted to tell Vivian Pershing how deceitful he was. Boy, did I have some news.

"But first I wanted to have it out with him. I went up to his office, but he wasn't there. I didn't want to hang around waiting, so I wrote the note you found."

"Why not go to his medical office?" Tawana asked.

"I didn't want to make a scene in front of other people. And I wanted to speak to Vivian before I went home."

"Go on," Frank said.

"When I saw his father's medical bag I knew he was still there because he always took it home. So I decided to leave the note sticking out of the bag so he'd be sure to see it before he left.

"As soon as I opened the bag, I saw the gun and the hospital ID bracelet. At first I was puzzled, but when I read Baby Girl Thomas on the bracelet, it was like a light went on in my head. I thought I would throw up. I fell back into the chair and sat there, feeling dizzy, not sure I could get up. Then I remembered he was in the hospital and thought he might go after Vivian. So I ran to the elevators."

"Why take the gun with you?" Avery asked.

"I don't know," Laura said, shaking her head. "I didn't even know I had till I saw it in my hand on the way to the eighth floor. When the elevator door opened, there he was walking straight toward me with that smile on his face. He yelled something and I know I answered, but I...can't recall what it was. I don't remember anything after that."

"How convenient," Avery said.

"Lieutenant!" Davis was on her feet.

Sam ignored her. "You don't remember arguing with him?"

Laura shook her head.

"Or firing the weapon?"

"No."

"Did you see Kramer anywhere?"

She again shook her head. "No, I'm sorry, but I don't recall anything until I woke up in the hospital room with Cynthia sitting next to me."

Davis pointed at Sam. "Don't say a word, Witkin. You know damn well amnesia can occur in a situation like this. We're willing to take a polygraph if you want."

"Lieutenant," Kramer said, "I think I can shed some light on what happened."

Sam continued to stare at Laura for a moment, then turned to him. "I guess it's your turn. Why don't you take it from the time you left your office carrying the plastic bag and went outside."

"Hold it, Bob," Barringer said and turned to Frank. "Captain, a point about the ground rules."

"What is it?"

"I don't want what my client's about to say to lead to any charges against him not having to do with homicide."

"I can't agree to that, Ms. Barringer. There are lesser charges that might be involved. Assault, reckless endangerment."

"No problem. Any form of attack on any individual is fair game, but no mickey-mouse crap for anything about the clock."

"Only if I'm satisfied it doesn't compromise our investigations about any victim, including Ms. Pershing."

She paused, then "Okay. I can live with that."

"Wait a second, Linda," Davis said. "What's this about a clock?"

Barringer turned to her. "I asked to be present when Dr. Sawyer examined Pershing, but the Lieutenant said no." She looked at Sam. "Too bad she never did. I would loved to have seen your face when I told you what Pershing said. Where there's a will, I find a way."

"The radio transmitter was your idea?" Sam asked.

Barringer grinned. "Go ahead and tell him, Bob."

"Linda had a security firm deliver it to me that afternoon. Their courier showed me how to set it up with the hospital clock I had with me. He said to make sure I put in a fresh battery. I taped the thing to the back of the clock when I returned to my office."

"It's a great toy," Barringer said. "State of the art, voice activated, smaller than a pack of cigarettes with a range of a half mile. The receiver has earphone jacks and a patch cord to record to a cassette or a minidisk."

Kramer leaned forward in his chair. "I was to switch the clock with the one in the solarium where Vivian was going to be seen by Dr. Sawyer."

"Why did you take the stairs?" Larry Foster asked.

"To limit the number of people who might see me carrying the bag. I might have to take the clock back and forth if Vivian was in the solarium when I showed up and couldn't make the switch or if I had to adjust the transmitter."

"Adjust?" Tawana asked.

"After I hung the clock, I was supposed to say a few words to test the transmitter. The courier was parked across the street and I was going to call him when I returned to my office to make sure he'd heard me."

"How'd you plan getting the bag by the nurse?" Foster asked.

"I still work there, detective. I wasn't going to Vivian's room, just checking out the wing."

Sam looked at Barringer. "And you'd be listening to the receiver in the morning?"

Barringer shook her head. "One of my associates would be in the parking lot recording."

"Pretty fast and loose, counselor," Sam said. "The bar association ethics folks might enjoy hearing this."

"Cut the bull, Sam. You had your own tapes running all afternoon."

"Please continue, Mr. Kramer," Frank said.

"Well, I took the stairs to the eighth floor and had just opened the fire door when the right-hand elevator opened and Laura got off holding a gun at her side. I started to say something but then I heard Thorpe shouting from my left. Then Laura raised the gun."

"Why didn't you intervene?" Sam asked.

"Lieutenant, you didn't see the look on her face. I thought she was about to shoot. I'm not a hero."

"And you could hear Prentice clearly?"

"As I told you that evening, I heard them both."

"Take it real slow now, Mr. Kramer," Davis said, writing frantically. "I want to get every word."

"No problem," he said, "but I don't have to do this from memory. I turned on the transmitter after I heard Thorpe shouting at Laura."

"And it worked like a charm," Barringer said, taking a small cassette player out of her briefcase. She stepped over to Frank and handed it to him. "Captain, if you'll do the honors. This copy's for you. Just press Play."

"One second," Kramer said. "Laura, this may not be pleasant."

"I'm up to it, Bob, " she said.

"Ms. Davis?" he asked.

"I trust what Linda told me about helping us."

"Go ahead, Captain," Kramer said.

Frank pressed the button. The next sound was clearly Thorpe's angry voice:

"...doing here? Where the hell did you get that gun?"

"You know damn well," Laura's voice answered. "From your precious medical bag. Is it really your father's or is that another lie?"

"Give the gun to me, Laura. I don't--"

"No more lies, Dr. Thorpe," her voice breaking. "I know all about your mother and I saw your brother's obituary. Only it's your picture isn't it--William? The nose almost threw me, but not those eyes."

"What are you talking about?"

"No questions, you fucking impostor." Tears in the voice now. "You didn't die in Saudi Arabia, did you? It was Cape Cod. But it was really Peter because you were about to be indicted. That's why you killed him and Congressman Devlin."

"Laura, I can explain. I was innocent of all that. Peter came to help. The explosion was an accident."

"Don't move! Now tell me, should I have the police arrest you or shoot you like you did Dr. Monroe? Was this the gun?"

"Listen, Laura, there's--"

"Stand still!" Her voice firm now. "Right there. Not another inch! Now--" The sound of a gunshot. Then another. Muffled sounds. Then Tawana's voice:

"Freeze, Kramer! Drop that gun! Now move away from them." A pause, background noises, then Tawana again. "Prentice's unconscious but seems okay, but Thorpe's taken a head shot..."

Frank hit the stop button, then looked at Kramer. "Did Thorpe go for the gun or try to attack her?"

"My sense is he did, Captain, but, honestly, I'm not sure. His back was blocking my view by the time the first shot went off. But he was moving forward all the time. He might have lunged for her or the gun."

"Of course he did," Davis said. "Laura was acting in self-defense."

"What about the second shot?" Sam asked.

"I don't know how the gun went off either time," Kramer said. "Laura could have still had her finger on the trigger when Thorpe lunged or fell into her or when they hit the floor. I hurried over and had picked up the gun when Detective Briggs rushed in. You know the rest."

"Not quite," Avery said. "Why did you pick up the gun?"

"Reflex, I guess. Get it out of the way."

"You went for the gun and held onto the bag? More reflex?"

"The transmitter was important."

"It wasn't on when I examined it," Avery said.

"No, I flipped the switch when you told me to put the bag down. No need to keep it on."

"Why didn't you tell us you'd recorded their conversation?" Frank asked.

"I didn't know. I wasn't sure the system had worked. Besides, I had to confer with Linda before I said much of anything."

"That's right, Captain," Barringer said. "Bob couldn't sneeze without asking me. When he told me what happened, I advised him to outline what he'd heard to you and demand to take the gunshot residue test. Once I spoke to the courier and checked out the tape, we'd figure out what to do."

"And I also wanted to talk to Laura," Kramer said, "but she wasn't in any condition. Then Marcia got involved and I couldn't. Anyway, Linda and I didn't see any harm in waiting a day or so."

"How about obstructing justice?" Sam said.

"Tell it to the judge," Barringer laughed. "Bob's kept nothing from you. We've verified the tape and arranged for this meeting. Plus you weren't pushing that hard to talk to us. Hell, I think you owe us lunch."

"Can't afford you," Sam said, but smiled.

"Lunch sounds good," Frank said. "Maybe we should all take a break."

They did, ordering sandwiches from Frank's favorite coffee shop two blocks away. Afterwards, there were only a few more questions for Laura and Kramer, before Frank sensed there was nothing else to cover.

He turned to Nick. "Are you ready to tell us about your 'media aftermath'?"

"At last," Nick said and distributed sheets of paper. "Vivian, Bob and I worked this up. We'd like it released this weekend after you've run it by your PR folks."

Frank and the others began to read:

*The Metropolitan Police Department today named Dr. William Thorpe as the person responsible for the recent string of homicides at Clara Barton Memorial Hospital.*

*Thorpe is a fugitive from justice. He is suspected of murdering Timothy Parnell, a former D.C. policeman, in Philadelphia this past April, and to have killed his brother, Dr. Peter Thorpe, in Massachusetts in 1991. Thorpe is said to have assumed his brother's identity when he forged documents and was later hired at Clara Barton in 1993.*

*Thorpe was shot and critically wounded this past Monday at the hospital and remains confined in the intensive care unit. Due to his condition, it is uncertain whether or when he will stand trial for his alleged crimes.*

*"William Thorpe fooled the medical community and law enforcement authorities in four states and the District for over a dozen years," Lieutenant Sam Witkin who led the investigation said. "We owe a debt of gratitude to the Philadelphia and Springfield, Massachusetts police in solving this case."*

*D.C. police were also helped by Vivian Pershing, chair of Clara Barton's board of trustees, Robert Kramer and Cynthia Ellis, its chief executive officer and chief of staff, and by Kramer's executive assistant Laura Prentice who confronted Thorpe before he was wounded.*

*Metro police detective Captain Frank Stephens commented on this aspect of the investigation. "We couldn't have solved this case without the discreet and active assistance of the Clara Barton executive staff over several months."*

*Two local attorneys, Linda Barringer and Marcia Davis, also cooperated with the police behind the scenes. Nick Mercante, a consultant*

*to the Department, also played a role in the investigation. The
Department plans to hold a news conference Tuesday morning where Ms.
Pershing and Mr. Kramer will appear.*

Sam shook his head. "Even if we accept everything we've
heard this morning, we can't go with this."

"Why not?" Nick said. "Sure there's some hyperbole in there,
but the basic facts are true."

"No one's called Thorpe a fugitive or said they believe he
killed anyone out of town."

"That's just wordsmithing. Work out the language. Call your
friends in Springfield and Philly and confirm."

"There is a lot of spin, Nick," Frank said.

"It's putting the best face on a bad situation. Just like that
drug company did years ago when someone spiked the Tylenol."

"Johnson and Johnson," Foster said.

"Right. The point is to paint Thorpe as a long-time villain so
that the hospital and staff can get out from under his cloud and
move on."

"And to give you some ink?" Sam said.

"That was my idea," Kramer said. "I wanted to make it look
like a run-of-the-mill press release."

"I can see Massachusetts and Pennsylvania," Connie said.
"What are the other two states?"

"Missouri and Colorado," Tawana said, "where the Thorpes
grew up and Peter practiced."

"I think this is just great," Marcia Davis said, waving the
sheet of paper.

"You would," Sam said. "A little free advertising and it
makes Ellis and your client look better than they are."

"Not so," Kramer said. "They've committed no crimes. They
wanted the killer caught as much as anybody and in their way they
both aided the investigation."

"I concur, Lieutenant," Vivian spoke up for the first time.
"My concern is for the hospital. I've seen nothing to suggest these
women did anything contrary to its long-term interests."

"All right," Frank said, standing. "I think we've been at this
long enough. We'll digest what we've heard and get back in touch

with you."

"Like when?" Davis asked.

"Soon."

"Will you knock off your surveillance of my client?"

"We'll consider that."

"And no charges of bugging or breaches of privacy?" Barringer asked, handing Frank the cassette and retrieving the tape player.

"We'll consider that, too."

"Good. Thanks for the lunch."

"Taxpayers' pleasure," Frank smiled.

He watched them all depart, then turned to his colleagues. "Comments?"

There were plenty. After they called it quits and he was alone, Frank picked up the phone to call home.

"Finally," Gail said. "The camp phoned an hour ago. They revised tomorrow's schedule. The bus doesn't get in until three-thirty."

"Good. We can have a long lunch. I'd like to invite Tawana and Sam to join us."

"To talk about the case?"

"Yeah. Wait till you hear how you folks over there helped solve it."

## SATURDAY, JULY 31

It was unusually crisp and clear for a midsummer evening in Washington, and the sky formed a starry canopy over the Potomac and Kramer's balcony where he and Connie sipped the champagne he had served at dinner.

"God, it's so beautiful here," she said. "There were times I thought I'd never be back."

"Because you thought I was guilty?"

"I admit there was a twinge of doubt when I heard about that gun in your hand, but more that you'd never invite me after I went along with Nick's plan."

"I'm glad you did. And you said your lines really well. Had

me going there for a while."

"How can you be so damn tolerant?" she asked, gripping his upper arm.

"Because I realize why you did it and in fact you guys helped resolved things more quickly than I could have."

"Do you believe I've buried Vic for good?"

"Never heard of the guy. I'm the only man in your life."

"I don't want there to be anyone else again. There, I've said it."

"Good."

"Am I rushing things? I always seem to."

"Your timing's fine. And, listen, there's something I'd like to run by you now that I'm out from under."

"Sure."

"If the police issue the press release, Clara Barton's reputation will rebound some, but fundraising's still going to be tough for a while."

"For sure," she said.

"So I'll need to devote most of my time to it, which means fewer hours in the office and more schmoozing around town. I can do that if someone's minding the store. A good deputy."

"You don't mean Laura."

"Cynthia."

"You're kidding?"

"No. Red, you should have heard her on the phone the other night. Something's happened to her, her outlook. I don't know what, but I want to take advantage of it."

"Will she do it?" Connie asked.

"I broached it this morning. She wants to talk to her brother, but she did suggest a name for the position. Chief Operating Officer. She laughed when she said it and promised she'd tell me why."

"You want my approval?"

"I want to be sure you wouldn't be bent about my keeping her on board."

"Bent means jealous?"

"Among other things," he nodded.

"I get it. First you wine and dine me, then you drop the hammer. You must be great at fundraising."

"Then you're okay with it?"

"I'm not worried about her, but just so you know, I am the jealous type."

"Here's another one for you. Laura as chief of staff."

"Oh hell, I knew that was coming next."

"Well?" he asked.

"But what about the publicity? I mean she did shoot Thorpe."

"She'll probably come out a hero."

"You seem to like reclamation projects. Is that why I'm here?"

"Actually it's for your tennis."

## SUNDAY, AUGUST 1

Nick and Kathy walked out the side door of Trinity United Methodist Church into a sunny afternoon. They had been married there twelve years before, and had recently help solve a series of brazen homicides that took the life of the former minister who had performed the ceremony.

"Not too long a service," she remarked as they walked toward their car hand in hand.

"August in Washington. Even Communion goes quickly." He turned on his cell phone and looked at the display, which promptly beeped at him.

"The White House need you?" she said.

"The prez could use some help, but it's a voice-mail from Frank." He worked the keypad then held the phone to his ear. He smiled and closed the phone. "They've cleared the press release. It goes public at four. They fiddled with it, of course, and e-mailed a copy to me, Vivian and Bob."

"So it's Bob now, is it?"

"Why not?" After climbing into the Camry, he turned to her. "I'd like to swing by the hospital on the way home. Would you mind?"

"You bringing flowers to Thorpe?"

"Funny. No, something's bugging me."

"Oh-oh."

It was a short trip and Nick soon pulled into Clara Barton's horseshoe-shaped driveway, went all the way around and stopped near the exit.

"Nicky, the sign says you can't park here."

"Technically we'd just be standing if you stay in the car and get behind the wheel. Drive around if you get any static. I'll be back in less than five minutes."

It was closer to ten when he returned. "Success," he said, taking over the driver's seat.

"Tell me what you're up to."

"I need to review my notes first."

"It's such a nice day and I have weeding to do."

"Weed away," he said, making the turn toward home. "We can chat later. I'm not going anywhere."

"Lucky me."

As usual, Kathy became totally engrossed in her garden. It was almost six when she called it quits.

"Sorry, I lost track of time," she said, trooping into the bedroom with Patches. Nick was on the edge of the bed watching the Buick Open with the sound off. "Am I too late to take a quick bath before dinner?"

"Take a long one," he said, eyes on the screen, as were Maggie's and Puffer's who seemed fascinated by the golf ball rolling on the green.

"Tiger Woods winning again?"

"Not today. Would you believe John Daly's going head to head with Vijay Singh?"

"Who's John Daly?"

He looked at her. "Go have your bath. Would you like a glass of wine?"

"If you're buying."

"Meet you on the porch."

He had crackers, cheese, sliced pepperoni and wine waiting on a tray for her when she and Patches joined him.

"Who needs dinner?" she said happily, settling into a chair with her glass and a plate.

"The press release is next to the lamp."

She munched a fully laden cracker, reading. "This is good, Nicky, very close to the draft."

"A little more hedging, but we figured that. Vivian's pleased. She called while you were outside."

Kathy sipped her wine, glancing at the release again and shaking her head. "God, what could have possessed Thorpe to kill his own brother."

"Perhaps he didn't."

She rolled her eyes. "Wait--let me guess. It was an accident like he said on the tape."

"If could have happened that way."

"Parnell was no accident."

"Hey, that's different. I'm talking about 1991."

"No, Nicky, a person can't change stripes. Thorpe killed Peter and everyone else."

"All right, then. Why did he go to Philadelphia to kill Parnell?"

"Oh no you don't. I asked you that two weeks ago. You thought Parnell might have had something on him."

"That was before I knew how Peter died," he said.

"What difference does that make?"

"Look, Thorpe might have been a crook in '91 but not a murderer. Let's assume Peter's death was an accident. It was also a way out for Thorpe. He might simply have taken the opportunity to assume his brother's identity to escape Massachusetts. After that, he had to live out the lie."

"Posing as Peter," Kathy said.

"Sure. Even his mother would never know. He goes into hiding, has plastic surgery and then resurfaces at Clara Barton. He's successful, moves up, and wants to be chief of surgery."

"But Stan Jacobi stands in his way."

"Correct. So he schemes with Cynthia Ellis. But maybe their plans won't work. That's not good enough for him. He wants a foolproof way to remove Jacobi. So he goes to the expert, Tim

Parnell."

"I'm not buying it," Kathy said, sipping her wine.

"Think a minute. Why else would Thorpe need Parnell if he already knew how to plan a triple murder and not get caught?"

"He was no amateur. He must have planned killing Parnell in advance."

"Probably. But he was also aware the police know all about motives and evidence. He had no motive to kill Parnell, but he did Jacobi. Parnell could tell Thorpe what mistakes to avoid, what little tricks might make the difference. Who knows, maybe Parnell convinced him to plant his own hair at the scene."

"That's some theory, Nicky."

"It fits what we know. I'll chat with Frank about it when we all come up for air."

"Too bad you can't run it by Thorpe."

"Yeah, but I've got another one for you to chew on."

"Today's visit to the hospital."

Nick smiled. "I thought you forgot."

"Never, but I'll need more Zinfandel if you're going to keep talking."

He stepped over and filled her glass. "Okay, everybody agrees Laura fired in self-defense."

"Of course, based on what Kramer said and the tape. Either that or the gun went off by accident."

"That's what I thought until this morning. I was filing away some stuff while you were getting dressed before church and something bothered me."

"And?"

"Bob's story doesn't quite wash."

"Are you serious?"

"Listen," he said, picking up a yellow pad. "According to my notes from Friday, Bob said he wasn't certain whether Thorpe lunged at Laura before the first shot."

"Sounds right to me. Thorpe was blocking his view."

Nick flipped a page. "Right, but he also said he saw Thorpe continually moving forward, so he might have rushed her."

"What's wrong with that?"

"Bob couldn't have seen a damn thing from where he was standing."

"Nicky, he was right in front of the fire door. Even if he were in the stairwell, he would have seen everything. The door has an safety window."

"Absolutely right. I checked. All the doors have one. And on most floors there's an unimpeded view to all the elevators from the stairwell."

"Most?"

"Yes, it depends on what's built on the rest of the floor. Hold on a minute." He pulled a folded paper from the file next to him and opened it on her lap. It was the diagram of the Clara Barton VIP wing.

"Here's the fire door," he pointed. "Now look at the three elevators across the lobby. Bob said Laura came up in the one on his right."

Kathy studied the sheet. "It looks as though you can't see that elevator from the door."

"You can't. I tried today. The wall of out-patient infusion center blocks the view. If Bob was in front of the fire door, he couldn't see the elevator open or Laura get off with the gun in her hand."

"Or seen Thorpe's back as he approached her. Why would he lie?"

"I'm not saying he did. Thorpe and Laura were shouting. Things happened fast. Bob said he hurried over after the second shot. Maybe it was after the first. Maybe he was moving all the time. And that's how he saw Thorpe closing in on Laura when the second shot went off. Maybe he saw what he wanted to see or what his mind told him was more likely because of the argument."

"All that doesn't mean it wasn't self-defense."

"Agreed, but it's also possible that after Laura warned Thorpe to stand still, he did back off and she moved toward him and then pulled the trigger. You really can't tell from the tape. I wish she could recall what happened. If she really can't, that is."

"Nicky!"

"Hey, it's just a thought. She's probably telling the truth. We both know all about dissociative amnesia from the Caruso case."

"Exactly. And she might recall someday with therapy."

"Won't happen. Laura's had it with therapists," Nick said.

"What about you? Can you let it go or will you tell Frank about this, too?"

"I've been mulling that over till you and I could talk. I mean it's just an idea. Speculation, really. And then I thought, why push it, what does it really matter? Legally or morally?"

"They'll never prosecute her and Thorpe got what he deserved," Kathy said.

"So there we are. We'll never know if Thorpe killed Peter or if Laura really meant to shoot him."

"I'm okay with that. Are you?"

"You always ask the tough questions."